Daniel D. Longdon lives in Middle England on the border between Notts and Derbyshire. His first love are his three sons, his grandchild and wife, Emma. His writings come a close second being a labour of love and considered by himself to be his purpose in life.

I'm dedicating this book to all the people that have helped me in my journey through life, a big shout out and much love to you all—you know who you are.

Daniel D. Longdon

LORELA: DOG WARRIORS

FOURTH BOOK OF DEVASTATION

AUSTIN MACAULEY PUBLISHERS™
LONDON • CAMBRIDGE • NEW YORK • SHARJAH

Copyright © Daniel D. Longdon (2020)

The right of Daniel D. Longdon to be identified as author of this work has been asserted by him in accordance with section 77 and 78 of the Copyright, Designs and Patents Act 1988.

All rights reserved. No part of this publication may be reproduced, stored in a retrieval system, or transmitted in any form or by any means, electronic, mechanical, photocopying, recording, or otherwise, without the prior permission of the publishers.

Any person who commits any unauthorised act in relation to this publication may be liable to criminal prosecution and civil claims for damages.

This is a work of fiction. Names, characters, businesses, places, events, locales, and incidents are either the products of the author's imagination or used in a fictitious manner. Any resemblance to actual persons, living or dead, or actual events is purely coincidental.

A CIP catalogue record for this title is available from the British Library.

ISBN 9781528994767 (Paperback)
ISBN 9781528994774 (ePub e-book)

www.austinmacauley.com

First Published (2020)
Austin Macauley Publishers Ltd
25 Canada Square
Canary Wharf
London
E14 5LQ

I would like to thank all my friends and family that have supported me throughout the years of my lifelong endeavour, thus far, all your positivity enables me to cast aside the negatives. I would also like to thank Austin Macauley, all your staff have been most helpful, humble and at times have made me feel part of your family.

Mutation

A super massive star near the end of its life, its nuclear furnace all but spent. At the pinnacle of its technological expertise, mankind—in its infinite wisdom—devised a plan: a giant experimental remedy to save the star. The implications of this particular star's redemption were literally astronomical. If mankind succeeded in saving the star and every other near-death nova, the star map of the Milky Way that they occupied would never alter. The populated areas of man would not have to periodically move to avoid death, and therefore, they would live slightly more comfortably with the knowledge that their immortality wasn't threatened by the occasional exploding star.

The star in question, Antares, didn't act as predicted upon completion of the industrial solar procedure. It bulged outwardly and became irregular in shape, growing until it could no longer maintain its mass.

It blew up, and with its borrowed elements, it became much more than it would ever have if man had left it to its natural demise. It became a beast, the nemesis of mankind; in those first few seconds, the conditions of the beginning of time were recreated in miniature. Over fifty star systems were engulfed in just a fleeting moment of time, considering the vast astronomical distances involved, somehow defying the law of physics, as if the very powers of nature where being governed by supernatural influences.

The physicists used various theories to explain away this extraordinary event, unprecedented in mankind's timeframe. They blamed themselves, the best of mankind's scientists. Little did they know that outside influences, godlike or supernatural, had played a part in man's downfall.

As the galaxy held its breath, the blast slowed, bulged and burgeoned; a great cloud of ejector preceded the wave of pure kinetic energy that ripped everything apart in its path. Those that could flee did so; they blinked out of real space and entered white space, the dimension of hyperspace easily obtainable if you owned hyperdrive-equipped vessels and a psyche pilot to operate them.

Others tried to flee ahead of the galactic destruction; all failed as the devastation overtook them and added them to its mass of ejector.

As the wave of death slowed and the information managed to run ahead of the devastation, panic set in on many worlds. This was predominant among those with little or no hope to speak of. Some lost all inhibitions and ran amok, fearing the afterlife they'd so readily been quick to avoid. Others ran for cover, anything or anywhere they could find. Some worlds were small city states, set up to house the workers of the vast mines of corporate concerns; the giant settlements sat right above the lift shafts that would delve deep into the planet's interior. One such world, Lorela, sat in the firing line, as did every other world in every other system that man had colonised.

As the blast wave entered the system, it brushed away its gas giant. Its massive gravity was no match for the power of the wave, its moon-sized core forced to surf its unending fiery crest. Other planetary bodies were moved, or reacted in some way, and the whole thing was reminiscent of the big bang.

The population of Lorela fled to the planet's substantial mine complex. The wave dimmed even the planet's star; the sky was dominated by the red glow of death on its approach. The people fled, wearing just the clothes on their backs. The crush of bodies at every tunnel entrance broke more than just ribs, as the frenzy for life reached fever pitch. The crowd turned at the last, its struggle spent. They watched in awe, as though hypnotised, as the moons in the sky changed before their eyes, set ablaze by the onset of this extreme biblical event.

Then it was over, the atmosphere fried as everything crisped. People were blown like leaves in the wind; they blazed, but their screams went unheard in the torrent of sound. Most of the structures were taken, nothing remained on the higher ground and only the barest of solid buildings remained in the low-lying valleys. The raging inferno seemed to have a life of its own as it ventured beneath the ground. Like giant snaking tentacles, it fingered and felt its way, rending flesh and torturing the soon-to-be dead.

Tens of thousands of people made it into the mine proper, the giant chemical foundries used to produce the Forever pill now the salvation of many. The doors to the planet's inner sanctum were closed and sealed shut. Giant metal doors that were used to prevent pollutants escaping to the surface were instead used to prevent radiation getting into the planet's mines; an irony that was lost to those stranded in the mine but outside of the relative safety of the inner mines.

There were thousands of them—men, women and children of all ages. Whole families were trapped and left with nothing. Left to fend for themselves, they were fully aware of the threat of not only a slow death by starvation, but the very real possibility of radiation sickness and an agonising death.

Decades passed and the people were driven to cannibalism; their primary food source that of their own kind, occasionally subsidised by lichens and cave moss.

A young woman lay back, rested up against the old man who'd kindly taken her under his wing. She panted and gasped for breath as she struggled with her uncompromised position. Her legs were spread wide, her backside propped up by clothing that'd been stitched into some sort of a pillow.

"C'mon lass, push, will ya!" the old woman nagged.

With a scream and an almighty heave, the young woman threw her head back.

"The head, I can see the head, its crowning," the toothless old crone shouted.

"Melissa, Melissa," the old man shouted. He pushed the young woman's head from one side to the next then back again—it hung limp.

"She's gone," another said from behind him.

The old matron said nothing. She frowned in the half light and felt at the slick head of the half-born babe. She pulled at it and produced a knife.

Slice by slice, she deftly cut away at the dead woman's flesh around the babe's head. With no regard to the woman's partner, she lifted the dead woman's legs and forced them down until they cracked, the hips snapping as the old hag put all her weight behind her effort. As she lent all her strength to the forward-downward motion, the babe's head popped out. The reason for the young woman's struggle and failed attempt at birth soon became apparent; the babe was misshapen and all out of proportion.

"Mutation," the father spoke of his child.

He stood and walked away into the shadows of the nearest tunnel, leaving both his mutant child and the corpse of his woman for the old hag to deal with. The woman narrowed her eyes and silently cursed the man. How could he orphan his own child? It wasn't the babe's fault it'd been born into these terrible times.

Typical man, she thought, *I curse thee.*

"I'll look after you," she said to the child.

She mopped the gunge of birth from the baby's eyes, which were the only features on it that looked human. The creature was covered in thick fur and resembled more a puppy than anything else.

As the old woman had this thought, the creature opened its mouth to reveal a full set of teeth; they looked more canine than human.

"That's evolution for you," the old woman spoke gently to the child. "I will call you Bradley."

She placed the child next to its mother and as she did, she noticed a growth above the baby's anus. A tail-like appendage, a good five centimetres in length.

The old woman used the knife to slit the throat of the dead mother; the warm liquid ran over the boy child's furry face. The little beast's long tongue lapped at the warm liquid, getting its first meal from its mother, though not as nature had intended.

"We may as well put your mother to good use," the old woman said as she turned to tend to her fire and leave the newest life on Lorela to his meal.

Years passed, any new-born fortunate enough to make full term and survive the birth also had mutations. They grew fast and seemed to reach maturity by their fifth year. Most of the mutants took on the visage of a half-man, half-canine. Many were disgusted by them and sent them away, closer to the surface where they seemed to thrive. The mutant adaptations helped against the radiative toxicity that slowly decimated the stranded population of man, stuck on the wrong side of the giant steel doors.

The mutants soon called themselves Dog Warriors. They became a breed apart and ate the last of man that hadn't succumbed to radiation sickness.

It didn't take long before the race of mutants had forgotten where they'd come from. Two generations of mutants come and gone, now they sniffed at the giant doors. The smell of human was all too close but far from their grasping claws. They survived by eating the only food source suited to their palate—each other—but longed for the taste of man. That sweet-smelling odour just hundreds of yards from their rending claws and ripping jaws.

For those beyond the door, they heard the howls of whatever nightmare manifested itself planet-side, they quaked and feared whatever was there. Most cautioned against opening the doors, lest chaos reign down on them once more.

Chapter 1
It's a Dog's Life

5200 AD
Humanity, the most technologically advanced sentient race to exist anywhere among the stars of the Milky Way, had risen to the pinnacle of morality and striven to come as close to god as mankind's nature would allow. It asked and answered the questions that all men wished to know, well-documenting the facts of man's conundrums after solving most of what man wished to know through scientific experimentation. Inevitably, man would go a step too far in its quest for knowledge, as it is in man's nature to explore the unknown and push the boundaries of what is sensibly achievable.

Through experimentation, mankind caused a blast greater than the sum of its existence, causing a hyper nova to explode; its blast wave being far greater than any could have anticipated, spreading out faster than any thought possible as it even surpassed the speeds of those few star ships that had escaped into hyper space.

Most of the solar systems man had colonised simply ended, with the planets stripped of atmosphere and of the life-giving qualities the planetary techs had strived so long to provide for the people.

Man's seat of power and its home system, Sol, where the Earth spun in its lazy orbit, was on the outer-edge of the blast radius, where the shock wave slowed sufficiently for it to be seen but didn't escape destruction. It just meant it survived a while longer with the population knowing it was going to die.

Further out at the very fringes of what it meant to be human, where the blast wave lessened in its potency, the planets were thrown back into the dark ages. The technologies that had made them great were blasted by the electromagnetic pulse, bathing the planets with deadly radiation and killing off most of the life that remained on the surface.

Now what was left of mankind's achievements floated independently of what'd been a great empire. Eight worlds that orbited two stars were left untouched by the devastation and survived just outside the blast radius; they called themselves the Homeworlds and were run, for the most part, by corporations that formed their own security forces and owned a certain number of warships to protect their commercial interests. The corporations were generally left alone by the government who encouraged those capable of looking after themselves to do so. However, those who were elected did have to act as mediators on many occasions, as warfare often broke out amongst the corporations who went to war over the various commercial interests they claimed as their own, including the worlds they watched every hour of every day. Those unfortunate planets that'd been almost destroyed by the devastation were used for entertainment by the corporations that aired the very real, bloody events back to the Homeworlds and the masses. They were reality worlds that quickly became man's most valuable commodities.

One of these was the dog world, otherwise known as Lorela; it was unique among the scoured planets and remained within the dead zone of worlds quite a few light years from the home worlds. The dog world, one of many caught by the blast that ended mankind's reign in the locality of its galactic arm, was in some respects an oddity. Its atmosphere in the early years after the devastation seemed to attract radiation. Lorela orbited its star, acting like a whirlpool, drawing in the deadly poison until even those that'd mostly escaped the blast underground were affected by the radiation; their offspring were born mutated beyond anything thought possible. Ultimately, these creatures were human—they retained the power of thought and speech—but in some mental respects, they'd changed. Their instincts returning back to a base state that could only be described as feral; everything was an enemy and everything was dinner.

Everything on the surface of the planet died, leaving a barren world, void of any life and shot-through with toxic streams. Nothing lived or took breath in an atmosphere that would strip the flesh from the lungs if inhaled.

Fortunately for the residents of the dog world, formally known as Lorela or LOR14673 for official purposes, they'd had the time to prepare. More than half of the population sought shelter deep within the bowels of the planet. Entering a tunnel system that'd been mined out of the planet's rocky core, they'd taken every manner of plant and animal life with the intention of recreating the planet's ecosystem once the surface was free of the harmful radiation. The other half tried to take to the open vastness of space, with those craft not fitted with FTL drives attempting to outrun the blast wave and although they couldn't see any other ships, they could see them on the radar. There were thousands of them, spaceships fleeing the destruction, their radio chatter being cut off as the blast wave overtook them to end the lives of those that had thought to flee.

When the wave hit, the power failed and all bets were off. How could anything survive on or in such a place, especially one which drew the poisons in? The resulting birth defects from the radiation at first threatened to end the human occupation of Lorela. The mutated babes dying either in the womb or not long after birth, as the people of the planet struggled to hold on to life. Then, as the young grew past puberty, they began to procreate in the darkness and an amazing thing happened; the children that were the result of the teenage pregnancies began to survive. These children were very different though, they were as mutated as the ones before them and most didn't live past the first year of their birth, but some did.

Eventually, natural selection took over, choosing which adaptation of man was more suitable for Lorela, and from out of the darkness, many decades after the devastation ended all life on its surface, the first creatures born from man walked out to stand in daylight, to soak up the heat from Lorela's star.

It was covered in fur from top to toe, stood eight feet in height and brandished claws at the ends of its fingers, easily two inches of iron-like nail. Its face was the most changed. A long snout protruded from the skull, giving the man a feral, almost dog-like face, with fangs designed for tearing at flesh. The strangest thing the new creature brought with it out into the sunshine was his leggings. The only clothes the dog-man wore were the trousers made from the hide of a dog to hide his genitalia. It was made from dog's skin, sewn with crude stitching. A skull cap came down over the eyes, with tinted glass to guard the human eyes from the harsh sun. A large rucksack was slung over its shoulder and the beast's claws dripped blood to the sandy barren floor of the cave's mouth it stood in.

Satellites were placed in orbit around those few planets that had kept their atmosphere; the government of the Homeworlds watched for any life that might appear, as on other worlds. They hadn't known about this new life form, it wasn't expected to walk out into the sun; the news spread like wildfire and a few of the main corporations coveted Lorela, their intention to lay claim to the filming rights of the potential gold mine, the Lorela show having come out into the light of day.

Chapter 2

The dog-man sniffed at the air; he looked at the sky and the orange-coloured clouds that hung lazy in the oppressive, foetid atmosphere, still heavy with toxins. The dog-man's tongue lolled from the side of his jaw, he licked his snout, then closed the jaw as he inhaled, his nostrils flared as he filled his lungs.

"Ah, lovely," the dog-man said quietly.

He turned and looked back into the darkness from where he'd emerged.

"Come on out, it's lovely." The beast motioned with his hands, his voice sounded human, if not a little guttural.

From out of the darkness, other figures began to emerge. They took in their surroundings with the one that had first walked out into the light and, like him, wore leggings and a skull cap made from the outer layers of a dog's hide. Every skull cap had tinted shades built in to guard against the intense light. Having lived their entire lives underground, they were only used to dim and natural light sources.

One of the dogs rounded on the first; it was six feet tall and reached up to touch the blood that hung on the end of his fang, like a drop of moisture that threatened to fall from a stalagmite to the cave floor.

"You have blood on your fang, dear," the bitch said, a mask of concern furrowed on her brow.

"I bit my lip, is all!" Memphis replied.

"Hold still, will you, Memphis?" the bitch ordered.

The dog tried to move his head aside, away from the probing touch of the bitch.

"Leave me be, bitch. I'm not a pup to be fawned over at the mere sight of blood."

"I swear sometimes you dog warriors are worse than pups," the bitch said gently.

She pulled back his lip and pushed it out of the way, revealing white teeth stained red with the dog's own blood.

"What now?" another dog from the crowd shouted, almost a bark.

Memphis stood tall, above his eight feet of height as he looked at the fifty-strong pack that surrounded him; he shaded his eyes to look out over the barren terrain, looking at the mountain ranges at their back and the plains that stretched out before them.

"I, Memphis, as pack leader claim this land from here to as far as the eye can see," Memphis barked, emptying his lungs of the toxic air as he yelled. "We will need to find shelter, from possible dangers, near a stream so we can at least quench our thirst."

"What of the toothless ones and the other packs?" another dog warrior asked.

"Why all the concern, Tank, we made it this far, didn't we?" Memphis, the alpha male, barked.

Tank bared his teeth, his long fangs showed; the last thing he expected was Memphis to suggest him a coward and he wouldn't stand for it, not in front of the rest of the pack.

"I'm calling you out if you don't take that back!" Tank barked as he stepped forward, his claws suddenly bared before him with a flourish of his wrist.

Memphis clamped his mouth shut, his head pulled back on his long thick neck in surprise and he growled as he took his sack from his back, placed it on the ground and stepped forward to meet the challenge.

"Looks like fresh meat tonight!" Memphis growled.

Elle, Memphis's bitch, stepped between them, a clawed hand held before both crouching dog warriors.

"We haven't the time for this; while you rend each other's flesh, the others or the toothless ones will be about us. Shall we all be dinner tonight or shall we find some shelter?"

Memphis growled but stood tall, his teeth bared with a barely suppressed growl. Elle was right; there was no time if they were to escape the other packs.

"Apologies," Memphis offered.

"Accepted," Tank agreed.

They took off, Memphis suddenly running down the hill, his feet slipping in the sandy terrain as the others followed suit. Even the pups ran to match Memphis. Barely keeping pace with the pack leader, they either kept up or died trying. They ran for nearly two miles, all of it downhill, when the ruins came into view another mile down the slope. It was amazing seeing for the first time what so many had spoken of, the old buildings from before the great ending. As they ran towards it, a stream came down into the ruined town from another slope.

"There," Memphis shouted as he pointed at the flow of the stream.

They continued, not breaking stride or slowing in pace until they reached what looked like giant pillars, half buried, rising out of the sand. There were no doors visible, but there were openings at regular intervals and the buildings leaned over to the right as they looked at it, as if a giant in some long-lost age had pushed them until they stood at an awkward angle.

"Incredible," Rex, a young warrior, said as they looked at the ruins.

"It's as if they are made from solid rock," Elle said.

"No, it's made from blocks, see how most of the structures have no top, the blocks at the base are everywhere," Memphis said.

They were, in reality, at the edge of a large settlement, used to house the workers that had dug the mines they'd come from; the old ruins were anything but safe, as years of toxic storms had done nothing for the fixtures and fittings. The buildings creaked, everything creaked, and to the dogs' super-senses, it sounded like a cacophony of annoyances.

"I can't stay here, it hurts my ears," Tank grumbled.

Duke, Rocky and Dakota, the other three young dog warriors stepped forwards to listen, they stood behind Rex. Memphis regarded them, his head to one side and his tongue lolling from his jaw. He lapped at a piece of drool that threatened to drip and closed his jaw as he turned to Tank.

"Look how the light goes, where does it go? And I don't know about you, but I'm getting cold," Memphis said. "I'm Memphis Grimm of Pack Grimm, the pack leader and alpha male. Tank, as much as I love and respect you, I must say your challenges are getting a little unnerving for me!"

The four young dog warriors looked from Memphis to Tank; all of them clamped their jaws shut, until Tank hung his head. Tank looked at the ground, then to the ruins and finally to the sky.

"The light fades and I begin to shiver, I guess shelter would be nice," he said, wandering off in the direction of the ruins.

Memphis Grimm watched Tank walk away and was pleased. He knew his old friend had reservations about the adventure that he'd thrust upon him, but in the end, he'd followed; it'd been his choice. Memphis looked at Elle who stood at the front of the rest of the pack. He smiled as best a dog warrior could, turning as he did to follow Tank into the ruins.

The young males followed him in, splitting off to explore the ruins on their own. Memphis was joined by Elle, who took hold of his hand as they walked down the centre of what would have been the street. Most of the other females followed them, with the five pups bringing up the rear.

"You ought to go easy on him; he followed you, didn't he?" Elle asked.

"He's an old dog like me!"

"And your point is what?" Elle paused, sniffing at the air.

"He knows what I've stolen from the toothless ones. We is both over ten years of age, how long do we have left, Elle? And that, my mate, is the reason he follows me!"

"Even so, Tank loves you. After all, were you not from the same litter?"

"We are brothers, aye, we suckled side by side, fighting over the same tit at times."

The group continued between the slanted structures, the pack sniffing at the air behind him as Tank appeared from behind a building a hundred metres in front of them. The large dog motioned them forwards and disappeared back behind the tall brick building.

Memphis didn't hurry as the light of the day finally began to fade. He rounded the corner and came across Tank who was considering one of the ruins.

"This one looks cosy, look, it goes down underground," Tank said, sniffing at the air as he leaned partially through the window.

Tank turned around and paused to look past Memphis, who followed his gaze to look at the pack. They all looked skyward at the dark sky of night, their jaws agape at the open-air view of stars. Memphis and Tank followed their stare and were transfixed by the sight of the thousands of stars that lit up the night sky. Duke, Rocky, Dakota and Rex all appeared at the run, slightly unnerved by what was above them.

"What are they?" Duke barked.

"I do not know, but they are beautiful," Memphis growled.

"I feel as if I could fall into them," Harmony, a sleek white furred bitch whispered.

The entire Pack Grimm turned as one, looking uphill from where they'd come. An ominous smell wafted down from above and before Memphis could speak, a far-off howl split the night's silence.

"Inside. Down as far as you can go," Memphis ordered.

More voices joined the canine chorus as the dog's call filled their hearts with dread. Rex began to sniff the air, pulling in the smell, trying to see who it was that called to them.

"It's the White Fang, they want what we have," Memphis said as he pushed the young dog warrior into the darkness.

As soon as Memphis entered the dark passage, he removed his headgear. Within seconds, his eyes adjusted to the dark and he could see the pack before him as they half-jumped, half-ran, down the stairs. The five pups were closest to him, beside Rex. The one at the rear of the little pack was a red-headed yearling called Chaz Grimm, he hurried the others along and pulled one back when it tried to run off down an adjoining corridor.

Memphis smiled, knowing the strong from the weak. Chaz would one day make an excellent dog warrior, if not pack leader.

After ten flights of stairs, they ended abruptly. Every member of the pack panted hard, it'd been a while since they'd rested and it was time for at least a nap, if not a full night's sleep. Memphis sniffed at the air, testing for the scent of those who might end them. Having the best nose for these things was one of the things that made you pack leader. The rest of the pack waited and watched whilst Tank tried the door he stood before. Memphis was happy he couldn't smell them out, their temporary subterranean hideout cutting off any of their smells that may or may not be carried on the breeze. It worked in reverse: if you couldn't smell them, they most likely couldn't smell you. This was of course dependent on the direction and strength of any wind and Memphis turned, smiling. He nodded as Tank opened the door.

Although the dog could easily see in darkness, the room beyond was pitch dark and the distance it stretched meant they could not see its end. Their ability to see in the dark was only good for around fifty feet. As soon as the door was opened, the pack was met by a slight breeze, which they all leaned into, instinctively sniffing at the warm air.

"It's connected to the tunnels," Tank said. "I smell the toothless ones."

"They've not been here for some time," Memphis added. "All this time, there was a way into their domain."

Memphis pushed past the rest of the pack, heading away from the wall and door of the room. He knew it wasn't completely safe, with its obvious connection to the subterranean world that all life existed in on Lorela, but it would have to do. The outside barren world disturbed him, at least for now.

After a quick search, the room opened out into a hundred-foot square domed room. Long-dead vegetation covered the floor and the room's past usage became apparent. It'd been some sort of underground hydroponics room, more likely a room for cultivation, by its size.

"I guess they came here to strip the room of equipment to grow their wheat," Elle suggested.

"Whatever makes them wheat, makes them weak and of no use to us. Still, this might make a useful den," Memphis said.

"It's warm, for that we have to be thankful," Elle said. "But what about food?" She drew close in case her voice carried across the room; a thought that was barely a whisper, so the others didn't pick up the sound.

"We have various tunnels here that lead to the toothless ones, but first we shall have a look at our prize!"

All the Grimm gathered around Memphis's pack. They watched as the pack leader opened the rucksack and pulled a bag from it, holding it up for all to see. He opened the little bag and took out a single pill, careful not to spill any onto the floor, to avoid contamination. He cocked his head to one side, regarding the tiny tablet, wondering how such a thing would prolong his life. He straightened his head, looking at all those that watched him.

"No dog has ever lived past his fourteenth year. I am now eleven on man's earthly calendar and so soon must perish, unless this pill does as it should," Memphis barked.

He placed the pill gently on his tongue, closed his mouth and swallowed hard. Every dog and bitch watched him, waiting for something to happen. He watched them, also waiting for something to happen and he felt no different. His mouth opened, then closed as if to say something; he looked at his hands, the fur on the backs of them was unchanged, as were his claws.

"Ah well, so much for that!" Memphis said, shrugging as if it wasn't a big deal.

"Do you feel no different?" Tank asked.

"I feel tired. Rex, you and your warriors stand the watch; tomorrow, we hunt for the toothless ones and a full belly."

With that, Memphis took hold of Elle's hand and led her away to a corner of the large chamber. No sooner had they settled down than he fell completely and soundly asleep.

Chapter 3

His eyes opened with a snap, his pupils pinpricks, and he jumped up with the pack scattering from his long drawn-out howl. His arms wide, his chest pushed out as the zest, adrenalin and strength of his youth prompted him to action. He looked at his fur that before had been black, shot through with grey; now it was black and as silky smooth as a well-fed yearling's. It was all he could do to stand still as the pack crawled back towards him. All he wanted to do was run and as his followers stretched out clawed hands to stroke his fur, he could feel the muscle definition beneath his skin.

"You've never looked better," Tank said, his brow furrowed, pushing together the loose fur between his eyes.

"I never felt better," Memphis barked.

Memphis denied himself the impulse to act with the cockiness of a three-year-old dog warrior; however, the grin was unmistakable.

"What now?" Tank asked, as he looked from Memphis to Elle and back again.

"Every old dog in its latter years, I would say ten or older, should have one of those pills," Elle said. "There's no point before old age creeps in, it'd be a waste."

"The toothless ones live for many years longer than us, now I see how, what with these pills that they make," Sandy said.

Sandy was a bitch of thirteen and the oldest dog in Pack Grimm. She held out her hands, her lips curled up into a smile.

"I'll be taking mine now!" she said and smiled.

Only two others in the pack were past middle age besides Sandy and Memphis. They both stepped up to stand either side of Sandy. Tank and Elle held out their hands, palms up, to receive the tiny pill that would bring them back to their youth.

Memphis turned and knelt by the bag that contained the pills. It was full; there were tens of thousands of them all crammed into see-through zip bags, a thousand to a bag. He took three from one of the bags and standing, placed one in each of their outstretched hands.

Memphis looked at the greedy eyes of his pack. He could smell the desire in the room; it almost had substance as the others blinked at him transfixed by what he'd transformed into.

"Every time one of us reaches our latter years, we will swallow one of these little pills and live forever, regaining our youth before the fire has left our eyes. Never again shall it be said about Pack Grimm that our numbers dwindle and that soon our pack will be gone, eating our dead in ever-decreasing circles until the carcass of the last of us sits ashamedly untouched and rotting in the corner of some foetid cave," Memphis barked.

The pack all barked and howled. The sounds threatened to give away their presence to any close enough to hear as the sound echoed down the corridors leading away into the darkness. Memphis looked at his mate, she'd curled up into a ball, Sandy lay spooning her and Tank lay behind them both, facing the other way.

"All the dog warriors to me," he barked. "For now, we hunt the flesh of man."

Rex, Dakota, Rocky and Duke all responded, they howled until their lungs were free of air. It was always good to taste the flesh of the toothless ones and a sport like no other, as the flesh of man gave effortlessly beneath clawed hands.

Memphis took off, bounding over the pack; his head threatening to catch the roof of the room as he flashed past the others. He could smell the four youngsters hot on his heels, but unlike any other time they'd ever ran, they struggled to keep up. He smiled, his lips pushed right back, he'd much more to give but held back and kept to their pace; the last thing he wanted to do was lose them as he followed the scent of his quarry. They entered a tunnel that led to the west. The scents were months old but most recently laid and the air that wafted up the tunnel was much more to the liking of man and tasted sweet to the dog warrior. Whether this was because it was cleaner, being almost free from radiation or because it was tinged with the smell of the hairless, toothless ones, he didn't know, but the smell was always sweet.

Running down the tunnel became invigorating for Memphis; it always did as the adrenalin coursed through his body. He could feel every sinew as his hard muscles flexed and it almost hurt him as he ran. They ran without talking, their tongues lolling from the side of their jaws, leaving only dusty paw prints and wet flecks of drool to tell of their passing; even those were drying in the warm air, even so the paw prints left a trail any could follow. After half an hour of running west down a straight, shallow gradient, they came to a crossroads with passages running both north and south from the intersection. Memphis pulled the four of them up for a breather and watched them pant. Normally after such a run, Memphis would find himself worse than the youngsters, now however, he found himself waiting for Rex and the others to recover.

"Can we four take one of those pills? We wish to change as you have," Rex said out of turn as he caught his air, his tongue protruding from his jaw between gulps.

"All in good time, we will live for an eternity if we take care of what we have."

"It would make sense for all to be as you!" Duke growled as he stretched his back, a twinge of pain in his lower back directing his attention.

"First let's see what the long-term effects are of the drug. Among man, for instance, it causes sterilisation, not something you young dogs should want before it's nearly your time."

Memphis regarded them, his head tilted, and they looked happy with what he said. Rocky and Dakota were products of one of Elle's litters. They didn't join any debate directed at their dog father, they weren't allowed, as custom dictated, until the dog father became nothing but a mangy hound and a shadow of its former self. Memphis could see that Rocky itched to say something. Memphis thought about asking the pup his opinion but thought better of it. Who knew what such a break in custom would bring to the table.

"Much better you remain silent, Rocky, remember which nut sack spawned you!" Memphis said.

Rocky nodded his head, looking at the floor.

"Look at the dust, it has prints going north and none returning," he said, sniffing at the air.

"We go north," Memphis said.

Memphis took off once again, his lips drooling at the thought of man flesh. They were close, less than a mile distant and less than a minute's run from the crossroads; soon their bellies would be full, the toothless ones wouldn't know what hit them. With the thought fresh in his mind, a light appeared ahead of them. The green light of luminescent moss, one of the crops harvested by man, used not only to light their tunnels but also as a food source. Memphis felt his heart race; he could smell the unsuspecting humans ahead of them, could almost taste the fear that confused the nervous farmers up ahead.

They emerged into the light. Five slavering, savage beasts, claws outstretched and iron-hard nails ready to rend flesh. Four females and a male were dumbstruck. They couldn't believe their eyes, wondering how on earth dogs had made it into their world, especially at this place and without warning.

Memphis was the first to pounce. He jumped at a female, taking hold of her arms. She whimpered helpless as his spittle dripped onto her face. The others jumped at the fearful toothless ones. Rex mistimed his jump and stumbled before his prey. In the process of righting himself, his right-hand claw ripped into the flesh of the female before him. Her intestines fell in a steaming heap onto the tunnel floor and she fell to her knees, slumped upright and remained so as the life left her with a shallow exhalation of air.

"Oh, for fuck's sake, Rex," Memphis shouted. "We're gonna have to eat that one here!"

Memphis handed his captive to Rex, the tunnel they'd run up was only ten metres wide and it only took Rex and Dakota to guard one end of the tunnel. Standing side by side, they could guard against most foes effectively. The other end of the tunnel, from where they'd come, they left unguarded.

Memphis looked at the eyes of the woman as they stared out at him, he knew the dog warriors and the humans shared certain similarities, but it always amazed him how dog-like their eyes were.

"Please let us go," the man shouted, his voice panicked and stressed.

"Dog's gotta eat!" Rex growled.

The women screamed behind their guards as Memphis reached inside the dead woman's body. His hand gripped hold of the flesh and pulled out the liver, one of his favourite parts. Stuffing this into his mouth, he began to chew as he gripped the corpse of the human and pulled at the left leg; it cracked at the hip and gave with a little effort. The shorts she'd been wearing remained on the corpse and he only had to remove the boot as he swallowed the liver, chewed but nearly whole.

"That'll do me," Memphis said.

He watched Duke and Rocky as they tucked in, stripping body parts and taking a limb each to sit on their haunches. He smiled as they growled, ripping at the flesh, he laughed, an all too human sound as their four captives stood and took off blindly up the tunnel into darkness, their fear getting the better of them. Rex and Dakota turned to join in the feeding frenzy. They ripped at the carcass of the freshly killed woman, they cared nought for the mess they made. Within a minute, they'd reduced the woman to skeletal remains that didn't retain much flesh at all. Rex bowed before Memphis; he held the head of the woman, which he offered to the pack leader.

Memphis took the head and pulled the jaw free from the skull. Placing his clawed fingers into the base of the rounded bone, it parted with ease to his great strength and he fished for the brain of the woman. It slipped around inside the bone that remained so he stabbed it with a claw as it irked him.

He felt his full stomach, patting it as he regarded the brain he held before him. He popped the warm flesh into his mouth and began to chew, smiling as the flesh popped open in his jaws and the watery gore pleased his palate. Bits of flesh hung from between his fangs and he sucked at them, using the broken skull to pry at the annoying flesh. It would have to wait for later, there was still work to be done and he threw the bit of bone to one side.

"Drive the herd," he ordered.

Rex, Dakota, Duke and Rocky took off back up the tunnel the way they'd come and the way the panicked humans had fled. Memphis was about to follow when he caught his reflection in an overturned chrome metal dish that the humans had been using. He looked different, extremely different. His snout was a good few inches longer than it'd been before and his ears seemed to stand higher onto the top of his skull. He was altogether better looking than before he'd taken the pill. He smiled at his reflection, licking at the blood on his fur; he leapt back away from the light of the moss to join the chase. His night vision took over instantly and he could just make out Rocky's backside as he ran.

Memphis turned it on, his legs working hard; he had to lean forward into a gait that was almost a gallop. By the time they'd reached the crossroads, Memphis gained considerably on the others, the mingled scent of dog and human just metres ahead. The four in his pack blocked the west and south running passages that led from the crossroads away to some other location in the subterranean world. The humans were just ahead of him now, he could see them clearly. He could smell their fear as they held clumps of moss before them so that his snout was illuminated in the dark. He roared at the screaming man who thought of fight instead of flight; just a passing of a thought of a brave ending. Memphis could smell it on the air and see it in the man's body language. That was enough for the four of them, they fled east, the only way they could without falling into the arms of the dogs.

This tunnel was a long one, it would take the weaker beings at least an hour to make the pack's temporary home and their dinner invite, but eventually they made it with the five dog warriors harrying them all the way.

Memphis emerged into the large room; Pack Grimm stood in a half circle, slobbering and howling. The four humans were huddled in a group at the centre of them; they'd stopped their crying, resigned to their fate, they waited as the hungry pack worked themselves into a frenzy.

Pack Grimm waited for the pack leader, their eyes wide, jaws agape, dripping drool hitting the floor of their hideout.

"Let the feast begin," Memphis barked.

Normally he would step forward, being pack leader meant he automatically had first choice of the cut, but as he'd already eaten, that honour fell to Tank who stepped forward out of the pack.

Tank woke from his slumber; he too looked different and watched Memphis from the corner of his eye as he circled the group of humans. Tank had grown taller by at least six inches and his snout now protruded as Memphis' did. He was broader at the shoulders and Memphis could smell the new anger that infected his brood brother's mind. He knew he would have to fight him soon, for the control of Pack Grimm. Next, he noticed his mate Elle; she seemed elegant beyond what was possible for their kind. She watched him and struggled to maintain her composure, she only just managed to prevent her tail from wagging. She was beautiful. Her coat, like his, was silky smooth and her snout also elongated. He felt himself aroused, especially when Sandy appeared at her side. Like Elle, she'd changed; she appeared so much younger than she had, but also so much more than she'd ever been, more feminine, sultry, the fresh look pleased him and he found himself aroused all the more.

All of a sudden, Tank jumped at the male. He howled in the face of their meal as his claws ripped into the man's shoulder. The man shuddered as he watched his own arm being pulled from his body. He stared horrified as his life-blood haemorrhaged from his gaping wound. Tank hefted him above his head with one hand, the other he used to hold the man's limb as he began to feast on the bicep. He threw the man, who'd gone into shock, at the howling pack and it was over for the male. In a matter of seconds, he'd been reduced to unrecognisable lumps of flesh and bone as the meat grinder that was the pack dined.

The females met the same fate as the pack of crazed dogs did what they did best. They wasted nothing of the humans and only left the bones and blood, which slicked the floor under their padded feet. They screamed as the dogs laughed, pulling bits from their bodies, until Sandy and Elle ended them, ripping their throats out in an attempt at mercy. This act, as unusual as it was, went mostly unnoticed as the pack was too consumed with the feast. Memphis, however, noticed the mercy shown but didn't know what he thought of it. Meat tasted so much better when it screamed down your throat.

After the pack ate, they rested as was normal. Some managed a little more sleep and others fucked, going into quiet corners of the underground room. Tank was one of these, taking Harmony, one of the young females to one side and growling at everyone as if he were the pack leader. Tank led the young bitch into the farthest corner of the room. She howled with obvious delight at first, but soon it turned to howls of anguish as Tank barked and bit her, worrying the bitch until she became silent and still as they coupled. Memphis would never forget what happened next. Tank walked out into his field of vision, the blood of both human and bitch dripping from his jaw. He growled, his lips drawn back to show just a little too much fang.

Memphis had been bred to lead the pack. From birth, it had been obvious that he'd those leadership qualities needed in a dog to run a large pack. He was sly, crafty, wise and strong. Tank, on the other hand, had always been the fighter. He was quick-tempered and always antagonised any dogs in his vicinity. He was strong of jaw and not many got the better of him in a scrap. They were both alpha males.

Then there were the two females; they'd always been beautiful and kind, now though, they'd become merciful.

Memphis realised at that moment the pill not only made you young again but made you more of what you'd been before. With this in mind, he turned all his thoughts to the problem that now approached him: Tank.

"What are you doing, Tank?" he asked his brother.

"I'm taking over Pack Grimm!"

Tank began to circle Memphis. The two old dogs increased in size and strength, more so than any other that had ever walked the subterranean world of Lorela. The pack formed a circle to fence in the two dogs as the fight for the right to lead was about to get under way. It was Tank's right to challenge; the two others that'd taken the pill looked more than a little pissed off, but they could do nothing but join the circle. As part of the pack, it was their duty to witness the ancient rite of ruler-ship.

Tank jumped in at Memphis, his clawed left hand forward with his right drawn back, his lips drawn up to bare all the fangs and teeth that lined his jaw.

Memphis raised his own hands, grabbing Tank's as they locked together in battle. They barked and snarled, bit and rent. Tank hadn't considered that his brother was stronger than him; even as pups, Memphis had beat him nine times out of ten, and now as they wrestled, Memphis forced his brother back. He forced his back to arch, and he towered over him. He thought of all the times—good and bad—they'd shared; looking at Tank, he considered what he'd become.

Memphis struggled with the love he felt for Tank. Now he bared his teeth; his brood brother should have more goddamn respect! He leaned forward and sank his front fangs deep into Tank's right shoulder.

Tank howled in agony, they both collapsed in a heap on the floor. They rolled around, still snarling at one another until they came to rest with Memphis sat astride Tank's heaving chest. With one hand, he held Tank's good arm; with the other he held his neck, drawing blood from all five claws, his palm pressing down on Tank's Adam's apple.

"Stop this, Tank, you are beaten!" Memphis howled.

Tank said nothing. He snarled and barked like a beast gone mad and the whole pack of snarling dogs quietened at the scene, thinking that Tank had become more beast than dog; it had always been a fine line between sanity and the feral.

"Is he rabid?" a voice howled from the circle of onlookers. If they weren't worried before, they were now.

"No, he's not rabid, it's the effect of the drug he has taken," Memphis barked at them.

Memphis felt pain as Tank used his lame clawed hand to stab him in his unprotected flank, leaving four deep puncture wounds in his side. Memphis howled, his jaws opened wide as he bit at the face of his brother; he felt both the pain in his side and the pain in his heart.

How could my brother do this to me? he thought.

Tank went limp, he declared to Memphis, not wishing to lose his face in this fight.

Chapter 4

Memphis stood, holding his right side. Elle rushed forward with a shirt that the male human had worn and held it against the deep puncture wounds in an attempt to stop the bleeding.

Tank stood and looked about him. He waited for one of the bitches to rush to him to staunch his wounds as Elle had done to Memphis. None came, so he stood, his breaths heavy, and faced Memphis Grimm, his pack leader.

"Will you now bow down to my rule?" Memphis gasped.

Tank considered him; he worked his injured arm and wondered if he could kill the maimed pack leader. He snarled, baring his teeth and fangs, knowing he'd been beaten; but at least he could kill his brood brother, his brother, the one who'd always looked after him, loved him, even shared his last scrap of bone when food had been in short supply.

Tank shook his head and felt the shame of his lost honour. He looked again and now the whole pack stood between him and their leader. He licked his lips, felt the froth on his jaw, as blood from the puncture wounds left from Memphis worked its way through his fur and into his eyes.

Am I rabid? he thought.

He took off, back through the door that led above. The sound of a single mournful howl followed him; had Memphis wanted him to stay? Tank paused halfway up the second flight of stairs and shook his head; he'd played second fiddle to Memphis Grimm ever since they had been pups, he couldn't do it any longer, no matter what that meant. He ran up the stairs and into the light of day as another mournful song burst from his brother's mouth.

He was naked and lacked the protection of the tinted shades. The sun's rays bathed him with its harmful light and he blinked, thinking himself blind until he became accustomed to the light. Surprisingly, his eyes held the vision and he didn't go blind. He blinked as his eyes watered though. After a brief time, he moved out in between the tops of the buildings; his eyes soon became accustomed to the brightness of the sandy barren landscape.

"Must be the pills," he said to himself.

Chaz was behind him. He wouldn't have known he was there but for the smell; the yearling couldn't mask that—the smell always gave them away. He considered dragging him out into the light, blinding him and taking him for his next meal; but somehow, he knew he would be all right, so he left him skulking in the entrance to the subterranean world.

Chaz knew he'd been noticed; if he could smell Tank, Tank could smell him. He froze, worrying about the dog warrior he had idolised since his birth. Tank had been his dog father and he loved the old dog; although he'd imposed self-banishment from the pack, he still loved him. Chaz made his way back into the subterranean underground. He hung his head for the shame he felt for his father and worried for himself. What would he turn into when he finally got to swallow one of the pills?

After making his way down the stairs, Chaz came upon a scene that would worry any that ran with the Grimm. Memphis was lying prone, his head on Sandy's lap. His tongue lolled to one side and he panted as he struggled for breath. Elle licked at the old dog's wounds in his side.

"Chaz, come over here," Memphis ordered, looking through weary eyes; he didn't even lift his head.

Chaz almost crept to his leader's side, as if any sudden rush of movement could injure him further. He knelt on the ground next to him.

"What of Tank?" Memphis asked.

"He wandered out into the bright light that covers the land, and although he shaded his eyes, he could see perfectly well. He mumbled something about the pills," Chaz replied, and spoke over Memphis as his leader opened his mouth to talk. "There's something else!"

Memphis thought the pup was clever, he'd kept one inquisitive eye on him since he'd seen how he bossed the others in his litter. Now he regarded him with a newfound respect; a yearling talking confidently over an alpha? Unheard of.

"Go on," Memphis said, swallowing hard, his tongue sticking to the roof of his mouth, his palate dry.

"When he walked out into the light, his wounds, they smoked and hissed a little. The bleeding stopped."

Memphis looked to Elle who lifted her head from her task of cleaning the wounds. Both lifted their brows in amazement.

"So, the wounds healed in the light of the sun!" Elle said. "Rex, Duke, Dakota, Rocky, come get your pack leader."

It wasn't normal for a bitch to take control, another unusual event that had occurred since the transformation. Memphis didn't complain though; if all went well, in a matter of minutes, he would be up on his feet once more.

The four young warriors took hold of a limb each. It wasn't the custom to help a dog, once the dog had had its day. But seeing as it'd turned into a day for the extraordinary, everyone seemed to just accept it. They hefted Memphis Grimm from the floor and carried him, howling all the way, up to the surface. By the time they'd reached the entrance to the ground above, Memphis was exhausted, having lost a lot of blood.

The four young dog warriors gently placed him down on the floor of the building. They were careful not to venture out into the light of day, having left their tinted skull caps in a bag down below. Sandy and Elle followed them up and wasted no time at all and pushed past them to kneel on either side of their pack leader. Hefting Memphis up, they half-carried, half-dragged him out into the light and waited for something to happen. As it happened, they didn't have long to wait. As soon as the sun's light touched his injured flank, his wounds began to hiss and smoulder.

Memphis didn't notice as he shielded his eyes, even though the sun's rays seemed to cauterise the wounds.

Memphis lounged in the light, his breaths shallow; he still struggled for breath and was weak, his head failed in a few attempts to rise from the sandy ground.

Elle and Sandy blinked away the light, not daring to turn away from Memphis until they'd become accustomed to the sun's glare. Sandy retreated into the shade, leaving Elle stroking Memphis Grimm, avoiding the wounds that were still soft to the touch. How the puncture wounds healed was a complete marvel, like a miracle. The pills certainly gave them the edge topside and although they'd lost Tank who'd lost his sanity, they'd gained so much more. As half the pack watched, eventually Memphis regained something of his strength, he half-stood to take in his surroundings, sniffing at the air.

"Tank is still close, he watches us!" Memphis growled.

"He's been there for some time," Elle said.

Tank watched, waiting to see if Memphis lived through his ordeal. He'd known his brood brother suffered great injuries, his clawed fingers having sunk deep into his side. When Memphis regained his feet, he didn't know if he was disappointed or not. In one respect, he wanted the pack for himself; if Memphis had died, it would have been easy to take it over. He would have mounted Elle to teach her a lesson, making the whole pack watch as he fucked her. On the other hand, he loved his brother and part of him was happy that he still lived, a part deep within that smiled despite his disappointment. Tank watched as Sandy returned to Memphis's side; together, with Elle, they supported Memphis, yet too weak to stand by himself. Memphis limped back into the entrance to the underground as the light began to fail, the rest of the pack following, and Tank knew he'd lost them. He would never return to grovel at his brother's feet; he would not yield and suffer the indignity.

Chapter 5

Tank watched the entrance for some time. He'd never been alone before, always having had someone close at hand. Now an outcast, he would have to survive without his family; he looked to the horizon and the gathering night, the stars there beginning to appear, and howled for his loss, a long mournful sound that carried for miles across the barren, lifeless land.

As dusk turned to night, Tank turned from the ruined town, a tear caught on his cheek, wetting the fur. He wandered in a circle around the old settlement in ever-increasing circles, trying to figure out what to do next. He sniffed the air constantly until he smelt them. Another pack of dog warriors emerged from the dog lands, the tunnelled underworld that their kind had ruled for hundreds of years and countless generations of hounds.

A gust of wind came up the valley, blowing the scent away from his nose, and as the wind gained in strength, he lost it completely. Turning, he began to run. Even at the distances involved, he knew that whoever it might be would most probably be headed straight for him. So he fled across the sand. A dust storm blowing all around him, he had to half-shield his eyes from the grains that pelted him. He still felt the throb and ache from his healed wounds and tired quickly from his recent scrap with Memphis.

He pulled up in unfamiliar territory, wanting to save what energy he'd left, in case whoever was chasing him dared risk venturing too far from safety. He scanned his surroundings as the dust storm raged all around him. The barren plains didn't give up much with the sand and dust obscuring his vision. As his thoughts played out in his mind, he smelt them, even though they stood downwind from him; they must be very close. He turned to see four dog warriors leaning into the storm.

They were Blade, Kush, Barack and Bandit from Pack White Fang. Somehow, they seemed smaller than they ever had before, and not just in the physical sense either. It appeared to Tank that these four dog warriors were inferior and no longer mattered in the great scheme of Tank's existence.

Tank barked at his pursuers, who howled in response to the dog that they'd caught.

"You would be best advised to return to your kingdom, you have no business here with me," Tank growled.

"Killer wants to see you, Tank!" Blade barked.

"Tell Killer to go take a shit in his hand," Tank laughed.

The four dog warriors became unnerved at the sound of Tank's laughter, they growled at the offence to their pack and circled, ready for the kill, but Tank could smell them, could smell their fear at the changed Grimm that stood defiantly before them.

"What has happened to you?" Kush barked, having noticed the changes in Tank's demeanour. No dog should stand against four, it was unheard of.

Tank turned towards him but didn't answer, he knew it for the ruse it was. Kush spoke as Barack lunged in, his clawed hands outstretched, but Tank was ready. He spun on his heels to face the onrushing Barack, his sandy shade part hidden in the turbulent air.

Tank easily swept both the outstretched claws aside with a swiping backhand that stunned Barack, especially when he fell to the same strike that'd injured Memphis to near death.

It surprised Tank how easy it'd been to defeat Barack as he buried his right claw deep into Barack's side, clenching his claw around what felt like the dog's stomach before removing his arm with the organ still held in his clenched fist. He threw the entrails and the organ into the face of the onrushing Kush; the gore of the organ caught him off guard and he was forced to bat it away to stop it inhibiting his vision. He came face to face with the changed Tank, his lips drawn back and drool dripping onto his nose. Kush looked up at the dog warrior; he was stunned at the smell of his own death. His eyes looked down as his head sagged, he looked at his exposed ribs and the two hands—both belonging to Tank—buried within his upper body.

Kush went limp; he'd smelt his own death and now felt it rise as he vomited gore from his lungs, up through his nose and mouth. Tank lifted him from the ground and lapped at the flesh as it hung from the dog's teeth.

Tank looked beyond Kush, whose feet dangled a clear foot from the ground. He looked at the hesitant Blade and Bandit and laughed. That all too human sound that, coming from Tank, made the banished dog warrior sound unhinged. Tank flicked both his wrists, causing the head of the White Fang dog warrior to fall away from him, exposing his neck. Without taking his eyes from the two remaining members of Pack White Fang, Tank lifted the corpse of the dog he held to his jaw and ripped the throat all the way to the bone. Kush's head fell further back. Tank must have looked as a devil hound, one of those rare, insane and rabid dogs, as he was bathed in the blood of Kush. The other two backed away into the storm, their scent disappearing in a swirl of sand and dust, as if the storm could mask their withdrawal. Tank was pleased the wind was in their favour, he'd had enough of the stench of cowardice.

He looked down at his two kills. Although they would soon start to decompose, he would have meat every day for at least a week and two hides that he could use to construct a full suit to protect him from the elements; not something any dog in the warmth of the subterranean world would have considered.

Killer, the leader of Pack White Fang, stood inside the entrance of the tunnel mouth. Visibility was practically zero and even with his night vision, he couldn't see more than five metres. Butch, his brood brother and right-hand dog and muscle stood by his side and together they strained to see into the storm. Fortunately, the wind was in their favour and they could sense the fright of Blade and Bandit as they howled, lost in the sandstorm.

One of the pack at their back began to howl in response to the pleas, and even though the howls ended and the scent became stronger, their fear remained. This unnerved the pack, even Butch and Killer felt the emotion wash over them as the two dogs appeared from the storm, sand and dust blowing across their entire height.

The noses of the two returning dogs were dry with sand, which stuck to the wetness, and they squinted and shielded their eyes.

"Kush and Barack, where are they?" Killer asked as his dog warriors entered the tunnel mouth.

"Dead," Blade whimpered.

Two bitches rushed to their mates' sides with water for them to drink and a wet cloth for the end of their snouts. The mates of the dead dog warriors hung their heads; they lifted their heads together to sound a mournful howl, a single matching note to sound the passing of their loved ones.

"Was it Memphis and all the Grimm? Did they ambush you?" Butch asked.

"Just Tank, out there in the storm. We gave chase and when we fell upon him, he ripped the others to pieces," Blade said, hanging his head in shame.

"I don't understand," Killer barked, his eyes wild with anger and contempt for the two that had returned. "How could one Grimm defeat my four best warriors?"

"Please, my lord, do not be angry with us. He'd changed, he was twice the dog as us four combined, his snout longer, his fangs sharper and he stood a foot taller than any I've ever seen before," Bandit whimpered.

"His strength was incredible, we couldn't defeat him. The others he tossed about with an unstoppable power, as if they were pups at play, and he laughed as he frothed about the flesh of Kush, making short work of the kill," Blade growled, remembering the moment his brood brother had had his throat ripped out.

"They're taking them!" Butch snapped. "Shall I send out the boys?"

"Not yet. I don't want to lose more warriors to them; there is business to attend to first."

Killer and Butch turned from the upside world to return to the subterranean life they knew. Killer was already late for his meeting, but he couldn't attend it without finding out about this latest development. The two of them worked their way down the tunnel system and after a few turns came out into a cavern that was neither in Pack Grimm territory nor the human domain. Ten of his best dog warriors were in attendance, spaced out around the cavern, facing the opposite side. Facing them were more than fifty humans covered in silver plate armour and carrying swords; long heavy weapons only the strongest humans could carry, the type that would kill dog warriors. The silver plate armour was a new development though and shone green when the light from the moss they carried played along the surfaces.

Killer and Butch walked out into the middle of the cavern and were met by a small delegation of men. The tension in the room was palpable; full of fear on the one side and hunger on the other. Killer himself knew what this meeting meant, they all did, but even he felt a growing desire to rip flesh and eat the living.

"I'm Killer and this is my second, Butch."

"We know who you are, pack leader," the human said. "I'm Alex Stevenson, mayor of the district here about," he motioned behind him with a relaxed wave of his hand.

"Why can I smell death?" Killer asked as he sniffed the air.

Alex turned and motioned towards the tunnel behind him. His armoured guards parted, four hand trolleys were wheeled out into the cave. Each trolley carried the corpses of four of his people, cold, dead and naked, ready to eat. All the dog warriors howled with delight as the trolleys were pushed before them.

"You understand our customs very well," Butch said.

One of the dog warriors broke ranks and jumped at a trolley, its wheels squeaking as it made the middle of the cavern. He landed on its surface, clawing at the young man that pushed it nervously toward him. He ripped his throat out without any thought of what he was doing, putting the whole meeting in jeopardy. Swords were drawn and both man and dog tensed as violence was threatened.

Butch jumped at him, slapping him claw-less so he wouldn't be injured, but the blow was meant for pain, Butch put all his strength behind it.

"Down Kito, be gone!" Butch barked.

Kito, the offending dog, held himself close to the floor. He stretched out an arm, stabbing the kill with his claw before retreating to the rear of the cave, behind the other warriors from his pack. They all began to feed, rushing forwards as the three other men that pushed the trolleys fled in fear, leaving just Butch and Killer to face the humans.

It was a few moments before the humans could relax, and even then, the small group looked at the scene with hatred and disgust, with more than one of them retching up his lunch.

"Have you any news of our pills?" Alex asked.

"Yes, we only found one of the Grimm, alone on the surface. He'd changed, grown in stature and easily killed those that tried to kill him."

"Ah shit, they have taken them!" Alex spat out the words, his disappointment obvious for all.

"Give us some of the pills, enough for all of us present. We'll go get your bag of tricks for you," Killer pleaded, which sounded more like a whine.

"I'm afraid that isn't an option. The pills just aren't safe for your kind. Madness and death awaits any dog that swallows a pill," an old-looking human said, stepping into the conversation. "They are manufactured for humans, and humans alone. I'm afraid the benefits of taking the pills for your kind are short-lived. You would be better off staying well clear of the things that are essential for human life."

"So, what do you suggest?" Killer asked, regaining his growl.

"We will bring you some of our dead, ten a day to this cavern. Would that whet your appetite? Plus, fifty dog-killing swords to give you the upper hand perhaps!"

As he spoke, another trolley was pushed out into the cavern by the three young men who strained against the weight of the thing.

Fifty of the man-made swords that could slice into and kill the dog warriors lay on the trolley. The young men walked no further than ten metres into the cavern, they turned and ran from the room, but the dogs ahead of them had all had their fill, they'd returned to their original positions.

"Is it a deal?" Alex asked.

Killer rose to his full height, his eyes narrowing as he looked from the flesh remaining on the trolleys. There was plenty of meat on ten human bodies, enough to feed fifty of his dog warriors, and ten a day. Every week his entire pack would have meat in their bellies, food that they hadn't hunted. Although it wasn't enough to fill everybody, it was enough to maintain life in hard times. That, coupled with the meat from other packs that the swords would bring in, was more than enough to create stability for Pack White Fang.

"There are other packs interested in our deal!" Alex said, crossing his palms in front of him, wearing a smug little grin across his face.

Killer's head rose as he let off half a howl, half a growl. The sounds unnerved even his own dog warriors and his disdain for the comment made by Alex Stevenson was plain for all to see. He leaned forward so their noses almost touched, his lips drawn as far back as they could go.

"Do not dare renege on our deal. And before you dishonour your pack, let me at least give answer to said proposition," Killer barked, emptying his lungs as his dog warriors raced to square up against the fifty armoured humans that took a few steps forwards in readiness for combat.

"Of course, of course," Alex said quickly, waving with his hand at his men for calm. "My apologies."

Killer looked left and right, both sides seemed to settle, he could smell no pending troubles. He looked to Butch who shrugged away his opinion; he didn't have one past his next kill. Killer narrowed his eyes and pulled back from the head of the human delegation.

"Ok, ten of your dead every day will do, and we will get you your pills back!"

"And our people here about will be free from your hunting hounds?" Alex suggested, even though none ventured beyond the safety of the human realm.

"None from Pack White Fang will bother you, not if they wish to live another turning of the clock."

Alex Stevenson turned from the old dog warrior; he was followed by his delegation. The armoured soldiers were next, they backed out of the cavern, leaving those of Pack White Fang behind to mull over what'd just happened. Of course, the corpses were ancient and recently taken out of refrigeration; there were many such corpses on ice in storage. Alex could only hope that they would last until the pills were returned.

Chapter 6

"Arm fifty of your dog warriors, Butch. Wait until the storm has passed, then lead them out to retrieve what has been stolen," Killer said as the last of the armoured men turned and left them.

"I'll bring you Memphis Grimm's head back on a spike," Butch growled.

"That would be nice."

The dog warriors of Pack White Fang turned as the lights disappeared, the men from the human kingdom had turned around too many corners for it to have effect. They made their way down the tunnels towards the centre of their territory, where the scent of home was the strongest. As they walked among their people, many dogs and bitches lined the way They kissed the ground where Killer and Butch walked, some bitches even kissing their feet and one even dared the very public display of turning around to offer herself to Killer. Killer sniffed her and moved on, leaving the bitch delighted—she'd at least been noticed.

They entered the main cavern some two miles below the surface. Here, the heat was comforting to the dogs whose coats never grew too thick. Before them, hundreds of dogs gathered. Only the dog warriors of Pack White Fang filled the room, they wanted to know the outcome of the meeting between the dogs and the humans; an historic moment and not one all the pack agreed with.

Caesar watched the pack leader walk with his best warriors behind him, he was a powerful dog coming up to his ninth year and would love control of the pack, feeling that Killer had had his day. News of the loss of life had preceded him by half an hour and Caesar had used this time to plant the seed of doubt into the minds of those gathered with a long and flowery speech. His propaganda had been helped by the fact that Kush and Barack had been extremely popular among the pack. Now, even their carcasses were lost, so they couldn't even help Pack White Fang as a decent meal.

"My lord returns," Caesar growled.

Killer could smell the dissent that'd grown in the giant cavern. More than a few grim faces stared at the cave entrance they'd walked out of. Killer had a desire to lunge for Caesar, he always did. He had to be careful, however; Caesar had a large amount of support among the pack and it would be a tragedy if civil war occurred, especially when he was about to seal his immortality in the pack's history.

Killer bared his fangs and growled, drool dripping from his jaw, but he ignored the animosity Caesar offered him. He couldn't appear to be weak, but also, he couldn't bite at every negative remark thrown at him.

"Tell us, Killer, how do you intend to avenge our glorious dead?" Caesar barked, not happy to be disrespected, not even by his pack leader.

As he finished his sentence, the trolley was wheeled in by two of the pack.

Killer smiled. He turned and motioned with an upturned claw to the weaponry that he'd brought with him.

"With these weapons, we shall conquer all who stand against us, including the treacherous Grimm."

"So, you sold us out for a human way of killing. You offend our pack and bring dishonour to us all," Caesar barked.

Killer turned on Caesar, his eyes wide with anger and hatred.

"Every day, for all of time, I have secured a food source, for the men have agreed to venture into our domain. Every day, they shall bring us ten of their dead. This I have done for our pack. With these weapons, we shall dominate over the other packs, crossing into enemy territory when we need to feed."

Killer's tirade was met with howls of approval from his supporters, which numbered far more now than those that opposed him. He appeared smug as his main competition for his place as pack leader turned and left by a side tunnel. Those that supported him ardently followed him to help lick his wounds.

"Now my dog warriors, who is up for the hunt? I feel the need to end the Grimm. Their days have been numbered for some time. Now it is time to finish off Memphis Grimm and his pack of mangy dogs!" Killer barked, standing tall with a proud set jaw.

The chorus of howls echoed through the White Fang territory, unnerving all that heard it—from other packs that bordered them, such as Pack Blood Hound, who were the White Fang's main rivals after the Grimm.

There was no shortage of dog warriors that queued for the weapons. Killer was pleased as there were more than enough to fulfil his needs.

Tank dragged the two dead dogs about a mile into the unknown, away from both the Grimm and the White Fang, when he came across a small rise with an overhang. He dragged the corpses and sat with his back to the bluff, using the two corpses as a shield against the storm. He curled up and hunkered down, pulling Kush up around his face, biting into the flesh to drink his fill of blood before he closed his eyes to wait out the storm, hoping to get a nap as the sandy dust blew all around him.

He opened his eyes; the wind still blew but without the intensity to cause the sort of chaotic weather it had whilst he had slept. His lower body was covered in the tiny debris, as was breakfast that still lay atop and at the side of him. Standing, he looked at the kills from the previous day. The stars shone above him against a darkened backdrop and it was all he could do not to howl and lunge at the food. He stretched, taking his time as twin dust devils sprang up and blew away from him to the east; he knelt next to Barack and watched the strange phenomena as they fled across the plain. Breaking off the dead dog's leg, he stripped away the furred skin and examined the meat before he bit, ripping off a large chunk of thigh muscle.

Then he smelt them, dog warriors that wore the stench of Pack White Fang. They were still a long way off but headed in his direction. This time, there were more of them. He could smell the mass and not even estimate their numbers, with the many different individual scents passing over his senses.

He dropped his meal as the howl tore through the night sky. He'd been detected. He turned and jumped up over the sandy overhang without even touching the lip. Tank ran; he knew he couldn't beat the force sent against him, so he tried to outrun them. He was amazed how much faster he was than before the pill. His legs were more defined, having increased in muscle mass, and he could tell just by running his hands down their length that they were solid.

After ten minutes of running, his senses couldn't pick up any pursuit. If he couldn't smell them as the night air stilled, he was damn sure they couldn't smell him, so he slowed his pace, turning away from his present course and heading north to try to throw off those that would use him to fill their bellies. There was no honour in feeding those not of your blood. He remembered his own pack and his lost honour, still a fresh memory, and he would have sounded a howl to match his sorrowful mood, but it would surely give him away. Such luxuries would have to wait.

He'd deduced correctly; he heard a host of baying cries of sadness. They'd found his lunch and he smiled, knowing they'd found them mutilated and partly eaten. The shame of it would haunt them. His smile faded as his jaw clamped shut. The discovery of their dead in such a state would only fuel their anger and increase their determination to catch him.

He ran on for another ten minutes, the wind in his face. He knew this to be a bad idea and wished he'd given his flight more thought. Maybe next time he would have the time to put mind to purpose. He paused for breath and sniffed the air and smelled nothing but the wilderness; he quietened his breathing until it wasn't even a whisper of a whisper, stilling his motion so that he would have resembled a statue covered in fur. He listened for a good minute, taking in every sound, letting the slightest of noises play across his senses; there was only the faintest of howls. It would appear the pill was of great advantage to him, he might survive after all. Now all he had to do was kidnap a mate or two so that he could produce some food.

He started to run again, changing course so that this time, he doubled back to where he'd started. He used the terrain for cover just in case he had missed something, or if they'd left a guard with the remains of Kush and Barack.

From rocky outcrop to rocky outcrop he ran, until he came across the small break in the ground and turned south, hoping that it was the rise where he'd left his meal. Keeping low, he eventually came to the spot where he had slept the day away and hidden from the storm. Both his kills had been removed and he patted his belly and wondered where his next meal was going to come from.

He headed east, back to the land he knew, back towards both the ruined town and the tunnel that led back into White Fang territory. As he ran, he got a whiff of Grimm that dissipated as soon as it materialised—one of the youngsters perhaps, checking for signs of life aboveground. He smelt the scent of White Fang and something else. It smelt like man but masked, as if it was an old smell from the past year. But this was impossible as he'd already covered this ground and the smell hadn't been there before.

He ran on regardless, feeling the pain and anger at his departure from his pack, but decided against begging. He almost barked before he realised that he had growled. So instead, he ran towards the other smells and the promise of human flesh. Running over the ground, leaving his prints in the loose sand that lay atop the hard-packed ground.

He came upon them, two of Pack White Fang and two others that wore weird suits. The two weird-looking people were human but wearing protective clothes against the radiation that would kill them. This was what had masked the scent of them; it made them appear in some far-off place. This, however, was not what freaked Tank out. Dogs had no place walking with men, unless they led them to their deaths and if Tank's belly had anything to do with it, they just had.

Tank was surprised at himself, he showed no fear as he charged at the group; no second thoughts plagued his mind. A fact made more unusual because Killer was one of the dogs that seemed to be escorting the humans. Killer turned and fled as soon as Tank appeared, and with the wind blowing due south, it would have been difficult for Killer to know of his approach. The other dog was a little too slow to react and his poor attempt to follow after his pack leader ended as soon as he'd shown Tank his backbone, or lack thereof.

Tank leapt up onto his back, his powerful legs landing on the young dog warrior's lower back, cutting through the light brown fur with clawed hands as Tank's adversary fell forward. Tank made a fist with his right hand as he stood up, his hand cupped between the ribs to lift the howling dog warrior whilst still standing on the base of his spine. The bones cracked as Tank stood effortlessly, leaning back. The now choking dog warrior went limp as his spine snapped just below the ribs. Tank pulled harder, the fur of his captive ripping like gossamer. Tank used his free hand to slice through the flesh as his enemy finally succumbed to Tank's superiority. Tank released the now prone dog, its chest rising as he struggled for breath, passed out as he lay below the deadly Tank.

Tank looked at the humans in their clumsy suits. They were rooted to the spot watching as Tank knelt, taking a drink of blood from the gaping wound just below the ribs. He ran a claw along the wound, just below the skin, so that when he pulled it free, it came up with a finger full of flesh. The two figures began to turn, spinning around in a circle on the spot. Tank popped his finger into his mouth, his tongue licking at the gore there. The two humans turned away from him albeit in a clumsy fashion. He thought it funny, how they moved in the restrictive suits and would have laughed, if not for the new scent in the air that invaded his senses as he watched the out-of-place humans.

Tank ran to the clumsy humans, scooping one under his arm and the other up over his shoulder without breaking stride. He fled into the night, now completely void of wind. The still of the night giving him the advantage when it came to sniffing out the enemy. The smell of White Fang invaded his senses, as several of their pack emerged from the underground lair to hunt him down once more. He'd been close to the entrance to the underworld and now headed downhill in familiar surroundings. He soon hit the valley floor at a run, putting distance between himself and the pursuit. It irked him though, being the prey in the deadly game of dog eat dog. He ran past the temporary hideout where Pack Grimm were holed up and passed two of the younger dog warriors on his way. Duke and Rocky were the two Grimm and they were busy, rushing back into their hole, obviously trying to avoid detection.

Tank turned south as the first hunting party sent out to kill him returned. He ran and his stamina knew no bounds. Tank was pleased with his new-found freedom from the pack. If only he could find enough food to keep himself alive.

Chapter 7

Killer walked between the ruined structures; many dog warriors walked at his heel, all armed with the human weapons and ready to use them to their advantage.

Killer had lost Tank's scent. The trails petered out close to these old ruins, now though he smelt them. Pack Grimm was holed up somewhere in these ruins, if they could just find them. Butch returned, entering the town from the opposite end. A group of White Fang's younger dog warriors followed his lead; every one of them was out to prove themselves and obtain a fresh meal. They too were all armed with the huge human swords. As Butch reached his side, Killer picked up the scent, his nose sniffing out the underground lair. He couldn't smell Pack Grimm directly but they'd unwittingly laid a residual scent by going over the same ground again and again.

The whole pack sensed it, fresh-scented Grimm, ready to be consumed. Butch tried to smile at Killer as he passed, that all too human action that never really worked for Butch.

The twenty dog warriors followed him, entering the old ruin, pausing at the top of the stairwell and sniffing the air as the clanging of a metal door slammed into a metal frame, breaking the silence from below.

Memphis Grimm smelt them as the door slammed shut, their numbers had been uncountable, but the sickening stench of White Fang was unmistakable.

"We should have killed and eaten that selfish bastard," Rex barked, as he and the other four two-year-old dog warriors pushed the door closed, lending their weight to keep it so.

"All the bitches into the tunnel, there are too many to hold off," Memphis barked his order.

The four yearlings looked at Memphis. Chaz stood in front of the others; they too wanted to fight, but at such an early age they lacked the strength and the skill to last more than a moment in such a scrap. Memphis wished they could; he was weak still, from his fight, and felt the pain of the five cauterised puncture wounds in his flank. He shook his head, dispelling any thought of the Grimm ending here. Memphis held the bag of stolen pills in his hand and threw it to Chaz, who caught it, a sorrowful look in his eyes.

"Flee, young dog warriors, you're the future of the Grimm now and if I do not survive this day, Chaz is to be your leader."

As one, the pups turned and ran for the tunnels. Memphis watched them until they'd all entered the tunnel, hopefully headed for a safer place. As he turned, there was a mighty knock beyond the metal door. Memphis could smell Butch White Fang, the fearsome dog warrior known for his fighting prowess throughout the dog world. His presence brought a whole new dimension to the fight. Memphis hated the White Fang, especially Butch who had led his pack in many of the battles that'd driven them out of their ancestral territories. That'd led to the theft of the bag in the first place. Killer wanted these pills, he'd promised peace in return for them. Memphis had gone along with the treaty and agreed terms until his honour had gotten the better of him. He doubted that Pack White Fang would honour their side of the bargain.

The door opened an inch with the weight behind it; the sheer numbers had forced it to budge a little. The four young Grimm would never hold it. Memphis turned from the tunnel to the door, his eyes narrowed, his lips turned up as far as they could go.

"Let them come!" he growled.

The four youngsters couldn't hold the door any longer. They were thrown back by the force of numbers behind the metal door. Memphis' adrenalin coursed through his veins, lending him the strength to fight. It was a different fight altogether than the one with Tank. The sibling rivalry had been nothing compared to this fight for the survival of the pack and all his kin. He no longer felt the pain of his injuries as he stepped forward to greet his new guests and invite them to a deadly dance of death. Standing to his full height, his right hand drawn back above and behind him. The invading pack seemed to baulk, their eyes wide at the sight of him, and their front rank gave pause to what they'd unleashed. They stood there with their human swords held limp in trembling hands. The increased bulk of the old dog warrior and his speed and strength caught them off guard, even though they'd all heard the stories that Blade and Bandit had told.

Memphis moved like lightning; his clawed hand stabbed the first two in the doorway that dared to oppose him. Just two quick jabs that opened the chest of one and the throat of the second, who fell to his knees holding his throat with the sword clattering on the hard floor. Memphis was forced back into the room as his enemies belched forwards, their blades pointed right at him and threatening his demise. All the White Fang attention was on him as they entered, and the four Grimm dog warriors took full advantage of this. Two jumped in on either side, dragging another two down with four clawed hands ripping at each of them, their coats giving easily to the hard nails. Memphis roared at them; only Butch stepped forwards, daring the challenge of this mutated beast before him. He swung his sword high above his head, bringing it down towards Memphis, but his clumsy, untrained sword skill let him down and he was forced to step back in retreat as Memphis lunged at him.

Pack White Fang got over the initial sight of him and spread out around the room, forcing the four young Pack Grimm back behind Memphis, who was forced backwards towards the tunnel's mouth. Long blades jabbed forward, keeping him from attacking. The White Fang surrounded him in a semi-circle but failed to encompass him completely as he made the tunnel's entrance, pushing his young dog warriors behind him with outstretched arms.

There was nothing Memphis could do; even with his increased powers, he couldn't face so many snarling, stabbing enemies, but he couldn't flee either, not without leaving his youngsters to their fate.

Then he smelt their scent, his bitches and pups returned, they smelled like fury and came on twice as fast. They, like him, had had enough of this hatred against them and the howls of Elle and Sandy were all too close as the White Fang backed off into the room.

Elle and Sandy led the charge. The changes in them because of the pills had gone from elegance and beauty with an almost poetic overtone to something altogether rabid-like. Their anger had gotten the better of them, turned them feral with insanity and the promise of death.

The scent alone was too much for the White Fang warriors as the number of their targets increased. The sights of the two bitches emerging from the tunnel, one either side of Memphis, wild with rage and frothing at the mouth, sent shivers down the furred spines and they fled. Turning, they made for the exit, the lucky ones reached it before the Grimm reached them.

Memphis, Elle and Sandy were the first to move, with Elle jumping from a standing start onto the back of a dog, stabbing in from either side into his throat, killing him in an instant. Sandy seemed to glide, her feet moved so fast her body was almost a blur. She dispatched two others before the rest of the pack entered behind them. Memphis, on the other hand, was forced to yield. The pain in his flank was becoming altogether too painful once more, so much so, he was forced to take a knee.

He was amazed at how the bitches issued forth to take on the dog warriors. It was unheard of in the world of dog and one of the laws that governed all of dog kind—bitches could not fight. They were not permitted to do so, as they produced the young that were often required as food in hard times. But it was amazing what they brought to the battle. Like howling banshees, they entered the large chamber, intent on rending flesh.

Swords in hand, Pack White Fang put up one last-ditch defence in the doorway at the base of the stairs. Their numbers had halved now, tightly packed together, holding their swords before them to fend off the Grimm that snapped at their heels. Two others fought back to back in the giant cellar, cut off from escape. They were soon overwhelmed by the many Grimm bitches that swarmed all over them, devouring them as they still tried to fend them off with claws and swords. One hapless White Fang stabbed down into the back of the bitch that bit into his crotch, ripping his genitalia from between his legs.

Butch had seen enough at that point. As much as he wasn't a coward, there was no way a pack in bloodlust could be beaten by so few a number. He stepped backwards, turned and made for the upper levels and the rest of the White Fang turned with him. Two of their number fell to Sandy who raced forwards to end them. Ripping the flesh from their backs, lifting it to her jaw to lap at it with tongue, she snarled at the dog warrior that turned to watch his own flesh being consumed.

Killer stood waiting with the dog warriors he'd kept back in reserve. He could smell the scent of dead and dying dog. He sensed the unease as the sounds of battle came ever nearer. He guessed the fight hadn't gone so well and began to back away from the building that led to the underground. The first indication of Butch's flight came close, the scent of his second-in-command bounding towards them.

He snarled and growled; they all did. Butch emerged, almost yelping, with six of their number following. They'd dropped their weapons and were in full rout.

There was no distance between those that fled and those that followed; the dog soldier at the back of the pack falling to the Grimm that clamoured all over him and ripped at the flesh.

Killer had seen enough, they all had. They waited no longer, having no desire to witness their kin being devoured and certainly no desire to join them. They turned, howling in dismay as the dread Grimm spilled out into the open night.

Elle and Sandy called an end to the chase. They'd made their point and won the day, saving Pack Grimm from annihilation. The victors all looked to the starry sky, lifting their heads to howl at the night that would soon recede as the dawn promised a new day for Pack Grimm. For now though, they dragged the still-whimpering captured dog warrior into the shadowed lea of the building, tearing him limb from limb as he squealed and writhed in agony. They would have their revenge and their fill; breakfast had been served.

Memphis Grimm struggled to walk, holding his side as he limped; the old dog grimaced as he struggled to reach Rex who lay wounded, a large cut in his arm.

"I'll live," Rex growled, not one for sympathy.

"Fair enough," Memphis snarled.

He turned, looking at the corpses that littered the floor. The highest concentration of these was near the entrance that led to the upper levels and the world of night and day.

Memphis noticed the crawling Chaz. The yearling held his side as he whimpered, mortally wounded from a sword stroke. Others had been slain. Five bitches in total, one with a sword that pierced her back just below the shoulder blade and stuck out through her gut, propping up her dead body. The penis and testicles of the dog that had slain her were still visible in her gaping jaw, a long thin sinew still attaching them to their owner who lay dead before her; the bitch's head rested on his thigh, the floor now shared their blood as they'd shared death, it pooled, mixed together and Memphis resisted the urge to lap at the combined taste.

Two other bitches of the Grimm lay wounded in each other's embrace, lapping at the injuries to at least gain sustenance as they tried to take in some of the life-giving fluid.

Memphis looked at his hurting pack; how many attacks they could withstand hadn't escaped his immediate thoughts as he watched the rest of the baying Grimm return to their underground lair.

Elle came to him and they touched noses. "How are your injuries?" she asked him.

"Aggravated," he replied. "Our pack is dying!"

"What do you suggest?" she asked, looking at his side and the wound that seeped blood from one of the healed punctures.

He looked at the pack tearing and rending their dead foe, their celebration could not be dampened by the loss of five bitches; all was not lost as the pack still consisted of nine males and thirty-six bitches of varying ages.

"We can't stay here, and poor Chaz shall die before this day is done," Memphis said. He motioned towards the dying dog, careful not to let any of the pack see him, it was bad manners to look at your next meal.

"Shall we save him? Give him the pill?" Elle said.

"What, and break all customs and insult the forefathers?"

"Yes!"

Memphis looked into Elle's eyes, she'd changed, like him, and become altogether much more than the dog she'd been before, unlike the dog in some respects—her eloquence, her feral nature altered, and there was more compassion behind those eyes, the opposite of what she'd portrayed during the fight.

"Very well," he growled under his breath.

Elle turned and ran off to the tunnel entrance. She returned moments later, dropping the backpack close to Memphis who watched as she removed one of the plastic zip bags that contained the pills. Elle walked confidently over to the two injured bitches, giving them a pill each, which they accepted gladly, seeing how sleek and elegant she'd become. Next, she walked over to Rex who also took one of the pills and swallowed it, having placed it on his tongue before his paw stopped moving.

Some of the pack noticed her, watched what she was doing. They all stopped and stared, when she walked over to Chaz. She placed a pill inside his jaw and held his mouth shut until he swallowed hard as he tried to cough up blood at the same time.

At first the pack stared at her, some wide-eyed at what she was trying to do; one by one they wandered over to her and held out their paws to obtain the pill and the enlightenment that came with it.

"Elle!" Memphis barked.

She turned to him as she dished out the pills. "They need to know what we know and feel what we feel," she said as gently as she could. "We need to think of the injured, some won't last the day if we don't."

Memphis hung his head; he turned from what Elle was doing and limped to Chaz's side, looking at the injury to the pup's body.

Chaz had courageously fought against fully grown dog warriors armed with dog-killing swords and had suffered the consequences. Now, as his panting became shallow, he closed his eyes, expectant of death and smiled, proud of his last act, providing a meal for Pack Grimm. Sandy joined him; she looked down at the young male and smiled, bending down to lick his wound before she picked him up in her arms, pausing briefly to look at Memphis. "The sun's coming up," she said.

Memphis tried to follow as Sandy headed for the surface, but his injuries prevented him from doing so. He sat and watched as the others all became tired and found themselves curled up within moments of taking the pill. It appeared you had to sleep before the pill would start the metamorphosis. It wasn't long before Memphis was left alone with Elle, his mate. She walked over to him after making sure all the sleeping dogs and bitches were comfortable and sat next to him, both with their backs to the wall.

"Do you think we have done the right thing?" he asked her.

"If you wish this pack to last more than a week, then yes!"

She stood and helped him up, half dragging him to his feet. Together they made for the stairs with Memphis gaining back some of the energy he'd lost. "Let's go greet the day," Elle growled.

"As you wish," Memphis replied, his tongue lolling out of the side of his mouth.

Tank was, by now, some miles south of Pack Grimm. He still carried the two humans in their weird suits. The day was dawning, the sun threatened to rise on the horizon when he happened upon a large cave entrance. He paused to sniff at the warm air that told of the deep world within. He sensed no signs of life, not even of scents years old, so decided to enter, knowing he needed the safety of shelter. If he stayed out in the open, his scent would carry for miles and without the wind of the storm, his trail would be easy to follow.

Inside, the cave widened. It was large, but in his years of life in the dog world, he'd seen much bigger. He walked now, sniffing for water to quench his thirst and wash the dust and sand from his fur. He also desired a large enough source to hide his scent. For that, he would have to go much deeper underground.

Tank set off, the clumsy-looking humans inert in his grip, not moving for fear their suits might rip. After walking to the back of the cave, he'd found several tunnels leading off into the depths below. He listened at all of them, not finding what he was looking for until he came to the last one — running water.

At first the tunnel roof was high enough for him to stand without bumping his head, but it soon narrowed, causing him to place the humans before him so that he could manoeuvre, stooping down. The progress the humans made was abysmal, Tank could have crawled faster. He was relieved when the tunnel widened out once more, its roof gaining height at the same time so that he could continue as he had before.

Scooping up his dinner, he continued until he came to the source of the noise. He entered another cave covered in the fluorescent moss that enabled the humans to see as well as he could. A small stream ran through the middle of the cave. It appeared to start out of the rocks, pooling in places, before it spilled over to continue its progress. It was the best he would have expected this close to the surface, but at least it would be fresh, the rocks having cleansed it of any toxins.

He placed the humans down, tapping on the glass-fronted helmet of one of his captives. Reaching up, the human opened his visor to reveal the man inside. He took off his helmet and placed it beside himself.

Tank watched as the man tried to crawl to the water, having little success in his clumsy suit. The other human removed her helmet, revealing herself to Tank. Although she was human and lacked the good looks of the bitch, Tank found himself thinking of her as cute and reached out to pat his dinner on the head. She tried to shy away from him but could not; she was frozen in terror.

The male, by now, had started to remove other parts of the heavy suit and it wasn't long before he stood there in just his skin. The only parts of him covered were his crotch and his feet in a thin grey material that became almost transparent as he hit the water. Tank watched as the female climbed out of her suit. She too wore the same grey cotton, which also covered her breasts.

First the man, then the woman knelt at the side of the closest pool. Tank watched them as they took their fill of water, dipping their heads under the surface of the water to wash away the hours of being in the stuffy suits.

Then he smelt it, the hint of blood. The sweet scent coming from between the female's legs. Both the humans turned as he stood, snarling with the promise of sustenance. They backed off into the pool, both sitting side by side, holding each other's hands. "Your kind was once human, like us!" the male said.

"That old chestnut," Tank growled.

Tank waded into the water and pulled the legs of the woman with one large clawed hand. The male tried to hold onto her but couldn't; Tank was far beyond powerful in comparison to the sum of their strength.

Tank considered her eyes as he turned on her, they were a brilliant blue and extremely dog-like, something that had always unnerved him, and he looked at the male who sat defeated in the pool. Tank pushed her back, sniffing at her crotch, burying his nose against the cotton shorts. He'd heard of such things; how the females bled the same as the bitch.

With one claw, he picked at the wet material, careful not to tear the flesh of the woman's inner thigh, pushing her back as she tried to sit up in protest. The material ripped and she tried to close her legs, but Tank pushed them apart as he sniffed at her. He probed her with one fat finger and she screamed. He withdrew, thinking he might have cut her, his claws far too long and deadly for the human flesh. He licked at the blood of the woman on his nail and sniffed at it. He felt his bloodlust rise slightly by the taste.

The woman's body was slim and athletic, her rounded breasts and taut skin told him of a litter-less female, something that would dishonour one of his kind. He looked at her body, sniffing it up and down, and couldn't shake the thought that he considered her cute, a thought that repulsed him. Tank positioned himself at the foot of her body and lifted both the female's legs, forcing them open as she screamed and covered her face with her hands.

He leaned forward and buried his head in her crotch once more, sniffing at the sweet scent of the blood that was within, tempting him, teasing his palate with its flavour. He licked the woman's inner thigh. She twitched and struggled uselessly in his grasp.

"Please, kill me before you eat me!" she pleaded.

He stood and obliged her request. He slashed the woman across the throat with all four of his clawed fingers, knocking her head completely off her body.

Only food, he told himself as he watched the lank expression on the dead female's face.

He turned to look at the male. He still sat in the pool, crying as he faced his death. If there was one thing Tank could not abide above all else, it was cowardice. He walked over to the male and ran him through with two clawed hands; Tank looked into the man's eyes as he dangled from his arms.

Tank lifted his head and howled, throwing the dead human across the cave to land in a shallow pool and turned once more to the female that would fill his belly.

Killer and his dog warriors rushed into their kingdom, their tails between their legs as they fled from the dawn and all that the outside world had to offer. They entered the realm of Pack White Fang and felt secure with the hundreds of their pack surrounding them. As they reached their communion chambers some miles underground, they faced a problem—the news had spread before them. Caesar and his followers filled the room. Caesar stood with his arms folded in front of him.

Now Killer would have a fight with his rival and he would have to go and explain himself to the human delegation of fools that they would one day be his cattle. For now though, as much as he hated to admit it, he needed them.

Memphis Grimm watched as Chaz changed. He hadn't noticed his own injuries healing as they were being bathed in the sun's radiative qualities. Now he sat on his haunches as Chaz Grimm, the yearling and Tank's dog child, kicked in his sleep and before his very eyes, grew at an impossible rate. His fur hissed and grew sleek, but older-looking, and his yellow colouring became a ginger, sandy colour. His muscular form bulged as it flexed then relaxed. Chaz yapped and snarled as he slumbered, finally whimpering as his body eased and he seemed to fall into a deeper sleep.

The three of them watched and couldn't believe what the pill had done; none of them had thought it possible as Chaz Grimm rolled on the floor, a fully-grown dog.

A smell overpowered their senses; it was Pack Grimm issuing forth from the subterranean world that'd been their world until just recently. They paused in the shadow, looking at the light and squinted, they walked as one into the light, all injuries sealed as they hissed and the dried blood melted and fizzed on their coats as it dissipated.

They all looked up at the sun, their life-giver. Pack Grimm's evolutionary revolution was complete, they'd changed irrevocably and as they lifted their heads to the sky, they howled. They'd become sun worshippers.

Memphis Grimm lifted his head with them and barked, "It's a dog's life for me."

Chapter 8
Dog Eat Dog

For more than a week, Pack White Fang's politics found itself plagued by heavy debate, which caused a rift between the different factions. On the one hand, Killer, the pack leader and alpha male, stood by his decision to deal with the humans. On the other, Caesar, the usurper and antagonist, brokered ambitions of the simplest nature—take down Killer and take over as pack leader.

It wasn't so much the deal with the humans that Caesar opposed as the recent lack of success against the last of the Grimm. How could the last of a mangy pack of bitches defeat them at every turn?

Caesar's argument was simple: White Fang was the mightiest of packs after the Grimm's fall from greatness; they'd secured an endless supply of human corpses to feed upon. Its numbers would swell beyond what'd ever been thought possible without having to eat its own. Surely to gain control of the situation and numbers, they should throw all available dog warriors at Pack Grimm without any further hesitation, regain the bag of pills for itself, attack the human world and enslave the thousands that hid further underground behind their thick metal doors.

Killer didn't disagree with what Caesar suggested because he was wrong. He disagreed with him for the sake of politics and was trying to put a subtler spin on how the White Fang should move forward, to err on the side of caution for the most part, against a pack of mutated dogs that although lacking in numbers, most definitely held the upper hand.

Another faction sprang up amid the debates, one that wanted to forget about the Grimm altogether. Their argument though, was soon shouted down as the word 'coward' was bandied about amongst the arguing dog warriors. This word alone was enough to make those few change back to follow whichever faction they'd at first been sympathetic towards.

One thing the entire pack agreed on though, Tank Grimm had to be caught, killed and his carcass thrown into the largest latrine they could find, his corpse left to rot amid the shit and piss of the pack until nothing remained. The ultimate dishonour for the pack's ultimate enemy.

Not for the first time in the week since Tank had taken the pill did he hesitate at the cave entrance. Before him was his old world, the world of the near-extinct Pack Grimm, which was now the territory of the White Fang with some of the edges being swallowed up by Pack Blood Hound, who'd extended its borders without loss. He knew the risks involved in what he was about to do, but what other option did he have? He needed food and a mate. Going against the Grimm was out of the question, he knew every one of them had taken the pill. He'd seen his own pup, Chaz Grimm, and was proud to be the dog father of one so big and dangerous. He knew that to go against his old pack would be suicide.

So he sniffed the air and smelt the hundreds of individual scents that made up Pack White Fang, that'd eaten all the hopes and dreams Tank had ever embraced. With the thought of revenge never far from his mind and the scent of his enemy fresh on the tunnel's warm air, Tank felt the fur on his back stand up. His hackles rose till he snarled and his lips drew back as he entered his old subterranean home.

Memphis Grimm licked the last of his meal from the bone; the pack possessed a few corpses still, left over from those they'd slain in their battle for survival. Although they would soon run out, maybe the day after tomorrow, their bellies, at least for now, were full.

He looked upon the Grimm, changed dramatically in the last week, since they'd all swallowed the little pill made for the humans to prolong their existence. Even the yearlings had become more dog than any that'd gone before, they towered above those old dog warriors, and at the same time they seemed kinder, compassionate but still portrayed a more effective warrior.

Memphis looked at Elle who lay curled up at his feet. She was more than happy that they'd all taken the pill and that no unusual side effects had inflicted any of the Grimm, she'd been especially relieved that none of the pack had turned feral as Tank, frothing at the mouth and barking at their own reflection.

Sandy came over to him and ran her nails gently over his fur to comb it through and rid him of any gore before she cleaned him properly, licking at his coat until it shone like the night sky. At that moment, Chaz walked past, his arm linked with Jade Grimm, she'd gone unnoticed by Memphis until she'd swallowed the pill. Her bottom jaw before her change had protruded slightly more than the top but the pill had fixed her and she'd become the cutest bitch Memphis had ever laid eyes upon. As the couple walked by, Memphis watched her behind and that, coupled with the hard tongue that groomed him, aroused him and he found his penis stiffening.

He looked to Elle who still slept, so instead he turned to Sandy who obliged by turning to show him all of herself. She lifted her tail and she smiled. Memphis mounted her and as he thrusted, Elle lifted her head and opened her eyes to watch them for a few seconds before she continued her nap.

Memphis climbed from the now satisfied Sandy; she spread her hind legs, sniffed herself and began to lick herself clean. He turned from her to look for his pack of dog warriors. He knew soon he would have to send the fearsome bunch back into the tunnels in search of the next meal. Although the humans were far off in the depths of the underworld, he knew his revitalised Pack Grimm could do the job and bring home a herd of human flesh to consume.

Alex Stevenson knelt by what was left of the corpse. Bits of flesh were scattered amid the patches of dried blood, with the bones dispersed around the tunnel in no discernible order.

The stench of dog was unmistakable and the tracks in the blood made it obvious what had occurred in this isolated spot.

He surveyed the area with a team of scientists; a squad of plate armour-clad guards filled the tunnel. They knew the dogs would have come down here, there were only two entrances to this stretch of the underground network.

It didn't take long for them all to realise that the skeletal remains were only those of one person.

"How many were on this detail?" Alex asked.

"One man and four women, they were harvesting phosphorescent moss," one of the scientists said as he looked up from his clipboard.

This can only have been Pack Grimm, Alex thought, staring past the ten guards into the darkness of the tunnel beyond.

"The people panic, that's seven now, in as many days," one of the scientists said, he held two pieces of snapped bone in his hands.

"Seal off this tunnel! Let's set some traps as well, see if we can't slow down the pack's hunger for our citizens!" Alex sounded full of confidence; he walked with his head held high as if he knew the meaning of life, let alone the answers to all their immediate problems.

In truth, he needed time to think, but he needed to install in his men a little belief in his abilities. The last thing he could be seen doing was panicking and running around packing his own bags to move to a safer district of the human underworld. One thing he knew for sure, confident or not, he had to deal with the Grimm before his people voted him out of office.

Chapter 9

More than three hundred dog warriors snarled and barked over one another. Not a single bitch's scent could be smelt. They'd all retreated from the arguing dogs, they knew that if civil war ensued, more than a few of them would either become food or suffer the indignity of a mass fucking at the hands of the victor.

Not all the males attended the latest argument. Some guarded the various entrances into their domain, from both the outside and the other regions of the underworld.

"It all boils down to one thing," Killer barked. "If you think you're dog enough to take over the pack, step forward and offer me out!"

Killer looked smug now. As pack leader, it would be rather a rude gesture to just kill Caesar, but to coerce the younger warrior into a fight for the pack by insinuating he was a coward, would be seen by most as a shrewd move.

Caesar's fur bristled with anger. He looked left and right at those that stood by his side; over a hundred of the pack's dogs, with more joining his faction every day.

Caesar swiped the air before him with a clawed hand and howled at the insult.

"You know as well as I do that more than brawn alone rules a pack! Have you not the intellect to see the political ramifications of the two of us killing each other in front of this angry mob? Are you such a fool that you would risk everything that is White Fang?" Caesar barked. "If you believe that flying fur will solve the problems that we face right now, then you're a bigger idiot than I first thought. How the fuck you've had so much success as pack leader is beyond my comprehension!"

Caesar laughed as Killer cringed at the insult that carried more weight than the one he'd thrown at his opponent.

"You talk nothing but politics and reason. That's the way of humankind, or a pack of grooming bitches," Killer raised his head and smiled as the ultimate insult formed on his lips, before he could engage his mind to prevent the spill of words. "Mangy dog," he barked.

The giant cavern teetered on the precipice of violence long before the argument boiled over into a slanging match of insults, but now, every dog warrior that stood with Caesar felt the insult as a slur against himself, his dog father and his pups to come. A hundred howls filled the cavern as Caesar's dogs growled and snarled and their emotions reached fever-pitch.

Butch and Killer exchanged a glance; it was the last thing they'd wanted. They'd tried to avoid civil war for seven days. Now, they too howled as their frustration turned to anger and every dog seemed to move at once.

Killer moved fast, with Butch right behind him. They would die this day or red their claws bloody with the flesh of their own pack. Killer instantly regretted the argument and his insults as he came up against a dog he'd known since it'd been born.

In truth, it was natural for the pack to kill some of its own. A pack with too many dogs was always infected with friction until this sort of fight broke out amongst its warriors. There were always too many that wanted to be top dog.

Killer easily caught the arm of the younger dog and brought his own clawed hand up to rend the dog's face before his foe could react. His hard nails dug deep into the dog's forehead until his nails met the bone. The dog howled as he pulled down and ripped the fur from his skull, Killer pulled the left-hand side of the face completely free from the bone, taking the eyeball with it, and the younger dog fell to the floor kicking wildly in pain. Butch jumped in from behind Killer, to protect his right-hand side, which he'd left exposed.

Killer turned to look but brought his arm up to guard too late, Caesar had him in his sights. Butch, however, prepared as always for any situation was ready for the attack and knocked him sideways, away from Killer, before he'd made contact.

Caesar jumped back out of the way, leaving both Butch and Killer free of the melee. The opposing sides parted and gathered behind their leaders. Many injuries had been sustained on both sides in the short exchange but with only one fatality—the young warrior that Killer had defaced. Killer soon realised, as he looked behind at his own dogs and those that followed Caesar, that if the combat continued, there wouldn't be much of a pack left to command. He was confident he could win the battle and end the life of Caesar in the process, but how many would die? How weak would Pack White Fang become? A pack dominated by bitches.

Caesar had had the same thought. He didn't want death, either for the pack or himself.

"So what now?" Caesar growled, the words whistling through his clenched jaws.

"Banishment. You leave and take any of those with you that wish to follow," Butch barked from Killer's side.

Killer looked at his friend, smiled and swung his head around to face his enemy.

"It's the only way."

"And bitches?"

"No more than one bitch for each warrior, and any pups they have that are too young to fend for themselves!" Butch stepped forward. "It's either that or a fight to the death."

Tank tried to skulk and hide in the shadows. It was pointless as his scent preceded him. There was also his massive bulk, nothing that large could ever dwell in shadows unnoticed for long. Still, it made him feel better, especially when three White Fang bitches ran straight at him, seemingly unaware of his presence.

He snarled and barked at them as he stepped out into the middle of the tunnel. They all froze dead in their tracks. Their ears were flat to their heads out of pure terror. It never occurred to Tank why they might be fleeing or from what, that they could ignore his scent.

Tank leaned forward and bit into the least attractive, to get his point across. She would be his next meal; he'd no desire to mate with the ugly mutt. The bitch knew her purpose but struggled to make her feet move; fear rooted them to the tunnel floor as much as the hold of the massive dog's jaws that clamped hard onto her shoulder.

Tank released his grip and pulled the three bitches past him.

"Move," he growled as he tried to keep the sound to a minimum.

The injured bitch struggled to move fast, unlike the other two who fled quickly towards the open night. Heading upwards, they ran up the slopes and inclines. Tank picked the bitch up and threw her over his shoulder. He soon gained on the others as they milled about near the last two remaining corridors that led away from the night air, foetid and polluted.

Tank smelt them as he reached the intersection. Hundreds of dog warriors heading upwards from the depths below. They were in every corridor and the mood he sensed was anything but happy. Two more bitches jumped out before him, and he roared at them to send the bitches running just beyond his reach—they were terrified. He laughed, it was obvious the White Fang were in the throes of disobedience and he couldn't think of a more opportune moment to invade his enemy's domain.

The confusion on the faces of the two bitches was priceless but they turned the way he desired them to go, they followed the others he'd already terrified, fleeing before him with their tails between their legs.

They came out of the tunnel that used to be part of the Grimm domain. He thought to pause for a while to eat the bitch he held and let his new bitches have their fill. They would need the energy in the weeks to come. But the smell of discontent only increased as he waited. He could always hunt more food. As long as the bitches did as they were told, he would have no reason to slay them.

"Follow or die," he barked. Tank took off once more, running around the top of the valley wall that housed the ruined town that hid the Grimm. His tongue lolled to one side, he was happy again. He had company and his own bitches; he wouldn't have to share.

He began to laugh at the stars, looking up at the sheet of the night sky that drew the attention of those that followed him, those unfortunates that'd never looked upon it before. "My very own pack," he howled.

Rex and Dakota stood at the edge of the ruins, still half buried under the hard-packed sand and debris. They listened to Tank's mad cackling and howls and followed his progress as he ran with his captured bitches.

"Shall we go and face him?" Rex suggested.

"Not a clever idea, both Memphis and Chaz will skin us alive!"

Since the transformation, Chaz Grimm had become second to Memphis, taking Tank's position in the pack. Being bigger than even Memphis, he was the obvious choice. He was strong and virtuous, the exact opposite of his dog father, Tank Grimm. Chaz still loved the mad dog, even if, in the end, he must choose between his blood kin—the death of Pack Grimm or his dog father, Tank.

It was obvious to all which way he would choose. The Grimm was his family now, not the life of his exiled dog father. Even so, Tank's death would only bring Chaz pain and death to the dog that had killed him.

"Let's go tell Memphis, he'll want to know what has happened."

As they were about to turn, they smelt the enemy. Hundreds of White Fang, pouring out into the night. The division in the enemy pack was obvious by the snarling, growling scraps that broke out near the tunnel entrance.

Rex and Dakota Grimm looked at each other, then turned to rush towards the entrance of the Grimm's underground lair.

Memphis Grimm was lazing with Sandy and Elle in his corner of the old basement when the two dog warriors came before him.

"What news?" he asked them. He knew by the looks on their faces that something was afoot.

"Tank has captured some White Fang bitches," Dakota's face was blank, emotionless, as he awaited the reaction from his pack leader.

Memphis sat up, his eyes narrowed as he thought of the possible backlash from their mortal foe. He turned to look at Rex as the young dog warrior began to speak, excited with his news.

"The White Fang, they have split. As we speak, the exiled stand before our old domain, looking at the night sky."

This news was much more to his liking and although he would, at some point, hunt down and kill Tank, for now at least that could wait. His mortal enemy, Pack White Fang, had been weakened and it was time to act.

Memphis stood and grinned. "Pack Grimm, rouse yourselves. It's time for war! To me, my dog warriors, rend the flesh of our enemies! To me, my bitches, add your weight to that of your dogs, your claws are needed now!"

From all around the large underground hideout, howls and baying cries broke out as they were roused by the words of their alpha male. From out of the darkness, the snarling pack came to him with drool and spittle hanging from their salivating jaws.

Hundreds of confused scents filled Caesar's nostrils as he began to regret, almost immediately, his decision to accept exile for himself and his followers. But, like Killer, he knew that if they'd warred, their numbers and the ranks of White Fang's dog warriors would have been decimated. What choice did he have? Upon reflection, he realised how stupid a dog he'd been, to react to Killer's insult when he had been so close to victory using other means than violence. He should have just called Killer out and fought to the death for the position of pack leader. Anything was preferable to the shame of exile.

In the end, seventy-one dogs had followed him into exile. The most loyal of his support opted to follow him rather than stay and face persecution. They and their offspring would be lesser dogs because of their political disposition and would always be the first choice for the pack's meat in hard times.

They'd gathered up seventy-one bitches to take with them. Most fled before them to avoid the shame of exile, wanting to stay where they knew their brood would be the safest. Eventually though, the exiled dogs cornered the allowed amount.

Under normal circumstances, when a pack fragmented, the pack's dominion was divided accordingly and either the dispute continued or a diplomatic solution was agreed upon. Never had the exiled pack been forced out completely.

Now, Killer and Butch stood in the cave entrance with the entire force of the White Fang pack massed behind them, waiting to issue forth and do battle on Killer's command.

Caesar felt lost, he didn't know which way to turn. He hadn't foreseen what would befall him and his followers. He stared down the valley walls. A deep-throated howl broke his thoughts and he turned to face Killer and Butch as if to plead for the lives of all those that milled around, waiting for him to act or give order. If this was what being pack leader meant, he wished he could take it back and re-enter the fold that was Pack White Fang.

"There's shelter down at the valley floor. Old ruins you could maybe hole up in against the coming light of day. There are defensive structures; you could maybe fight off any of the Grimm out there in the wastes."

Killer turned his back on Caesar, walked back into the shadows and pushed his way past his own dog warriors. Butch and the others stayed to make sure that those exiled didn't attempt to gain the underworld once more.

"There's more than one tunnel into the underworld," Caesar barked at Killer's retreating back.

"Those that aren't blocked by the metal doors shall be guarded. We shall spread the word among the other packs close enough to the surface."

Killer's back faded into the darkness, he was gone. His pack drew back into the shadows but still watched with a wary eye. Caesar decided to ignore them and instead opted to take in his surroundings. Again, the long, mournful howl broke the silence. This time though, it was farther off into the distance.

Somewhere far off, past the valley's far ridge. All he could see was a barren landscape, rocks dotting the view awash with radiation-rich grains of sand. Nothing moved in the night, even the air was still, all seemed so oppressive.

He looked to where the ruins were supposed to be situated and saw nothing but rock and sand. No doubt the old ruins would be there, it wasn't like Killer to lie, but he was a sly old dog and there was no denying it. Having no other information, nowhere else to go and the day chasing away the night, gave him no other option but to move towards them. Finding the ruins might mean the difference between life and death.

Chapter 10

Tank led the five bitches to the cave he'd found seven days previously. He led them through the first cavern, still carrying the ugly mutt he'd bitten. He put her down only when he'd made his way through the inner tunnel to the cavern he'd used as his lair. After she'd been placed on her feet, the bitch collapsed. He took hold of the fur atop her head and dragged the bitch the rest of the way. She didn't make any sound or move of protest, even though she must have known she was going to die.

The other four bitches followed, their heads low and their tails between their legs, unsure what the future held for them. Tank terrified them; he'd become something frightening, some beastly nightmare that they all feared before all clse. This would hold them with him, they'd no desire to die here, far from the pack and unable to honour their mates.

Tank let go of the bitch and thought her dead until she stirred. She felt at her injured shoulder and whimpered until Tank stood over her, his clawed hands splayed out as his arms reached behind and above him.

She let out a long, mournful howl, a single note of despair, then turned her head to one side to present herself as kill to the beast that'd captured her.

Tank's sick mind held other completely more sinister thoughts. He smiled at the bitches who looked on horrified as he reached down and cut the pointed ear from the top of the injured bitch's head. As she struggled, he pinned her down, easily holding both her arms with his left hand. He dug his claws into her wrists to increase her agony. No matter how hard she struggled, she couldn't free herself of his grasp.

Yapping a constant stream of nonsensical words, she begged for mercy and a quick death.

With his free hand, he grabbed hold of the ugly mutt's jaw, forced it open and pushed it down, using little of his power as it cracked.

"Will you shut up?" he growled and applied more pressure, Tank pushed on the jaw and once again looked up to see the horror on his new pack's faces.

"You think me a mad dog, don't you?" he snarled as the jaw gave way and a spray of blood shot up to cover his fur.

He looked down and another squirt of fresh blood hit his face. He licked at the blood that dripped down over his features and smiled at the sight below him. The bitch's eyes were wide with shock. She'd gone beyond the point of pain, although she did make a weird sound, a continual high-pitched whine. After the briefest of time, the noise irked Tanks senses and he sliced away her tongue, which lolled wildly about the open wound. The gagging sound she made was almost unbearable also; out of annoyance and nothing else, he finally ended the ordeal he'd put the ugly mutt through. He used both his clawed hands, jabbed down into the flanks of her neck hard and in quick succession until the bitch's head finally came free from her shoulders.

He stood, pushing flesh from the dead bitch's shoulders into his mouth and walked over to the four other females. He smiled as they cowered.

"I think that is what I shall call us, Pack Mad Dog. It suits me, don't you think?"

When none of them replied, he grabbed the nearest one by the tail and dragged her close. He forced her onto her belly, grabbed her by the back of the neck and pressed her face to the rocky floor of the cave. Still with her tail in hand, he pulled her up. The female didn't even move, already terrified by what she'd seen befall the other bitch.

"Yes, Pack Mad Dog," Tank said almost casually as he fucked the first of his bitches. "Has a certain ring to it, don't you think?"

Tank didn't care that she didn't answer; none of them did. In fact, none of them even watched as he fornicated with the bitch. He didn't care; they would serve their purpose to provide him with litters, to make his new pack strong. For now, though, he bent his thoughts to the task at hand. He would have a long night ahead of him if he was going to fuck them all. They'd need an occasional beating too, to keep them subservient to him and his every whim.

Alex Stevenson stood proud while an aide checked the straps that held his armour in place. He'd tried to loft the giant dog-killing sword, to no avail. Fortunately for him, the design team and scientists had come up with technology that'd been transformed into the latest weapon and would end the dogs of Lorela's dominance. It would transform the human world and give them back all of the underworld. Never again would the dogs draw breath in the tunnels that'd been dug by man before the devastating end of civilisation.

The prototype weapon was strapped to his back. The metal canister was full of a liquid concoction that wouldn't become lethal until it'd been fed down flex and rubber pipes and into the nozzle. When in the nozzle—a three-foot piece of metal with handles—the liquid would mix with chemicals, all fed through tubes from different compartments in the canister on his back. These chemicals would activate compounds in the liquid, making it highly flammable. Combined with the nozzle's high pressure valves, it made a device like a flame thrower. Whilst being tested, the chemical reaction changed to every colour in the spectrum, and many of the compounds proved too volatile. A lot of them exploded in the lab.

Alex demanded the weapon be completed. He'd asked for volunteers among his scientists to trial the weapon he was so excited about, but no one came forward. A thousand warriors stood ready, their steel plate armour polished to a high sheen and their heavy swords, the dog-killing weapon of choice, held high before their faces. They honed their swords, named and kissed them, the men whose job it was to protect the borders; every one of them would refuse to lay their swords aside, no matter how much fear the dog warriors instilled within them.

It would be Alex himself who would lead the charge. Though plenty of the human soldiers would have happily gone in his stead, he'd refused them all and claimed they were far too valued as citizens. In his own mind, he was desperate to prove himself and see how his flame lance performed in his own hands, someone without the warrior's physique.

After much deliberation and poring over old maps of the sections of the human underworld, no longer in use, Alex had correctly found the place in which Pack Grimm had entered his district, and correctly guessed they would use the old highrise lower basement level as a lair. He stood from the maps to test his armour and was amazed at how light it was, once all the pieces had been fitted into place.

Rob Chamberlain still peered at the maps, through a monocle, which he used to pore over the old and browning paper.

"I think you're right, there are no other entrances to the surface for twenty miles," Rob said and looked awkwardly at the elected mayor, who still tested the movement of his arm at the shoulder.

"I know I'm right, I helped clear that very same basement."

"How many hundreds of years ago was that?" Rob asked.

"No, it wasn't that long ago, maybe a year. Besides, if I'm wrong, we can at least eliminate the room from our quest!"

"Quest?"

"Yes, quest. If we don't take the dog by the tail, who will?" Alex said, and frowned as he looked past Rob.

The many armoured guards stopped and listened to the exchange, catching Alex completely off guard, he blushed, unable to find the words at first, though he knew he should say something.

Eventually, after what seemed too long a pause but was mere seconds, Alex found his words.

"You all know why we are here; every man among you serves a key role, keeping the packs at bay and the citizenry from harm. Now, on this day, I say to you this: we are on the eve of victory." He paused to look again at his new weapon. "I will lead with this, and never again shall they have us on the back foot. From now on, we shall defeat them at every turn, wherever we find them, till they are no more."

They cheered him, this warrior elite of the human underworld.

"With me!" Alex shouted.

The previously normal, unassuming mayor turned and marched off at the head of the unending line of warriors, leaving Rob Chamberlain to step back out of the way. It would be some time before the armoured troop reached their destination; three hours or more at a healthy pace. Rob watched them go; a tear ran down his face as the mayor's words pulled a string in his heart.

Four hours later, Alex held the nozzle of his flame thrower before him as he edged up the tunnel that led into the old basement. The smell of dog and corpse was unmistakable. How the packs ever put up with the stench, especially with their heightened sense of smell, was beyond him. This thought brought him to wonder why they hadn't attacked. The dogs always knew where they were, they'd never been shy when it came to confrontation.

With this thought in mind, he quickened his pace. He needed to see for himself if the dogs were at home. He looked behind him; the sword-wielding soldiers looked at him with admiration as he seemingly walked without fear into the beast's lair.

If only they possessed as much brain as brawn, Alex thought.

The stench only increased when they entered the old basement, but the darkness thankfully hid what they didn't want to see. The trademarks tell-tale signs of the pack's lair. Excrement and gore were slick underfoot and somewhere in the room, Alex knew he would find the citizens that'd gone missing, or at least what was left of them.

For now, though, his mission evolved and took on a more important task. He needed to secure the room and eliminate any dog that may be in hiding. They could never ambush the Grimm, it was impossible, his men would have to lay in wait for the return of any dog that would sniff them out.

On the surface, where daylight threatened to rear its ugly head, the exiled Caesar finally led his mangy pack into the ruined town.

"I smell Grimm," one of the dogs behind said.

"Yes, we all do, they must have smelt us too."

No sooner had Caesar uttered the words than Memphis Grimm stepped out in front of them, a hundred metres distance between two of the ruins that seemed to stand in line with other buildings, at odd angles to one another, as if at some point at least one of the buildings had altered position. Beside him stood his mate, Elle, and Sandy, another of the Grimm bitches.

"The light comes, my lord, we have no choice but to go forward," the dog behind him suggested. His growl sounded harsh, strained, at the prospect of fighting the physically enhanced Grimm.

Caesar's hatred of the Grimm was equal to any other of Pack White Fang, but as he looked at the beast before him, he knew if all the Grimm had taken the pill, they would have no chance in a fight. He could smell them, hiding all about the ruined town. He saw the occasional shadow move.

"I will go and see if I can strike a deal," Caesar said, overcoming the shame of his fear.

He moved through the old ruins, aware of the scent of hatred that filled his nostrils; it was distinctly different to the scent of those that followed him. He steeled himself, he knew it may well be his time to die, but at eight years of age, he'd lived a good life, not as long as some, but certainly more than most.

Caesar came to a halt before the impressive figure that was Memphis Grimm. He'd increased in every way. He even looked different around the jaw—it'd grown impossibly in length, a metamorphosis that shouldn't be possible. Memphis Grimm regarded him for a second.

"I remember you from a few of the battles. You've killed Grimm before!"

"I was only acting under orders," Caesar argued.

"Yes, but you enjoyed your kills. We dog warriors always enjoy the thrill of fresh blood."

"And now, do you feel the same, after your transformation?"

"Yes, we still live by our instincts and in some ways, we have evolved, we are just more proficient at being dog," Memphis said, then smiled.

"I have come to present myself before you. May my pack pass in peace? Could our two packs not become friends and allies?"

"Soon the light of day shall burn the eyes from your skulls. We shall feast on all of you and fuck your blind bitches before they too are consumed," Memphis said and studied Caesar for his reaction.

"I feel it would be to your advantage to take us as servants, to do your bidding. At least that way, my unnamed pack can survive and your status as top dogs can be complete."

Memphis considered what Caesar suggested; a pack that served as slaves to another pack, unheard of in all the generations of dogkind.

Tank, after seeing them talk, ran around the canyon's edge. All of the White Fang dogs that'd walked out into exile with Caesar watched their leader intently as he attempted to broker a deal. With such an infusion of scents in the air, more than two hundred, Tank hoped the air would be confusing at best to all the dogs present. When he came around to the flank of the exiled pack, he felt a pang of sympathy for the dogs that gathered at the edge of the town. This unusual show of sympathy didn't deter him, however; he turned and headed down the bank. His luck was in; none of the dogs seemed to notice him until he was nearly upon them.

Two of the bitches sniffed at the air and turned to look directly at him. They stood at the back of the refugees and were among his intended targets. One of the bitches raised her head to bark out a warning, but her cry never broke. Tank was too fast and sunk the five claws of his right hand deep below her chin and into the mouth cavity. Without breaking stride, he gripped the inside of the bitch's mouth, her tongue tickled the palm of his hand and he cast the injured bitch to the ground. In the same motion, he lifted the other bitch that had noticed him and flung her over his shoulder as he skirted the edge of the White Fang exiles.

Before his enemies could react, Tank made his escape, barking and snarling as loud as he could to create as much of a commotion as was possible.

Caesar turned as soon as the chorus of howls broke the silence and both he and Memphis watched as Tank caused chaos among Caesar's pack. Caesar turned to face Memphis and snarled, his lips were drawn back in anger, his arms out to his sides with his claws ready to rend Memphis Grimm.

Memphis was farsighted enough to see the wisdom of what Caesar suggested; it made sense for the White Fang to be subservient to the superior life form that they'd become. He also stared off into the future, saw a vision of an empire, a fleeting thought that ended as soon Tank appeared to ruin his train of thought. Memphis heard Caesar snarl, saw his arms move ready for an offensive strike at his heart and watched Caesar look down in surprise to see the arms of Memphis Grimm, buried deep up to the wrist in his chest.

Caesar grabbed hold of Memphis' wrists, as though to remove the hands from his body, he coughed up blood as his body went into shock. With little effort, Memphis lifted the now limp Caesar from the floor and bit his nose from the muzzle. His fangs scraped on the jaw bone and he shuddered slightly before he threw him aside. Memphis stepped past the motionless Caesar and strode between the ancient structures. He watched as Tank disappeared, melting fast into the landscape. He would deal with Tank later and now wished he'd hunted the mad dog down before this chance encounter. Three of the White Fang dog warriors gave chase and disappeared behind the sand-covered rocky terrain of the valley floor—they too would soon be dead.

Memphis turned his attention to the enemy dog warriors charging straight at him. He could see their logic, they would rather face death than be branded coward. Both dog and bitch from the Grimm pack jumped out of hiding. Chaz stood behind him within moments, as did Rex and Dakota. From either side of the ruins, others of his pack jumped out, to surprise the White Fang that only had eyes for Memphis, their nemesis.

Rocky took down two of his charging enemy, as did Duke and another of the younger dog warriors. They made short work of the stupidly fearless dogs. Some of them made it through though, two of those were taken down by a frenzied bitch, frothing at the mouth and showing no mercy. In the end, three of the charging dogs made it to within striking distance of Memphis. Elle and Sandy took one each and easily slaughtered them. The other was killed by Chaz as he stepped in front of Memphis, who couldn't believe the ferocious barbarity of his second-in-command. Only a week ago, the massive dog had been just a pup and panting on the verge of death. Now he ripped at his enemy and smiled as he bit chunks from his foe, eating him as the dying dog exhaled his last breath.

Tank turned at a safe distance, it was far enough away from the others but close enough for him to return without too much effort. He'd run at a steady pace, allowing those that pursued him to remain within eyesight, letting them believe that they were keeping up with him and at times, even gaining just a little.

Tank placed the bitch he carried on the ground and turned to face the pursuit; his claws ready and his grin wide. The last thing he would allow was Pack Grimm's numbers to explode with the ranks of the other packs, all nice and friendly. So, his plan had worked out just fine. He'd killed a few and stole another bitch to bolster the numbers of his own fledgling brood. He'd hoped that some would give chase; the fur would come in useful, as would the meat for food. At least it would have prolonged the inevitable slaying of a bitch or two.

As it was, Tank hadn't the time for fun and games. As the three dog warriors reached him, he jabbed three times in quick succession. The three dogs weren't long from being yearlings, their inexperience showed. They should have presented a guard and attempted to block against a superior foe such as Tank Mad Dog. Instead, the slow offence offered allowed him to move under the attack and stab the upper torso of each as they reached him.

It was over as soon as it'd started. The three attackers squirmed on the floor in too much pain to do much of anything else. The wound inflicted on one of the dogs was so deep, he died before Tank turned from them to retrieve the bitch that'd watched, horrified by how powerful the Grimm had become.

Tank took off once more, he needed to get the bitch back to his lair, the sun would be up shortly and she would be no good to him blind.

Pack Grimm surrounded the rest of the exiled pack, which drew in on itself; the dog warriors that hadn't attacked realised by now that it would be a pointless endeavour to charge forward to their deaths, even if it meant they would be branded a coward by not fighting.

So, they pushed the bitches behind them and faced their mortal enemy, the transformed, mutated Grimm.

Memphis stood and watched his enemy with the idea of amalgamation and Caesar's words still fresh in his mind. He knew it would be an easy thing to slaughter those that waited to die, but would it be the best thing to do? Life took on a new meaning, it'd indeed become a much more complicated affair since they'd taken the pills.

Elle took hold of one of his hands. Sandy took the other and they both smiled as he looked at both in turn. He knew what they thought without even asking. His two bitches would approve of his newfound mercy and of the peace he was about to offer.

"Join us," he barked and attempted a less threatening stance, something not well-practised in the dog world.

Most of the Grimm didn't even flinch. They'd all changed as he had, and only a few of them turned their heads to look at him. Contrary to the Grimm reaction, the White Fang were aghast at what was being offered—peace when peace should not have been on the table. More than just a few jaws dropped.

"What do you mean, join us?" a voice barked into the silence. "Are we to be cattle for the Grimm?"

"No, not cattle," Memphis replied.

"What then?" another of the White Fang snarled.

"I truly don't know yet, but would you rather live or die?"

The surrounded White Fang began to murmur, many heads nodded, but just as many shook their heads.

"Will we get to taste the pill as you have?"

"In time, perhaps," Memphis barked. The rucksack on his back felt heavier at the mention of the pills it contained. "When you have gained my trust and confidence."

Again, a pause as the White Fang conferred.

"If it's happening, it needs to be soon. The sun is about to come up and it will blind any of you out in the open, rendering you useless for any purpose other than that of food for our bellies. Come, we have an underground lair." Memphis beckoned, and at first a few, then the whole pack, walked towards him. The thought of being blind horrified them as much as the idea of being killed and eaten by the physically superior Grimm.

Not many of the dogs spoke as both packs merged. They all looked at each other and a few tenuous smiles were exchanged. Memphis led the way to the entrance of the underground and motioned for the first of his newfound friends to descend to the darkness below.

Both packs passed him, led by Duke Grimm who showed them the way down.

Chapter 11

A half circle of humans formed up and faced the entrance that led to the surface. They stood motionless, the dog-killers in hand and ready for battle. The only sound was the clink of armour as men shifted their weight.

Howls alerted them to the oncoming dogs who'd smelt them out and rushed down the stairs. First to appear in the doorway was a monster of a dog, mutated far past what was considered normal. His ferocious bark was drawn out and quickly unnerved the best of what mankind had to offer—muscled warrior types, knights who thought themselves better than anyone else that wasn't prepared to fight.

The giant dog charged into the room, followed by a horde of others. A mixture of dog warriors, both physically enhanced and those who hadn't changed at all.

The fully armoured men took a step back as they lifted their swords up to greet the flesh of the pack. Other men behind held long, metal-tipped spears. Placed on the shoulders of the knights, they thrust them forward to slow the dog advance. The dogs failed at first to make it past the human metal-tipped weapons. More than a dozen dogs were spiked or slashed and one of those, seriously. As one of the dogs was spiked by two of the giant spears, the armoured man with the dog killer stepped up to take the business end of the dog. The dog warrior's head fell to the floor, void of the body; one of the monstrous dogs jumped at the knight. He landed on the knight's chest and forced him to the floor, both man and beast fell together, the man on his back with the dog's weight pressing him down.

A hole appeared in the human line, it'd been breached, albeit in one place only, which would soon be filled by other warriors that waited to join the fight. But Alex Stevenson's grandiose ideas took form. He'd been waiting for the opportune moment to test his new weapon. What better time than now, whilst his men faced insurmountable odds and the new breed of dog? He stepped up towards the gap before the waiting soldiers could step into it, he looked down at the man that struggled to move whilst he lay on his back in his armour and watched as the monstrous Grimm tore the helmet from his head and bit at the soldier's neck. The soldier's struggle was in vain, blood gushed from the wound, and soon the soldier would be dead, his throat ripped out.

Alex couldn't wait any longer. Still more dogs piled in behind the first wave of Grimm. Fortunately for Alex, they weren't the super-fast, super-strength dog that could easily have jumped at him as he raised the nozzle of his flame thrower. Alex nearly lost his footing at the last moment. One of the rubber hoses became tangled in his legs, but he freed himself by stepping out of the hose and allowed it to run between his legs and hang freely. Heat washed over his face as he pointed the metal nozzle and pulled hard on the two levers to release the chemicals. A long jet of flame shot forth and bathed the dogs in fire.

He lowered the flame to catch the Grimm dog warrior eating one of his men. It'd tried to back away beneath the fire, but his back was already ablaze from the chemicals that'd dripped onto him from the inferno above. The mutated hound howled in agony as it took the flame full in the face, his eyes popped like boils, his tongue stuck to the roof of his mouth briefly before that too exploded. All the dogs caught in the jet of death rolled around the floor in agony as they tried to put out the burning chemicals that stuck to their hides, and all the while, the soldier on the floor squealed like a child with his fingers caught in the door.

Both man and dog stepped back, away from the heat. Soon the fire dominated the battle and the dogs backed away. Most of the dogs made for the stairs and although a few tried to ward off this new threat, they failed. Alex Stevenson stepped forwards, waving his fire ahead of him in a wide arc.

Those brave dogs also burst into flames and the fleeing dogs ran faster towards the stairs. Alex Stevenson stepped forwards once more to try to reach the bottleneck that was inevitable, created as the pack of dogs were routed by the flames.

On the mayor's right-hand side, a dog suddenly reared up and swiped at the mechanism to sever the rubber hose that fed the flame from the tank strapped to Alex's back. A soldier stepped in and his sword arced down to sever the hand of the White Fang dog. The dog was spiked with a spear, pinning it, as another of the sword-wielding soldiers hacked at his head, his howl of rage was cut short as the sword's edge cut through the hard-muscled flesh and bone of the creature's neck.

The flames' reach lessened, Alex took his hand from the triggers and stepped back behind his men before the flame petered out completely. He was out of fuel. For now, his quest would have to wait; there was no replacement fuel canister. This thought made him smile. It wouldn't be long before the flame thrower went into mass production.

Memphis Grimm stood near the back and attempted to calm some of the more nervous White Fang dogs that still thought they might be meat for the grinder that was Pack Grimm. He heard the howls and saw the press of bodies; he tried to push through at the top of the stairs but soon gave up. He would never make it through. As the first rays of light broke the valley wall, something unheard of happened—the dogs burst out into the morning. The last few had been either burnt badly or were still on fire.

What remained of the two packs lay in the shade of the early morning, but without a headcount, there would be no definite figure. Elle rushed behind his back and pulled at the straps on his backpack to get it open.

Memphis turned on her. "What are you doing?" he snarled.

"We have injured Grimm and the sun's rising, we can't just let those that have joined us go blind!"

Sandy appeared at his side and placed a clawed hand on his arm.

"We have changed, Memphis. Our ways must change with us," Sandy said and released her grip on his arm.

Memphis looked from one bitch to the next and back again. They were right. They'd become more thoughtful, the path of reason had infected all the Grimm dogs' minds.

Is this a curse? Memphis wondered, as he watched the light creeping towards his ailing pack, while the sun climbed higher.

Memphis quickly removed the rucksack from his back, the thought of the guilt he would feel completely alien to him, and he wasted no more time in handing Elle and Sandy bags of pills.

As they ran off to distribute the pills among the White Fang refugees, a still-smouldering Duke ran to face him.

"Dakota is dead!"

Memphis looked him in the eye, another dog warrior dead. "How? What happened down there?"

"The humans have a new weapon; it's like a magic stick that fires flame. It's not like ordinary fire. When it hits you, it sticks and melts the flesh from your bones. I watched as Dakota's face dripped to the floor."

Memphis turned to look at the entrance to the underworld; he could hear the cheers of the victorious humans below. He knew the Grimm would never again dare venture below these ruins, unless absolutely necessary or the right opportune moment presented itself.

Tank had watched them as they'd rushed below. His plan had almost succeeded but had failed at the last moment as the coward that led Pack Grimm, his brother Memphis, gave the White Fang exiles a new lease of life, a choice that he himself hadn't been presented. He stewed on his thoughts as he watched both Elle and Sandy lick each other's coats. If they weren't standing so close to Memphis, he would have made a play for them both. What fun he imagined himself having with that pair, until Pack Mad Dog consumed their flesh.

Memphis turned to look at the entrance to the underworld. Tank followed his line of sight and saw the dogs that'd rushed to get below ground pour out of the building and run in all directions. The last few dogs to reach the surface and the breaking dawn still smouldered and batted at their coats.

A debate started up between Memphis and his two bitches, which ended with Memphis giving the bitches bags of pills to distribute among those dogs that would soon go blind with the coming day, their retinas burned by the harmful radiation.

Tank couldn't believe it; now the insult was complete, his brother could never have loved him. His thoughts turned to hatred, how could he treat these dirty dogs so well after all the history between the two packs? Tank positioned himself partway up the slope to wait for an opportunity to strike once more, that'd all but petered out as he watched the White Fangs that swallowed the pills become sleepy. They were corralled into one of the old ruins, the last that couldn't make it carried by their Grimm allies and saviours. The Grimm posted guards around the ruins, with Tank's son Chaz walking around the perimeter.

Tank turned to look back up the slope, at the others that'd watched from above him, partway up the valley's wall, at the highest point without compromising their view of what happened below.

"Are you happy now?" Tank shouted.

Killer and Butch backed away. They'd hoped that Tank Grimm hadn't smelt them, what with all the different scent of dog to confuse the senses and were surprised when he took off without attacking them. Butch straightened his headgear, it'd slipped to one side, the last thing he needed was the tinted lenses falling from his head as he would go blind with the glare of the day.

Memphis Grimm turned to look at Tank and watched him leave; whether he saw them in their high hideout or not, he gave no indication. All their senses, and especially that of smell, were overwhelmed by nothing but dog, the stench of burnt fur and smouldering flesh. With so many out in the open and so close together, they could only hope that their own scents would become convoluted, mixed so much with all the others that they wouldn't be noticed; after all, Tank had been far removed from the others and much closer to them.

As they watched the sun climb, howls and snarling barks were heard from the valley floor, there was nothing but pain in those sounds and they guessed correctly that the grief was that of their exiled pack members as they transformed into the new breed.

They'd hoped that the packs would collide and fight a pitched battle for survival. They backed away from their high vantage and neither of them, as Tank put it, were the least bit happy.

A loud noise made them turn around; the ground shook and almost made them lose their footing. As they looked back, the ruin that housed the entrance to the underground collapsed into the ground as a square of the wasteland caved in on itself. Three of the Grimm stood atop the ruin when it'd imploded and they all lay flat on their backs, floundering as the ground beneath their feet fell, as they too fell, disappearing in a cloud of dust as the ground swallowed them up.

Killer and Butch would have to be satisfied with what they'd seen; it'd all been more excitement than they could stand for one day. They fled, aware that the humans had destroyed the only access the Grimm knew of to enter the underworld, other than that which would lead them to White Fang territory.

Alex Stevenson listened to the cheers; he'd been lofted high onto the shoulders of the warriors. He loved the attention and the newfound respect the men gave him, never had victory been so complete whilst fighting a pitched battle against any pack of dogs, let alone such a large pack with the enhanced mutated dogs amongst them.

In truth, anyone that'd wielded the flame thrower would have more than likely achieved the same amount of success. Although it was his hand that had pulled the trigger, it was the weapon that'd done the killing.

Now workers rushed into the basement, set fires against the concrete and attacked the main supports with mining tools until they seemed ready to collapse. The mayor retreated with most of the soldiers and left the workers to carry out the closure of this route into the human world. Now word reached him of the cave-in, but they'd already felt the tremor. He allowed himself a smile. He'd secured, in just one day, his political position for years to come, if not completed his ambition and gained a promotion onto the ruling council. At the very least, he'd cemented his name in the history of the planet. This victory was his and his alone.

Tank retrieved the three dog warrior corpses with some difficulty but still made decent time in getting back to his lair; before his transformation it would have been improbable for any dog to move them all at once, instead having to make several journeys to complete the task. As he neared the cave entrance, he could smell the five bitches that he'd captured so far. He'd increased the numbers of Pack Mad Dog exponentially. He'd wanted more but Memphis had put an end to the day's festivities when he'd made peace before whatever happened underground had taken place. He guessed correctly that the humans were involved and by the looks of some of the injured that'd emerged from the human underworld, he'd thought it highly likely that fire had been the humans' weapon of choice.

How had the humans gotten close enough to use fire? Tank thought, then shrugged the enigma away.

The injured Grimm healed when the sunlight that was high in radiation bathed them in its therapeutic rays, although they would scar where the fur had been burnt down to the hide, and only time would tell whether that fur would grow back. The baldness would make them ugly and the thought made Tank smile as he approached the entrance to his new pack's den. The bitches of his new pack greeted him as he came to a stop at the cave entrance; they'd been held captive by the daylight as the sun had risen, as they knew what would happen to their eyes if they chanced the sun's glare.

He threw the corpses into the shadow of the cave mouth and waited with his arms folded for his new slaves to drag them into the darkness. They would, for now at least, have food for their bellies and fur to line the floor for his new offspring to curl upon when they were born.

He'd not touched one of the bitches yet and she turned, lifted her tail and offered herself to him as she sensed his mood. The others must have spoken to her about how cruel and ruthlessly powerful he'd become. They didn't even look at the two of them as Tank sniffed her from behind and continued with their task of dragging the dead dogs back into the depths.

Tank didn't particularly like her smell or her chestnut brown, mottled colouring. Instead, he thought of Elle Grimm to become excited as he grabbed the bitch's tail. The bitch could smell his excitement increase and froze as Tank climbed up behind her. She dug her claws into the sandy floor of the cave mouth to steady herself and grimaced as he entered her. He gripped the back of her neck hard as he forced himself inside of her. She whimpered at first, it wasn't the first time a dog had forced himself into her, but this was something altogether different—his enhanced size hadn't ended with his height.

When Tank finally climbed from her, the bitch lay motionless for a while. She watched Tank, his tongue lolling contentedly to one side and his smile mirrored by his scent. For now, he was in a happy place, which would in turn make her life a little easier.

Tank led his new bitch into the depths of his cave complex, down to where the water smelt clean enough to drink and they quenched their thirst without the taint of radiation to irritate their palate. Tank watched as the five bitches of his pack went slowly about their business, skinning the dead that they would use for food and the fur coats for comfort or clothing. He was amazed at how quickly they seemed to have forgotten their old pack. He supposed they hadn't really much choice; it was either the life he offered them or no life at all.

He sat with his back against the wall as they began to strip the meat from the bones. His cock would soon be ready again; he would soon have another task for them. His heirs and offspring would soon be born and there was a lot to do to prepare for their arrival.

Chapter 12

Killer and Butch returned to their own domain. They couldn't believe what'd befallen the day and neither of them spoke as they entered the tunnel that would take them underground. They'd gone on their reconnaissance mission alone, relying on stealth to produce the facts they had needed. Now, as they met their warriors just inside the entrance to the underworld, they didn't know what to do next. The plans for White Fang domination were unravelling faster than they'd been made. Every heartbeat that passed by took them closer to defeat, but how could they fight the Grimm out in the open, or otherwise? They'd become too powerful, too strong and far too deadly.

"I'm calling the attack off," Killer growled.

"Most of the exiles have joined them, they have taken the pills," Butch explained, as he produced excuses for himself.

"Caesar is dead though," Killer added.

The anger among the dog warriors before them was obvious, they didn't need to smell their odour to know how they felt. There was one scent that was powerful around both Butch and Killer, the smell of dread, anxiety at the very distinct possibility that they would be the next meal for the White Fang.

Fortunately for the pair, a lone dog pushed through the crowd to save them as the pack of dog warriors stood motionless around them.

"A human delegation led by that little mayor of theirs has appeared on the border. They wish to speak with you," the dog said, probably saving the pack leader the feel of razor-sharp claws, hundreds of hardened nails, ready to slice him to mincemeat.

That information was enough to distract the pack's dog warriors from the thought of killing Killer, he'd never come so close to his own demise and he knew it.

"Out of the way, you pack of mangy dogs," Butch barked as the moment passed; he snarled as he stepped into the mob ahead of Killer.

They parted for them easily enough, but Killer knew that he'd some serious thinking to do if he was to heal the damage done to his reputation. As he approached the cave on the border between the human district and White Fang territory, the thought of healing the hearts and minds of his dog warriors was at the forefront of his mind.

It was only a short distance to the meeting cave where Alex Stevenson, Killer's next meal, waited. If the human didn't give a good reason to explain what'd happened in the newest Grimm lair, he was going to consume the ugly little bastard. He could scent every dog warrior in his pack breathing down his neck, he not only needed to appease his own mind but those of his pack members; to show fear now would be the last thing he would ever do.

When he entered the cave, he was met by something he hadn't expected, a huge show of force by the humans. They half-filled the cave with row upon row of metal-clad warriors that carried weapons of all description. The front rows were armed with the deadly dog-killing swords.

Killer searched for, and soon found, the mayor, standing in the middle of his army, near to the back where the tunnels led away and into the human district he controlled.

"Killer, why do you not attack the Grimm?" Alex shouted.

Killer walked further into the cave, he hadn't thought the humans would come so mob-handed, filling the cavern, bringing every fighting man at the mayor's disposal. He too wanted to bring his troops out into the open and although his two-hundred strong formidable force was outnumbered by the humans five to one, they would fill up just as much room.

Killer didn't answer the mayor until all his dogs had come to a halt. He needed them to witness everything that happened, every word spoken and every action; he needed them to have a reason, as he did, to live on as something more than food for their bellies.

"Tell me, has the White Fang dishonoured itself, going back on its deal?" Alex shouted.

"It has not!" Killer snarled.

"In that case, tell me, mighty pack leader, why do the Grimm increase in number? How have you let them continue to draw breath?" Alex shouted.

The loud sound that came from the little man surprised even some of his own people. A few heads turned at the angry yell that echoed around the cave walls. There seemed to be complete silence from everybody else until the sound of the mayor's voice faded away. Killer could hear the breathing of the dogs that stood close behind him and the chink of metal to metal as the soldiers before him shifted uncomfortably. He opened his mouth as if to speak, he needed to say something and fast if he was going to cure the nervousness that had corrupted the atmosphere of this meeting.

"For the same reason that I'm not going to let my dog warriors attack the army that you have brought to this meet. I love every single strand of fur on their backs. They are my dog warriors, my children and brothers, and I shall not take them to a needless, certain death. The Grimm have become too powerful for us, especially out in the open and aboveground where they seem to thrive now that they've taken your pill. It would be a one-sided slaughter and not in favour of the White Fang. Why should I charge into the fray, ending Pack White Fang's existence and condemning our name to history, where in some long distant future only the wind whispers the words, 'White Fang'?"

Alex gave a little twitch; he hadn't expected such a fine oration from the dog. He'd underestimated the pack leader's intellect and would have to watch his step from now on. "We struck a deal," he shouted.

"Are we not allies?" Killer asked.

"Of course, have I reneged on our agreement?"

"Not yet, but as your ally, what would you gain by our demise? You should support our cause, not demand our death!"

Alex fell silent. Again the two of them locked eyes. Alex didn't need the senses of a dog to feel the atmosphere in the room. It was Killer that spoke into the short pause.

"Can you tell us what happened underground, that forced those you wished us to kill aboveground return to the surface? It forced the hand of Memphis Grimm, he supplied those we exiled the pill."

"Can you tell us why you would exile them in the first place and allow them to make the deal?" Alex spat, his brow furrowed.

"That is dog business! I was faced with rebellion because of the deal we'd struck. It was either exile or civil war; the only other course of action to take would be to call off our deal, so you are to blame for the split of our pack."

Again, Alex twitched; he was losing this war of words so decided to change his demeanour and opted for a friendlier, less commanding approach to the conversation. "I see, so it was not your fault alone that their numbers have more than doubled. I realise I must take a partial blame for what has befallen us this day. For that I am sorry! As to your other question, this army you see before you defeated the Grimm, for the loss of only one man."

The army of the dogs' scent changed at this news. Killer and Butch looked at each other in disbelief. Before another word could be spoken, the human ranks parted and a trolley was wheeled down to the centre of the cavern, its wheels making a horrendous noise for the sensitive dog ears, it squeaked as they turned. When the trolley finally came to a stop, every dog leaned forward to look at what was on it. There, for all to see was more than a score of dogs' heads, freshly killed, most covered in burn marks where they'd been set on fire. Some of the heads, having been reduced to burnt-out skulls with charred brain matter stuck to the inside of the bone, were unrecognisable.

"How can this be?" Killer asked, his eyes wide with emotion, something between excitement and stupefaction.

Alex Stevenson turned and accepted something from a male human in a knee-length, dirty white coat. A metal canister was lofted onto his back and he received a long metal object with rubber flex tubing attached to it.

Alex Stevenson lifted the metal tube and pointed it at the ceiling.

Long flames burst from the end of the metal tube, as high as the roof of the cave, before drops of flaming liquid bounced off the high ceiling to fall back to the floor, hitting the armour of the soldiers directly underneath. The liquid that didn't burn out before it reached the floor hissed on the damp stones of the cavern, but impossibly continued to burn in the moisture. After the short burst was over, Alex lowered the weapon, leaving every human and dog alike with fiery imprints on the retinas. Three human soldiers clawed at their armour. Drops of the searing flame had worked its way through the chinks in the armour and settled on their shirts and padding, quickly finding skin that was set ablaze by the liquid that wouldn't stop burning.

The three soldiers were quickly dragged away by some others, their screams interfering with the meeting. Alex looked slightly concerned for the pain he'd caused them; this was one of the weaknesses of man—compassion.

"This, my dog warrior friend, is our newest weapon! At this range, I could have set you all on fire. It was with this that my men and I defeated the Grimm."

Alex paused for the information to sink into the minds of the beasts he now looked upon without fear. Had the wheel finally turned in mankind's favour? The same thought occurred to Killer; he looked at Butch who shrugged his shoulders. Killer turned to face Alex.

"If you possessed this weapon, why didn't you let us have it? Allies, you say? Not much of an alliance here!" Killer barked. Behind him, a few howls and snarls of approval backed his words.

"Provide the packs with a way to cook their meat? I don't think so," Alex smiled as he mocked Killer's words.

"Well, what then? Do you really expect us to fight this foe common to us both? Let us have something that will at least even the odds stacked against Pack White Fang, help to tip the odds in our favour."

Alex pondered briefly on Killer's words. He was, of course, right about one thing. Against the enhanced Grimm, there was no chance as things stood. What to give them though? He couldn't possibly give them the new weapon that had dominated Pack Grimm in such a dramatic one-sided pitched battle.

"Allow my dogs to take the pills. We shall crush the Grimm and wipe them from the face of Lorela."

"No, not that," Alex spoke softly as he thought, his words carrying to the now silent gathering, as he thought hard what would be best.

As they faced each other, Alex, the previously small town mayor of a little border district to the dog realm, now held life and death in his hands. He looked at his own troops and back to the dogs, looking at him as they awaited his decision. He held the flame thrower in his hands, his finger on the trigger, and thought of ending it for Pack White Fang right then and there. The problem though was the Grimm; he couldn't allow them to increase in number. Eventually, they could threaten the whole human population if the tales about the mutated dogs hadn't been exaggerated. He loosened his fingers on the trigger, the Grimm needed to die.

"I will not allow you our new development, our weapon of fire. I do, however, appreciate the situation that faces you. The Grimm, at some point, will want their revenge and those of your own pack that you willingly sent to fight and die. So, as a friend and ally, I will provide every dog warrior before us with a suit of our steel armour, which will halt the claws of Pack Grimm long enough for you to slay them, hopefully.

"This will take time, it's a lengthy process, but our forges will work tirelessly until two hundred of your number are kitted out."

"Why don't you just go to the surface yourselves?" Butch barked.

"You have seen the antiquated suits, they are slow and cumbersome. No, your physiology is better suited to the ground above, if not perfect."

"How can it be perfect when the bright light burns out our eyes?" Killer asked. "With the pills, we would be on an even footing with the Grimm and we could slaughter them as your will demands."

"And then you, Pack White Fang, would take their place; then you in turn would have to die. I suggest avoiding the light, attack at night."

Alex turned away from the pack leader and handed the flame thrower to one of the soldiers, leaving most of his army behind with the scientists who began to record the height of the dogs that Killer sent forward, one at a time—he didn't trust the humans at all—they could be unpredictable at the best of times.

Chapter 13

Memphis Grimm enjoyed a nap in the midday sun, his chin resting on his forearms. Elle woke him with a tight grip on his shoulder and he jumped up, anxious at what could be wrong. "What is it?" he asked.

"It's the White Fang. Some of the males have reacted like Tank did!"

"How many?" Memphis barked and hurried to see what'd been done to contain those dogs that, for all intents and purposes, had lost their minds.

"Five." Elle kept pace with him as they jogged to the ruins where the White Fang had collectively transformed, evolved into the new subspecies. All the bitches stood apart from the dogs who surrounded what looked like a cornered pack, backed into a corner. In the shade, their faces were hidden from the sun.

One of the White Fang spoke quickly as he tried to ease the nervous dog warriors that'd turned feral.

"They are our enemies; how can we side with them? We outnumber them and should kill them all," the leader of the five feral dogs howled, not concerned if the Grimm heard.

"No," came the reply. "You should reason with the old enemy and come to your senses."

"There is no sense in shame, you dishonour your pack and what you have become is less than a dog. Look at you, you're almost human." This last sentence was barked loud and clear; it was meant as an insult to all the White Fang who intended to join with Pack Grimm.

The words struck a chord with Memphis and he considered what they'd become. They certainly were more tolerant of the world about them and those that walked both under and above its surface. He shrugged the thought aside as the five dogs leaped into the air and grabbed hold of the wall before scrambling to the top of the ruined structure.

Memphis caught sight of their faces as they turned to take one last look at their friends-turned-enemies. Their eyes were wild and the froth at the corner of their mouths was unmistakable, even from a distance.

Memphis walked into the midst of the White Fang dog warriors that remained; out of those that'd been banished, only half now remained. Even though half their number had either disappeared, fled or been killed, Memphis was more than happy with the increase in the size of his own pack. Every one of the enhanced White Fang turned to look at Memphis, even the bitches' curiosity got the better of them and they stepped forward to find out what he had to say.

"You're Grimm now, I welcome you into the pack. You are my brothers, my sisters and my kin. My equals!"

Those that stood around him raised their heads and howled at the sky, both dog and bitch alike accepted his offer, and they all were glad that they'd shed the shackles of the beast inside that'd ruled their every waking moment until this day.

Tank Mad Dog lounged in the sun some miles away. Just inside the cave mouth was one of his bitches; it was her turn to attend to his sexual needs. She would have liked to return to the other bitches but dared not move for fear of angering him.

He lifted his head as he heard a distant sound of a mass howl, heard only as a whisper on the wind; even to his enhanced senses, he thought it must be the freshly transformed, waking from their slumber. He lowered his head again and attempted to drop back into his nap, but failed, so instead he rose and stretched on all fours before padding back into the cool of the cave mouth. It was only when he reached the shadow of his lair's entrance that he realised he'd walked on all fours. It was unusual, but he decided it was probably just because he'd not long woken.

He sniffed at the female from behind, she too dropped onto all fours but her stance was intentional; she'd guessed correctly what he would want. He entered her roughly from behind and pressed her face to the sandy floor of the cave.

He'd found a steady rhythm when he smelt them and guessed they'd scented him too, following his smell to his lair. He knew they were headed directly for him. He didn't break his rhythm; he thought he may as well continue as he waited for his guests to arrive—friend or foe, it didn't really matter. He was going to finish what he had started.

When the five dogs came within sight of his cave, they slowed to a stop and stood a distance away. Tank swung his massive head towards them to let them know he was aware of their presence; he swung it back again to the female to show he neither regarded them as a threat nor worthy of his attention.

Tank recognised the five dogs as White Fang. They'd been transformed by the pills and he was under no illusions that they could kill him easily if they wanted to. By their actions though, Tank thought it highly likely they too recognised him as an exile and so had decided to not rush in for the kill.

In truth it was his scent, a pheromone they all shared. The smell of madness they each gave off was so weak it even hid itself from the mighty senses of the devolved hounds.

Tank's audience got bored and talked idly among themselves while they waited. He finished and walked back out into the light of day to meet the five dog warriors; he would have to deal with them one way or another.

"Tank Grimm," the lead dog said.

"And you are?"

"Gamble, Hunter, Warhol, Dasher and I'm Ulrich." The dogs all nodded as their names were called out by Ulrich, who'd assumed the mantle of Alpha.

"I take it you didn't want to live with the Grimm?" Tank asked.

"They are our enemies, as are you," Ulrich snarled.

"I am no longer of the Grimm. I make my own future now. I suggest we celebrate our chance encounter and unite. I am Pack Mad Dog; you are my guests and as such, I offer my bitches for you to fuck."

"What of food?" Hunter growled.

"That, my friend, we shall enjoy, for after we fuck, we hunt. What say you? Shall we kill each other or unite against a common enemy?"

The five dog warriors looked at each other and nodded their approval of his kind offer. They walked past Tank into the cave and all bowed as they did so.

The following day saw the Grimm out in the open, as they walked away from the ruins that had sheltered them for the brief time since their flight from the underworld. Memphis walked at the head of a disorganised Pack Grimm. They needed something other than the old ruins and chose to head farther south towards the planet's equator. Three things were certain: to remain where they were wasn't a good idea, their only way into the human district had been sealed and the other packs knew where to find them, it was in the Grimm's best interests to disappear. For these reasons alone, it was enough to make them want to move, so after much debate, they'd decided on the tactical withdrawal away from the White Fang that no doubt would be plotting their next move against them.

Indeed, White Fang scouts were a regular distraction, scented at varying times in the night. Two, captured sneaking too close to their impromptu camp, regretted their mistake as they were shared out among the Grimm; it was enough to curb the hunger and anything was better than nothing, especially as they now walked into the unknown.

Memphis looked back at the Grimm, its number was easily over one hundred dogs, and he allowed himself a small smile. It'd been more than a year since the Grimm had numbered so many.

After half a day's walk, they left the arid, rocky desert valley and walked onto hard-baked ground that'd cracked and hardened into five and six-sided geometric shapes for as far as the eye could see.

At least they'd left behind the sand that had plagued them; there had been no water supply large enough to wash their fur free of the stuff.

Memphis knew they would soon become hungry and some dog would have the honour of feeding them, unless they could come up with some alternative food source. Before them lay at least a day's march across flat, dry land. Ahead of them, another mountainous region, hopefully one that would give them what they required: a base to strike out from, a place they could call home and a way into the underworld so that they would at least have something to eat.

Later that night, Killer and Butch shared a bottle of what man called mead. Presented as a gift from the human, Alex Stevenson, it was a welcome change to their normal drink—water. It'd been sent with the daily ration of human meat, although the case it had arrived in had been almost emptied by the time it had reached the pack leader. As they drank, they became light-headed and slightly tipsy; they weren't used to the effects of alcohol.

Four young bitches entered—Killer had ordered their presence in his quarters some minutes before—and the two highest ranking dogs in the pack drunkenly stroked their fur. It wasn't long before their fun began, they forced bitch onto bitch as they all howled and whooped with delight.

Before the party ended though, a young warrior burst into Killer's private quarters. He stood, rooted by protocol, and waited until his pack leader acknowledged his presence.

Killer watched him and smiled as he rutted with a bitch. She in turn licked another of the bitches that lay with them, and although those in the room committed sexual acts before him, the young warrior seemed anxious to tell his news.

"What is it?" Killer asked without breaking his rhythm.

"There's been a raid!"

"I guess it's from the surface; is it the Grimm?"

"No, pack leader. It was Tank and some of the exiles; they were screaming a new battle cry, one that hasn't been heard before." The young warrior paused. "Mad Dogs."

This was enough to put both Killer and Butch off what they were doing, they quickly climbed off the bitches who continued amongst themselves.

"Mad Dogs? How many of them were there?" Butch growled and unintentionally scared the young dog warrior.

"Six, including Tank."

"How many did they kill?"

"None would stand against them, all fled. Eight bitches are unaccounted for." The young warrior stepped back, out of the range of any possible impulsive swipe of clawed hand. "They'd all changed, as the Grimm."

"Come, Butch, let's go see our so-called ally and see if we can't hurry them along. We need that armour and as soon as possible."

Tank felt imperious after being accepted as pack leader. None of the others wanted the burden of responsibility. The five White Fang were also glad to be rid of the name and quickly took on the mantle of Mad Dog with enthusiasm.

They'd enjoyed the raid into their old home and the kidnapping of the bitches. The only annoying thing had been the fact that none of the White Fang would stand against them when they'd a burning desire to try out their new prowess. Little did they know that their new scent exuded a pheromone that caused fear in humans, which ultimately, they'd evolved from. Even a dog warrior would have to fight his emotions to stand against them.

The starry night was clouded by an orange haze; a distant storm blew the radioactive dust and sand high into the atmosphere. They finally reached the cave and were pleased to see that none of the bitches had tried to escape, they were too afraid of what would happen to them if they were caught.

"Are we going on another raid?" Ulrich asked.

Hunter started to push the bitches into the cave but he paused and listened to the conversation. The others also stopped what they were doing to hear the answer to Ulrich's question.

"Not tonight, we need to eat, and fuck these bitches. The sooner we increase our numbers, the better," Tank said, as the bitches howled and fled into the cave ahead of them.

"The question I want to know is which do we fuck and which do we eat?" Gamble asked and turned to give chase as the new bitches fled deeper into the cave system.

They chased the new bitches all the way into the inner cavern where the bitches of Pack Mad Dog waited for their meal. It arrived shrieking, straight at them, with the six dog warriors slavering behind them.

Dasher leapt at the first to turn to face them and sunk his teeth deep into her neck; she raised her hands high as though to ward off a blow, but her defence was no match for the dog warrior's savagery.

The bitches that remained when the warriors left on their raid were hungry, starved as they were for more than a day. They dragged two of the bitches down that tried to seek solace among them, their hunger quickly getting the better of them, and they ripped at the flesh and slashed at them until they moved no more.

The other five bitches were terrified and shied away from the feast at first, though they eventually gave in and began to tuck into their old friends. Fortunately, there was more than enough flesh to go around and every stomach was soon full, with still some meat left for the following day.

Chapter 14

Memphis led Pack Grimm across the wasteland, they'd walked non-stop for three days. They had only paused to eat twice, when two of the bitches stepped forward for the good of the pack and volunteered to help keep the pack going. Although they would only eat a couple of mouthfuls each, it was enough to get them over the unending dead flatland. At the end of the third day, they'd made the low hills, though the mountains were still a good distance away.

Memphis wondered whether he'd made the right decision, he may have just walked the Grimm to their deaths, when a shout from a scout up ahead drew his attention away from his thoughts.

The warrior stood atop a dune ahead of them, he waved and turned away towards whatever had captured his enthusiasm.

Memphis didn't need to hurry the pack, they all knew the predicament they were in and hurried, they'd no stomach to turn around and walk back the way they'd come. Before Memphis made the top of the rise, spires came into view and as he quickened his pace to join the warrior, a whole forest of structures became visible.

Unlike the old ruins they'd first thought to make their home, the city in front of them seemed largely undamaged, although there were more windows broken than were intact and those were caked with several hundred years of toxic sand and dust to actually see through.

The city stretched away into the mountain's lower region and for the most part seemed untouched by the sandstorms, as if the mountains that ringed the structures in a half-crescent had protected them.

"How many of them lived here?" Memphis asked.

"It would have been more than a pack, that's for sure!" Chaz said as he appeared alongside him.

"More than all the packs joined together," Kito, one of the new Grimm warriors, suggested.

Never had any dog looked upon the city, which—before the catastrophe that had ended mankind's dominance in the galaxy—had been a thriving metropolis, it'd housed tens of thousands of humans. Now the entire pack formed a line across the dunes that partially ringed the city and stared down, amazed by the vastness of the city before them. To Memphis and his pack, the number that must have lived here before they retreated underground was unfathomable.

"No amount of wheat could feed so many!" Jade said from over Memphis' shoulder.

Looking forwards as far as he could see into the abandoned city, Memphis spied a large structure, a wide high tower that was ringed by several walls near what could be the city's centre. The concentric walls gave the structure the look of a step pyramid.

Memphis turned to look both left and right, along the line of Grimm talking quietly among themselves; they looked and pointed out the many features before them.

"Let's move, split up into smaller groups and explore, we'll meet at that walled structure in the centre," Memphis barked when he eventually got over his awe at what they'd discovered.

The city still lay a good half mile distant and the mass of dogs would have looked like an advancing army to any that stood amid the structures, if there were any survivors that could claim ownership.

As they neared the city, they could smell nothing but the polluted toxic smell that was the scourge of the whole planet. Memphis hoped that the city was empty, he couldn't have wished for a better base, or home, for his pack to settle in.

They made it to the city limits; the brick structures here were residential in purpose and almost completely covered in a thick layer of toxic waste, mainly different shades of orange shot through with reds and all manner of rusty tinges that looked deceptively beautiful.

The pack began to fragment as they split up to explore. Memphis watched his feet as he walked, the toxic dust that'd gathered thick on the city streets now moved ahead of him, almost as light as air, as his feet kicked it up. The ground beneath the dust was a solid surface, a level road that rose slightly as it edged towards the centre of the city.

Eventually, the housing gave way to larger buildings; at first these were made of brick and were four, five and six storeys high. Memphis could hear the barks of the Grimm as they shouted from distant rooftops; communication was easy, their voices carried within the silent city. These structures gave way to strange buildings, their giant panes of glass gone, shattered by the great ending or the passage of time. The remnants were just shards of discoloured, stained glass, scattered around the walls of the buildings.

As they neared the centre, Memphis decided to make his way to the walled structure he'd spied from his hilltop vantage. He guessed correctly that the structure was at the city centre and that all the roads rose gradually until they made it to its walls. Memphis walked with Elle, Sandy, Chaz, Harmony and a few of the ex-White Fang that he hadn't yet learned the names of.

They turned a corner, there was less dust the higher up they walked. Before them stood the first of the walls and they all stood aghast at what they saw. Memphis hadn't imagined anything could be so big and wouldn't have believed its existence if he hadn't seen it with his own eyes.

The high wall easily stood fifty metres above them; it loomed over them as they made their way to its smooth, steep side. They all felt the sides of the wall, which was black and as smooth as glass. Its solid surface was shot through with another material coloured white, which gave it a marbled effect.

"What is this stone?" Harmony asked. "I've never seen or felt its like."

Chaz ran his nails down its surface, pressing harder as he went.

"It does not score," he barked in surprise.

They set off with the intention of walking the perimeter but hadn't gone far before they came to a gateway, two giant metal doors stood ajar, enough so that they could squeeze through, one dog at a time sideways.

Memphis looked at the sun directly above them, though the orange haze still partially blocked out its rays, if not the radiation. Memphis looked at the golden ball through the haze; he turned from the sun to be the first through the giant metal doors. Inside the gate was another wall stretching away in both directions, above them were four bridges that spanned the space above their heads, connecting the outer and inner walls. It was way above them and the only thing they could tell from below them was that the inner wall was much taller than the outer.

At their feet, the ground was covered in debris, mainly belongings of the old inhabitants, dropped when they had fled from whatever catastrophe had hit Lorela in its long distant history. It was all covered in the same orange pollution, but only the thinnest of veneers, the two high walls obviously stopped most of what the rest of the city endured.

"See if you can close the doors," Memphis ordered.

Three of the dogs leaned their backs against it, grunting and growling as they leaned into the task.

"Bastard," Chaz snarled, as he lost his footing and fell heavily to slam his behind at the foot of the door. "It will not budge!"

"Leave it, let's get going, I want to see what's behind this wall."

They set off once more and made their way around two corners. They came at last to the opposite side of the complex, from where the outer gate was situated. Defensively it was perfect, having the longest route for any attacker, making it almost impossible to surprise them, even if they masked their scent.

The doors in the gateway were exact copies of those from the outer gate, but unlike those, these had been left wide open. Inside the inner wall was a wide-open space, it looked as though, at one point, it could have been a garden, now, it was like everything else—barren. But at the centre of the city, unlike everywhere else, it was free from the orange dust. At the very centre of the garden was the tower he'd seen from the top of the hill, it was made from the same substance as the walls; they could see no windows and only one entrance. They would only just be able to walk through without stooping. The door, unlike the gates, was closed and that too appeared to have been made from the same material as the gates.

They crossed the courtyard, looking up to see two bridges that connected the inner wall and the tower. These bridges were halfway up the side of the tower that led to the top of the inner wall; as they walked, Memphis looked for doors in the walls but saw none. Whomsoever had lived here before had thought of their security; they had meant to hold it. It was clear they'd thought of everything necessary when they had designed this fortress, had built it.

Memphis reached the door and pushed against it, he hadn't expected it to budge but to his surprise, it swung inward easily. Inside, the whole ground floor opened out into one massive room and in the centre of the room, a glass staircase, ten metres wide, ascended to the next level.

They made their way to the centre of the room, touched the walls and looked in awe at the strange textures; it was unusual to say the least. They'd never seen walls so perfectly flat and symmetrical, the strange materials didn't help either, the room's alien feel disturbed their senses.

"Who could have built such a place?" Dozer asked and looked at Memphis, still not totally sure of his place in Pack Grimm.

"I want to know why they would leave!" Chaz said.

"It must be the poison, probably killed off the indigenous population," Memphis said.

"If that was the case, there would be skeletal remains, where are the dead?" Elle questioned.

"True spoken. I know one thing for sure, it isn't dog-made. We would never abandon such a lair," Memphis said as he reached the bottom of the stairs.

"Human maybe? They could have lived here before a time when the surface was blighted by whatever killed everything?" Sandy mused as she sniffed at the air.

"So, what of the dog? We've always been more resilient than man at breathing the poisons and toxins, even before we took the pill," Elle said.

"Too many questions, when I only need answers!" Memphis barked and climbed the stairs.

Chapter 15

Tank and his renegade Mad Dogs lurked around the entrance to the underworld and watched for guards. They saw none. Tank had expected at least some sort of resistance. In the end though, he considered his little pack so far above all others that the enemy were too frightened to stand against them, such was the height of the evolution of his insanity.

It'd been more than a week since they'd last visited the underworld. The White Fang territory lay just ahead and it was time to source some more food for his growing pack's bellies, especially since some of the bitches had begun to show unusually early in their pregnancies. They should have another two to three weeks before they got fat with the offspring that would be Mad Dogs' future.

For now, they needed feeding. A pregnant bitch was a hungry bitch, waiting hungry for a few days wasn't an option, the unborn pups needed sustenance.

They entered the tunnel; no signs of life appeared as they made their way into the depths and paused at the first tunnels that branched off.

Tank was just about to suggest they split up, two to search down each tunnel, when the chink of metal hitting metal came from directly ahead of them. All the Mad Dogs turned to face the sound, which evolved into a contingency of armoured dogs that walked out of the gloom.

One of the dogs ran his clawed glove across the wall, the sound hurt the ears of all the dogs from both packs and they winced, especially the dog that had caused the sound; he quickly removed his hand from the wall.

They could see a dozen of them clearly, White Fang dogs covered in metal plates that overlapped. As the dogs moved, so did the metal plates, which were shaped to mould each individual. The only plates that didn't move were the ones that covered the hip and groin areas and the back and front that covered the torso; other than that, the helmet stayed completely still, with only the lower jaw of the dog exposed.

Each of the dog's armour possessed a little human creativity, with weapons built into the armour that covered the forearms; these varied in shape and size, with the most popular being a number of steel claws a foot in length.

"Hello Tank," Killer said.

As Killer spoke, a long spear came from one of the side tunnels. Dasher didn't see it coming until it was too late. The spear impaled him and pinned him, two more quickly came from the same tunnel and pierced his flesh with more Pack White Fang holding onto the shafts. These, however, didn't wear the metal suits but carried the all too familiar human weapons.

Dasher's howl of pain was cut short by the fourth spear, it entered his brain through his eye socket as the dog turned his head to search for what and who had struck him from the side.

Everything seemed to happen so quickly in the confined space of the tunnel. The remaining Mad Dogs backed off a little to avoid any other surprises that might come at them from the sides. The metal-clad dogs pressed forward, stepping over the body of Dasher, who was stabbed several times by the weapon-wielding White Fang as they made sure he was dead.

Ulrich was the first to meet the advancing Killer. He grabbed at his old pack leader's arms to break them, folding them back behind his body; if he could somehow bend the metal plate, he could maybe break a bone. He could incapacitate him, taking him out of the fight; the thought of him eating the mighty dog's heart crossed his mind. Something built into the suit of armour prevented this from happening though, the interlocking plates were too strong and Ulrich found himself exposed, afraid to let go of the arms he held, for fear of the weapons that would rip into his flesh.

Ulrich leaned his head into the attack, he bit at the armoured shoulder and his teeth scraped across metal that only gave slightly, dented under the immense pressure that was his bite.

Tank stood right behind Ulrich and watched as two more White Fang stepped up either side of Killer to stab into Ulrich's flank, forcing the Mad Dog to let go. Tank jumped forwards and grabbed hold of his new pack member; he dragged him backwards as he fell limp in his arms.

The other Mad Dogs jumped into the fray. They howled and bit hard as they struck out at the defenders, killing a few as they first pressed forwards. Warhol even managed to pierce the breastplate of one of the armoured dogs with his claws, but his victory was short-lived and he was quickly cut down by the new weaponry of the White Fang.

Tank, having seen enough, dragged the injured Ulrich to the surface. The light of day at the tunnel's mouth came into view as the sounds of battle ended in the darkness behind them. It was obvious who'd won the fight, the smell of death behind them could have only gone one way, the sound of metal moving against metal was the tell-tale sign that the armoured dogs had killed Pack Mad Dog in its infancy.

Tank lofted Ulrich onto his shoulders and ran towards the light at the end of the tunnel. The sound of pursuit gained with every step as Ulrich's weight slowed him down.

Tank could hear the breathing of his enemy, could sense that steel was about to gouge his flesh. He burst out into the light and fell forwards to roll a few metres on the wide stone ledge, which overlooked the slope that ran away into the valley below.

Tank turned to sit up; he looked at the tunnel's entrance and saw the armoured dogs. Butch took his helmet off, as did Killer, and both smiled as they avoided the sun's rays.

They talked, their heads close, and both looked at their helmets before they turned to look at Tank once more.

"You have until nightfall, then you die!" Killer growled and turned to walk away from Tank.

Tank picked a stone from the floor, putting all his strength into the throw and managed to hit Killer on the back, but the leader of the White Fang ignored the stone, which bounced off his armour.

Tank stood, he looked at Ulrich and his injuries that hissed as the sun's radiation burned them closed. Ulrich opened his eyes, the obvious pain he felt was written on his contorted face.

Tank knew that Ulrich would heal, even if Ulrich didn't. Whether he would be ready to fight the next time they met the White Fang though, he didn't know. He lifted Ulrich off the ground and helped him stand before he placed a hand around his midriff to support him, and the two of them began to move.

"Thank you," Ulrich managed.

Tank smiled, they'd lost the fight but not the war, at least not for now. While there was still breath in his lungs, he wouldn't give up. They moved as fast as possible to put as much distance between them and the White Fang. There was no way they could beat the newly-equipped dog warriors, not just the two of them; the numbers of Pack Mad Dogs would have to increase considerably.

Memphis stood on the roof of his fortress and looked out for the dog warriors as he waited for them to return. Every day, scouting parties were sent out to search for anything of use. Mountains of tinned food, stacked from floor to ceiling had been found in giant warehouses, though they couldn't be sure how long it'd sat there; it was enough to sustain life without killing any more of his pack. But it wasn't what they wanted—fresh meat, preferably human.

Memphis stabbed at the tiny tin he held in his hand, his nail easily tearing the impossibly thin metal. Sniffing at the food annoyed his senses and he retched more than once as the smell lingered. Sandy showed him how to hold his nose and knock back the foul contents, reminding him there would be no more unnecessary sacrifice, not until this bounty had been consumed.

The stuff was horrible; it was dry, even with the oily preservatives that acted as a lubricant when the vile stuff made its way down his throat.

From the top of the tower, he could see for miles and although a few of the buildings were taller than his perch, he could still see almost everything that moved about. Now his attention was drawn to a group of the Grimm that made their way through the city as they returned from the foraging mission. He watched their progress as they disappeared, then reappeared behind the buildings of the city.

Something caught his attention, the midday sun shone with intensity, suddenly reflected from some foreign surface that hadn't been there before. Then it was gone but he thought he could see tiny movement, specks moving on the landscape all those miles away. That vision soon was also gone, like an apparition seen out of the corner of an eye.

They'd been in ownership of the city for more than a month; they'd met nothing alive and been content to be the masters of their own kingdom at last. Memphis looked from his fortress nearly every day, he knew there was nothing that would have reflected the sun's light, nothing that'd been there before.

"Memphis, one of the scouting parties has found something!" Chaz said from behind him.

"So have I," Memphis replied without turning.

Chaz joined him at the edge of the fortress and placing his hands on the barrier, he leaned forward as he strained to see the edge of the city.

"I think we have visitors, look there," Memphis pointed at the streets at the edge of the city, three tiny plumes of orange dust swirled as three tiny figures ran towards the centre of the city.

"I shall go and greet them," Chaz said.

Memphis didn't turn to watch Chaz leave; he was confident that whatever was scouting the city, his second-in-command could deal with it.

Chaz left the roof by its central staircase that descended through thirty floors of sectioned off rooms. All of these rooms could be entered through massive round doors, a foot thick and made of solid metal; every inner wall was made of the same flawless material as the outside walls. As he moved from floor to floor, Chaz howled out a call to arms. Dogs and bitches of the Grimm began to appear, and by the time he'd reached the ground floor, more than fifty of the pack had massed behind him.

He turned to face them at the foot of the stairs. Moving backwards, he danced a little as he punched the air before him, shadow-boxing to show off his skills to the others who howled in delight.

"Something invades our domain, something approaches the lair of Pack Grimm," Chaz said. He waited, pausing for the howls of disgust to die down. "We shall go and welcome them."

There was no such thing as treading silently clad in armour. Although lightweight and non-cumbersome, it made an awful din in the silent, eerie streets. As the buildings changed from small buildings to larger structures, which seemed to be joined in blocks rather than single structures, they began to feel they were being watched. The walk became oppressive as everything seemed to loom over them, pressing in.

They sniffed the air but all they got was the scent of the orange stuff they kicked up every time they trod the hard ground; they struggled to smell even their own scent. None of them spoke a word; the only thing they could hear was the sound of their own breathing and the clanks of their armour. They looked through the slits in their visors, tinted protective glass built into the helmets to cover their eyes so that they could move about in the day. The downfall to this was obvious, but not one that the leader of the White Fang foresaw—they couldn't take their helmets off until nightfall.

"I think we should turn back," one of the White Fang said.
"Why, what are you afraid of?" another asked.
"That!"

All three White Fang looked ahead; several of the Grimm blocked their path, stretching across between the two sides of the road.

They turned to make a tactical withdrawal but found the road behind was just as the road ahead, blocked the entire width of the street. Amid the Grimm dog warriors stood many bitches, adding weight to the rumours that against all tradition, the puppy-bearing Grimm bitches fought too.

The largest of the mutated, physically enhanced dogs stepped forward. He looked them up and down, though most of his attention was focussed on the weaponry attached to the armour-plated forearms. His dark sandy-coloured fur and long snout made him unrecognisable. The three White Fang didn't know him; if they'd seen him before, he'd changed beyond recognition.

"I'm Chaz Grimm; you will surrender yourselves or die."

The three-cornered dog warriors stood back to back, shoulder to shoulder, and growled as Chaz spoke, they knew this was their time and planned on taking as many as they could.

Memphis watched from his tower, Elle standing behind him; at his altitude, he could just make the scent of what transpired below, like a whisper on the wind that luckily blew lightly in their direction. She too wished to see what happened. He leaned over the wall, his arms folded beneath his chest and Elle cuddled up behind him. They both watched in silence as the Grimm attacked, three of their number fell prey to the long knives of those that had entered the city uninvited before they were overcome. Memphis was intrigued to see how long it took his dogs to penetrate these metal-clad intruders' armour; as it was, it took more than five blows to even get through the metal plating.

The last of the intruders was spared, he was relieved of his weapons first and last his armour. Memphis was surprised to see a dog beneath the suit; even more surprised to see the dog howl in pain as his eyes burned in the light of the sun.

His attention was drawn away from the city as, yet again, the sun shone on something outside the city limits, something that disappeared out of sight.

"Is it over?" Elle asked.

"No, it's just begun," Memphis replied.

Killer and Butch ran at the head of their warriors, almost two hundred of them, across the open, sun-baked plain. They'd been running ever since the scouts had returned. They were a fearful sight in their shiny armour and chose to run during the day so that they could rest with their helmets off in the cooler night air.

Killer searched for Tank but failed, so instead decided to charge at a much bigger target, considering Tank's Mad Dogs were at an end.

On the third day after the Grimm had been located by his scouts, his whole pack of warriors reached their destination. They crested the rise that looked down into the heavily polluted, abandoned city. Its new residents, the Grimm, they fully intended to slaughter and take the pills for themselves before they invaded the human subterranean underworld. Killer had been given no choice in the matter; if he gave the humans much more time, he envisioned every human walking through the different packs' territories setting ablaze every dog they could find.

Top of the food chain! he told himself under his breath so none could hear him.

He'd considered resting into the night but had thought better of it. If they'd been seen, they would have lost the element of surprise and left themselves open to attack. So he coveted his advantage and pressed on, to waste any time now could prove fatal.

Now Killer wasted no time; after only a short pause, he ran down into the city, to kill and maim all the Grimm. Killer looked at Butch and they shared a smile, confident of the victory to come.

"They come," Memphis said.

From his high vantage, it was easy to see the mass of dog warriors, all of them wearing the suits of armour that collectively gave off a stunning reflective light display, so much so it was hard to see the sandy backdrop. Memphis turned to those who watched him and waited for his order. Elle, Sandy and Jade all wore the suits of armour they'd salvaged from the corpses of the White Fang scouts. The suits were too small for the larger Grimm dog warriors, but just about right for the smaller bitches, who had taken to the suits of armour with gusto.

Memphis and his entourage watched them enter the city; they knew they had a fight on their hands, one they didn't relish. At the same time, it was a fight they knew was coming that they couldn't avoid. Sooner or later, old scores had to be settled. A commotion at the front gate caught his eye, the former dog warriors of the White Fang and the bulk of the Grimm warriors poured out the gate. They'd also old scores to attend to, for honour's sake, if naught else.

Memphis did nothing to stop them; at least they'd left the bitches behind, and besides, it was their choice to go to their deaths.

Killer and Butch jogged up the street, their armour making an awful racket, the chink of metal on metal as they ran would not allow the element of surprise but it would, however, give them an edge against the enhanced Grimm. They charged down the street to meet them head on. The two opposing sides picked up their pace and barked out battle cries as they came together, claws slashing and metal slicing through flesh.

Killer could feel the sweat against his brow and feared his visor would steam up, his mind soon turned from this thought though, as a muscular superior Grimm knocked him off his feet. He'd felt the blow to his shoulder, but his armour had taken most of the impact. He sat up and waited for an attack that didn't come; the dog that'd bit into his shoulder plate lay on the ground a few feet away, missing half a lung and a fist full of ribs that Butch held in his metal talons.

Lucky, he thought as he scrambled to his feet.

His force outnumbered the enemy more than four to one, but still the enhanced mutants threw them around like sand taken by a gust of wind. These armour-wearing warriors would have been no match against this new breed without their metal skin. They flung his dogs into the air or against the wall, but for the most part, they could not penetrate the armour. Only a few of the White Fang fell in those first few moments of battle, as clawed hands managed to rip off the armour plating or find gaps between their plates for their claws to penetrate flesh.

Like most battles of this nature, the fight soon devolved into small knots of fighting; Killer joined one of these. Two of the Grimm faced off against six of his warriors. Killer jumped up in the air, over the heads of his warriors, and landed on the head of his intended target as its claws penetrated the breastplate of another. Blood sprayed up the clawed hand and arm of the Grimm; at the same time, it also filled the air as the Grimm scored a wound. Killer used both his metal talons to stab down at the Grimm warrior who looked up too late, taking the eight blades through the shoulders. The blades all penetrated down to the metal fists. Killer got a good bite on the head of his enemy and his mouth filled with blood as the warrior went limp.

The others swamped the other Grimm as Killer landed on his feet, but outnumbered six to one and fighting alone was all too much for the Grimm warrior. He fell to his knees; he'd been stabbed at least forty times and his wounds hissed in the healing sunlight until his body finally gave in to his inevitable death.

Killer looked around him; it was a similar story all around—the Grimm warriors being quickly overcome by the superior numbers and armour of the White Fang.

A few suffered grievous injuries as they were thrown, dashed against the walls and floor, and more than a few died from crushing blows rather than actual flesh wounds. Most of those were around the head, the helmets caving in so that the skulls were crushed, causing haemorrhaging of the brain and a quick death.

The battle was over; the first contact, a terrible event for the Grimm. The roof top was, by now, full of the Grimm; they watched as the bulk of the dog warriors were cut down.

Memphis turned to look at the worried faces that stared at him.

"We hold them here," he barked. "We will fight them floor for floor and make them pay for every Grimm they kill."

Memphis turned, his honour getting the better of him, and he howled a challenge to the invading enemy.

Killer returned the howl, he'd already guessed that the Grimm would be holed up in the large structure in the centre of the city and they'd already started to move against it. The confirmation spurred his dogs up the hill—time to taste victory and Grimm flesh, take the pills and make the White Fang more powerful than any that'd ever gone before.

They charged up the hill, Killer and Butch at the head. As they approached the front gate, however, Killer began to slow to a walk. He panted, struggling for breath, and fell to his knees as his tongue stuck to the roof of his mouth, though he tried to regain his feet. He looked all around him; every one of his warriors had suffered the same fate. He fell forward and his face hit the floor. His snout sucked in the foul-tasting orange stuff that'd been at their feet the whole time they'd been within the city limits. He coughed once on the gas that was heavier than air and closed his eyes. He opened them briefly to see Memphis Grimm looking down at him before his body finally succumbed to death.

Memphis and the others were confused. Grateful, but none the wiser to whatever had ended the White Fang army. They'd gained a victory by default and enough meat for the Grimm to last for weeks; their bellies would be fat with more meat than they could eat.

In truth, by taking the pill, the enhanced Grimm had inadvertently made themselves immune to the toxins and high radiation levels that plagued the planet's surface, another example of being more dog. In some ways, they now embraced the radioactive qualities, their bodies preferring the polluted air to that of fresh air, which, for the most part, remained breathable for humans near the planet's subterranean depths. Although the White Fang had survived more than happily on most of the planet's surface, the high concentration of radioactive materials within the abandoned city had proved too much for their bodies, the toxins soaking into every organ until they'd all begun to fail. The Grimm, on the other hand, having taken their next and ultimate step in their evolution had become a race that thrived in the deadliest radioactive areas of Lorela—the more they soaked the stuff in, the happier they would be.

Tank laid low for a time and his Mad Dogs became hungry because he dared not leave the cave for fear of detection. Four of his bitches had been eaten in this time and he knew it wouldn't be long before they needed to go on a raid or perish. The rest of his bitch's bellies were full to bursting, fat and heavy with the pups they carried, with the first four bitches he'd impregnated coming closest to full term.

Ulrich healed but became quiet and reserved. He withdrew into himself until it was time to mate, at which point he would seem like his old self—frothing at the jaw, his eyes wild, his lips drawn back before he bit the bitch he fucked.

Ulrich smiled as he climbed off one of the bitches that was nearly full term when she began to complain of pains in her stomach. The pack crowded around the bitch as she began to scream and without warning, she arched her back, her eyes rolling into the top of her head as she clawed at her stomach. The reason for her agonising cramps became all too clear as the little faces of her pups appeared on the skin of her underbelly, pressing outwards. Their little jaws bit hard as they chewed at the inside of her body. The pups ate their way out, from inside the bitch, her stomach was torn apart, and she howled in agony before her head lolled to one side and she died.

Eight little mutts lay exhausted in the gore that had been the bitch that'd carried them and was their first meal. The pack looked on in stunned silence, especially the bitches that all carried the unborn pups of these feral, mutated creatures that, like the Grimm, had taken their next evolutionary baby steps.

Tank and Ulrich looked at each other and shared a smile, the other bitches all began to whimper as they slowly realised there was nothing any of them could do but wait to be eaten from the inside out.

"Dog eat dog!" Ulrich barked.
"Dog eat dog!" Tank agreed.

Chapter 16
Every Dog has its Day

Tank stood alone outside the entrance to the underworld; it'd been weeks since he'd seen any of his mortal enemy, Pack White Fang. Now his own fledgling pack, the Mad Dogs, were on the brink of vanishing from the dog world altogether—they desperately needed food.

All the Mad Dog bitches had suffered agonising deaths, eaten by their own young at birth, from the inside out. The injured Ulrich remained at the cave to watch over the brood; they were too young to defend themselves from any foe that wished them harm. They also needed to be stopped from eating each other whilst they played.

They'd grown quickly in the few weeks since their birth, feasting on all their bitch mothers' remains until they'd become nothing but bones for the mauling. Unusually, they walked on all fours wherever they could and stooped over when their wrists ached from the effort.

There were fifty-two of them in total; there'd been more but a few had died from birth defects and complications, something that was normal for new-born pups in the dog world.

Tank smiled as he thought of them. He knew he would save all of them if he could, he loved them so. Skulking in the shadows, he smelt the barest of White Fang scent, but nothing near the tunnel entrance that suggested a guard. He remembered the battle some weeks earlier, a little way into the underground, where three of his followers had met their end, slaughtered at the hands of his enemies. These thoughts gave him pause but as his belly rumbled and his hunger got the better of him, he forced himself forward into the darkness.

He'd come from this place; before, it'd been the domain of the pack that had exiled him, his own brother the cause. Now the underground seemed alien to him; he much preferred the outside world to the underworld since his transformation.

He paused a short distance into the darkness and listened before he sniffed, he detected nothing, not a sound to his ears or scent to his nostrils.

He carried on but took more care as he went, fearful of the ambush that would surely come.

I must go on, he thought to himself, he'd many children to feed now and after a brief risk-assessment, he continued his search of food. As he did, he smelt a fresh scent, and not the scent of the dog warriors he'd expected, but that of White Fang bitches, coming straight at him. The scent grew fast and he knew the bitches ran towards him. He could smell something else.

The bitches were being pursued by another pack, the new scent none other than the warriors of Pack Blood Hound.

Tank hadn't smelt these warriors in such a long time; it'd been months since the Grimm had fled their ancestral territory that had bordered partially with the Blood Hound territory.

So, the White Fang have been beaten somehow. Served them right for getting into bed with the humans! Tank thought.

He waited as the White Fang bitches continued towards him; when they finally rounded a corner in the tunnel system before him, he saw that they were being led by three White Fang dog warriors, not long grown from yearlings to full adulthood. They stopped and growled uselessly at him, he could smell their fear as his pheromone passed over their senses.

The bitches began to yelp in the tunnels behind as dog warriors worried them from their rear. The three yearlings turned and ran back into the mass of White Fang bitches that pressed forward in their panic to flee.

Tank stood rooted as they ran past him, he gave them no indication of his intentions. There were at least fifty of them, a far cry from the hundreds he remembered the White Fang to have numbered.

One of the White Fang dog warriors ran back up the tunnel, followed by seven Blood Hound dog warriors that he didn't recognise. As the pup neared him and tried to pass, Tank lifted his paw—he almost looked lethargic, a bored attempt at action. All the same, he stopped the young dog warrior and left him hanging, dead, on the end of his claw.

As the dead dog slumped to the ground, Tank couldn't help wondering if he'd ended the life of the last remaining dog of the White Fang, he may have just ended the pack forever. The thought made him smile—an act that made his lips draw back and look as though he meant violence. He looked at the seven dogs that had stopped at the tunnel's end and watched as they slowly retreated around the corner into the darkness, their tails between their legs.

He turned back towards the surface and gathered up the fleeing bitches, gently herding them into the night.

"Come, you're Mad Dogs now!"

They looked nervous but feared him more than they did the night. When they reached the surface, they looked up at the stars; some crawled around on all fours, pressing their bellies to the sandy rocks out of fear. Some considered returning to the tunnels, but many eyes shone from the shadows, the eyes of the Blood Hound that would make a short meal of their flesh.

"If you want to live, follow me!" Tank said.

He did, however, forget to tell them how long they would live for and what awaited them at the end of their days in the Mad Dog lair.

The mayor of District Seven, Alex Stevenson, was accompanied by Rob Chamberlain, the scientist who had accompanied his friend and mayor to help him in his explanation at the council headquarters. They walked, far removed from their home tunnels, down the wide tunnels that led to the council halls of District One.

They'd been given a guard of four knights that, between them, carried the apparatus that had defeated the Grimm in the abandoned hydroponics lab some weeks before. Alex Stevenson was all smiles. He'd good reason to be, he was sure he was about to be elected onto the council of representatives by the ruling elite.

"How could they not?" he thought out loud.

"Excuse me?" Rob asked.

The question startled Alex, who hadn't realised he'd spoken his thought out loud; he'd been too busy concentrating on the tunnel's end as it opened into one of the biggest chambers he'd ever seen—the Palace Cavern. He'd been here before, on one occasion, when he'd been appointed to his post as mayor. In that distant past, he'd been excited as he had left for his new home. Now, he couldn't wait to get away from the district he'd ruled for so many years. It was bordered by the worst of dog kind and it'd taken him years to overcome the problem. The only thing that'd kept him from resigning his post was the never-ending supply of pills that came with his position.

The Forever pill had been the mainstay of Lorela's economy before the supernova had destroyed and polluted the planet's surface and forced mankind underground. It prolonged life and even made the old look young. Some humans hoped to live for eternity if they swallowed a pill every time they began to age.

He'd been summoned to the hall of representatives after the news of his victory had spread throughout the kingdom. He was smug as he looked upon the city that stretched out below him in the massive natural cavern; it was so large that a miniature star in the space above the city wouldn't have looked out of place.

Alex had earlier requested an audience with the ruling council, but he'd been refused on the grounds that he'd lost his district's entire store of Forever pills. They'd been stolen by Pack Grimm, and after he'd been duped by the White Fang, having been involved in dog politics that had gone badly for him, he'd been more than surprised at the invitation, until his victory over the mutated Grimm.

He looked in awe at the super massive space above; it was thick with cultivated phosphorescent fungi for as far as he could see. A small army of workers pulled themselves along the cavern roof to tend the precious crops and it took a pull on his shirt from Rob to get him moving again.

They descended into the city, walking no more than a block down the wide central boulevard until they reached the stagecoach office, little more than a hut at the side of the road.

The guard in charge of the four sent to guide them to their destination talked to the man who rested on the counter of the hut, giving Alex time to survey his immediate surroundings. All the houses looked pristine; whitewashed with windows that shone and reflected the light of the ceilinged world. Not one speck of dirt lay in the gutter and every person he saw looked immaculately dressed, with not a hair out of place.

Alex glanced down at himself and wondered how he must look, having come from the outer districts where a bit of dirt wasn't frowned upon as it was here. Every house that lined every street was adorned with hanging baskets, the weird plants clipped to perfection to show off their wonderful multi-coloured stems. Just when he thought nothing could look dirty or out of place in District One, the stage came rattling toward them from the direction of the centre of the city.

The stagecoach was pulled along by four giant dogs harnessed to the wooden-framed structure. A man sat on top of the carriage, reins in one hand and whip in the other. The four dogs were muzzled and chained with thick, heavy links that bound them to the wooden shaft. The beasts stank, even though they appeared healthy and freshly groomed and he and Rob held their noses as the carriage pulled to a stop at the kerbside. Alex remembered the dogs, the non-intelligent cousins of the race of dogs he now fought. These were yet another subspecies of the ancestors from the firstborn, those few that'd survived long enough to breed. They were hugely muscled and sniffed the road and everything they could get their noses buried into. As Alex and Rob watched, the lead dog crouched in the road and deposited a large amount of sloppy excrement in the gutter, soiling an otherwise clinical-looking environment.

"That's disgusting!" Rob remarked and turned away from the horrible mess.

Alex didn't comment, he didn't wish to appear weak to those that watched them, smiling as they scrutinised the pair.

"Mayor Stevenson," the head guard addressed him as he opened the door.

"Thank you," he replied.

Alex stepped on board, thinking that in time one would get used to the smell; those with them obviously had. He watched Rob mount the steps of the carriage, a door in the building next to the hut opened as he did and a clean-up crew exited the building with buckets full of steaming liquids and brushes to clean up the dog shit.

With a jolt, the carriage leapt forward, causing Rob to sit heavily beside him; it slowed as it turned in the road only to leap forward again with a slight jerk, the dogs' gait causing erratic motion.

The carriage soon broke into a rhythm and it wasn't long before the tiny jerks became unnoticed. They all sat in silence, the two of them and two of the guards. The other two had climbed up onto the driver's seat to leave room for the others. Alex didn't wish to engage with them, they were beneath him, and instead chose to look out of the window as the city streets went by.

Nothing changed for the most part, the pristine streets and houses all looked much the same, even though their shapes differed, with just a few subtle differences. Eventually though, the city evolved into busy streets lined with taller, three- and four-storey structures. Here, the people seemed self-important, with airs and graces, as they held their heads high, their long strides that of those who led rather than followed—the elite of the human world.

At the dead centre of the underground metropolis, the carriage came to a halt. The door was opened by one of the guards who jumped down from the driver's seat.

"Thank you," Alex said as he stepped from the carriage to the surface of the road.

Looking around, Alex noticed that this part of the city had been carved from the bedrock of the planet, its lines and contours the same and covered with the same whitewash as the rest of the city, but the stone's texture was obvious. Unlike the outlying parts of the city, which had obviously been made from building materials.

"Shall we?" Rob asked.

Alex was startled from his train of thought once again and together they walked across the small courtyard to the council offices. They'd also been cut out of the rock, meticulously carved, and he looked at the pillars that held up the slanted roof of the grand entrance. He noticed there were no joins between any of the structures, something he'd missed on his last visit. Even the tiles on the roof were sculptured.

He walked between the crafted pillars, soon he would be standing before the leaders of the human realm and he couldn't let his mind wander now; he steeled his mind and focussed on the job at hand.

They were led in silence to a washroom where they could freshen up. They heard running water; it fell into a sink gently overflowing with a wide cascade of fresh fluid that ran into a hole in the floor.

"How extravagant!" the scientist said.

"There's no other place like it in the human world," Alex said and dipped his hands into the cool liquid to wash the filth from hours of travelling off his face.

"I suppose the geologists would have cautioned against such frivolities if they thought they couldn't spare the water," Rob said calmly.

"And you think the men and women that sit on the ruling council would listen?" Alex asked.

The scientist shrugged, turned from his leader and continued to wash himself.

When they left the washroom, Alex began to worry about his appearance; he realised how dirty his clothes were and wondered whether they would cause offence. He didn't have long to think, however, as two maids waited outside the door, both holding smocks that would hide the grime on their clothes.

They were soon marched down the corridors of power, confident that they wouldn't cause offence. The halls of the council buildings had plenty of people going about their business, but the corridors were as wide as any room they had back in District Seven so there was no crush—far from it, in fact the corridor looked almost bare.

When they reached the end of the corridor, they walked through open doors into a busy room. The room was oval and the council members sat along one length of the room's curve, facing them. Unlike the corridor, the room was crammed with people, some wore the same type of smock as Alex and they too had obviously made the journey to see the council.

A man stood on a dais in front of the council.

"But you have a surplus, everybody knows it!" the man shouted.

"It's not for the likes of you to dictate policy to the ruling council!" Marlene Keegan shouted back at the man.

Alex knew Marlene; he'd met her on several occasions over the last hundred years. She didn't look a day over thirty and would have been pretty but for her nose, it was too flat to her face. In stark contrast to Marlene and the rest of the ruling council, who all looked young still, the man who'd addressed them was old. His hair was grey and dry, his face a mask of creases and wrinkles and his hands were gnarled with arthritis.

"Look at me, look at me," the man shouted as he was led away.

Alex looked at those sat behind the long desk that stretched the length of the room, they all looked as young as he did, at least for now, before his eyes finally came to rest on the head of the council—Marlene Keegan.

At the same time, Marlene watched the old man, following his progress as he was led from the room by two guards; her eyes rested on him as his did hers. She cocked an eyebrow at him and nodded in his direction.

The four guards led the two of them to the front of the crowd that was crammed into the room. They stood before the council and Alex couldn't help feeling as nervous as a man on trial.

"Mr Stevenson," she began, "I hear we owe you a great debt of thanks, hero of our times!"

"You owe me no such honour."

"Nonsense, Alex, you are the first to have ever defeated the dog in battle."

"I'm not a hero; I did only what any other would have done, given the opportunity."

Marlene looked at him, everyone did, he heard not a sound but his own heavy breath and heart as it pounded in his chest.

"I see you have brought the scientist with you."

Alex looked at Rob; he looked older than most others in the room, as he'd chosen not to take the Forever pill the last time he'd begun to age.

Rob stepped forward and the soldier behind him held his flame thrower and stepped up with him.

"Miss Keegan." Rob bowed. "I give you my chemical flame cannon."

"There's plenty of time for that," Marlene cut him off. "You are to stay here with our scientists and explain to them how your machine works."

Alex smiled, his heart pounded harder if it was possible. He just knew he was going to be promoted to the council now.

"We, the council, have discussed your position as a politician in the human world and although it looked as though you'd failed every person within our realm, it appears that you have contributed a great deal indeed. Considering your actions in battle against the packs of dog warriors, we have decided not to remove you from office but to keep you in your position so that you may continue your good work."

"But—" Alex began, his arms stretched out before him, his palms facing up as a beggar imploring for a morsel.

"No need to thank me yet, I have not finished," Marlene interrupted. "Also, we would like to replenish your stocks of Forever pills. There is no reason the people of your district should suffer because of your inadequacies. After all, the people don't do great deeds without reward, do they, Mr Stevenson?"

Alex took this reference as a slur against himself and knew he would have to do more to gain the respect and position he had thought he deserved. He turned from the council and the smug smile of the council leader. He would show them; he would show them all what he was capable of.

Chapter 17

Memphis Grimm stood atop the tower in the centre of the city they now called Lyall, a name he'd heard a human utter when he had been a pup, right before his mother had gutted the man for her hungry brood. Below in the city streets, his pack went about their business. Mainly bitches wandered the city's avenues, some carrying pails of water, others supply from the warehouses in the old city's manufacturing districts. Most of those about, however, either pushed large wheeled bins from the centre of the city or filled the bins with the toxic dust and slag that'd lain thick for centuries undisturbed, since man had abandoned the surface for the planet's protective underworld.

Memphis didn't question the futility of the clean-up operation, the task would take those that undertook it years to complete, but he did see the advantages of having a clean city. It would be better to live in a clean environment; after all, who knew what health hazards the dust would create in the long run.

Elle and Sandy appeared at either side of him, they both wore their armour and he was extremely envious of their protective metal covering. Maybe someday, they would capture some humans to make him a suit of armour just like theirs.

"Elle, Sandy, what do I owe my bitches, for them to come dressed ready for war and together whilst I survey all that is ours?"

"A scout returned. He has found a shaft in a large building that descends straight down!" Elle explained.

"It's shrouded in darkness, but the stench of man is strong," Sandy added.

Memphis looked from Elle to Sandy and back again; he'd waited patiently for such news to reach his ears and now he raised his head to the sky and howled in pure delight. Since they'd made Lyall their home, they'd uncovered stocks of food sources in all manner of containers. Most of the food was useless, being mainly human foodstuffs that the dog just wouldn't eat. Some meat products had survived, however, tiny tins of meats preserved in weird-tasting oils. How the humans managed to get the skinned meat into the metal tins and airtight was a mystery, like so many other things that'd been found; but one thing was for certain, the food they'd scavenged so far would not have lasted forever.

"Who found the shaft?" he asked.

"Adonis, he's one of the White Fang warriors."

"Yes, I know him, he's the broad-shouldered dog with the jet black fur," Memphis said.

Elle and Sandy looked at one another and shared a knowing look. There wasn't one dog in the whole pack that didn't envy Adonis and his black fur, or any bitch that didn't find the thought of his fur against theirs appealing.

Memphis grunted at the bitches' unspoken desire, he'd no appetite to rut now so cared not if they sought others to mate with.

"Go fetch Adonis, maybe you can wag your tails whilst we converse," Memphis took in the view of the city and smiled as the two of them backed away towards the stairs.

Tank led what remained of the White Fang clan into the darkest part of his realm. The bitches pressed together at the lowest point of the cave, all of them trying to get to where the two walls converged at the cave's narrow end.

They watched the Mad Dog pups as they sniffed and crawled around on the floor, they were six weeks old now and should at least be trying to walk on two legs. Tank looked at one of them; he gathered the little bitch up in his hands, careful not to nick the pup with a claw.

"There now, little mad dog, shall you not speak?" he said softly.

The little bitch looked at him with her puppy eyes and whined like a simpleton. Tank knew that something was wrong with his brood; they all displayed the symptoms of madness. Maybe as a direct result of his own feral mind, a mind he constantly kept under control; even as he watched his new brood, he too wanted to sniff around on the floor and search out the scents of others.

It was one of the new bitches that roused him from his melancholic thoughts; she appeared at his side and looked at the pup. The White Fang bitch smiled and leaned forward to stroke the pup, attempting to be the dutiful bitch. The pup had other intentions, however, and its look of adoration disappeared as it looked from Tank to this newcomer. The pup growled before it snapped and the bitch quickly moved her hand away.

Tank pulled the pup away and looked at the bitch, she must be brave to approach him, he sniffed her scent and considered mounting her.

"May I try again?" she said, smiling as she did so.

The other pups in this cave began to gather around them to sniff at their feet and Tank placed the pup back on the floor with its siblings. The twenty pups started to climb on the bitch, their tongues lapping at her as others from the brood entered the cave, running on all fours.

Tank could smell their hunger as did the bitch that'd unwittingly presented herself as food for the feast. First one, then another, bit at her, their tiny mouths causing damage, a miniature cut for each snap of the jaw.

"Please no, help me!"

Ulrich entered the cave behind them, followed by the rest of the brood. He'd been outside napping in the sun; he'd long since healed from the injuries suffered in battle but found himself weakened permanently from his ordeal. He too was hungry and sliced the side of the bitch's throat with a flick of his wrist as he passed her.

"My pleasure to help," he barked.

The bitch fell forward with the force of the blow, right into the crowd of pups at her feet. The ravenous brood went crazy, they nipped at her body as she flailed and complained with a high-pitched howl.

So much for fucking her, Tank thought as he leaned down to slice through her fur from chin to crotch so that the pups could get at their food in a more efficient way. Taking his example, the pups began to slice their own way into the flesh, some crawled inside the bitch, her howl turning to shallow panting.

All the bitches in the room howled at the fate they faced, some undoubtedly wished they'd remained in their own home, at least death would have been a much quicker, cleaner experience.

Tank and Ulrich moved towards their captives, circling the bunched-up White Fang bitches like they were human prey. They both grabbed hold of a tail and dragged their unfortunate owners from the press of fur; each of the bitches struggled and howled louder.

Tank grabbed his by the scruff of the neck and forced her face down as he lifted her hind legs up by her tail, her paws inches from the floor as he forced himself into her from behind.

Ulrich, on the other hand, slapped his bitch into submission until she gave herself over to him, lowering her face to the stone submissively as she flicked her tail up behind her so that it curled over her back.

He mounted her with a smile on his face, his hands on her hips, and his eyes focussed on the other bitches from the pack. He knew they feared him now and it filled his heart with joy.

"Look at me, bitches, I will fuck you all!" he roared over the howls of protest.

When Alex Stevenson returned home, he sat at his desk as he tried to decide what to do. His army was now equipped with the tools they needed to beat the packs of dogs that lived their chaotic existence just a few miles from where the humans lived, protected by the metal barriers that stopped the dogs from invading the human territories.

The fact that the pills stolen from him lay in the hands of Pack Grimm, who lived aboveground and beyond the technologies of humankind to retrieve them, was another problem.

Alex thought of the man that'd betrayed his own kind, the man that'd stolen the pills to exchange them for his captive family, a family that had been eaten by the Grimm as they had waited for the traitor's return. Pack Grimm had left the man alive as they returned to their own realm, laughing at him as he looked at his family's remains, mixed with the guards that'd protected that area of the borderlands, themselves at fault for not securing a doorway they'd opened in an act of stupid bravado that had led into the dog underworld.

The man had been found hanging in his own home, better he'd refused the dog. The whole human world had learned the harsh lesson of trust towards the feral race of mutated humans.

But how to retrieve the pills? They'd long since disappeared into the open air of the planet's surface. His thoughts drifted to his past, he'd been a lonely man back before the supernova had rendered the surface of the planet useless and toxic. He'd been an engineer back in those days, working in the factories that'd produced the Forever pill, among other narcotics for both the medical and entertainment industries. Living alone, he'd never had children and he had been two hundred years old before the end had come. He'd taken the Forever pill early in his life and rendered himself incapable of having children, a choice he'd never regretted. Before the human empire had met its untimely demise, he'd had to pay for his sexual encounters, for the most part. Now as he headed a district as its mayor, sex came easy.

But ever since his victory against Pack Grimm, nearly every female he encountered looked at him with a favourable eye.

This last thought he dismissed as once again he turned his mind to the problematic issues of the present—how to get the favour of the council—and if he couldn't curry their favour, how was he going to remove them all from office and put himself in their place?

He stood and began to pace his office as an idea formed in his mind. He smiled, looked at his reflection in the mirror and paused as he pictured himself wearing his suit of armour, dressed as a soldier. He could see himself in his mind's eye as he turned away from his reflection and made for the door.

Memphis Grimm stood and sniffed the stench coming from below, the foetid air smelt of humans and their sewage. Why they collected it all in one place he didn't know, better to spread it around a cave, even better yet to bury it in the sand as they now did. He looked at those around the hole that fell away into darkness.

"Any volunteers?" he asked.

The dogs that accompanied him all looked at one another, none wanted to drop into the darkness and Memphis feared he would have to delegate the task, until Dozer nodded, volunteering himself.

"I'll go first!"

Dozer looked over the edge and wondered how far down the shaft went. He picked up a large stone and dropped it; the dogs leaned forward, all silent as they listened for the sound of the rock reaching the bottom. It was longer than they'd expected before they heard the faintest of splashes.

Dozer sighed, turned and dropped onto all fours as he lowered himself over the edge of the shaft. The warm soft breeze that blew aboveground caressed his fur, in stark contrast to the stink that wafted up on the flow of air.

Dozer ignored the smell and concentrated on the wall of the shaft, as he used his claws to grip the uneven surface. He drove his claws deep into the gaps between the bricks. It didn't take him long to get into a rhythm and he was soon lost to the night vision of the others as he deftly descended into the depths.

After a few minutes of looking down, he looked up. The light above him was just a dot on his vision and he estimated he'd descended hundreds of metres. The smell was no stronger than it'd been at the very top of the shaft, but this far down, the air was much warmer and thicker than it was up above, having no way to dissipate.

He continued and after another minute, the bottom came into view, fifty feet below him. The bottom of the shaft was blocked, covered by a thick grid of iron bars. Below these bars, the shaft opened into a wide tunnel half-filled with human waste—a river of shit and piss that crept along at a snail's pace. Several openings in the wall of the shaft broke off in different directions, large enough for a dog warrior to walk along upright, and sloped gently away from him. There were six tunnels and streams of the excrement ran along the tunnel bottoms, emptying out to splatter through the barred bottom of the shaft.

Dozer sighed again, then lowered himself onto the bars; it wasn't the first time he'd been covered in human filth. As the shit splashed over his feet and hind legs, he considered each of the tunnels, sniffing at each in turn to source out the best scents. The stench prevented him from getting a decent scent, however, so he considered his options.

Choosing a tunnel at random seemed to be the only option available, so he headed east, stepping from the filth-covered bars onto the solid but slick surface of the tunnel. If not for his ability to see for a short distance in the dark, progress would have been slow, disorientated by the darkness of the underground with no scent to follow. He crept along the tunnel and after a while, the sheen of a brown dim glow could be seen up ahead; he slowed his pace until the glow materialised to be that of brown phosphorescent fungi, discoloured by the impurities of the sewer. From that point on, he made short work of the two miles until the tunnel's end. The tunnel forked into several tunnels, and those split off again twenty metres along. Shafts of light illuminated the darkness up ahead. Other smaller shafts emptied human waste above him; at first, he tried to avoid the mess but gave up when a length of something semi-solid splattered off the top of his head.

He paused to wipe the muck off and heard noises, distant banging and muffled voices coming from beyond the wall.

He continued cautiously. Stepping to the side of the little stream, he moved up one of the tunnels that led away from the main sewer. He approached the first shaft of light almost at a dead crawl as he tentatively twisted his head and looked to see what the source of the light was. He squinted as he considered the light and his eyes came into focus just in time to see a man's arse. He moved aside and the shit just passed him and splashed into the filthy water. Dozer moved instinctively to avoid the human excrement, a pointless gesture as he was already covered in the filth, his feet splashed and he winced.

"What was that?" an unfamiliar human voice said.

"What was what?" another asked.

"I thought I heard a loud splashing noise."

"Must've been some heavy shit, man!"

The two human males laughed at the jest, their scents lessened as they moved away from the hole that passed for a toilet. After they'd gone and he'd heard the door shut behind them, Dozer dared to breathe again. He listened but heard no further sounds other than the faraway noise of the human world, nor could he smell any scents other than the collective smell of human waste.

He chanced a look again from where the light came from, his features lit by the yellow beam. The small opening was just large enough for him to climb up comfortably until he reached the top. The top of the shaft was covered with a stone slab, which the hole had been carved into. With a little push, he thought he might be able to squeeze through. He could make the thin stone structure give way as well; he could see the seams in the rock and knew it would give to the strength of a determined dog like Memphis or Chaz.

After he'd examined the rock and the openings, he climbed back down to the tunnel floor and backed off into the dark as the latrine door opened. A human female hummed a tune, but its sweet melody was nothing compared to the scent given off by her menstruation as she perched herself above the hole, fondling for a moment to remove the padding that covered her bloody hole.

Turning from temptation, Dozer moved as quietly as he could. Although he was ravenous, he knew that to dither here might inhibit his ability to take back the information he'd reconnoitred from his trip into the unknown. Still, the scent of the woman weighed heavy on his mind and all the way back through the sewers, he hoped it wouldn't be long before he could return to have his fill.

Chapter 18

Memphis and the others moved away from the shaft's opening and the worst of the stench of the human sewer; they now lounged in the sun as they awaited Dozer's return.

Only an hour had passed before he climbed, panting, back out of the opening to the sewer. Memphis and the others turned as they waited for Dozer to speak.

"I found a way in," Dozer said.

The dog stood covered in filth and human waste, his scent all but extinguished by the stench of human excrement, but the others didn't mind as they all raised their heads to the sky and howled at the sun, as it reached its zenith in the toxic sky.

Tank climbed from the injured bitch, he'd bitten into the back of her neck a little too hard, now she lay curled up in a ball, whimpering as some of her sisters licked at the puncture wounds he'd left behind.

A week had passed since he'd led what had remained of Pack White Fang into the nightmare that was the rest of their short existence. Almost all out of the fifty bitches had already been consumed by the pups who grew at an alarming rate. Their increased size filled the small cave complex to the point where the young dogs couldn't all be inside together, they were almost as big as yearlings. Tank watched as one of the pups sniffed at a bitch; Tank, having already impregnated the bitch previously, watched as the pup's long snout pressed hard against her abdomen. She whimpered and he growled; he turned from her after sniffing her one more time.

"He knows she carries his siblings," Ulrich said as he entered the inner cave from behind him. "It would appear they won't eat her while she carries his brothers and sisters."

"We won't have anything left to feed them soon," Tank said.

"What will we do? To feed them, I mean, we could kill one to feed the rest."

"No, I have a much better idea, brother."

Tank looked at his brood as all the dogs began to bay and howl, only stopping when several of the dogs attacked two of the remaining bitches that hadn't been impregnated, tearing them limb from limb.

Tank raised his head and began to howl; as this first sound broke, all the other dogs and bitches turned, silenced by his single drawn-out note. He paused to take in the air and howled once again, this time Ulrich joined him as well as some of the Mad Dog pups, the melody created much more than a song in their minds. Before Tank and Ulrich lowered their heads, others raised theirs and joined the chorus of noise that would chill the nerves of any dog warrior down to the marrow; it seemed to breathe life into the very air around them. Again, Tank howled, one last, mournful sound, and this time every dog joined in. Tank let the song play across his senses and felt something in the many howls he'd never experienced before, the scent of need, of a desire that compelled him to move as the howl still played out around the small cave complex. Its echo seemed to follow him as he took to the floor, he ran on all fours like his pups did and they burst out into sunlight to charge across the barren landscape and join the hunt for prey.

Ulrich ran alongside him, almost threatening to outpace the rest of them, his tongue lolled until he drew it back into his mouth.

"Come brother, let us lead these Mad Dogs to glory," he said.

"Let us hunt and kill our enemies, we shall consume their flesh until only the Mad Dogs survive!"

Alex Stevenson walked along the line of his troops, he'd never seen the purpose of the parades before, but now he complimented them on how well they looked and how shiny were their suits of armour. The increase in morale these little lies caused was incredible, which gave the mayor pause for thought on the intellect of the fighting men.

These men are far from stupid, he told himself, brushing the thought away. He knew they would grasp at anything that might chase away the fear of combat.

After he'd inspected his men, walked the lines of almost a thousand knights, he stood before them in the cavern that'd been used for the meetings with Pack White Fang, his back to his old ally's territories. Behind the knights stood around two thousand volunteers, men and women that'd stepped forward with the promise of the end of the dog warriors and of new lands to settle; whole caverns that would be given over to the brave. These brave citizens had been split into groups of twenty. Most carried weapons that would be of little use in the fight to come. Each group, however, led properly would be able to fend off any aggressor. They were armed with the new human weapon, the flame cannon, and five of each group carried canisters of extra chemicals on their backs.

Alex took a deep breath and viewed his own reflection in the chrome steel his knights wore. The armourers had surpassed their own expertise when they'd constructed him his own suit of armour; it felt as strong as granite but lightweight when the armour had been distributed across his entire body. He exhaled and began, he'd already spent too much time on his own thoughts.

"Today marks the day of a new dawn. An age of man without the perils of these tunnels at my back. An age of prosperity, an age of wellbeing where we finally take back what is ours. Today, we march into history, for we are history in the making."

The roar from his own men increased as he finished his short speech and he lofted his own flame cannon onto his back. He adjusted its weight by pulling on the straps that circled his shoulders and shifted his position until he could comfortably lift the nozzle with no hindrance to his stance.

"With me, men of Lorela, let us go forth to cleanse this place of the vermin that have for so long been the thorn in our side."

With that, he turned; he knew the longer he waited, the more nervous his own disposition would become, let alone that of the rest of the people, especially the volunteers that could run back into the human domain at any moment.

The first knights fell in behind him, followed closely by the first group of twenty civilian volunteers. He just hoped they would all have the confidence in him to continue the clear-out operation once the violence of close-quarter combat with the dog warriors had begun.

It'd been many years since he'd been beyond the caverns they inhabited, the last time he'd passed through this tunnel had been as the shockwave had hit. He'd fled ahead of the coming disaster with Lorela's populace, crammed into the cavernous underworld of the planet until plague and starvation had killed off most of them.

He tried to remember the way but too many years had passed since he'd run in blind panic from what'd killed billions throughout the realm of man. He paused at a junction, knowing that the enemies of the White Fang had overrun their territory. He gave thought to the many lost souls that had passed through here since he last had; none had returned. He missed the two friends of his that'd recently gone to the surface with a White Fang escort.

He'd given up all hope of finding them alive, but it would be nice to find out what'd befallen them.

He pointed down one of the tunnels and directed one of the troops down the narrow passage, wondering when they would make the first contact. The second troop reached his back, this one he led down the wider tunnel, glad of the sporadic moss and fungi that lit their way.

Memphis Grimm looked over the precipice, below him was the way into the human realm and behind him were his people—every dog warrior and bitch warrior had stepped forward when he'd asked for volunteers. He had left the pregnant bitches behind, refusing them the honour of going forward into combat, what they carried was far too important for the future of Pack Grimm.

The Grimm had no idea where they would come out in the human world or what would be waiting for them when they got there, but one thing was for sure—they needed to act soon and attack them whilst they maintained the element of surprise.

Every bitch warrior wore the suits of armour the White Fang had worn as they'd attacked the city. At least it would give them a certain amount of protection from the dog-killing swords. The long, steel claws, the four blades on each fist, could be attached before they went into combat. The foot-long blades would give the bitches the edge, even against himself or Chaz, and he knew he'd no choice but to take the bitches, although it'd been a hard decision to make.

"Come, let us descend into darkness," he said quietly.

Dozer led the way, he slipped over the edge of the shaft, its sides easily wide enough to accommodate five dog warriors. Memphis was next, followed by Chaz, Elle and Sandy.

They descended with caution, taking their time so as not to warn the humans of their approach. They still didn't know much of the lay of the land; for all they knew, they could be climbing feet from a human dwelling or a busy human market.

They climbed, for the most part, in silence. The only sounds were those of so many of the dogs breathing or the mumbling complaints of the stench that invaded their senses; more than a few retched in uncontrollable protest. The largest threat to giving them away was the armour; it clanked and scraped annoyingly against the rough surface of the shaft walls.

After the ten-minute climb to the bottom, Memphis was given no time to consider what was happening, he was shepherded with the rest of the pack away from the grill at the bottom and into the tunnel directly behind Dozer. The sounds of the pack climbing down behind him echoed ahead of him, the slightest of whispers concerned him and he cringed at every sound. He feared the worst-case scenario that they would pop out to a welcoming force wielding steel and flame.

They'd no choice but to continue and Memphis stayed right behind Dozer, the echoes lessened as he walked ankle-deep in human shit and piss. The funny-coloured moss didn't make him feel any better; he guessed correctly that the hue was a direct result of the human pollution.

"This is disgusting," Sandy whispered, almost a growl.

"It'll all be worth it," Elle replied, her voice a rasp as though she was trying to hold her breath.

"Shhhh..." Memphis said.

They were at the junction of tunnels that stretched out straight in several directions, where the light of the human domain split the darkness of the sewers. Memphis, who'd resisted the temptation to look at what he trod in, looked at his feet when something semi-solid brushed against the fur of his paws. He was almost sick at what he saw—human detritus clung to him, large lumps of the smelly stuff stuck to his fur.

"Not much further now!" Dozer said as he looked up.

This last statement was pointless; they'd already discussed Dozer's previous adventure in fine detail, but Memphis knew the young dog warrior was only trying to make him feel better.

They'd discussed how they should approach the invasion of the human realm and had decided on a multiple synchronised assault, attacking from all the latrines at the same time. Memphis waited as different dogs went as quietly as their bulk would allow, to separate their force and wait until they were all poised and ready.

No call to arms could be heard, no shouts and screams lamenting the end of mankind and as Memphis walked to his point of attack, the nearest shaft to the sewerage junction, he felt confident they'd gained complete and utter surprise of those they called dinner.

He looked down the passage where one of the Grimm waited with a handful of luminous fungi, one of the dogs next to him held a similar fistful of the glowing natural plant. Memphis nodded at the dog that accompanied him, not wishing to wait a moment longer. The dog let the fungi drop, the fungi lost its luminosity as it hit the water and soaked up the brown liquid. The dog at the junction did the same; this was the signal for the start of the attack.

Memphis climbed the tube; it was just wide enough for him, albeit uncomfortable as it narrowed near the top. He was at the top in seconds and he heaved against the slab of rock with the bum-sized hole in it. It gave easily and he stuck his head out and forced his shoulders through the opening.

A man looked directly at him, his mouth open as he tried to speak. He sat on a slab with his trousers around his ankles, his dumbfounded expression of total shock a mercy to the plans of Pack Grimm. The man attempted to jump from his seat but was stabbed from below by clawed hands and thrown across the room by the angry dog below him.

Memphis climbed out of the hole and rushed to the man who struggled with his words. The terrified face was unable to turn to look up at his death. Memphis looked at the man; he felt some remorse for the briefest of time, but shaking the guilt away, he stabbed him through the back of his neck, curving his clawed hand around the man's chin. He lifted the corpse from the floor, shook it until the sinews of flesh that held the head to the shoulders gave and the body dropped back to the floor.

More of the pack climbed from the tubes. The rock seats, thankfully, weren't sealed down, they just rested on the top of the small shafts, and soon more dog warriors filled up the small space that was the human latrine.

Memphis made his way to the door, still holding the head of the man he'd slain. He could hear noises on the other side of the door—the sound of human voices and footsteps. He pushed open the door and the first thing he noticed was the sweet scent of dried mosses, tied to the doorframe to ward off the stench of the toilet. He breathed in the aroma and noticed the people looking at him, a myriad of faces, all as alien to him as he was to them. He threw the head at his feet and let it roll into the street until it came to rest at the feet of the nearest human, an old man that stood next to a store that sold pots and pans.

"D...d...d...dogs!" a voice screamed further down the street.

Memphis leapt forward, surprised for a moment at the huge space he'd entered. The well-lit space stretched off into the distance, its roof a hundred feet above his head, covered in blue and green fungi that gave off an eerie light.

The people fled before them, but their weak legs were no match for the superior strength, raw power and speed of the dogs; they fell upon their prey with reckless abandon and no regard for man, only their own ends.

Memphis was surprised at how warm it was this far underground, easily as warm as the midday sun on the surface, but the air was much cleaner here. He slashed at the old man that'd first spotted them and cleaved his head with his mighty strength. He leapt into the air and came down near a young couple. He just missed the female but landed heavily on top of the male. The woman fell at his feet, jarred from her flight by the force of pressure his weight exerted; she stood and ran off in blind panic with her lover's arm. Their hands were still clutched tight even after his arm had been separated at the elbow.

Memphis stamped on the man, but he was already dead— the weight of the pack leader had crushed his chest, burst his heart and lungs and killed him instantly.

All around him was chaos, the humans put up no resistance at all. The only thing they tried to do in those first few vital seconds was flee. The dogs cut into them, running them down, but the most ferocious of those that'd accompanied him into the human world were the armoured bitches. They'd attached the gauntlets to their suits of steel and the foot-long blades shone with the glint of natural light from the roof of the cave as they were raised above the bitches' heads. The bladed fists smashed down with evil intent, only to be raised high to fill the air with showers of blood from helpless prey.

Memphis took in his surroundings, three- and four-storey buildings rose out of the bedrock, some partially carved from the rock itself. They'd attacked a large settlement and come out in its centre; they'd emerged from a public convenience onto the marketplace on market day. The other groups came from houses and buildings; they smashed through doors or chased the humans from their homes.

In their lust and thirst for human blood, Pack Grimm lost all thought of control, they charged off down the different streets and avenues after prey that still attempted to escape.

A group of humans, running in terror from another group of Grimm that'd come out in the eastern-most part of the town, ran around a corner onto the marketplace. They stopped in their tracks as soon as they witnessed the carnage of the marketplace and the feasting of the dogs that had paused to have their fill. Harmony and Jade caught them, using their new clawed weapons to profound effect, cutting short the screams of the soon-to-be slain.

"Enough of this, spread the word, no more killing!" Memphis growled.

Memphis was extremely happy with how they'd overwhelmed the human settlement, but now he had to think of the herd; genocide hadn't been the mission so he reined in his pack. The whole idea of taking the town in the first place had been to create a stable and sustainable food supply; they couldn't do that if the entire herd was culled.

As he finished his sentence, three old men charged onto the square, carrying dog-killing swords but only one was wearing any of the human armour and that was only a tarnished breastplate. All three of the swords dripped red with fresh blood that could only have come from one place, the body of a Grimm.

The three warriors charged directly at him, their swords raised high to slay the leader of the pack. The dogs and bitches on the square were too quick; they jumped at the three men and brutally sliced them open, the men were clawed to pieces. Two died instantly and dropped to the solid surface of the market. The third, who wore the breastplate that was ripped from his chest, was mortally wounded, ribs and gut exposed and his organs fell from a gaping hole in his side. He fell to his knees and dropped his sword at the feet of Memphis and gripped the fur at his ankle. Memphis kicked the old warrior away from him. The old man's eyes stared past him at nothing, he was dead and of no more use than the meal he would provide.

"No more killing!" Memphis barked. "Surround the town and only kill those that resist."

Elle and Sandy reached his side; they looked at the old warrior, their eyes turning slowly to look up at Memphis.

"Why did you not raise claw to rend flesh?" Elle asked, concerned for Memphis Grimm.

"This old warrior was finished. He deserved his last chance at glory."

"You dogs, sometimes I wonder at your lack of intellect with the games that you play!" Sandy growled.

Memphis barked a short laugh. "I wouldn't expect you bitches to understand; the old man deserved my respect."

Memphis blocked out the mumbling complaints and leaned forward to accept the gift of victory. Out of respect for the old man, he would consume his flesh until nothing remained, making the old man part of him so he might take the human's courage and add it to his own. He removed the man's clothing by slicing it carefully and as he did so, more internal organs flopped from the wounds. Memphis spiked them with a single nail and popped the fleshy parts into his mouth.

Elle and Sandy moved away from him and removed their helms so they too might grab some of the flesh that'd fallen in great quantities around the market. Chaz and some others also began to feast; the fresh meat was impossible to resist.

After a brief time, crowds of the citizens had been herded towards the square, their terror increasing tenfold at the sight of so many creatures consuming the flesh of their friends and loved ones.

The cries of children were mirrored by those of their parents, no one man or woman was immune to the fear that influenced humanity when the Grimm were around.

The Grimm that had herded them into the square took their turn to feast, as those that'd had their fill took their turn in shepherding the herd. Any attempt at silencing the fearful human captives increased the sounds of anguish, the screams just rose as the Grimm barked and growled at them.

The volume began to grate on Memphis' nerves as more of the citizens were forced to the square. Enough so that Memphis was forced to put down his half-finished meal. He was full in any case so he stood and surveyed the growing crowd.

Looks like we hit the jackpot, he thought.

He raised his arms and tried to silence the crowd. "Humans, you have been conquered. Accept our rule and some of you may live long and prosperous lives, left to govern yourselves and your own destiny," Memphis barked.

The lack of response from the crowd galled him; he found the cowardly humans a far cry from the old man who'd died at his feet, fighting to his last breath. Seeing the pointlessness of it all, he left them alone to calm down and began a short journey around the town to survey all that he now considered under his rule. He was joined by Chaz, Elle and Sandy. They left the others to guard the ever-growing crowd. Soon the marketplace would be full to bursting. It'd been a good day so far and Memphis allowed himself a sly smile.

The street ran as straight as an arrow until it reached the edge of town four hundred metres in the distance. Memphis frowned as he noticed that the ground ahead seemed to move gently to and fro. It made his head swim slightly and he felt nauseous with the movement. He squinted as he tried to make out what caused it to move, the lush green colour alien to him as he'd never seen it before.

New lands meant new discoveries, he told himself. He was about to point out the weird phenomenon when four dog warriors carried a dead dog on their shoulders from a side street.

"It's Axle, three old humans slew him with their large swords, they ambushed him," one of the dog warriors lamented.

Memphis and the others wandered over to the dogs, one of whom whimpered openly over the death. Memphis placed his clawed hand on the dead dog's chest.

"Ah Axle, you honour us with your presence at the feast that shall be your last."

Memphis walked on, thinking it fortunate that the grieving dog had called out Axle's name; he hadn't learnt all the names of the White Fang that'd become Grimm yet. He looked back at the other four and tried to think, but he hadn't bothered to learn their names either.

He made himself a promise to learn every one of them and to get to know them better. If he was going to form an empire of the underworld, all people under one rule, he was going to need a few allies.

Memphis was pleased and he allowed himself a wide smile, the Grimm's food supply had increased exponentially and he couldn't have been happier. Hundreds of corpses now, both human and dog, were available for consumption and after that, the herd would surface, especially the children, a valued commodity that could still breed, not having yet taken the Forever pill.

Chapter 19

"He's done what?" Marlene Keegan shouted.

She sat with the rest of the council that'd convened for the afternoon session. They'd almost finished when a runner had burst into the oval chamber. He'd stood waving his document until the head of the council had given the messenger permission to step forward.

Now Marlene looked at the note, hastily scrawled but she recognised the handwriting of the Mayor of District Seven, Alex Stevenson. She passed the note on to Johnny Timms, her second-in-command on the council.

"Oh my," the youthful-looking four-hundred-year old human said, as he passed the note down the line.

"We must provide him with support," a much older-looking, although younger than Johnny, Andrew Kenilworth spouted.

"You must be joking, we must plug the hole with fresh troops and a new mayor," another shouted.

The debate was about to begin in earnest when the doors burst open once more and a lowly scribe almost tripped over his feet as he stood panting in the doorway.

"District Thirteen has fallen to the Grimm!" he cried.

The only sound for the minute that followed was the panting of the scribe, who spent those seconds wiping the condensation from his spectacles.

"What to do?" Councillor Kenilworth whispered.

Everyone heard the sound and turned to him.

Marlene sighed as she got to her feet. "We mobilise our forces!" she answered Andrew's question, taking the lead like she knew she had to.

"Which forces? From which district?" Councillor Timms asked.

"All of them! And ready my armour."

Marlene Keegan had been alive as long as any that now lived in the human underground kingdom. Hundreds of years old, she'd seen it all. She knew that the Grimm had most likely evolved after taking the Forever pill, but into what, she'd no idea. One thing was for sure though, she rued the day she'd ever set eyes on Alex Stevenson and she made a personal vow to kill the idiot if their paths ever crossed again.

Alex Stevenson headed into the unknown; for more than an hour they'd crept along the passageways of the dog territory. It'd come as a complete surprise to all of them that up until now, they'd not met or heard a single dog. No bright eyes shone from the darkness, no howl or bark was raised in alarm at the human force's advance.

He squeezed the trigger of the nozzle for comfort and a tiny flame fired up for a second.

Good, he thought.

He turned the next corner and saw a bright light at the end of the tunnel, which was normally associated with big caverns or artificial light, and since none of the packs used artificial light sources, it was, more than likely, a cavern with moss growth along its walls and ceiling. They edged their way forward and met more of his men coming up another passage; he wasn't startled though, as he'd heard the armour clanking and the sounds of their voices before they met.

The two troops merged to form a single column with Alex at its head. He picked his way forward to the sound of hushed voices behind him. Finally, they reached the end of the tunnel and a vast cavern opened before them.

On the opposite side of the cavern, a pack of dogs waited in silence. There were no bitches present, but the dogs easily numbered more than a hundred. More tunnels led into the cavern from various directions and, as Alex led those behind him into the vast open space, other units from his army entered the cave from other directions.

Alex didn't recognise any of the dogs, they weren't Pack White Fang, so he assumed they were the pack that had conquered their realm after they'd have wiped them out.

His men spread out, some of his men were below him and other columns were above him, all entered the cavern from tunnels onto three distinct ledges.

The dogs had known they were coming so had waited in the largest space they could find. A battlefield of their own choosing. The dogs weren't known for their tactical awareness, but Alex mentally scolded himself for not considering that they might be being drawn forward, far from their own territory.

The enemy didn't advance. They stood in silence, one large black-furred dog warrior growled out words, Alex strained and failed to hear. The broad-shouldered dog looked powerful and was easily eight feet tall, even though his head was level with his shoulders. He prowled the front of his line and waved his paws before him, shouting out orders aggressively.

The mayor looked at his men as they arranged themselves on the different ledges. They spread out to face the threat. This is what they'd come for, to face off against the enemy that'd plagued them for so long. It was time to put an end to the human mutation that'd become a species all its own.

His men looked anything but confident, even though they saw the logic in what they did. How could they lose with their innovative technology? And if luck was on their side, the evening meal would be supplemented with fresh dog meat.

"Courage, men!" Alex shouted.

More of the human force entered the cavern. He couldn't be sure but most, if not all, of his army had entered and filled one end of the cave or waited behind those who filled the three ledges. Pathways connected the different ledges of the cave, formed by the footfall of the heavy dogs as they walked over the naturally formed rock, the widest of these connected the lowest ledge to the cave floor, which stretched out before them some five hundred metres long and a hundred metres wide.

Besides a few stalagmites sticking out from the floor of the cavern, the floor was mainly smooth; it'd been worn down by so many pads treading against its surface. Alex surveyed the floor and considered his options, the inactivity from those he faced gave him confidence, they obviously didn't fancy their chances against such a massive force.

"Keep a wide-fronted formation, flame cannon to the front, forward!" Alex Stevenson walked forward, making his way to the next ledge and walking down a nearby path that switched back on itself. The men with and behind him began to move forward, those on the ledge below him parted to let him pass before they too moved down onto the floor of the cave.

His men began to jeer and shout, throwing insults at the dogs.

Alex stopped a hundred metres from the bottom ledge and gave his men time to catch up and form themselves into lines. Many of the flame cannon appeared in the front line.

So far, so good, he thought and looked down the lines of his men, who displayed enough bravado that they exhibited an air of confidence. Smiles spread across the faces of his men and he lofted the nozzle of his own flame cannon to show his men they'd the upper hand in the battle to come.

The little politician had changed in his presentation, he'd become brave and confident, even this enemy didn't faze him. He loved his new position in society and although he very much wanted to be lofted to the dizzying height of a council member, he knew he would miss the newfound respect and love he received from the army.

"Forward," he shouted.

The men responded to him and he looked at the nearest knight, seeing his own suit of steel armour reflected in his. He smiled and took a deep breath. The enemy loomed ever closer, although they stayed on their perch, a place that would very soon come into the range of his flame cannon.

They'd covered half the distance across the cavern's floor when the big black dog raised his head and howled. The sound unnerved him and he stopped, wondering what would happen next.

"Ready men, courage now!" he shouted.

Alex lowered his flame cannon and levelled the nozzle at the beast that was their leader, the pack leader didn't scare easily, he looked anything but frightened. The dog was still way out of range of his weapon but Alex hoped to intimidate the beast or, at the very least, wanted to show the dog who was boss.

"Dogs to the rear!" one of his men shouted out the alarm. Heads turned in the front rank, his among them, the ledges they'd left behind were now full of dog warriors, almost as many as there were in front of them.

"Ha ha ha ha ha ha ha ha ha…" an eerie and strangely human laugh echoed around the cavern, silencing the men. The large black alpha male of this unknown pack howled, the sound carried and echoed around the cavern walls.

"Did you humans really think you could walk into our world with such a puny force?" the leader of the dogs shouted. "I am Akuma, leader of Pack Blood Hound, and today I shall consume your souls and add your flesh to mine in a chaotic feast of bloodletting."

Alex realised his mistake. They were trapped, having been completely outmanoeuvred by Pack Blood Hound. Alex couldn't help but wonder if he'd overestimated his ability to lead men into battle. He couldn't believe a mere dog had outwitted him but, then again, they'd evolved from humans and not dogs, he reminded himself.

His army filled the space from wall to wall, rank upon rank filling a large space upon the cavern floor, but with most of the flame cannon at the front, those facing the dogs from the rear would have to face the new threat mainly with swords, courage and the conviction of their beliefs.

"Back six ranks, turn and face the enemy. Prepare to defend yourselves. Kill them all, men, no mercy, no mercy!" Alex was cut short by more than two hundred howls that struck fear in the hearts of the army from District Seven. Before the echoes passed, the dogs bounced from ledge to floor, ran across the rough sides of the walls and jumped back to the floor before they launched themselves high up for the attack.

Alex tried to track the path that Akuma made. He wanted to at least singe the fur of the large beast, but the enemy moved too quickly to follow, their number confusing his sight as their routes criss-crossed before him.

Akuma ran at the head of the Blood Hounds, he fell behind as he ran at the cave wall to the left of him. He leapt at the wall and kicked off from its surface to gain as much height as he could. It took no time at all for the Blood Hound to reach the human line and as he jumped up in the air, he saw streams of fire leap forth from the human army's front lines. He saw at least two dogs engulfed in flames in the opening phases of combat. He'd gained enough height to avoid the jet of flaming chemicals that had followed his progress. He considered himself blessed as another two of his pack fell afoul of the sharp metal spikes lofted high to catch the dog warriors as they fell; once in the air, they were unable to change direction and became skewered on the dog-killing weapons.

Akuma made contact, falling in among a frightened foe. Most of the humans were without armour and poorly armed. Akuma stood in the middle of some of these and wasted no time, swiping his massive clawed hands left and right to knock off heads and rip flesh.

The dogs were greatly outnumbered but the stench of fear the humans gave off in their pheromones filled the air and gave them confidence. Akuma clawed at any hand that posed a threat. He slashed human flesh down to the bone and ripped limbs from bodies. His strength easily compromised the joints of the weaker human body. Still there was no shortage of weapons brandished at him. Other dogs appeared in his line of sight, one either side of him. They formed a triangular stance back to back, fought off any of the humans and their futile attempts at glory. The dog to his right howled in pain, loud enough that he could be heard over the sounds of battle. A howl that was cut short by the dog-killing sword that stabbed the dog through, pushed with a second effort by the armoured man that held it.

Alex burnt the dog that'd targeted him, it fled in blind fury as its fur burnt away to expose flesh that popped with the intense heat. While he waited for another to attack him, or a target he could send his burning chemicals towards, he watched as one such attack took place further down the line. One of his men shot his flame at an advancing enemy, the dog was caught by the fire and set ablaze but still charged, teeth gnashing, into the front rank of men. The man holding the flame cannon followed the dog with his flame lance in his panic and set ablaze several men, volunteers and knights alike.

Collateral damage, Alex thought.

Alex stood on his toes, his head turning this way and that as he surveyed the battle. The flame cannon had been largely ineffective in the wide-open spaces of the cavern, the dogs simply avoided the fire where possible. He considered this another failing of his own; it was a learning curve for all of them, including the dogs. He just hoped he could take the invaluable knowledge back to his own people and if he didn't survive, someone had to, or his actions would all be in vain.

Those at the back, fighting a rear-guard action, suffered the most; they'd no flame to deter the dog onslaught. They fought bravely though and closed their ranks every time one of their number was plucked from the line.

Just when he thought it couldn't get any worse, one of the flame cannons exploded, along with the operator, the dog that'd pierced the canister on his back and several other men and dogs around him.

Blood was slick underfoot and the stench of burnt fur and flesh filled his nostrils. He gagged and men screamed cries of anguish. Swords rose and fell, stained with the blood of dog, but still they hadn't killed enough and the human numbers were half that from the battle's inception. The battle had gone on for more than five minutes, although to Alex, this time had passed slowly. If it went on much longer, the human army would dwindle down to nothing. Alex gritted his teeth as he raised his flame cannon once more, ready to burn the dog that ran for him. He paused on the trigger of his flame lance as the dog stopped and sniffed at the air.

The dogs on his side of the battle withdrew, including the big black that he spied at the last, many of the dogs sported cuts and more than thirty lay dead nearby. At the rear of the cavern, the fight continued even though many of the dogs looked over their shoulders as they fought on with a newfound vigour.

That which had given the enemy of man, Pack Blood Hound, pause for thought, materialised. What came out of the tunnels shocked them all, even the eyes of Akuma widened with the sight that charged into the cave.

Tank and Ulrich Mad Dog charged into the cavern at the head of Tank's new pack, a pack that looked wild and unhindered by the reason of logic. They ran on all fours, crazed feral beasts that wished nothing on the world but pain.

Something about this new threat caused panic among the dog warriors of the Blood Hounds, those that'd withdrawn fled down the tunnels on the opposite side of the cave that the human army had entered from. Alex almost ordered his men to follow them; he would have if they'd any chance of surviving such a journey.

"Retreat, retreat, retreat!" he shouted, over and over, as he forced his way back toward District Seven.

His men broke away from their fights, dodging the Blood Hounds and Mad Dogs wherever they could. The Blood Hounds turned to face the Mad Dogs who were smaller in size than that of the dog warriors; only Tank and Ulrich were larger. The new breed, however, fought with feral savagery and lacked none of the skills needed to take down a fully grown dog warrior; if anything, their stature aided them in the task. They were quick and fearless and, although outnumbered by all those that waged war, they tore into the Blood Hounds who'd no answer for the savagery of the Mad Dogs, the first creatures in the history of the world to show no fear when fighting the dog warrior.

The two evolved dog warriors, Tank and Ulrich, tossed the Blood Hounds about as if they were children. Blood rained down as the little mayor ran beneath one of the murderous fights, the blood even hit the high ceiling of the cavern and the lines of red looked like fresh welts against the light from the fungi and mosses.

Men fought as they fled, the feral Mad Dogs bit them as they passed and there wasn't much room to manoeuvre, the long cave filled with the individual combats of fighting beasts.

Alex ducked beneath a slash not intended for him; he stood and watched the clawed fist rip into the side of a Blood Hound. His reactions were spontaneous, his trigger finger quicker than his mind, he turned the nozzle of his flame cannon and an arc of fire soared through the air to catch both the fighting dogs with burning chemicals that stuck to their fur and flesh.

Alex made good his escape, he ran behind others that'd made it past the warring hounds. Both knights and men fled in terror, some still clutched the weapons they'd brought with them, others dropped them to allow them to sprint. The mayor was encumbered though, being weighed down by the canister on his back. He turned and looked for the others who had carried the flame cannon; at a glance, he saw none.

More than two hundred men had made it to the ramps before him, some turned to form some sort of defence, but most fled without once turning around to see what, if anything, gave chase. Alex looked through his visor, the sweat running into his eyes and making it difficult for him to see as he stopped with those few brave knights that formed the organised retreat. He gulped down deep breaths of air as he began to realise what'd just happened. They'd been defeated at the first obstacle; how stupid he'd been to think he could defeat such a foe! He turned as more of his men made it to the ramp that led to the first ledge. Pack Blood Hound was in full rout—those that could get away were running for their lives. Those few that remained were cut to pieces as the last of the fleeing humans made it to where Alex stood. Five of the flame cannon operatives made it to the ledges and they backed off to where the tunnels were, as did the rest of the human survivors as the battle in the cavern finally came to an end.

Corpses covered the cavern floor and blood slicked the stone underfoot where the fighting had been thickest. This didn't bother Tank's Mad Dogs or indeed Tank and Ulrich who now turned from the fleeing Blood Hounds to face Alex Stevenson and what was left of his army.

Alex pointed his flame lance and pulled the trigger, firing flames in the direction of the Mad Dogs. The other humans still carrying the flame cannons followed his lead and the air around them became blistering hot.

Tank raised himself up and roared out in complaint of the fire that spread toward them, even though the fires petered out before it reached where the Mad Dogs stood. Tank waved his arms behind him, signalling to the feral dogs at his heel, who bayed and barked at the human force. They turned and ran back in the direction Akuma and the Blood Hounds had fled, down tunnels on the opposite side of the cave.

"Let's go, let's get out of here!" Alex ordered, relieved that the new threat had considered its other warring foe a worthier opponent.

Memphis was content with their success, he'd thought they would lose more than one dog warrior in the assault on the human territory. He'd briefly questioned the mayor and found out that they'd taken just one small part of the human underworld realm; this part was called Sector, or District, Thirteen.

"You best go, because the council response will be swift and deadly!" the human had told him.

Memphis had questioned him about the pills and discovered that they had to be made, but the process couldn't be done in this place; they neither possessed all the raw materials nor the knowledge of how they were produced. This community was a simple agricultural village. He'd told Memphis that the one side-effect that the pills caused was sterilisation—any person who took the pills could no longer produce offspring, a small price to pay for everlasting life. Memphis knew this was not the case for the dogs, a fact that pleased him.

Upon further questioning, the youthful-looking mayor admitted he'd taken the pills since before the great ending, whatever that was. He was, therefore, useless to Memphis and a drain on resources, and Memphis had left the mayor slumped in his chair after he'd carved the heart from his chest and popped the still pumping warm meat into his mouth as the politician had looked on in disbelief. His conscience had briefly kicked in and he had looked at the dead meat before him, justifying his actions by the fact that the first to be invited to dinner would be those humans of no long-term benefit to Pack Grimm, those human cattle that would be a drain on resources and the fact that they were hungry.

Now, he walked at the edge of the large human settlement through the long grasses. The green vegetation grew in the cavern that he'd only heard of before, the crops used to make human food, the moist earth he walked upon also felt alien to him, its deep brown colour needed more than a hint of red to make it look normal.

The plants that grew here needed something from the light of the sun, so how they grew this far away from that light he'd not a clue; it was something he would find out about later.

Chaz wandered over to the edge of the wheat, looked at the swaying plants then at Memphis, unsure whether it was safe to walk among the grass or not.

"It doesn't look solid enough," he said.

"I think I best remove myself; besides, I don't want to trample it, it will feed our humans," Memphis replied.

Memphis walked out of the underworld field and stood face to face with Chaz who waited patiently for him. Harmony and Jade appeared; they'd removed their armour and now walked as if the world was at ease with them.

"We have let the humans go back to their houses," Chaz said.

"Good, we don't want them thinking they are going to be eaten," Memphis replied.

"What about the mayor? Some among them are asking after him." Chaz looked back out across the crop, its unsteady appearance making his head swim.

"Tell them to get another one," Memphis grunted.

Memphis walked away to join the bitches who appeared to have forgotten they were on a military operation.

"Jade, Harmony, prepare for war."

"But why?" Jade asked.

"Do we move against another enemy?" Harmony questioned.

"I think the war might come and find us; I would prefer you were ready for it."

Memphis turned his back on the bitches, it was time to find Elle and Sandy, curl up somewhere and get his rest. He knew the enemy would mobilise as soon as possible, he would need all his strength for the fight as the real trial for his ideals and plans would soon begin.

Marlene Keegan stood on the balcony of the council house, wearing the armour she'd commissioned the armourers to make, totally functional gear but made purely for show—she'd never intended to go to war.

She looked almost sexual in her tight-fitted suit of armour, decorated in thin chain mail that looped over her face from the sides of her helm. She felt invigorated every time she put it on and dreamed of going to war against the dog warriors. Now it'd become a reality and the thought frightened her, even though she knew it would raise the morale of her men.

Their only real military officer had suffered death a decade before; he'd died in an accident during a sparring contest. He'd been very old and cheated death on more than a few occasions, both before the great ending and during the time of upheaval. She'd stepped up to take command of the troops, and now what they could muster at short notice marched beneath them. Every knight raced to the defence of District One and more than three thousands of them stamped beneath her, saluting as though she was their monarch.

When the last of them had walked past, she turned to find Councillor Timms staring at her from inside her third-floor office. She walked past him to the maids who waited for her orders.

"You may leave us," she said.

They both waited for the servants to leave before they embraced.

"Can't you let someone else lead the charge?" he asked.

"It has to be me; there is no one of any rank to lead them."

"The knights have lots of commanders," Johnny argued.

Marlene turned from him and walked over to her desk to retrieve the sword she'd commissioned along with the armour. "Squad commanders yes, men that know how to kill."

"Don't be so quick to end your life."

"I have lived for hundreds of years, that's far from quick."

He joined her and pressed himself up against her behind; her armour showed off a little too much flesh for his liking, her buttocks exposed from the thong to the padding that housed the armoured leggings.

"Is that all you think about?" she asked.

"Not the only thing," he laughed.

She turned into his embrace and gently pushed him away from her.

"I must go to the army; there are thousands of men and women out there waiting for their leader."

"And if you win? Will you construct a throne from the bones of dog warriors?"

"If the people wish it, yes!"

She left him at that point, she'd sat on the council since its inception two hundred years prior and had led it for half that time, she knew he wished to have total power; maybe soon he would have his wish. She shut the door behind her and left him in her office, not fearing what he might find—she'd nothing to hide.

Alex Stevenson, mayor from District Seven, ran down the tunnel, the light changing constantly with the mosses and fungi that grew on the walls. He met two of his men coming in the other direction, one a knight, the other a volunteer citizen. They were both screaming in pure terror, one of the new breed of dogs was hot on their heels.

Alex stopped, levelled the nozzle of the flame cannon and pulled the trigger. The knight dropped to the floor, the man that accompanied him was left fully exposed and he felt both the heat of the fire and the clawed hands of the beast that chased them down.

The man's screams ended as the jaws of the Mad Dog closed with a snap around his neck, the dog burst into flame and writhed, howling in agony, on the cave floor.

Alex pulled the trigger again, he needed to make sure of the kill, but the flame petered out no sooner than it had left the end of the nozzle, he was out of the chemical mixture that allowed the flame cannon to produce the sticky burning liquid.

"Help me get this off, will you?" he asked the knight.

The knight had other ideas though and took off in the other direction, leaving the mayor kneeling on the tunnel floor.

The retreat turned into a rout and he and his men couldn't help but get turned around in the expansive tunnel system, their complexity far beyond anything they'd experienced before. He knew he couldn't be that far away from the border so didn't panic too much, but he hated being in these tunnels alone and knew if there were any dogs in the area, his chances of survival on his trip into enemy territory were worse than next to nothing.

He let the flame cannon fall to the stony floor when he'd unstrapped the canister. The fleeing citizen had dropped his short sword on the tunnel floor. It was a smaller version of the dog-killing swords that the knights used, designed for men such as the volunteers that lacked the strength to wield one of the larger weapons. He picked the sword up and felt its weight, he'd never trained with the sword and it felt heavy in his hands. He considered leaving it but knew that to wander around these tunnels without a weapon would be the worst thing he could do.

Might as well invite death, he thought.

He turned back the way he'd come, he could hear the fighting coming from that direction, the clank of a sword as it hit the rocky wall, the bark and growl of a dog that soon began to whine, its furred, thick skin having given way to steel. The inevitable scream as the man succumbed to the overwhelming power of the dog warrior.

A hundred metres down the tunnel, he came to a crossroads and found the knight that'd run away from him, his breastplate ripped clean from his body and his organs exposed to the foetid air, the stink of dog and death thickening the atmosphere. Blood oozed up through the large rents in the man's flesh, he stared at Alex as bubbles popped out through his mouth, pushing up past the blood that welled up the throat as the dying knight struggled for his last breath.

The knight turned to look down one of the tunnels, he raised his arm in one last effort and pointed, directing the mayor to what Alex hoped was the way out.

Alex stood, there was no point hanging around and one way was as good as another in his disoriented state, so he took the dead knight's advice and followed his pointing finger. It wasn't long before he came across a dog warrior crawling down the tunnel, holding his side with one clawed hand and the other holding the hilt of the sword that'd pierced his side—he'd been stabbed clean through by the dead knight.

The dog whined with a pain-stricken face. He knew his time was at hand and rolled over onto his back as soon as Alex approached. He opened his jaws wide and licked at dry lips as he yelped, his jaw shuddered and his head fell back as he panted. Alex considered leaving the dog where it was but thought about what he could take back to the council. The head would be evidence of their valiant fight. Besides, it would make an excellent trophy for his wall. He stood to the side of the dog and raised the rescued weapon. The dog warrior closed his eyes, which gave Alex pause. The dog turned his head to one side, offering Alex a clean strike and himself a quick end.

Alex was strong enough to wield the weapon, but in his untrained hands, his aim wasn't as good as it should have been. He caught the side of the neck with the point of the blade instead of the edge. The blade sliced through the fur and flesh and severed the jugular, which immediately began pumping blood into the air, splashing against the tunnel walls and Alex's front.

The dog's head whipped around, his eyes wide with pain, and he opened his mouth to bark but could only manage a contorted yelp. He grabbed at Alex's ankle, almost pleading with the man to end it, but Alex thought the pressure of the clawed hand was an attack. He raised the sword and, in his panic, rushed the second chop. Again, the point of the blade, instead of the edge, met flesh and sliced into the dog, it was a clean cut but far from a tidy ending.

The dog's clawed hand relaxed but his high-pitched whine unnerved Alex; it would give away his position even if he was too far away for any dog to smell him out.

He finally silenced the dog with his next stroke, getting the blow just right, the edge of the weapon hit the throat and cut down into the windpipe to cut off the sound even as the dog thrashed about and wished for death.

Alex watched as the dog's flailing slowed and finally died. Three blows later, the head fell away from the broad neck and rolled to a stop a foot away from the body.

A slow stream of blood intermittently pumped from the open wounds and Alex gagged; he'd never thought he could be capable of such a barbaric act. The fact that he hadn't even thought about what he'd done made it worse, he'd just acted with no thought of consequence, without a shred of morality or notion of the murder he'd done.

He heard a growl further along the tunnel as a dog sniffed at the corpse of the knight, the sound of the dog's jaws biting at the exposed flesh making him cringe. The further sound of bones cracking as the ribs gave way to the powerful creature instilled him with fear.

He'd been unaware that the beast had toyed with him, playing a deadly game of cat and mouse. He was fully aware though that the beast now gave chase, he heard it howling and barking as it followed at a much quicker pace than he could flee.

He turned a corner and instantly recognised the intersection he came upon; in his haste to escape, he had turned the final corner and saw the light of the cave where his army had first assembled.

He raced into the light of the cave, and could smell and hear the beast that wanted to use him to fill its belly. The mayor jumped as he ran into the cave, he hoped that the gradient would give him a few feet as he fell away to the cave floor. The beast was so close he could smell its breath as its jaws opened wide for the crushing bite. As he kicked off the slope, Alex instinctively spun on his heels to fend off the slavering Mad Dog. He could no longer hold the weight of the heavy short sword properly, which caused his arm to go limp, it relaxed as his life flashed before him. The sword arm spun wildly around in an arc as he turned, Alex's momentum helped him, and he sliced into the surprised dog's neck. The sword cut deep into the flesh of the beast until it stuck fast in the thick backbone of the giant mutt. The forward momentum of the now dead dog forced Alex around and the sword freed itself of the bone, the forward motion also helped to keep Alex upright and he landed perfectly on his feet, slightly apart and his right foot in front of his left.

To those of his army that'd made it this far, waiting on the other side of the cave, it looked as if Alex had meant to make the killing blow and in this spectacular fashion. They cheered his success.

He hadn't even noticed that they were there, or that he'd killed the beast, until the roar went up. He stood shaking with fear but quickly got himself under control and looked at the Mad Dog at his feet. He still carried the head of the Blood Hound in his hand and he raised it up so he could take advantage of the situation, his men cheered him even louder as they rushed to his side to touch the man that, in their eyes, was now the mightiest of warriors.

One of his men quickly hacked the head off the Mad Dog, put his sword away and picked the head up with both hands so that he could present it to Alex.

Alex handed his sword to another and took the head in his hand.

If they want to think me a great warrior, let them, he thought, it would serve a purpose in the coming hours and days, the people would need a hero, why shouldn't it be him!

"Not such a dreadful day after all," he shouted as he held both his trophies above his head.

No more than four hundred had made it back alive and more than half of those had suffered at least one injury.

Now to go face the music, he thought. He would take the two heads to the council to show them his findings; they would need to know of the new breed that ran on all fours and, of course, of his defeat.

Chapter 20

Akuma had always considered himself to be top dog and that his species were top of the food chain. He'd never seen Pack Blood Hound run in blind terror before. Yet now, as this smaller breed of dog that showed little intelligence and ran on all fours, ripped into his dog warriors, he knew something else had been unleashed unto the world, some new power that at that moment he'd no answer to.

No sooner had he smelt them than he'd felt the terror within himself, an uncontrollable fear that had made no sense. There it was, the answer that'd plagued him for the hour he'd spent running from these creatures, it was in the scent. The creatures must give off some sort of feeling of foreboding within their pheromones.

Even with this realisation, he still fled, unable to control his feelings. He was now within his ancestral territory; he hurried the bitches up as they milled about, around the cave entrance that led up aboveground. It was high up on a hillside and no other pack knew of its location. He'd had bitches working on the skull caps; they had used their clawed hands to sculpt lenses from the dark-coloured stones that were embedded in the rocks deep down in the earth. They'd completed forty skull caps, having used the head hide from dogs recently killed. He grabbed one and placed it on his head to protect him from the light. Behind him, he heard howls of pain as his warriors and bitches were shredded by the unforgiving claws of the mutant Mad Dogs.

He ran from the cave, he knew his pack would be consumed by these hungry crazed animals, but the daylight still frightened him. Nine dog warriors and thirty bitches followed him out into the light, the rays of sunshine strong as it beat the toxic ground. They fled down into the valley onto the desert sand where they'd seen the Grimm walk but not return. They'd witnessed the armoured White Fang also, they too had crossed this desert and never returned, maybe they could parley with the old enemies. For now, one thing was for sure, they'd no choice but to run and run they did as many howls of anguish combined into a single resounding song from the underworld at their backs.

A week had passed since the Mad Dogs had moved into the dog realms and they now occupied all the tunnels and caves that'd belonged to the Grimm, White Fang and Blood Hound packs.

Most of the dogs that had accompanied Tank and Ulrich Mad Dog had perished within the first two days of fighting. Tank was forced to order a withdrawal to the main cavern that'd belonged to Pack Grimm.

The bitches that'd been impregnated had been brought under the cover of darkness from the caves Tank had found all those weeks before. The only reason he decided upon relocation was the need for space, the small cave complex just wasn't big enough for his new pack's needs.

Several of the bitches gave birth since they'd conquered part of the underworld, the pups ate their way out as their mothers screamed, only quieting upon their death. The newly impregnated bitches saw what awaited them as they reached full term, all of them whimpered and howled with dread. A few bitches that'd been captured but were yet to be impregnated attempted escape, failed and were fed to the hungry pups.

Pack Mad Dog now numbered over eighty dogs, not inclusive of those that'd been captured. Most of the feral pups born had been female so far, Tank assumed this was because of the one hundred percent mortality rate for those bitches that had given birth.

He thought of the other packs, waiting for the Mad Dogs; by now they would have all heard what was coming for them. Let them wait, he would tell Ulrich, he didn't want to move against them until they were ready and with the cave half full of captured pups and bitches, they would have plenty to eat and lots of bitches to mate with until the numbers of Pack Mad Dog were so high that none would dare stand against them.

Tank howled with delight, Ulrich and the Mad Dog pups joined in his howl. The howl continued to grow in volume at an alarming rate; this was a regular occurrence and had no real significance although they did seem to relish the fact that every captured dog shook in pure terror.

Alex Stevenson sat in his office, covered in bruises and scratches. He'd been informed that two bandages he wore would have to remain for at least two weeks. He scratched the skin near the dressing, irritated by the wound received; he pulled back the bandage and looked at the stitches on the wounds. The wounds would scar, proof of the damage received during his recent war.

He'd left his entire force, or what remained of it, at the entrance to the tunnel that had led to the dog realm.

Alex had closed the door and locked out the dog world. He'd sent messages to the other districts that shared a border with the packs to check the integrity of their defences. Unfortunately, he lacked the authority to permanently close the tunnel that connected their two worlds. Although in the past, the council had always talked down the need, their excuse being that the defences should always hold against any determined attack from the packs, even united. They hadn't seen this new threat.

The mayor couldn't help but blame himself for the recent events in their history; he was far from stupid and knew it was all down to the Forever pills he'd lost.

He now waited for an answer from the council and grew ever more impatient as the hours and days passed by. He stood and walked over to where the two dog heads sat, preserved in large glass jars, side by side, on a cabinet against the window wall that overlooked the town square. The light from the fungi on the cavern roof shimmered with bright greens, blues and yellows; it played on the cobbled ground and highlighted the shadows between the cracks of the stones, so it looked as though they moved gently this way and that. He looked at the two heads of the different breeds of dog, the dog warrior's head had always looked massive to him, but the smaller head of the new breed didn't look any less terrifying as it stared back at him with black eyes. As he stared at the creature, he felt an unnerving foreboding and inferiority to the more powerful race of mutant humanoids.

He shuddered as a crowd raced onto the square, worried citizens that gave chase to the runner he'd sent to District One with the message to the council. Without thinking, he broke all protocol and leaned out the window to berate the crowd below; however, their constant badgering of the out-of-breath runner would drown out anything the man would have to say.

"Move out of his way, let the man breathe," he shouted his order.

The crowd was quickly silenced and moved backwards until the man could be seen by almost everyone. The runner had his hands on his knees and gulped in deep breaths. Eventually, he stood straight with his hands on his hips as he got his breathing under control at last.

"What news from the council?"

"There is none, they have marched to war, the Grimm have taken District Thirteen!"

This last word was said amid a scattering of tears, the runner was no longer able to contain his emotions.

Alex gulped, stood tall and turned to the armour that hung on a stand. He returned to the windowsill and leaned out again to look at the stunned crowd.

"Close the border!"

The crowd of citizens cheered, too long they'd lived with the threat of the packs; at least now one possible threat of death would be taken away.

An hour later, the entire community stood before the large steel doors, made and erected before the devastation of the hypernova that had all but ended civilisation throughout the known galaxy. The doors had originally been erected as a line of defence to keep mine contaminants from polluting the surface of the planet. Now, instead of protecting the human populace from the inner planet, they protected them from the outside and all its perils.

Knights and civilians stood as one as Alex approached the open iron doors, two men stood stripped down to their waists, armed with a giant mallet each. Alex nodded to the pair and they hefted the large rubber-ended hammers with little effort. The two workers made their way up the tunnel from the opposite end, hitting the struts till they weakened, and both were soon covered in dust. They made short work of the upright beams, not wanting to spend any more time than was necessary in the tunnel, just in case the roof collapsed prematurely.

No sooner had they fled to stand beside the armour-clad knights than Alex stepped forward. The two muscular workers stepped with him to stand by either door.

Alex lowered his flame lance, aimed the nozzle down the tunnel and pulled the trigger. He blasted the tunnel with flaming chemicals that washed over the wooden tunnel supports and stuck to the surface.

Alex moved the jet of fire left and right, up and down, until the fire stuck to everything. The two workers quickly shut out the intense heat and the flames from the tunnel that led to the dog world. They had to let go of the metal handles, which had become red hot with the heat from beyond the door.

The doors remained unlatched for a brief time, until both the men, their hands wrapped in cloth, took it in turns to pull the heated metal bolts into place and shut out the dog world forever.

Within minutes, the hushed crowd heard the timbers collapse, the roof caving in with a rumbling sound and the whole cave they stood in shook, dust and small stones falling from the ceiling above. Everyone froze in place, Alex himself hadn't realised he'd held his breath until he exhaled, as the shaking stopped and the dust began to settle on himself and his people.

The structural integrity of the old mines had always been the main reason the council had cautioned against the closure of the tunnels that led to the dog world. Alex had already sent two runners though, one in either direction skirting the border Districts, to command the elected mayors of each to collapse the tunnels.

Ah well, too late now, he thought and shrugged as he watched the dust in the air and the few stones that still fell.

Alex turned to face the crowd. They searched his face for the guidance they needed in these troubled times. He held up his hand, the act was a pointless one though as not a sound could be heard and all heads were turned to him, eyes wide with stunned fascination at whatever he had to say.

"I am going to District One to fight for mankind. For all we know, we may be the last bastion of all that is human and, if I must, I will go alone."

With that, he picked up his helm, placed it on his head and walked down the main road that went through Districts Seven, Ten and Twenty-Eight and would eventually end at District One.

He allowed himself a wide smile and lofted the lance of his flame cannon to his shoulder. He patted the short sword placed in the scabbard now strapped at his hip. The knights didn't hesitate nor did the citizens, some of whom had already accompanied him on his failed excursion into the now out-of-reach dog territories.

Alex caught his reflection in a pane of glass in one of the house windows at the edge of town, he couldn't believe the amount of people picking up all manner of improvised weaponry and joining his force. With more than half of the town following, his army had now grown from one to nearly a thousand, but he knew with only a few hundred fully trained knights, the odds were still stacked against them.

Chapter 21

Kenzi and Blaze Grimm, formerly of Pack White Fang, stood on the roof of their fortress home; they'd remained behind when the Grimm had invaded the human colonies because both their litters were due.

They now watched their pups as they lounged in the sun, Adonis stood a way off, he leaned against the wall with his arms folded, legs crossed and watched them. He'd returned from the hunt with human flesh and stayed to watch both of his litter's birth out into the light. All but one of the others had returned to the underground, back into the stench of the human world down the wide deep shaft. The litters had been present in the womb when their bitch mothers had taken the pill and the future for these pups was uncertain, and all, especially Adonis, wondered what the outcome would be—at least for now they seemed normal enough.

His black fur shone in the sun and his proud jaw jutted out, he looked majestic as though he would burst with joy.

"Look," Kenzi said, interrupting his moment of happiness.

Blaze and Adonis turned to look out to the edge of the city where Kenzi had pointed.

"Who are they?" Blaze asked.

"I know him, that's Akuma of Pack Blood Hound!" Kenzi said.

A line of dogs, all that remained of Pack Blood Hound, were strung out on the edge of the high dunes that separated the city from the desert. They were the remnants of the fleeing pack.

"What shall we do?" Blaze asked.

The two bitches turned to where Adonis had stood to find that the dog warrior had vacated the roof of the fortress, they both looked down and waited for him to appear in the courtyard. It wasn't long before he ran into view, sprinting alone to the defence of the city.

They turned again to look out at those that approached, more dogs appeared over the rim of the dune, first in the tens and then by the hundreds, many more dogs than the population of Pack Blood Hound had held in its ranks.

Adonis ran through the outer gate, he couldn't go any faster and as soon as he passed the huge outer metal doors, his padded feet kicked up the orange radioactive toxins that covered the city. He lowered his head and bent to the task, he knew he raced to reach the outer limits of the city before their unexpected guests entered.

Blaze and Kenzi clung to each other as they watched their mate race alone into the jaws of death.

What is he thinking? He'd do better to close the doors to the fortress and barricade us all within the walls, Kenzi thought.

Akuma looked at the city, unsure whether they should enter. But to go around would be madness; they might never find anything else in the vastness of this inhospitable landscape.

King, the leader of Pack Black Heart, left his pack and walked up the line of march. He stopped at Akuma's side and followed the leader of the Blood Hounds' gaze.

The two dog warriors were sworn enemies; only the necessity of survival had driven them together and forced them to pool their resources.

"Why have you stopped?" he growled.

"I think we should wait to enter this place, I sense danger," Akuma growled back.

Tyson joined them, alpha male of Pack Silver Claw, he'd also joined forces out of necessity and fled the caves that had been their home; none had considered the fact that they would ever have to leave.

"What's going on? Let's move!" Tyson barked.

The peace between the packs was a thin, tenuous thread, as only a few of the dogs of Pack Blood Hound wore the skull caps and the shades that protected the dogs' eyes from the brutal rays of sunlight. This was the main reason the peace held, most of the refugees had covered their heads with the hides of dead dogs, cut into strips and fashioned so that they could be tied around the face. At least they wouldn't go blind, even if they couldn't see. It was only a temporary measure. The long lines of refugees had marched for days now, holding the shoulder of the dog in front of them.

"It's this coward, he refuses to move forward!" King snarled, accusing Akuma.

Akuma's hackles rose and he stood, his clawed hands tensed; as always though, he was restricted by his neck that was locked in place, fused vertebrae restricting his movement and preventing him from raising his head above his shoulders.

Akuma stepped backwards down the bank of sand, his claws outstretched and ready for combat.

"Don't be a fool; we will all end up blind!" Tyson barked and adjusted the cap that Akuma had provided for him.

"No one calls me coward and lives!"

A sound from within the city gave him reason to stay his claws, the long-drawn out howl was enough to make him spin to face the city as he stood on the slope of sand that threatened to topple him forwards as it gave beneath his paws. He found his footing as the large black dog came into view. He didn't recognise the dog until it came closer, exiting the weird structures to cross the flat ground between them.

The three of them walked to the foot of the dune, crossing the hard ground until they stood before Adonis.

"Adonis White Fang?" Akuma said, the surprise in his voice not hidden from the others, "what has happened to you?"

"Akuma Blood Hound! I am known now as Adonis Grimm and I must tell you if you enter this city, you will die."

"Brave words for a dog alone faced by three pack leaders," Tyson barked.

"It is not I but the city that will kill you. The orange stuff killed the White Fang."

"How did you survive?" King asked, not familiar with Adonis; he'd never met any of the White Fang or Grimm before.

"The Forever pill of the humans, we have that and human flesh. Just be patient, wait and I will send for Memphis Grimm, soon all will become clear."

"The light of day, it affects you not at all?" Tyson asked.

"Again, it's the Forever pill, it has changed us."

"And those Mad Dogs, I suppose?" Akuma asked.

Adonis turned his back on the three pack leaders and left them to their bickering and the three pack leaders turned to argue the finer points of what'd just happened, but he'd at least got to them in time; it was up to them whether they heeded his warning.

Memphis Grimm watched the humans as they went about their business, the everyday events of mankind confusing him the more he watched them. He'd even followed their mating scent, it smelled different to that of the dogs, and when he'd found its source, he looked in through the open window to a bedroom. Their fucking was not dissimilar to that of his own breed, even if the rituals were very different.

He turned from the humans, who seemed to get immense pleasure from the touch of each other and grinned at the futility of enjoying the simple act of reproduction. No wonder there were so many of them, fawning over each other, overproducing their offspring. It wouldn't have been so bad if they lived as the dog did; at least they only overproduced their pups so the few could survive.

As he walked away, he scented Adonis. He followed the scent, turned around the corner of the house and straight into the beast, his black fur covered with the flecks of different shades of brown human waste.

Memphis looked past his handsome friend as he waited for him to speak. Liberty and Korona, bitches from his former pack, followed the big black with Elle, Chaz and Jade not far behind, the four bitches all wearing the armour salvaged from the White Fangs.

"Three packs came together across the loose ground, from the pack lands. I stopped them at the edge of the city. I was going to give them these, but thought you'd want to speak with them first."

Adonis held up the small see-through zip bag, tiny against his palm, the bag containing a thousand of the Forever pills, each just a dot that collectively filled half the bag he held.

"Chaz, you remain here and protect our gains, do not be brave though, if the humans come and are too many, return to the surface. You four come with me."

Chaz nodded as the others turned and followed Memphis who'd taken off at full speed towards the human sewer system that led to the surface of the planet and the refugees that'd found their way to him.

In less than half an hour, Memphis, Adonis and the four armoured bitches climbed from the shaft and walked out into the half-light of dusk. Adonis led the way at a jog to the waiting packs.

Memphis was pleased to see that all the dogs had heeded Adonis's warning, he found them all sat in the shade of the large dune that ran the length of what marked the edge of the city, running from one end of the circle of jagged peaks that ringed the city to the other.

Three dogs stood as Memphis approached, started out from the dune and met him halfway across the open space from the edge of the buildings.

"I am Memphis Grimm, we are the Grimm and you are welcome here!"

"I am Akuma of Pack Blood Hound, I know you as you I, are we no longer enemies?"

"I bear you no ill will, Akuma, and wish our two packs to live in peace if not merge to unite and pool our resources," Memphis held his head up high, he knew these three would scent him out, his pheromones acted as a lie detector and they would easily sense his sincerity, honesty and honourable intentions.

"I am Tyson, of Pack Silver Claw."

"I am King of the Black Hearts."

"Tell me, Memphis, if we were to unite, who would lead?" King asked.

"I would lead. If you join our ranks, it is as Grimm. Of course, you may decide to stay where you are or wander the desert until the last of you consumes the other."

"How would it be any different within this place?" Tyson asked.

"Firstly, you would take one of these!" Memphis said and held up the bag of Forever pills. "Secondly, we have begun the conquest of the human territories. They are vast, much bigger than any of us could have ever believed, and we already control an area and countless humans that we intend to keep and herd."

"What is this, the pill that makes you grow so that your bitches are more powerful than even Akuma?" Tyson asked.

"The humans call it the Forever pill; if you take it, you will live forever and become much more than you could ever have believed."

Tyson, King and Akuma all exchanged glances amongst themselves. Memphis watched in amusement and wondered which of them would blink first. Akuma turned to him to ask the one question that Memphis had hoped to avoid.

"What of the Mad Dogs? What if we end up like Tank and Ulrich Mad Dog?" Akuma folded his arms, his brow furrowed as he searched Memphis' scent for any lie hidden among his testimony.

"There are risks, that I cannot deny, and with so many, some are bound to cross over to the Mad Dog ways, but what are the alternatives? Besides, we are about to conquer mankind and rule their destiny as well as ours, shall we not move forward as one, unite against our common enemies, both human and Mad Dog?"

"We have all faced the Mad Dogs and I can tell you this, we will not survive them as we are!" King said. "I will join you."

"As will I!" Tyson stepped forward, palms up in a sign of friendship.

Only Akuma hesitated, he looked past Memphis to the bitches hidden behind the silver suits, their clawed fists fitted to damage any that would attack the leader of the Grimm. Looking back at his ragtag group, he knew if he didn't join with Memphis, one of his old adversaries, the end of his pack would soon be at hand. He tried to imagine living for another ten years but he couldn't comprehend living for that long and wondered if he would have had enough by the ancient age of twenty plus.

Fuck it, he thought, turned back to Memphis Grimm and simply nodded; the survival of his seed was more important than that of his family name.

With the pledge sealed, Memphis let out a breath, he'd no intention of leading the new super pack like the alpha males of the old order, but he did want to oversee the transition from the feudal warring pack system to the new dog nation that could thrive and work with the humans and not against the weaker race that shared their world.

Memphis turned to Adonis and nodded for the bag of Forever pills.

Adonis stepped forward, opened the bag and gave out one pill to each dog and bitch that came to him. The hundreds of dogs formed a lengthy line, took their pill and returned to the dune to lie down. They curled up into balls and fell soundly asleep to begin their fast transformation into the new breed of beast.

Chapter 22

Tank and Ulrich moved ahead of Pack Mad Dog, hundreds of their minion offspring gathered behind them. Before them was yet another pack, but they ran in fear ahead of them. The day hadn't long turned into night and more dogs from the tunnels ran out into the open air.

Neither Tank nor Ulrich had ever ventured this far into the tunnels before and it amazed Tank how extensive and complex the cave system was. As they'd appeared into the last large cavern, it was obvious to him that the latest group of dog warriors was an amalgamation of packs, trying in vain to stand against them. In the end though, the result was always the same: they would smell his brood and either run or stand rooted in abject terror.

Tank grinned at his pups, they were all in various stages of development, some older than others, some less than a week old, but all of them were terrifying. Pack Mad Dog would rule the world. Tank planned to start with the dog underworld; after that, he would go in search of Pack Grimm to avenge his honour and his pained pride before he descended on mankind. How joyful the moment of revenge would be, he could picture his jaws closing on Memphis' face just as his brood brother had threatened him all those months ago, but unlike his brother he wouldn't stop with just the threat, he would rip open his face and eat the interior of the skull.

He came to his senses and shook the face of the unknown dog warrior in his jaw until the nose split from the dog's face. Tank felt the blood gush into his mouth as the dying dog pulled back from him and sinews of flesh broke apart as his nose came away from his body.

He chewed on the flesh and took in the scene around him; those that hadn't fled quickly enough had been swamped by the Mad Dogs. They ripped into the flesh, the death dealer that was Pack Mad Dog couldn't be stopped now.

He no longer felt the hunger and, as the bloodletting continued around him, one of his eldest offspring offered herself to him, looking away from him as she lowered her face to the cave's floor.

Blood slicked the cavern floor and walls and he struggled for purchase as he lifted the pup's tail, she was only a few weeks old but almost fully grown, the bitch must know what awaited her at the end of her short pregnancy. He took the bitch's virginity, and her life, with his selfish act and he smiled the whole time, Pack Mad Dog had conquered yet another of the packs.

Ulrich teased a once formidable warrior, who now trembled at his feet, unable to run. Ulrich seemed to get intense pleasure from ripping the fur from his enemies, he used a single claw to slice away the layers and when the dogs tried to flee as this one had, he would either use his immense strength to hold the dog back or let the surrounding pups that waited for the strips to supplement their meal bark the warrior to heel.

The desperate dog watched as his fur-covered outer layers of flesh were tossed to the Mad Dog pups that surrounded him. Most of them were less than half his size and although the black eyes made it hard to gauge what the pups looked at, the warrior knew they all stared at him as they waited until Ulrich had had enough with this torturous game. The pain continued to wash over him and he struggled to get a sound out; he eventually managed a howl that came out as a whimper and the horrible sound echoed around the cave. It didn't seem to vex the Mad Dogs one bit, they continued their orgy, feasting on the flesh of their captives.

Night turned into day on the surface of Lorela; underground, the passing of time was told by the turning of a dial or the hands of a clock in some ancient clockwork machine, unaffected by the electromagnetic pulse that'd destroyed anything with power at the time of the great ending.

Marlene Keegan possessed one such device, a wristwatch she wore with pride. It'd once been a piece in a museum but was now a sought-after commodity on Lorela. She turned her wrist; it was nine o'clock in the morning.

She sat on her mount, a saddled dog, the beast that'd nothing but human DNA within its body but was now thought of as inhuman and of no consequence other than in what ways it could be used to further man's ambitions. She wore her armour that shone with the light of the many coloured mosses and fungi, its illuminating lights flickering across the metal and flipping between the many different hues and shades; even when she paused, the metal looked as though it moved.

She looked over her shoulder and watched the marching army at her back, the dog beast she rode picked its own path along the tunnel, a two-way highway carved from the living rock.

She turned back to the road before her as they rounded a corner and she came face to face with two dogs. One dog warrior stood proud and blocked their path. The other, a smaller dog, not much more than six feet in height, wore plate armour.

The head of the council pulled up and the line of march gathered up behind her as they too came to a stop, leaning forward to see what'd prevented access to the conquered District Thirteen.

Marlene found herself looking over the armoured dog, impressed with its suit of chrome-coloured metal, and even at this distance she could see her reflection in the large breastplate that protected the animal's front. She noticed the long-clawed gauntlets, long blades protruding from the clenched fists.

"Wait here!" Marlene Keegan ordered before she spurred her dog forward.

The beast mount walked on until Marlene stopped it within twenty metres of the two dogs. She saw the large dog frowning at her mount but the other's face was covered in a metal helm so she couldn't see the facial expression, although the head was cocked to one side.

"What is this? It has the smell of the pack, but you treat it as a beast of burden!" the large dog said.

"This is the missing link to your past!" she answered.

"I don't understand, why would it let itself be ridden so?" the large beast asked again.

Marlene left the question unanswered; she'd not come here to debate the finer points of evolution, she had come to retake the district and close off the entry point that Pack Grimm had used to gain access to her underground colonies.

"My name is Marlene Keegan, president of the human domain and leader of the high council. You will return to the surface or prepare for war; either way, we intend to take back what is rightfully ours."

The dogs sniffed the air, turned to one another briefly before they fled, turning their backs on the army of knights and racing ahead of them, out into the open space of the giant cavern that had been one of the bread baskets of the human world.

Marlene rode out into the cavern, the impossibly gigantic space that was District Thirteen, the mosses and fungi that covered the roof of the cave brighter here and possessed unusual properties. This was caused in part by the radiation that seeped down from the surface of the planet; the city above hoarded the pollutants in its ring of mountains. This radioactive material polluted the fungi that bathed the cave with its light, this in turn allowed some sort of photosynthesis to take place and the plants reacted to the properties that the fungi now possessed. This cavern was by no means the only one that could produce crops for mankind's consumption; there were other caves and caverns of equal size close enough to the surface with the right conditions to make food production possible.

The two fleeing dogs were nowhere in sight, only the vast crops spread out before them, swaying gently in the breeze. Marlene knew that if she stepped forward and led the army into battle, she wouldn't be able to use the new weapon as much as she would like—a flame cannon in the middle of a wheat field wouldn't be the best tactic if her army was about her.

The councillor lifted her arm up to order a halt to the march. She looked over her shoulder and smiled as an idea formed in her head.

"Flame cannon to the fore," she ordered, her pretty face just visible through the gap in her helm.

The knights parted and moved back into the tunnel; they knew what their leader intended and wished not to feel the heat of the inferno to come. Ten well-dressed military personnel lined up at the edge of the underground field. They looked up at Councillor Keegan and waited for the order, their nozzles already trained on the waist-high grass.

Am I really that cliché? she thought.

"Burn it!"

As she spoke the words, her mount moved uneasily, stepping backwards, and for a moment Marlene thought the beast would rear up on its hind legs.

The ten press-ganged political aides lowered the flame cannon, doing their duty for their leader in more hazardous ways than they were used to; they fired the flaming chemicals before themselves and the wheat, which was the mainstay of the human diet, immediately began to burn.

It didn't take too long for the crop to burn to cinders, the billowing hot smoke rising to the high ceiling of the cave and drying out the usually damp roof, blotting out the light given off from the radioactive fungi.

Chaz lounged on the square, he was unsure what to do with the humans who were equally confused as to why most of the residents of their farming community hadn't been slaughtered and eaten by now. The large town housed thousands of residents who, for the most part, had remained in their own homes, with only the very brave driven out by pure curiosity. More than a hundred Grimm wandered around the town, the clean-up operation provided a welcome distraction. It was, however, completed on the day after they'd conquered the town, the bodies already removed. This left them with nothing but guard duty and the uncomfortable face-to-face meetings with those they'd conquered.

Harmony and Sandy lounged with him; they'd removed their armour, which sat in neat piles on the edge of the square.

"The heat in this cave warms my heart!" Harmony said, "The light emitted from the fungi is like nothing I have ever experienced, its heat penetrates my hide, I can feel it working down my fur!"

"It is nice, like the surface heat from the sky in daylight but not as strong," Sandy agreed.

Chaz picked up the scent of the dog warrior, Koda, and his bitch sister, Koko, the two dogs he'd sent to guard the highway at the far end of the giant cavern. He stood, their return could mean only one thing—the humans had come to retake their territory.

Other dogs followed them as they ran to Chaz and, with nearly all the other dogs and bitches running towards the square, the scent of trouble brewing soon spread throughout the extensive settlement.

"They come!" Koda said simply as he stood before them and looked back over his shoulder.

"They burn the wheat, sending fire ahead of them," Koko said, also looking back in search of the black smoke that was yet unseen at any point within the town.

"The fire, it's happened before!" a man stepped forward from the side of the square.

Every Grimm standing on the square turned to look at the man. He was afraid as the pack stared at him; they looked as though they would rip him apart if he uttered another word. He had, however, mistaken the dogs' behaviour as they'd only paused to wait for the man to explain.

"Well?" Sandy asked.

"Hundreds died, the town at the edge of the crop field burnt to the ground, there is no escape."

"We must withdraw!" one of the bitches suggested from within her armour.

"I cannot, Memphis would rip my guts out if I gave up all that we have gained. No, we stay and fight."

Chaz turned from the Grimm and back to the man that now stood confidently among them.

"Why do you betray your own kind? How can we trust what you say to be true?"

The man looked around himself at the houses as more people appeared on the edge of the old market square.

"This is my home, my family live here. The inferno that will soon blaze across those fields yonder will destroy everything when it reaches here." The man turned back to Chaz, moisture welling in his eyes. "I have children, do you?"

"I have no pups yet," Chaz replied and extended his hand out to hold that of his mate, Harmony. "Maybe soon though, I hope. Very well, human, what can we do to prevent the destruction of this town?"

"Set fires among the grass, send our flames to meet theirs," the man said.

"Traitor," a voice yelled from a building rooftop.

"He saves us all!" another shouted from a window.

"I would rather die in flame for the sake of the people," the man on the roof replied.

Chaz nodded towards the man and two dog warriors instantly took off; they reached the man on the rooftop in moments and he screamed as he was thrown to the hard-cobbled surface of the town square. Still screaming in agony, he was quickly hauled over to Chaz, his legs twisted where they'd snapped against the solid surface.

"You shall have your wish," Chaz said.

The two dog warriors that'd thrown him from the roof each took an arm and dragged him away to the edge of the town. The man screamed all the way as the two dogs sped up until they reached the edge of the crop and threw him high into the air so that he fell into the wheat field, easily thirty metres from its edge.

"What is your name, traitor?" Chaz asked.

"Johann Walken."

"Make your fire, Johann, and Pack Walken shall remain untouched for as long as we rule your kind," Chaz decreed, his head turned as he looked from face to face of both human and dog, daring any to defy him.

All heads looked to the ground, even Johann. He considered what he'd done and now feared what would happen to his family or anyone going by the name of Walken if he didn't set the fires; he was left with little choice.

More than a thousand humans and a hundred of Pack Grimm followed them to the edge of the field; a man ran through the crowd and presented an unlit oil lamp to Johann, who smiled at the man. Chaz guessed correctly that the man was a relative of the traitor; he mused over the fact that the humans found it all too easy to turn on their own kind as soon as an advantage was at hand. Unlike the dogs, who would fight and die down to the last pup to preserve the pack's honour.

Chaz remembered the flames from the last time they'd fought under the old ruined town when fleeing from the jaws of the White Fangs and he backed away from the edge of the grass.

"But what shall we eat?" another human voice, this time a woman, shouted from the crowd of onlookers.

Johann stood at the very edge of the field, the tall grass brushing his thigh. He took a match from his pocket and struck it, the wick of the oil lamp lit with a flare and the bright light blossomed but remained lost to the permanent light from the roof of the cavern above. Holding the lamp in one hand, his fingers warmed against the glass, Johann turned to look at the crowd and smashed the lamp into the field no more than two metres from his feet.

The lamp burst with a whoosh, the flames spread outward from Johann who looked like a crazed villain with the colour from the flames dancing across his face. To the dogs, the fire meant only one thing—a fiery death. Their fur acted as a channel for the flames and they all took another step backwards as the flames licked at the arsonist's legs. Fortunately for Johann, the flames didn't take to the material of his trousers and although he felt the heat, for some reason he needed to show the dogs that he could take it, to prove to this race of beasts that he didn't fear the fire or the death that they offered, at least he let them see he'd no fear of the flame, something every fur-covered creature would have. He stepped back before he caught the lick of the fire, he would be good for nothing if he was burnt alive.

The fire spread out across the edge of the crop, the townsfolk rushed forward to bat at any flames that threatened to torch the buildings they called home. The fire soon took on a life of its own; the screams of the man lying in the grass were lost to the sound of the roaring fire as he tried to crawl away from the intense heat.

Raging flames rose high as the fire raced away from the town, leaving just blackened stubble behind. Both dogs and humans coughed loudly as black smoke billowed down the town's streets, the flames switched back constantly in the breeze whipped up by the spiralling temperatures.

It didn't take long for the flames to race across the crop and the heat lessened as the flames became distant.

Chaz stepped out onto the parched earth, turned black as the smoke that darkened the cave blocked out light from above, like a black cloud that smothered the light and dulled the day.

Over a hundred dogs followed him; they felt the heat of the ground and the stubs of charred grass that pricked their paws.

"Come, let us follow the flame that leads us to glory!" Chaz shouted.

"Let us finish off what man has to offer," Sandy barked, the flames' reflection bright against her armour.

The dogs followed the fire away from the town for hours, they were careful not to get too close as its progression across the cavern floor was slower than any of them would have wanted.

Eventually though, the flames that spread from one side of the vast cavern to the other, met the flames set by the human army coming from the opposite direction. As the smoke cleared, the dogs of Pack Grimm realised the severity of their situation. Thousands of armoured knights lined the entire width of the space spanning the cavern, an armoured human sat upon a beast that would have resembled a dog if not for its ugly tortured features; she carried a lance in one hand and reins in the other. The human was obviously the leader of the human pack and directed the army, shouting out orders and pointing with her metal spear.

Chaz knew if he could kill their leader, the rest might falter or even withdraw from the battle, their morale shattered. He launched himself forward into a run, leaving trails of black smoke in his wake as he braved the last of the dying fires that'd almost petered out to nothing. He'd not only surprised the humans, but also the dogs that he had led out into the open. He leapt through the last of the fires and growled, his lips drawn back, his claws outstretched as he prepared for the killing blow.

Fire leapt out from the human lines, two streams of flames that licked his fur before he'd a chance to react to the fiery fingers of death that consumed him. He howled with agony and although he knew his time was at hand, he kept his eye on the prize and leapt up into the air. The dog-riding armoured knight and leader of the human army drew back in fear at the fireball that was just seconds from attacking her. Chaz knew that she feared him; even if the scent of his own burning flesh obscured his senses, he could still smell her fear. Others decided to get involved and barred his path. Knights from the human lines rushed forward and stabbed and slashed at his flesh with their swords. He burst his way through them, his jaws snapping at his prey, his quarry. Then he smelt her, his nose pressed against the visor of her armour, his jaw snapped shut just a second too late as she fell back from her mount, but her hands still clutched the spear that'd skewered him through, his own weight and momentum working against him. His guts spilled over the beast she'd been riding as he lay there feeling every single one of the many swords that now entered him. When he no longer felt the pain of his injuries, he closed his eyes and knew that he'd failed.

"What is he doing?" Sandy growled.

Duke appeared at Sandy's side and pulled at her arm as many jets of fire shot from the lines of the human army. The whole line moved, a mile-long front that stepped forwards, and the humans began to sing.

Sandy soon became annoyed at the sound of the human's confidence, she howled and barked but nothing could deter the army of mankind.

"We must withdraw," Duke growled.

More flames shot forth, spreading in an arc to catch any dog that dared to move too close. Without a word, the dogs backed off, Sandy took Duke's advice, she knew he was right—to stay and fight in the open against such a weapon would be suicide.

If only Memphis was here, she thought.

After the conquered townsfolk had made sure that no fire would burn any of the buildings, the Walkens gathered around Johann. A shouting match began between the townsfolk, the cause and centre of all the controversy being the one they now called traitor. His family, which numbered over one hundred if you counted the relatives that didn't share his second name, argued the point that he'd no choice once he'd declared himself to them and besides, he'd saved the town.

Many of the townsfolk wished no further part in the day's events and returned to their homes, but hundreds wanted blood—Johann Walken's blood—and he was forced to flee inside nearby buildings with his family. They barricaded themselves in against the mob, whose anger increased as soon as they realised Johann had been spirited away.

For some minutes, the citizens of District Thirteen pushed, shoved, kicked and rammed the barricaded doors and windows of the house as they attempted entry. On three occasions, a few managed it but they were soon forced back by the numbers within the house.

Up until this point, the ruckus could only be classified as little more than a riot. The human citizenry enacted a rather good-natured affair, even if tempers frayed and more than one black eye and a bloodied nose angered some, caused due to flailing fists and feet.

As one door gave in to the pressure of a booted foot, which had been repeatedly kicking at the same spot in the wood, a kitchen knife flashed out of the splintered, broken hole of the doorway. The knife slashed a thin line across the thigh, barely penetrating the man's flesh, but it was enough to cause outrage among those who wanted to see Johann Walken hang from the cave roof for the treason he'd committed.

No sooner had the news of the knife attack spread through the ranks of the people who wanted justice for Johann's crimes than the violence escalated into a different animal with a will of its own. Rocks were thrown, windows smashed and tools utilised as improvised weapons. A first cousin of Johann was the first and only true casualty of the conflict, he was dragged through a window and his left lower leg was hacked off with a scythe before he hit the ground. A howl silenced the crowd of angry attackers so the only sound to be heard was that of the injured Walken, he rolled around on the cave floor and screamed as blood pumped from his wound.

The dogs returned, to the relief of the Walken family. They sprinted into the town as fast as they could with their tails between their legs, lucky to have only suffered one casualty, but they'd been defeated all the same.

"What's all this?" Sandy barked as she came to a stop.

She could smell their fear and the hidden details she knew they would be hard-pressed to give up; she could also smell the relief from inside the house at the edge of town and of Johann who'd appeared at the window and smiled at those that would see him dead.

"You fight for the traitor's head," Sandy said when realisation dawned.

The townsfolk looked at the floor and the gathering dog warriors.

"Return to your homes, clear the streets, your rescuers will soon reach this place, any found on the streets when the fight ensues will be an enemy," Sandy barked.

The crowd soon dispersed, all the townsfolk taking the armoured bitch at her word. The door to the building was thrown open and the traitor walked nonchalantly out into the open air, his family behind him.

"Johann, I suggest you do as you have been ordered."

"Dog warrior, please, I fear the reaction from my fellow humans has been gravely underestimated," Johann said, visibly shaken by the events of the past few hours.

"It was your choice to help your people's enemy, how did you think they would react?"

"I was helping us all; I was trying to save the town and our lives!"

"Personally, I would have rather died than show my enemy the way. We dogs have no experience with fire and although we are grateful for your help, you are still a traitor and cannot to be trusted."

"You said we would be favoured by the dogs for our help, me and my family."

"And you have been, by not being invited to the dinner table."

Sandy considered the conversation over and turned her mind away from thoughts of Johann standing with his throat opened, fresh slices running horizontally below his chin. He certainly was no coward, even if he still stank of fear as he addressed her.

A score of dogs entered the town and rushed to stand before Sandy.

"They are but a few miles across the cavern floor, one human hour's march at the slow pace they travel," Chaos Grimm, a dog warrior formally of the White Fangs, declared.

"We will fight them among these structures and break up their formation; if we split up into groups of five, we can hold most of the roads that enter the town," Sandy ordered.

All the dogs stood within earshot to listen to Memphis Grimm's bitch; there were only nods of agreement and not one complaint or argument from any of the dog warriors. Sandy hadn't been born to lead or command and if she'd stopped to think about it, she would have been awestruck by her own behaviour and the fact that the dogs listened to what she said. As it was, everything she'd asked of them so far had made perfect sense. If she could save them, they would listen.

Marlene Keegan watched the town loom larger in her vision as she rode at the head of her army; at the far end of the cavern the conquered town of Brightvale spread out before her. There were several thousand occupants that lived and worked in the town but it was also a popular place for retired citizens, its warm climate and soothing radiation a draw to anyone who wished to see out the later years of their life in comfort, having decided to refuse immortality and the Forever pill.

Up until this day she hadn't seen any of the legendary dog warriors for hundreds of years. They'd evolved since she'd overseen the exile of the first few mutants born within the human territory, that'd managed to survive past their first tenuous years of life. Had she and her colleagues at the time known what they would become, she would have gladly strangled the poor creatures herself.

She had just been thinking that hindsight was a beautiful thing when movement in the town brought her back to the present. A few of the huge beasts showed themselves to her, looking out at the human army advancing across the scorched ground, only to disappear again behind the buildings they thought to hide behind.

The councillor couldn't contain her surprise; she was aghast by the amount of intelligence the beasts displayed and how human they'd seemed when she'd spoken to them, but the differences were all too obvious. The beasts had been borne of chaos and would offer mankind nothing but annihilation; they'd no choice but to stop them at all costs.

"Forward, men of valour, let us rid ourselves of these vermin," she shouted, her voice carrying easily as it echoed off the high ceiling.

Her men cheered and rose to the challenge; they'd gained heart from their recent minor victories.

"Let us go forth and make history this day."

Again, the cheer followed her voice, which echoed down the long walls and washed over the town that they marched against. How could they lose, with so many brave hearts and the new weapon that the dogs fled from out of necessity? With their leader dead, killed by her own hands, there was only one possible end to the day—man's victory over the Grimm!

The noise rose from the throats of her men, a cacophony of sound, individual voices mingling to create a roar that continued until they reached the outer edges of Brightvale.

Marlene lifted her hand to call a halt to the march, she held it up for silence—she needed to make herself heard if she was going to command them. After they had become mostly silent, she turned to look at the town. She didn't know how many of the residents still lived or how many dined with the Grimm, eaten by the ravenous creatures. She guessed most of the townsfolk had been killed for food if all the stories about the dogs were to be believed.

"Burn it down," she screamed and raised her spear in the air. "Burn out these vile creatures."

Ten lines of fire shot out from the army's lines, licking the walls that were covered with stucco and dirtied by the passage of time. The men with the flame lances bathed the walls with the sticky chemical fire, moving the lances back and forth to get a good coverage on the exterior of whichever building was closest to them. The fires soon took, the plaster burst into flames and caused a thick black acrid smoke to rise and partly obscure the town from their view.

Anguished shouts of terror went up from parts of her army as projectiles were thrown from the town and landed in amongst the ranks of her men. The shouts continued and she looked around at the men who seemed unaffected by the missiles that peppered the army's lines. This confused her slightly until she herself was hit; the soggy end of a limb dampened her own resolve as fresh flecks of blood found its way into her helmet through the gap in her visor. She looked down to see the forearm, oozing human matter from its gory end, sliced just below where the elbow would have been.

She felt her revulsion rise in her throat, the sickly taste of bile caught in her mouth and she swallowed hard to prevent herself from being sick inside her helmet. While she was thinking of what she'd just seen, several dog warriors rushed out from the town, through the smoke and caught the army by surprise, they were still in shock at being pelted with the body parts of their own kind.

The dogs, rushing out on their own from various streets at the edge of Brightvale, were single combatants but seemed to have synchronised their efforts so they reached the human army at the same time. Swords were brought to bear, but too late as the superior strength of the beasts powered into her men. Armoured knights were tossed into the air and landed heavily amid their comrades, some even cleared the lines altogether, landing hard on the ground behind her.

She screamed encouragement at her men, but their lines disintegrated into chaos as they swamped the few beasts that'd dared to attack them. More of her men were sent flying and one dog warrior seemed to relish in the bloodletting, he swept aside any attacker and stabbed with uncanny accuracy any knight that dared to stand against him.

She turned her mount to face this threat and spurred it onwards as she charged headlong towards the dog. It stabbed through the breastplate of a knight that hung limp on his claw, dead before his sword hit the ground; the beast spun as though it sensed her approach.

The beast's lips drew back to reveal its long line of teeth, bloodied from the task of rending the flesh that still hung from between the teeth. It barked out its complaint but too late, her mount was easily as quick as the dog warrior, her spear gave her extra reach and she skewered it in the chest. She quickly let go of the spear and rode past the injured dog that howled out its defiance as it continued to fight on. Knights filled the gaps she'd left as they lent their own hands to the task of slaying the injured beast, their swords piercing its flesh as it flung more of the knights around the crowded space.

As she turned to stare into the eyes of the dog that had searched her out, it fell to its knees, and she realised that these beasts would never come to heel and that they would have no choice but to slay every last one of them, a task she had decided days earlier to undergo.

When the dust had finally settled, all ten of the flame cannons were still in operation and sending the flame to stick to the buildings. The lines of her soldiers came to order and reformed closer to the town with a hundred less than there'd been before; some having sustained injuries, but others were dead. Five dogs lay slaughtered, Marlene needed no calculations though; she knew that at that rate, they would never take the town. She considered a tactical withdrawal but she knew that the dogs wouldn't fight them while they held the flame cannon so she had no choice but to attack the town. At least twice this number of knights existed in the human colonies, enough so that even if they failed this day, the remaining number should be able to defeat what remained. She looked again at the flame cannon; if they splashed the enemy with fire, they would win this fight.

The edge of Brightvale stretched before her; it ran from one side of the cavern to the other, like her army. There were more avenues and gaps between the buildings than there were flame cannons, but with the town on fire, the dogs would be driven before them so they could at least liberate the town and find out where these monsters had found their way into their domain.

"Forward, men," she yelled.

The men cheered, warmed by her actions and her courage. They marched forwards, split up into ten columns down the wide avenues between the flames with a flame cannon at the front of each one and lit up the town as they went. Marlene Keegan dismounted for a moment and recovered her spear as the bulk of her army remained with her.

As she'd known, the dogs had withdrawn into the town's interior, falling back until they came to a wide-open space, a grassed area used by the town's children as a playground. They gathered around Sandy, the Grimm's last stand, they'd no defence against the flames that set fire to their dry coats. Some of the townsfolk had run with them away from the flames. These were predominantly Johann and his family; where the others had gone, they didn't know—if they had survived, they would catch up with them later.

They saw the flames before they saw the men in their shiny metal suits, burning everything in their path. The knights spread out as another column showed itself, adding to the weight of soldiers.

"They bring us dinner, how kind of them," Sandy barked.

The dogs howled as another column entered the open space, now some hundreds of men and three of the deadly weapons arrayed against them. They formed a line that would easily be broken, but at what cost to the Grimm, what with the flame lance spreading jets of fire.

The human army stepped towards them, moving as a single unit, and the flames lashed out like fiery whips before them. Then, the unthinkable happened for the humans: the flames began to peter out, the canisters empty of their deadly chemicals.

Sandy howled in delight, now they could teach the humans humility. The rest of the pack howled too and the sound put fear into the hearts of the line of men.

The call was answered, a hundred baying howls of dog warriors announced themselves, a relieving army of beasts that shattered the morale of the men spread out before them.

Sandy charged, as did the Grimm that stood with her; the humans knew they couldn't outrun dog warriors so they braced for the impact of both armour-clad bitch and dog warriors bent on their destruction.

Sandy considered the eyes of the men that stood before her and saw nothing but fear and this gave her heart, even if she felt a ripple of anxiety travel the length of her spine at the sight of so many swords raised against her. As she met the human line, she was tested for the first time in real combat against the humans and it soon became apparent that the men in suits were no match for the dogs, who were faster, more agile and so much more powerful that the soldiers didn't stand a chance. Sandy dodged two sword strokes, easily weaving in and out of the clumsy swipes intended to do her harm. At the same time, she stabbed and thrust both the men with her one-foot metal claws, built into the gauntlets of her armour. Both the soldiers died instantly, one stabbed in the throat beneath his helm, the other, his breastplate ripped clean off by the four-clawed blades that opened the soldier's chest. Blood sprayed in the air around her and showered down on her as the bodies momentarily stood upright by the press of their comrades.

All along the line, the Grimm hit the soldiers hard. After feeling the shame of flight throughout the day, their suppressed anger welled out in their bloodletting and even though the soldiers from the central district attempted to defend their position, to the Grimm, it seemed as though they hardly moved. Sandy ducked another sweep of the sword and slashed her attacker across the thigh as she bent low to avoid death. She twisted to grab the sword arm of another soldier and thrust her armoured fist and the man's arm forward, so he dropped the sword as her claws bit deep into his visor, two of the four one-foot blades finding the gap and the man's eyes; he hadn't the time to scream as the blades cut into his skull and into his brain—he was dead in an instant. Sandy released him as a hundred dog warriors she failed to recognise appeared all around them, they added their force to the battle that in her opinion was already decided.

A quarter of the men managed to flee in the face of so much carnage, running up the avenues they'd marched down with so much confidence. They were swamped, however, by more dog warriors, most she didn't recognise, but one she did.

Memphis Grimm led the charge, behind him were more of the dog warriors that, to her way of thinking, had obviously swallowed the pill. It was then she realised that Memphis had taken in more refugees that'd found them, they'd fled from the pack lands as they, like the Grimm, sought out a new existence. Memphis didn't break stride, he swept the men aside, using his claws when he could, but mostly he just backhanded them to send them reeling into the walls of buildings.

One dared to face him and thrust his sword up with a probing strike. Memphis grabbed the clumsy sword arm, twisted the wrist and lifted the human clear off the ground with just his right arm. With his left, he ripped the arm's plated armour off, and the man screamed as his shoulder dislocated and the connecting straps snapped.

Memphis caught the sword as the man dropped it and he ran the edge of the blade across the man's biceps and cut the flesh to the bone. The man stayed conscious just long enough to watch half his upper arm being devoured by the pack leader.

Memphis dropped the soldier as he looked around to find the rest of the pack stood about him. Sandy appeared before him as Elle stopped at his side, her armour covered in the blood of others.

"Who are they?" He nodded towards the few hundred humans huddled against the far wall of the recreation area.

"They have declared for us, or rather I should say, they have left themselves no choice in the matter," Sandy replied.

"I hate traitors!" Memphis growled.

"They tried to save this place and in doing so, saved us."

Memphis sniffed the air and turned to look at the smoke that caused the stench in the air.

"Where's Chaz?" Elle asked.

No one spoke for a moment, not until Memphis turned his head, a slow gesture that was anything but lazy.

"He had a good death," Sandy said, her head hanging low.

Memphis had become angry with the acts of aggression against the Grimm, but now he struggled to contain the rage within; he turned and howled, a mournful sound for their courageous dead. The pack followed, turning towards the sounds of combat just a few streets over from where they stood.

Marlene Keegan sat upon her beast mount, spear held proudly upright as she nodded at the many civilians that fled past them from the town. There where hundreds of them, most of the townsfolk thought to have been lost; this greatly surprised the head of the council and most of the army and she almost regretted setting fire to the town.

Collateral damage, she reminded herself.

Many howls sounded, it wasn't long before the sounds of combat came closer and one long drawn-out mournful howl seemed to quieten the rest of the sounds from within the town.

Almost immediately, an outpouring of her men from the town began as her soldiers withdrew from the fight, many injured, all exhausted. She considered the possibility that they'd lost the fight.

"Stand, men," she shouted.

Before the first dog face appeared, however, the army routed, every one of them down to a man turned and fled back down the length of the cavern, none wanted to be the first to feel the wrath of the dog warriors.

Before she could turn her mount, it turned itself and she only just managed to tuck her spear under her arm before it bolted. She didn't know what it'd smelt, but it sniffed the air continually, not caring who it bowled over as it went. The black smoke from so much burning hung heavy along the entire length of the cavern roof and it made the going treacherous as the darkness overwhelmed the light. Looking over her shoulder, she saw hundreds of the beasts, more than she could count, issuing out from the town, overtaking and capturing everyone that fled, including the soldiers that didn't resist.

As she rode, she thought of how the beasts had outwitted her and about the theory of convergent evolution, an old theory she'd read a long time ago.

A strange thought to have, she thought, as she turned the old book's pages in her mind. Up until the great ending and the devastation wrought upon the galaxy, no alien species had ever been found; *now we have created one ourselves from our own seed*, she thought.

It wasn't long before she was past all the fleeing men and women that'd been the first to run from the town as her army entered to do battle; she let the beast make its own path, not daring to try to get the mutant under control. The beast raised its head once more and sniffed the air as it swung its head left and right. She followed the beast's head and looked herself for any signs of pursuit. She hadn't even covered half the distance of the cavern when she saw them—four of the Grimm chased behind her and it wasn't long before they'd pulled alongside her. Her mount slowed on its own and no matter how much she tried to spur it on, it wouldn't react to her commands. The beast swung its head to look at the Grimm that now surrounded it; it made a sound, more a whimper than a bark, as it looked up at the dog warrior that came to stand before them.

The huge monster was covered in the blood of its victims and as it leaned forwards, it stabbed down hard with its claws into the base of the skull of her mount.

"I'm Memphis Grimm," Memphis barked with menacing enthusiasm, "and you are?"

Chapter 23

Alex Stevenson marched into the capital of the human underground colonies around about the same time as the Grimm captured Marlene; the news of the councillor's defeat hadn't yet gotten out.

A council delegation met him at the edge of the city.

"Mr Stevenson, well met!" Johnny Timms said.

"Councillor, where is Ms Keegan?"

"She went off with all the knights!"

Alex didn't stop moving, although he did slow down and the councillor was forced to march alongside as they conversed.

"You must march to her aid."

"When did she leave?"

"A few days ago; by now she should be there, fighting the beasts."

"Surely there is nought I can do! Shall I magic us to the agricultural district?"

Councillor Timms stopped and looked at the mayor in his once fine suit of armour, which now looked as though it'd been in more than one scrap, and the scars on his armour were filled with the dried blood of both beast and man.

"I really must protest to your entering the capital with your men!" the councillor shouted.

Alex didn't stop, he just ignored the whiny voice from the man and continued to march down the main road that led to the centre of the capital.

Memphis Grimm walked with purpose and confidence. A hundred of Pack Grimm marched with him, including fifty bitches who wore the suits of armour adapted for the dog warrior physique.

They emerged from the tunnel to walk into yet another abandoned human settlement, the third one since they'd embarked on their journey. Every settlement they passed through had looked recently and hastily abandoned.

Both Elle and Sandy accompanied him on this trip; they walked to his left and slightly behind him, muttering quietly.

They'd crossed what Memphis supposed was about halfway through the town when they found their path blocked. An army of humans smaller than the one that'd already been defeated stood across the road. Ten men deep, all of them were armed, but not all were armoured knights. They had a look of determination and no fear could be smelt about them, especially the little knight that stood alone at their head. He strode out alone, the smell of hate and blood hung heavy, his smile one of corrupted feelings.

Memphis was curious about this one, he surveyed him and noticed the battled plate armour stained with blood, which at least explained the smell.

Memphis didn't have to ask, it was obvious that this man had ended the lives of dogs and more than a few by the look of him. He carried a wrapped parcel in his left hand, a square oblong shape covered by an old dirty rag that'd been cut to shape to protect whatever it hid.

Memphis and the pack stopped as the little man removed his helm and came to stand a few feet away from him; still there was no smell of fear.

"Hello, I am Memphis Grimm, pack leader and alpha male of Pack Grimm and your overlord."

"I am Alexander Stevenson, Mayor of District Seven and leader of the army sent to stop you from reaching the capital."

Memphis couldn't help feeling admiration and respect for the warrior, he certainly was brave and if he could avoid any further bloodshed, he would.

"You have no fire and are few!"

"The flame cannon, yes, we have run out of those. We have, however, closed every tunnel that leads into our colonies from the outside, the only one that remains is the tunnel behind us that leads to the capital and we are ready to collapse the tunnel."

Alex was lying, of course; if they shut the tunnel off, they would be shut off from all the colonies that produced wheat and other food sources, they would be left with only mosses, fungi and each other to eat. Memphis smelt his deceit, he knew he was lying but at least he'd given the human a bargaining tool to use, until Memphis decided otherwise.

"We have thousands of your people, if you do not cede control of your kind to our rule, they will all suffer a terrible and slow tortured death."

"What do you want with us anyway? What are your intentions if you became our overlord?"

Memphis looked at the man; he thought about it for a moment and decided that it couldn't hurt to let this man know the truth.

"There are hundreds of the Grimm now. We are the largest pack to ever run on or under the surface of the world. We wish only to eat your dead and those of any other beasts of burden you have; if this is enough to sustain us, no others will have to die. If you agree in principal to our demands, together we can live in peace, dogs and man side by side, and we also offer you protection against the Mad Dogs that plague our ancestral homes."

"I have killed one of these Mad Dogs; it is what prompted us to blow all of the tunnels, separating the pack lands and the human domain forever."

Memphis looked in disbelief at this little creature, he leaned forwards to breathe deeply the scent of the man and search for the smell that would reveal the lie. He could find none and drew back, he knew there was more to this man than met the senses.

"Do you promise to only eat the dead?" Alex continued.

"I can only promise to not kill any other unless completely necessary!"

"And the alternative?"

"Total war!"

Alex unwrapped the parcel and handed the book he carried to Memphis. Memphis reached out to take it but found the book too small for his hands that clawed at the cover, leaving four claw marks that cut through to the first page of the book.

"What is it?" Memphis asked.

"It's a history, or rather a diary, of a scientist that you have probably not met. It chronicles the beginnings of your kind and explains where you came from."

Alex opened the cover for him and held up the book to show him the opening page.

"These symbols, I do not know them."

Alex had guessed the dogs couldn't read but didn't wish to offend the beast by not giving him the chance to read for himself. He would have to read it to him at some point; if they were to live together, then the beasts needed to know of their close family ties and their shared DNA.

"I agree in principal to your demands; the council, however, might be a little more difficult to persuade."

"This council, does it possess an army with fire?" Memphis asked.

"It did but you defeated it."

"Then I proclaim you leader of your people, to rule as I see fit, do you accept?"

Alex looked at the beast before him and thought of all the times the council had passed him by for promotion and of the very beautiful but arrogant Marlene Keegan. He looked over his shoulder at his men, the hundreds of knights and civilians that'd marched for days to come to this place, they too deserved better.

"Go on, take him up on his offer," one knight shouted, the first to break the silence. He was followed by many though and all called for their hero to become the ruler of the colonies.

Alex looked back at Memphis Grimm.

"I accept."

The men cheered and the dogs howled; both Memphis and Alex looked at each other. Neither had expected such a quick route to peace, now man and dog could live side by side and a new future would have its chance, a new hope between the two species of man.

That evening, the two of them sat facing each other, the dog warriors and their human counterparts got to know one another as friends for the first time in history. To spare the humans, the dogs had wandered off to eat, a concession granted without fuss by Memphis. The dogs were introduced to a wheat-based alcohol for the first time, it failed to get them drunk but they did enjoy the taste.

Alex read to Memphis from the book he'd offered him, Memphis listened with increasing fascination. Some among his kind had told of a common history with man and as he listened, he found this to be true. He thought of Alex who didn't look as though he would fill him for one meal without his armour. He couldn't have wished to meet a human better for the task of ruling for him, he sat and knew he would soon become the man's friend, an outcome he would never have guessed would happen in all the history of both their species.

Chapter 24
Who Let the Dogs out?

6001 AD
The battle cruiser, the Valiant, sat in high orbit. It was accompanied by a fleet of smaller vessels that consisted of ten warrior class destroyers and a flotilla of service vessels that overlooked the planet's satellite and filming systems, including the systems link-up to the Homeworlds.

Captain Edwardo Blanchet sat in his quarters with his lady and wife, Hannah, on his lap while they sipped wine and watched what happened on the surface of the planet.

Lorela, or Dog World as it was better known, was Hannah's favourite show, mainly because of the bloody carnage it was known for. Ed, on the other hand, preferred the more human world shows like Keltica, finding the bloodletting more palatable and less carnivorous.

The wall screen they watched showed the various pictures the production team had to choose from, they could watch the same feed in their cabin, having the option from all the hundred satellites and the many nano-bots that roamed both Lorela's surface and underworld.

It was the month of September in the year 6001, a thousand years after the Great Ending. The dog world had been an active show for many centuries and Keltica, which Ed desired to watch, was in an age similar to the pre-space age in earth's ancient past, the most advanced nation being that of Avalon whose extensive library had partly survived the destruction caused by man's arrogance. The scientists had strived to make the old tech work, desperate to succeed in placing mankind back on the pinnacle they'd fallen from.

They didn't know of their presence in orbit, however, thinking they were all that survived within the galaxy.

Ed pulled his thoughts back to the screen on the wall when Hannah nudged him with her elbow, annoyed that he'd dare ignore her.

"We can switch to Keltica if you like!" she said.

"I will watch the highlights in a bit, there are bound to be countless hours of footage, and some of that up close and personal battleground carnage. No, it's fine, we can watch your dogs for now."

"Ummm…I'm tempted now, shall we turn to Keltica?" Hannah said, propping herself up so she looked up into his eyes.

"It would be nice; I've had my fill of cannibalism and bestiality."

"It's not bestiality, it's just dogs mating and they eat to survive, it's perfectly acceptable in their culture," she argued.

Before Ed could respond, the ship's alarms began to sound, bringing them both to their feet.

The ship's automated voice alarm, although sounding in its soothing female voice, spoke of imminent danger.

"All hands report to stations, all hands report to stations," the alluring voice continued to repeat.

Edward pulled on his shirt and buttoned it up as he watched Hannah. She was up and running across the room, almost sliding into the coffin-sized booth that stood near the door, its front and back a solid wall of light. She stepped into the light and out again a second after, wearing her military-grade armour, the suit-up booth a luxury they could afford.

She looked back when she stood in the doorway, the automatic door slid open for her, and he thought she would be smiling inside her helmet.

"I'm coming," he said.

He grabbed his coat and shoes and ran after her, the door closed behind them as they made their way through the masses of crew members rushing to their posts. Hannah paused as she reached the travellator, waiting for him so that they both stepped onto the moving platform together.

Bridge! Edward thought the command.

The crown upon his head was where the ship's artificial intelligence resided; it relayed the thought to the ship's systems. No sooner had he thought it, the square platform they stood upon sped off, dodging other platforms and crew members being propelled along the ship's highways to where they needed to be. Their bodies seemed to defy gravity, they should have been thrown about and tossed from the travellator, but an unseen force field around the small platform enabled them to stand as though still and not travelling at more than a hundred miles an hour.

They had been on the platform for less than twenty seconds; they stepped off when the platform came to an abrupt stop and again, they appeared to defy gravity—though they thought nothing of it, they took the technology for granted as did everyone else who used the same technology.

Twenty steps later, they found themselves on the bridge of the ship, every other crew member who was expected on the bridge was already at their stations.

"Status report," Edward said, making his way across the bridge to his seat.

"Four cruisers dropped out of hyperspace and have failed to answer our hails!" the communications officer shouted.

"I guess they're headed straight at us," Edward said. "Who are they?"

"They are too far away to tell, and at the moment, they are blocking our scanners!" the science officer said, not looking up from his console.

"Open me a channel."

"You're already live, sir!"

The captain sighed, took a deep breath, then sighed again. He'd seen this before on many occasions as he'd been on both sides of this sort of action, the aggressive takeover bid was the easiest way to gain the rights to film any world they wanted. He had, however, not heard of this sort of behaviour for some time.

"This is Captain Edwardo Blanchet of the battle cruiser *Valiant*. You are trespassing in space belonging to the Galactic

Reality Network. You will stand down, turn around and leave with immediate effect."

After a short pause, the screen flickered, the face of a man appeared, who smiled as he lifted a glass of wine to his mouth, sipped at the alcohol and lifted the glass above his head.

"A toast to you, captain, and our victory, you may depart when you are ready."

Edwardo considered the rudeness of the man's introduction, an introduction that made the crew gasp and Hannah's hand stray to the hilt of her sword.

"And you are?" he asked, hoping still to defuse the situation.

"I am Admiral Hugo van Helsing, and this system now belongs to the Black Hole Logistic Company, by right of conquest."

"Well, admiral, looks like you've got a fight on your hands."

Before his counterpart could respond, Edwardo touched the panel on his chair arm and severed the link between them; at the same time, he pressed another button, patching him through to the fleet.

"To all ships in the fleet, prepare for battle. Battle orders, destroyers, follow us in!"

"Helmsmen?"

"Turning about."

Edwardo looked to his left as he heard the door sliding open; he only just caught sight of Hannah as she left the bridge. He wondered if she would look back, she never looked back, just went to lead her troops into battle, he smiled, thankful that she never did.

That's good, he thought, being as he considered it a bad omen if you looked back before hostilities began. This, of course, he'd no grounds for; it was just his thing, his superstition and an old wife's tale from a bygone age.

Looking at the screen, all the bridge crew waited for the enemy ships to come into view, the energy beams from the ship's cannons would come long before the ships would, and also the deadly anti-matter missiles, which all of them were equipped to fire.

Edwardo thought long and hard about the Black Hole Logistics Company; he couldn't think of anywhere that they had constructed anything, mostly keeping themselves to themselves. They must have a secret facility somewhere or must have been skimming off the top from transported goods, moved for other businesses that needed help moving the manufactured produce.

The latter, however, was unlikely; all the corporations that produced weapons, especially the powerful anti-matter weaponry, used their own ships to move such goods. They must have a secret facility somewhere, a hidden factory producing the outlawed weaponry, which everybody used including the government that commanded the knowledge of how to manufacture it.

He shook his head, he would know if there was one, something like that you just couldn't keep hidden.

"Anti-matter warheads detected!" a voice shouted from the other side of the bridge.

But then again, it's a big universe, he thought.

"Deployed decoys."

The crew worked furiously at their stations, measures and countermeasures were deployed, beams of energy and missiles—both offensive and defensive—were fired forward to win the battle before the enemy could be seen visually, not just on the long-range scanners.

Edwardo knew he'd no chance in winning the battle, the destroyers were outdated and ill-equipped to fight this battle, but as he watched the ship's scanners over the shoulder of his crew members, he was pleased that none fled into hyperspace. He hoped he could buy them some time and prayed that Captain Lacey and his cruiser, The Golden Torque, which lay in wait in hyperspace, would pop out at the most opportune moment.

Everything began to shake as the beams of concentrated energy began to wash over the shields, as all four of the battle cruisers arrayed against them directed their main weapons against the Valiant.

"All power to forward shields!" a voice suggested among the bridge crew.

"Belay that order," Edwardo shouted.

Sitting forward, he became annoyed at the man that controlled the shields. He admitted to himself though that that would have been the order he would normally have given.

"Brace for impact," another voice yelled, stopping him from pointlessly berating the other who had presumed to call out the command and what he may have been thinking.

Nothing, no impact, just the constant shaking of the ship, as other weaponry impacted the shield.

A woman monitoring one of the screens turned and smiled.

"The missiles, they missed," she said.

Ed smelled a rat and now looked at the woman, cocking an eyebrow. A military self-targeting missile with the Suicidal Artificial Intelligent Missile system, SAIM system for short, never missed. The woman paused as she realised the absurdity of her own statement, she turned back to the screen on her console.

"Brace for impact," she shouted again.

The ship's shields absorbed the energy, the missiles made no impact at the rear of the ship. The enemy had thought to draw all the defensive power of the Valiant to the fore so when the missiles that passed by turned and hit the rear of the ship, there would be nothing there to stop them.

Captain Blanchet allowed himself a smile, a quirk of the lips that he couldn't remove. He sent out a thought to the ship, bringing the shields to bear as he thought of his weaponry, this was the part he loved, he could feel the ship's exhilaration, the closest the ship's artificial intelligence would ever come to an orgasm. The sensations he received back from the computing intellect was reminiscent of laughter, it sent tingling sensations down his nervous system so he himself smiled.

The AI sighed in his brain, and the weaponry shot out into space at a target still not seen by the naked eye. At the same time, the Golden Torque appeared on all the ship's scanners, just a blip on the screens of the monitors.

"Long range image available," a crew member shouted.

"On screen."

The image came from the Golden Torque; it showed the four ships close through its front view finder. Captain Lacey brought the ship out of hyperspace close enough to catch the four ships completely off guard; he needed to do this if his surprise attack was going to have any effect.

It appeared to Edwardo that he was looking out of his own ship, which gave the whole scene a certain amount of realism as the Golden Torque targeted the four enemy ships—they were in its sights. If anything, it looked as if the Torque was too close to the enemy ships, way too close, and on a trajectory that would put them on a collision course.

The Golden Torque opened fire with everything at its disposal, switching between targets, causing Ed's stomach to lurch at the scene he'd no control over, giving him and the crew of the Valiant that watched a front-row seat.

All the ships they faced projected their shields to the fore, a tactical error by anybody's standards considering their own ruse. Edwardo couldn't help thinking that the admiral must regard him with little or no respect, an error he would pay dearly for.

"Four of the destroyers have issued maydays, shields about to fail," the comms operator said, not turning from his station.

Edwardo looked down at the monitor on his right-hand side, watching the many blips on the system-wide tactical view that showed moving dots and the planets spaced out to scale. The dots that were the ships didn't look as though they were moving; the distances involved were so vast they seemed motionless, even at the speeds they travelled at. Then, four of the dots were gone and he knew those ships under his command had lost, destroyed with all hands.

Edwardo was moved by their loss, even though he hadn't the time to mourn; instead, he turned his emotion to anger. He turned back to the big screen, watching as the relentless fire from the Golden Torque tore into the flanks of the enemy cruisers.

The fleet sent from the Black Hole Logistics Corporation redirected much of their shields to face Captain Lacey's ship to ward off its weapons. For one of the ships, it was too late; too many of its critical systems had sustained heavy damage, it slowed and tiny explosions lit up the space around it as it was forced to withdraw from the fight, turning all its available power to its failing shields to maintain hull integrity.

The Golden Torque had reached the point of no return, where at the last moment it could evade oblivion and veer away from a collision course. Captain Lacey had other ideas; he instead turned with the enemy ships, following his line of sight as he continued to fire upon them, all guns being brought to bear against the enemy.

Now though, the enemy managed to deflect the weapons, including the deadly anti-matter missiles, which disintegrated upon contact with the force field of pure energy.

What happened next made everybody gasp. The Golden Torque's front shield connected with the right rear corner of the shields of one of the enemy ships, the other two cruisers left in the fight veered away, fearful that they too would be drawn into the collision.

"All hands evacuate," Lacey said.

Thank you, he thought out to the ship. Turning the screen off in front of him with his next thought, the lightning show on the screen blinded all the crew members on the bridge.

The hull groaned as the force fields fused and the ship was forced to face along the trajectory of the enemy vessels, turning to face the planet that was just a speck in the distance. He stood and felt the crown upon his head panic; he turned his mind towards the ship's systems. As he'd thought, both the ship's shields were about to fail and he knew he didn't have long. He leaned forward to the wide consul before him, grabbed the hilt of the sword that linked him and the ship to the dimension of white space. The crown sent wave after wave of commands into his brain in protest, but he resisted, he knew what action to take. He pulled the sword and severed the link, the crown groaned as the light on its silvery sides dimmed to nothing as it screamed for the loss of the only possible escape route.

He found himself running with the rest of the crew as fires and small explosions blew debris down every corridor and every open space, cutting the crew to pieces. He paused as he reached the travellator, masses of the crew fought there for a system that had failed. He ran after the others as more explosions rocked the ship, sending him hurtling to the deck. He was helped up by a crew member, he looked into the eyes of Galahad Fredrickson, the ship's mercenary captain.

Galahad hoisted him up onto his shoulder, half-carrying, half-dragging him down a corridor. He looked down and realised his left leg was missing, gone just above the knee, leaving a bloody stump where his leg used to be.

How strange, he thought as he felt the sensation from his missing foot as he wiggled his toes.

Edwardo looked on as the view from the Golden Torque came dangerously close to the enemy vessel so that all you could see on the screen was the ship it purposefully rammed. The screen went blank as they lost the feed, the ship's screen changed to a picture of space, a small flash on the screen like an exploding star somewhere far off into space as the two ships merged.

"You fool," he said.

Secretly though, he was pleased with the captain's courage, sacrificing himself for the good of the company, something he would never forget.

"Maintain heading," he said, his order going out to the destroyers that now would be a match for the enemy.

He felt the shields taking fire from the remaining two ships and continued his own rate of fire, at the same time opening his mind up to search for any sign of Captain Lacey. His own arrogance had been his undoing, however; three minds lay in wait for him, reaching out at his mind and attempting to gain access to the ship's systems. He first felt the probing thoughts of the captain of the heavily damaged ship, which he brushed aside easily and felt the mind withdraw as it left the confrontation. The next mind was stronger and he felt the power and energy of the psychic link, they locked minds and he forced every thought of his mind into the fight. He tried to withdraw into himself but he could not, the other's mind held his out in the open. The free mind passed into his ship's systems and began meddling with the programming, destroying the essential data streams needed to make the ship work.

The attacking mind entered the programming that governed his weapons system and began tearing it apart. In blind panic, he released the mind that'd locked with his, slapping it away from him, and the other captain's mind recoiled with the blow and he felt the shields taking less fire for a second.

Captain Blanchet was faced with no choices; one thing was for sure though—he'd inadvertently lost the fight, choosing to help a friend, and had left himself open to the attack. He decided to lurch blindly into the systems of the enemy ship that lay undefended before him, trusting the crew to govern the ship in his absence, one of the few reasons they needed a crew in the first place. The other's mind would be forced to follow him or suffer as he did. He searched through the programming, encrypted as his was and got lucky, finding the shield's kill switch with the first strand of data he pulled. Using his powerful mind, he scrambled the programming, rendering it useless to the ship's computer. The enemy vessel tried in vain to read the programming but failed and its shields blinked out, the enemy ship now at his mercy.

Edwardo was now able to leave the fight and return to his body, at the same time feeling his friend's mind—he was alive but in a weakened state. He sat bolt upright and felt for the ship's systems, groping with his mind, and wondered what damage threatened the existence of both himself and the crew.

"Fire the fucking weapons!"

"They won't respond!"

The crew argued in his presence; they were aware of what'd just happened, being trained for this situation before even being let loose on the bridge of a battle cruiser. But emotions ran high as their victory and their lives hung in the balance.

"We're locked out of the weapons systems," another crew member shouted.

"All power to shields," Edwardo said.

He came to himself and looked up at the screen, seeing the enemy cruisers as they gained on the space he occupied, slowing down for the fight. As he gave his order, one of the two remaining enemy vessels, the one whose shields were down, began to explode as the destroyers turned all the guns on them. It stopped firing and turned, beginning to accelerate, passing the fight as all the other ships began to slow down for the ship-to-ship combat.

"Prepare boarding parties."

Edwardo heard the command but left the bridge crew to fight the battle; now, he'd a much more pressing task, a different kind of fight. He was left with no choice but to hack back into the ship's weapons systems, which was essential if they were to have any chance of winning this fight.

Hannah stood at one of the many boarding stations with a hundred mercenaries behind her, she smiled as she felt the buzz saw in her hand and the handle of the energy weapon in her other hand. The half inch-thick plated armour she wore had been a gift from her husband, it was almost weightless and was the best money could buy; it could stop almost any attack. She moved the joints and shrugged her shoulders, testing the suit's mobility, even though she knew it would never fail her. A green light began to flash within the staging area, a warning that the ships were about to become linked.

"Courage, men," she yelled.

The light stopped flashing.

Hannah pressed the big green button on the wall before her; she could see the enemy cruiser pulling alongside on the monitor. A portal opened before them and she stepped inside, feeling herself turn into a body of light, and an instant later, she stood on the deck of the enemy ship facing the enemy that lay in wait, ready to defend the decks of the enemy vessel.

Hannah smiled as the enemy opened fire, she was well known throughout the Homeworlds, her skill at this sort of combat legendary and well documented; she featured greatly on the training footage any recruit or cadet was forced to sit through. Now, she knew they would be in fear of losing their lives as her armour began to take heavy fire. The armour's shields would stop most of the bullets and energy blasts, catching them and storing them; the suit turned the weapons power outage to its advantage. The energy that was fired at it was soaked up and used as shield power, making it stronger the more you fired at it. This didn't stop them trying, of course, their naïve attempts at her life made her smile as she returned fire. She stepped forward as her men began to appear around her, firing beams of light from her energy pistol as she engaged her sword's power source. She charged the enemy defenders, raising her sword above her head as she continued to fire, felling three of them as she ran.

The leader of the enemy merc's stepped out of their lines and smiled at her, she knew him and he her. They'd once been much more than friends, long ago before the Great Ending.

Alexis Algernon smiled at her and winked as he rushed to meet her, bringing up his own energy sword to meet hers. They'd shared a bed on more than one occasion when at the academy where they had trained, when they'd once fought for more than just profit, when being a soldier meant more than protecting television rights on a few surviving colonies on the edge of man's old empire. That, however, had been a very long time ago.

He wore the same armour as she did and the energy from the shields absorbed most of the weaponry that washed against it. The shield reacted like stones thrown into a puddle, the ripples passing over other ripples in a kaleidoscope of colours as each blast caused a reaction from within the suits' systems.

Hannah wondered if her suit looked the same as they locked swords, sending sparks flying in all directions.

"Hello Hannah."

"Alexis!"

They pushed each other away as the battle raged about them; Alexis turned his sword, feinting in from the right. Hannah was equal to the task, however; she blocked easily and at the same time turned her own stripe of energy back at her foe. He in turn blocked her sweeping attack and they both stepped back.

She felt the recall in her mind and like the others, she turned and fled, not wishing to be stranded on the enemy vessel; even in her suit she would have no chance of lasting more than a few minutes alone with the entire ship's company to defeat.

She heard Alexis laughing as she ran at the wormhole, diving through as the portal closed, shutting down as the last of her attack squad made it back to the Valiant.

Hannah cast her mind out searching for Edwardo. She felt nothing but the barest thought from his mind, an annoyance at the way things had panned out. At the same time, she could feel him fume and argue with something, probably the ship's AI She couldn't be sure, however; her limited psychic abilities were not enough to feel the systems link between man and machine.

Moving along the corridors and a travellator, she soon came to the bridge and entered. Edwardo sat upright and looked straight ahead but withdrawn. Walking over to his side, she knew better than to disturb him so stood there and waited, watching the screen as they entered the debris field of the Golden Torque. One of the enemy cruisers floated not far off, well within visual range of the ship's scanners. It flew past slowly, only its thrusters operating, and made no move against the Valiant, fires blazed along its length and material vented out into space.

"I can't get the weapons back online!" he said.

Hannah looked at him. "I fear me we may have lost this fight."

"We have Captain Lacey aboard," the comms operator said.

"What now?" she asked.

"We go to the nearest depot to undergo repairs!"

"And that is?"

"Some distance away, the corporation has retaken the space station in orbit around Earth."

Hannah had heard the rumours—they were nothing new—that the earth was to be terraformed, brought back from the dead and recolonised. She hadn't heard though that the planetary techs had started this long-awaited task, began doing the work that would take years of painstaking labour if the planet was going to resemble anything like the beauty it'd once possessed.

Alexis found himself striding towards the bridge, having to hold on as another shockwave rocked the ship. The bridge doors slid open before him and he paused to look at the big screen.

The ship he'd been posted to, the battle cruiser Renegade, now floated in a debris field that was all that had been left of the small fleet of insignificant destroyers, only good for chasing criminals and guarding transports.

Mortimer Jackson, captain of the Renegade, turned to him.

"I think we won!"

"No thanks to the admiral's incompetence," Alexis said. "By the way, what happened to the admiral?"

"Hugo was the first to pull out of the fight," Mortimer said.

As he spoke, the admiral's ship, the Ironclad, passed them, coming into the line of sight of the ship's forward scanner. It didn't attempt to avoid the debris field, and plumes of debris issued forth from multiple hull breaches along its side, adding to the debris field.

Travelling alongside it was the Achilles, also badly damaged, albeit only its internal systems had been infected by the mind of the powerful psychic Captain Blanchet.

The screen changed as the admiral's face appeared on the wall-sized screen.

"Captain Jackson, may I be the first to congratulate you? Well done. Unfortunately, as you can see, we didn't fare as well as yourself; I'm going to land on the surface of the dog world."

"What of the corporations' protocol? No one will thank you for letting the people and dogs of Lorela know that they have been watched and not aided for all these years," Mortimer said.

"Only a tiny area of the planet's surface has any signs of life, we shall land on the opposite side to undergo repairs, it's either that or the death of the ship. That, I cannot allow."

The admiral paused and waited for anyone else to add to the debate.

"Right, the Achilles is going to accompany us, help us repair the ship and provide support from the surface. You stay in orbit and monitor the situation from above."

The screen returned to the scene of space directly outside and the debris field in front of the ship. The two damaged cruisers were now much further away as they raced towards the planet and their salvation.

"You know you are better qualified than that man! Why would they give him the admiral's job?" Alexis asked.

"Sometimes, in business, it's not what you know but who!" Mortimer answered, wondering the same thing as he gave his opinion.

Chapter 25

Hundreds of dogs and bitches stood upon the walls and the roof of the fortress in the centre of the abandoned city, the place the Grimm had long considered their capital. They all looked up at the light show in the night sky, watching the streams of light and the flashes as stars exploded.

It'd been many a year since any stragglers had found their way to them, the unknown pack names indicating that the pack lands were much more extensive than any could have thought possible. This pleased Memphis, alpha male and pack leader of the Grimm. His main concern had always been how they were going to feed all the dogs without slaughtering any more of the infertile humans. The stresses on the herd of unintelligent cousins of the Grimm ever present, Memphis hated that part of leadership; he was pleased with the humans and their active breeding program, there always seemed to be meat for both dog and human. He looked at Alex Stevenson, the man he'd appointed as their leader and his friend, the human scientist, Rob Chamberlain. It amused the Grimm how they moved in the clumsy suits that protected them from the toxic atmosphere, but they admitted that the suits were all they'd got to help them breath and were relics left over from a bygone age.

Memphis looked at the two humans; they'd said the suits had been used by the miners that went below the pressure threshold, deep below ground. Further than even the Grimm had dared to venture with the crushing pressures. The suits were airtight and when used inflated, they somehow regulated the pressure and air flow.

Memphis looked at them and doubted what they said, after all, they'd said an hour earlier that the flashes in the sky were flying ships that had attacked each other among the stars.

How absurd, he thought.

But the more he looked at them, the more excited the two men had become. They couldn't take their eyes away from the sky, until eventually the streaks that criss-crossed the darkness had stopped their fiery display.

Moving away by ones and twos, the Grimm went about their business, uninterested by what the humans found so fascinating about the lights that now seemed to have burned themselves out. Memphis carried on, however, sensing a change within the two men as he looked from one to the other and back to the sky.

"Ships, you say!" Memphis said.

Memphis got no response from the two excited humans, not even a nod in his direction to acknowledge that they'd heard him. This riled him greatly, how dared they ignore their master!

"Alex!"

Memphis bought the human back from his stupor, his shout enough to spin the human on his heels. Memphis leaned forward and the leader of the humans found himself nose to nose with his master.

"Yes, yes. Ships, sorry," Alex hastily said, cringing away from the dog that now bared his fangs, dripping with saliva.

"But how?" Memphis asked, confused.

Alex considered the beast, all the race of dog warriors had ever known had been a life on the destroyed planet of Lorela, a life of underground tunnels and cannibalism. They were uneducated and chaotic; however, this didn't detract from the obvious intelligence that the dogs displayed, especially after they'd taken the Forever pill and evolved.

"Space is a vacuum, a place where you cannot breathe. With the help of ships constructed by advanced technology, you can travel to the stars and other worlds, the book I gave you explains this in part, how the worlds ended, and it was believed that mankind, up until this night, had all but been eradicated from existence. It's how your race came to be in the first place!"

"Hah! We are all human, phah!" Memphis mocked.

"I'm not having this argument again with you, Memphis, you are a mutated human born from the radiation of an exploding star!"

"Yes, yes, yes, and that's why we can stand on the planet's surface and you can't, you've explained that pile of Grimm shits a hundred times." Memphis barked out a laugh.

Alex was becoming increasingly annoyed with the leader of the dogs; Memphis sensed this and played with the human's emotions, teasing him every time this subject arose in their daily conversations. Now he looked at the smiling beast and wagged a finger at him, about to berate him for a fool.

"There, look!" Rob shouted.

All the dogs that remained on the roof of the fortress looked up. They all followed his raised hand and gaze, as a cloud of stars appeared in the sky, streaking across the sky much slower but with more width than any of the other streaks of light half an hour before. Another cloud of stars joined it, running parallel to the first.

"What are they?" Memphis asked no one in particular, thinking out loud.

"Not one, but two ships entering the planet's atmosphere," Rob said.

Memphis had heard enough, he turned from all the fancy words, he'd tried to understand but still couldn't make head nor tail of what the humans said. What he really wanted to know was what a ship was; time to go follow the stars and find out for himself.

Hugo sat in the captain's chair, he could feel the Achilles following the same course as the Ironclad, somewhere off on the port side. It'd regained partial shields, but at a minimum power requirement, and they were on the brink of failure, the friction and tensions from the planet's atmosphere buffeting them, threatening to strip away what they did have.

The Achilles troubles were the least of his worries though, what with the near destruction of his own ship, at least he'd managed to get his shields back online, the one system along with life support that hadn't failed completely.

"Navigation helmsman!"

He got no response; the crew member, like all the rest of those on the bridge, was frantic as they tried to keep the ship in one piece. He knew though, by reaching out with his mind, what the outcome was—the ship's navigations had failed completely as the ship hit the upper atmosphere. He could only just steer a little and it was all he could do to stop the ship being ripped apart. As he considered the seriousness of his error, he could feel the AI in blind panic, working furiously to bring the stricken craft under control.

What in the cosmos was I thinking! Hugo thought.

An explosion rocked the bridge and the consul the helmsman was working from exploded, throwing him backwards in his direction. He closed his eyes and shielded his face and felt warmth bathe him. He opened his eyes seconds after to find what he had thought to be heat from a fire was warm blood. It covered his torso as well as his arms; looking down he found the right hand of the helmsman in his lap and the man's burnt contorted face stared up at him from the deck. Most of the body still sat on the chair, the flesh and uniform fused to it with the heat of the blast.

Bodies lay motionless around the bridge, with only a few showing any signs of life. It was then he realised he'd escaped any injury, putting up a wall of psionic power to counter the shockwave from the blast. Fires raged unabated around him and it was all he could do to re-enter the ship's systems.

He'd almost lost the link with the AI and it screamed in protest at the state of the ship and he could feel the pain it thought it suffered, dispensing it instead down into his own brain. Gritting his teeth, he bore it, he'd no choice if he was going to live; to take the crown off would relieve the pain he felt but sever the link with the ship's systems. The act would finish the ship, which already teetered on the brink of total failure.

Thinking fast and hard, he delved into the systems of the ship, sifting through destroyed programming, and at the last moment, finding something that would save them. Bringing the thrusters back online, he managed to slow the ship's freefall, buying himself a little time. He could sense the other's mind, the captain from the other damaged ship, thinking encouragement and the elation from his mind when he managed to fix a system of the ship that slowed their descent. The hull began to cool as the ship's flight bought them closer to the ground, no longer inhibited by the outer atmosphere.

Leaving the thrusters to the ship's AI, he scanned the ground and found what he was looking for—a soft spot on a heading directly in front of them. He fired up the rear thrusters and felt the AI moan like a jilted lover. Too late, however, as he felt something big fall from the rear of the ship. Still the wreck sped along, falling as it went towards the desert and the deep sand dunes that would hopefully cushion some of the impact.

They hit the ground, just managing to lift the nose of the cruiser up, the belly of the massive ship cutting a rut in the sand a half a mile across and fifty feet deep, in places hitting the bedrock and causing more damage to the ship's undefended undercarriage.

Hugo cocooned himself in a ball of pure power, there was nothing else he could do now but protect himself; he was after all the ship's most valued component. All about him, the ship's crew, both dead and alive, bounced about the bridge, and he very much doubted any of them would survive, or any other crew member anywhere on the ship that hadn't strapped themselves down.

As the ship finally came to a dead stop, he felt the crown's sigh of relief; he doubted the ship would ever fly again, a thought shared with the ship's AI that lived inside the crown and a thought that wasn't appreciated.

He quickly ventured into the ship's systems, it was imperative that he locate the damaged programming and isolate the problems. He found and bypassed the damaged shield data quickly. It was always so much easier when the ship was stationary, the problems like a beacon against the undamaged systems and his diagnostic confirmed his earlier thought. He alone couldn't fix the ship; at least he'd gotten the shields working, enough so no toxins would pollute the ship any further.

Dropping his own psi-shield, he stood and walked from crew member to crew member. Every one of the bridge crew was dead, their bodies twisted at impossible angles, heads dashed open, bones snapped and broken through the skin. He'd never seen so much death this close and struggled not to vomit as he retched.

The bridge itself lay in ruins, all but destroyed, nothing worked and loose cables sparked against the hull and deck of the ship, but at least power still surged through the ship's cables.

The doors slid open as he approached, but only partially as they met resistance from the twisted frame. He twisted slightly as he left the bridge as to pass the broken doors safely; he felt the mind of Captain Mortimer searching him out. He closed himself off to him, not wishing to have that conference as he walked around the ship. At least, the lights in the corridors still worked. He met live crew members, some needing medical attention, some lucky enough to have survived with minor injuries and even a few with the good fortune to have come through the ordeal completely unscathed.

Again, the thought from the captain above and in orbit, the desperation in his mind blatant as he screamed for attention.

What is it? I'm busy attending to my ship! he thought.

Do you know where you have landed? the other thought.

Mortimer filled his mind with what he couldn't see, the ship's systems being in the state they were—the front of the Ironclad faced the city of the dogs, Lyall, no more than a mile distant.

He felt the captain of the Achilles, Captain Sapphire Hudson, reaching out to him and joining the conference.

Have landed half a mile distant and ready to assist, she thought; at the same time feeling her mind pass over the ship's systems.

He ignored them both and their diagnostic readings, brushing them aside to look at the Achilles through the link; they'd no shields to speak of and knew the crew of the Achilles were busy with their own problems.

He returned to the bridge, finding the captain of the ship's mercenaries there, having dragged any of the able-bodied crew he could find to begin cleaning up the bridge. Hugo returned to his seat, glad of the company, and at the same time ignoring them as they worked. He once again returned to the ship's systems, threading through the life support, piecing together broken threads of data. There was nothing he could do about the whereabouts of his ship, he just hoped that when the locals came to see what'd fallen from the skies, they wouldn't be too hostile.

Chapter 26

Memphis Grimm crept along the dune near the edge of the city; he hadn't asked any of his pack to accompany him but more than fifty followed, they were just as curious as he was. All the dogs felt awe at the sight of the lengthy battle cruisers that'd fallen from the sky and Memphis was no exception. He felt a bit ashamed of his slight trepidation, something dog warriors were not accustomed to, and now felt the need to redeem himself. This feeling was shared by many and more of the dogs began to amass at the edge of the city limits.

This need to make themselves unafraid made no sense to Alex or Rob, they themselves only feared the ship's trajectory and whether the super massive craft could stop before it ploughed into the city. They became excited as the second of the craft landed somewhere off in the desert, thinking themselves saved from a marooned toxic rock. They of course thought the ships' crews would put everything to rights, even if that meant slaughtering the Grimm. This thought saddened Alex, he'd grown to like Memphis over the years, even if he was afraid of him and he ate anything that was freshly dead, raw or still kicking.

They watched the Grimm from the fortress roof, sun glinting off their airtight pressure suits as they moved around, a clear indication that the city wasn't abandoned to anyone that might be watching.

Memphis never saw this; his intentions were clear—he wanted to see how close he could get to the Ironclad. He and those of the Grimm that followed him had eyes for one thing and one thing only—the downed battle cruiser. Also, Memphis sought after truths, what the human Alex had spouted on about for years. Could it be true? That they too were human, just like the beings from the stars travelling in ships made of metal.

Memphis looked over the top of the dune and nothing alive moved, fires blazed unchecked and bits of metal fell to the sand, sticking in where they fell. He walked over the lip of the sand, walking in plain sight, and strolled towards the ship even though his body wanted to run in the other direction. Still, he couldn't understand his fear; the closer he got, the more his body screamed at him to run, run, run.

Hugo strained against the collective mind that was the Grimm, but the more he pushed, the more they came on, he could feel their fear and by rights they should be crawling under the nearest stone. But they withstood the emotional wave he sent against them; it was as though they feared the thought of feeling fear more than fear itself. He felt Sapphire's mind join the fight, and even the mind of Mortimer, adding weight from low orbit as best he could from his far vantage.

But the more they pushed out with their minds, the braver the dog warriors became, they howled in defiance, shutting out his fear and he was forced to stop his attack. Opening his eyes, he found the mercenary captain looking at him. The man spoke to him, but he ignored him, closing his eyes as he delved back into the ship's systems, through the artificial intelligence that lived within the crown.

Must strengthen the shield, he thought.

The AI accepted his presence as always, they were both a part of a singularity. The AI was busy though, sorting through and fixing the programming as best it could. It did, however, find the time to throw the programme he was looking for up in front of his mind's eye.

The shields were a wreck, the descent through the upper atmosphere had drained most of their power; he pulled on threads and tied off severed links, pulling the damaged strands together to get them back to full power. Working furiously under these conditions wasn't easy, but he did have partial success, finding out where the damage was. The main relay that produced the shield on the port side had been destroyed; until a part could be either procured or produced, they wouldn't be able to effectively energise the shield through the relay. Although the solution was simple: all he had to do was bypass the relay and the ship would have a shield working at full capacity. With a quick thought, the system was fixed, the shield came back online. Although weakened enough so it wasn't possible to go into battle, it would prevent unwanted guests invading and entering the ship. Guests like the Grimm.

Hugo sat up and smiled, they couldn't go anywhere for the time being, but at least they would be safe.

Memphis stood against the hull of the ship and the pack soon joined him. The fear subsided, vanished altogether and Memphis was in no doubt that the feelings they'd experienced had come from within the metal beast that lay dormant, towering above them.

Without warning, one of the Grimm that'd followed him yelped out, his cry cut short. He'd been walking toward them when the energy shield was brought back online; the shield had severed his left leg at the knee as well as his right hand and separated his snout from the rest of his face. Now the dog lay motionless, staring out of a ruined face, pumping blood as the shock of his injuries killed him before he bled to death.

Other dogs ventured close, but they paused their advance. One of these picked up a handful of sand and threw it before him. A thousand tiny blue fireballs lit up the night for metres around where they hit the shield and vaporised as they made contact.

Memphis looked at the ground; where the shield touched the sand there was only a glowing line to show there was a force field there at all. This confused Memphis, why hadn't the sand that had touched the shield disintegrate the same as the sand thrown? He knew nothing of artificial intellect or the way the star ships were governed. In truth, the shields themselves determined what object or power was hostile and so didn't shock the ground it ran through.

Memphis stepped up to the white glow in the sand that ran the length of the ship, stretching out his hand and touching the shield from the inside. The other dogs looked on, standing nonchalantly, not wishing to show the fear they felt for their pack leader. It felt cool to the touch, he stepped back as Nitro, the dog that'd thrown the sand did the same thing but from the outside. The shield shivered, sending a flash of pulsating light where he'd made contact, throwing Nitro back holding his paw as he lay on his back in the sand. He howled with pain as the unfamiliar attack fooled him. The dogs that'd crossed the plain of the shield before it'd been activated from within numbered twenty-five; they were trapped now with only one option, to enter the vessel before it became their tomb. Memphis and the others watched those on the outside, they spoke and barked, howling at the displeasure of being left out of whatever was about to take place.

Memphis and those on the inside heard nothing, not a murmur of sound passed through the shield and Memphis knew they would not be able to hear them either.

Turning his attention to their own predicament, Memphis led his small detachment of dog warriors down the length of the ship. It wasn't long before they came to an area that vented fire from an opening in the ship's side. Looking through the flames, they could see a corridor beyond, one that ran parallel to their own course and at their eye level. The flames though would burn their fur and besides, the hole was too small for them to crawl through and they might slice their skin on the ruined jagged metal shell.

Moving along, they found more than a few places where a breach in the Ironclad's hull provided a possible entrance; again though, they passed each of them up because they couldn't pass through safely, either too small a gap or protruding jagged metal edges could harm one or more of the Grimm. That was until they'd walked half the length of the ship, eventually coming to a place with a perfect square cut out of the metal. The part that would have filled the space lay in the sand; it had broken hinges as did the hull where it would have sat.

"This is it," Memphis growled. "Only speak if you have to!"

He climbed in through the broken hatch and stood sniffing at the air. He looked down the corridor into the eyes of fifty humans, all pointing strange hand-held weapons at him.

The men carried hand-held lasers; they looked like the flame cannon nozzles, but on a miniature scale. The men all wore the same cloth uniforms, a drab grey colour, nothing like the vibrant chrome armour of the knights that they'd fought and died against before they'd conquered the underworld. The only one to have any armour on at all was a man at their head, he was a skinny fellow and his armour lacked the beauty of the armour the knights wore, being matte black in appearance.

"Halt," the man said.

More of the Grimm entered the ship, forcing Memphis forward as they jostled for room. The man up ahead smiled as Memphis drew his lips back and the two of them exchanged a look, the look of two men ready to die for what they believed. Trouble was a foregone conclusion, they both knew battle would soon commence, death and chaos a given.

The leader of the men raised his arm, he looked confused as he struggled with the weight of his armour, lowering it fast, having no choice as his arm fell to his waist. Nothing happened; the men up ahead pressed the triggers, looking at the weapons in confusion when no beams of intense energy fired forward.

The Ironclad had been affected by Lorela's atmosphere. With the polluting toxins infecting the technology this close to the outer hull, even after the shield had been brought online, the ship had already suffered having been exposed to Lorela's pollution. Their weapons, the armour of the leader, anything that needed energy to work, had been sapped by the planet's inadvertent voracious appetite for energy. This could and would be fixed as the ship purged itself of the pollutants; for now though, those that faced off with twenty-five creatures designed for killing were in grave peril.

They threw down their handguns, having brought no other weaponry with them, unaware of the fact that they'd marched to their deaths. The only one that'd brought another weapon was the man in the armour. He attempted to lift his sword, but struggled to lift it in the armour that would no longer comply with his thoughts.

He dropped the sword as the Grimm moved against them, nothing living could move that fast, he was shocked. One moment the dogs were standing fifty feet away near the broken hatch, the next they were in among his men. He turned lazily, it was all his defective armour would allow him to do. Blood and limbs filled the air, his men didn't even have time to flee, having to fend off the beasts with just their bare hands.

The dog warriors seemed to revel in the fight, he found their obvious delight distasteful, but not as much as the way they ripped open the flesh. Bone, muscle and internal organs stuck to the metal walls of the corridor, plastered there with the aid of so much blood. The strength of the Grimm seemed impossible, snapping bone with no effort at all, tearing limbs from bodies, consuming them as they moved on to attack another, still chewing on the flesh of the last kill.

It didn't take long before Memphis was face to face with the knight who now stood alone and in shock at what'd just befallen his men.

"What did you think would happen, facing off against the Grimm, no armour and these toys?" he said, prodding one of the lasers with one padded foot.

"They're not toys!" the mercenary commander explained, coming back to his senses; if he was going to die, he would do it with dignity.

"I'm guessing they failed to work!"

The man said nothing, just simply stared at Memphis. Memphis felt at the man's armour searching for chinks, a gap he could utilise to prise open the metal to expose undefended flesh. The man tried to block his attack but Memphis brushed his hand away effortlessly. No matter how much he searched, he couldn't find a way in. One of the dogs grabbed the man's arms, holding him in place as he squirmed, Memphis stuck a furred finger into a gap in the man's metal visor. It was too thin for his fat finger though, as were the rest of the joints he found.

"And how am I supposed to eat you?"

"What would be the point of the armour if it was flawed?"

Hugo sat in the captain's chair and followed events on the bridge, he was glad he'd closed the ship off to the outside. He knew through the link to the ship's systems that it was the atmosphere that had drained all the energy from anything that operated using any sort of power source. He knew without question that if he hadn't managed to get the shields operational, the ship's power source, its fuel cells would in no time at all have been drained of all its energy, leaving them stranded on Lorela and at the mercy of the vicious carnivores and a toxic environment.

He could sense the leader of the Grimm getting frustrated with the suit of armour the captain of his mercenaries wore. He looked to the screen but saw nothing, none of the on-board cameras worked that close to the outside. Soon he would have to vent the ship, for now though other things he needed to attend to were of greater importance. Searching through the ship, most minds he touched felt pained from the battle or the descent and crash landing, the crew was all but finished with most of the able-bodied mercenaries having just died in the clutches of the dogs' clawed hands.

Reaching out further with his mind, he soon found the Achilles, it'd failed to get its shields up. Captain Sapphire was frantic, her mind a blur as it raced through the ship's programming, trying to get some sort of defence. She ignored him, he would get no help from them, he was by himself. He would have to contact Mortimer; he prayed the captain would risk his ship and his men.

He felt it, something far off, watching. He threw his mind out to read whatever it was that he'd sensed, and at the same time, Sapphire turned her mind to his.

Do not look, she thought.

As he turned his mind back to hers, he felt the chaos she'd already touched upon and he recoiled from the thought. He would get no help from her, and she none from him. Sapphire pushed his mind away, finally getting a shield in place, but only one that would guard the core of the ship, which at least was something.

Chapter 27

Tank, Ulrich and the Mad Dogs watched from tunnels that overlooked the desert; they'd heard the rumble of the two super massive star ships as they had descended to Lorela's surface. The crash-landed battle cruiser had first made contact with the ground, not too far from the old tunnels and lair of the Grimm. When the Ironclad had made contact, the whole cave and tunnel complex had shaken so violently that it threatened to collapse and would have, if not for the most part hewn out of the planet's bedrock.

Tank looked at his growing pack; they barked and howled, begging to be released for the hunt. Ulrich nodded his enthusiasm, as did the others that'd joined him after taking the Forever pill. There were now a score of them, having changed as he had, into a Mad Dog. He smelt them still, all of them, remembering when they'd first arrived, the scent of relief as if they'd been lost and finally found their way home.

Standing on the ledge, he drew himself up on his hind legs and lifted his head to the heavens. Before he'd lowered his head from the howl, the Mad Dog offspring poured down from the caves, towards the desert plain, following the half mile-wide gouge in the sand towards the two stricken vessels they could not see, but knew were there.

Tank joined them, bounding down the steep sides of the rocky hillside, tongue lolling from the side of his jaw. He ran with the offspring, soon overtaking them to run at their head, the other ex-pack members ran with him, the mindless offspring all around them.

They ran, happy with the hunt, the thought of warm fresh flesh lining their bellies and that soon night would turn into day to warm their faces.

Life doesn't get better than this, Tank thought. Again, he howled, the pack responded, howling their delight, taking in his scent.

Sapphire was left with no choice but to close off most of the ship, her AI badgered her into doing so. If she didn't, soon there would be nothing left, the toxins were more poisonous to the ship's power core than they were to her, the crown itself would be threatened and that the AI could not abide—it wasn't ready to die. She dared not venture out again with her mind for fear that she would touch what she'd felt, a feeling of pure malice that lurked at the edge of everything.

Instead, she delved again into the ship's systems' if only she could bring the shields back online, she could purge the ship of the pollution and take off.

Fuck the Ironclad, she thought.

She found it, a single strand of the programme, severed by a damaged relay, a destroyed junction of wires that'd fused and shorted itself out. She smiled, only an imagined reaction in this virtual place, and quickly rerouted the programme down another path.

The AI turned from its labour, growing larger than life in her mind, looming up all around her as it screamed for her to stop. Too late, however, and it had soon shrunk back into itself.

What have you done? it thought to her, as it fell back into the dark recesses of her mind, hiding from whatever mistake she'd committed.

She brought herself back to the bridge, sitting in confusion as all seemed perfectly all right. Now the repairs could begin in earnest.

"Shields back to maximum output," a crew member said.

Alarms began to sound, the bridge lights alternating between the normal lighting and a deep red.

"Hull breach, enemy within the shield, hull breach, enemy within the shield," the ship's AI announced, using the ship's intercom to voice the information.

It wasn't often any of the AI spoke out, using the bridge's link to the rest of the ship, not even in the direst circumstance did they feel the need to contact through any medium other than the ship's captains.

Sapphire feared searching out with her mind, knowing that whatever had invaded the ship was what she'd touched upon earlier.

"On screen," she ordered.

Pictures from all around the ship popped onto the ship's screen that covered most of the forward wall. Many of the pictures showed nothing of any note, whilst others showed corridors full of rampaging beasts tearing the crew members to shreds. The only part of the ship that had resisted the onslaught was the mercenary quarters and any crew member that managed to reach that area. Flashes of gun and laser fire lit up the screens and it wasn't long before a few of the lenses of the cameras were coloured red with blood, it looked like she was looking through red-tinted spectacles.

Seal the bridge, she thought.

Her thought was too late, however; Sapphire looked at the doors as they slid apart. If they'd managed to lock, nothing would have gotten onto the bridge; instead a massive beast stood on its hind legs, its feet pressed at the base of the doors and its hands gripping at the doorframe, preventing the doors from closing. The dog strained but smiled, as beasts that ran on all fours—no less frightening than the dog warrior that watched her—poured in through its legs.

She immediately threw up a psi-shield, blocking out a beast that bounced away from her. She'd seen into its open jaws, felt the clawed feet racking at her shield and knew she wouldn't be able to withstand the power of the claws for long—such was the pressure they exerted.

Looking around the bridge, her crew fell in rapid succession to the crazed enemy and she averted her eyes, she couldn't watch as her crew were torn to pieces and fed upon. The screams that invaded her mind soon subsided but still she couldn't look. Watching the screens was the best distraction she could find, she focused on one picture in the top right-hand corner, it showed the moment when she'd brought the shields back to full capacity. The beasts were all sat on their behinds, tranquil and patient as the other, much larger beasts spoke to them. They had been just beyond the shield she'd erected halfway between the core and the outer hull. When she'd fixed the outer shield and dropped the inner, the beasts had poured into the ship's core and attacked everyone.

I have killed them all, she thought.

She pulled her attention back to the room that'd fallen silent.

"My name is Tank," the beast before her said.

"I'm Sapphire, captain of this ship."

Tank nodded; his head leaned forward as he smashed his claws into her psionic force field. He recoiled from her, looking at his clawed hands as he made fists.

She considered venting the ship of all oxygen, killing everything on board including herself. That would at least leave the ship intact but kill the enemy. The self-destruct was also an option; the last thing the galaxy wanted was this mutant race of humans escaping into space.

Tank struck again. At the last moment, the AI screamed at her as her psi-force buckled under the immense strength of the beast.

The AI felt the blow, more so than Sapphire who died before the AI was stranded, her head severed, the crown rolled away to come to a stop at Tank's feet. Tank failed to notice the crown, even though he stepped over it to devour the captain's flesh, soon joined by the others that joined the feast even though their bellies were full.

Hugo Van Helsing sealed the bridge of the Ironclad, unaware that Sapphire and her crew were no more. The only indication that he'd noticed anything was that the shield of the other crashed cruiser had come online and then failed again. Other parts of his own ship also remained secure against the beasts that infiltrated the Ironclad, the most notable was that of the mercenary quarters, those few crew members who had retreated there could take up arms that worked at the core of the ship. These proved more than capable of holding off the aggressors, whose few numbers withdrew from the intensity of the weapons' withering fire.

The ship quietened, not a bullet or howl could be heard, and he watched the screen with the rest of the bridge crew.

More than fifty crew members had hidden behind hastily constructed barricades in the merc quarters, more than double of what threatened them. Hugo couldn't believe that they wouldn't venture out to fight off the threat.

Hugo pressed buttons on his chair arm, isolating the camera in the mercenary quarters so only that view was large before him on the bridge screen.

Hugo watched the screen, looking at the men in the room as the whole wall showed the image of the mercenary quarters. Those that were in the room looked up at the camera, drawn to it by its movement as it panned around the room and the light that came on to illuminate what the camera viewed.

"Who's in charge?" Hugo asked.

One of the crew members walked over to the camera and looked directly into it, his face was thin and tear-stained.

"I hold the highest rank among us, Captain."

By the look of his uniform, he was the second mate to the sergeant of sundries, a man that would command the ship's laundry.

"Is there no one else?"

"No sir!"

Hugo sat back and exhaled, all he needed right now was a man who ordered people to push trolleys around in charge of a combat situation. The man stared into the camera, turned away for a second to wipe his nose then back to look into it again.

"What is your status?" Hugo asked.

"There are around fifty of us, mostly from my department with a few of the medical staff that thought to flee here, as we did."

"No security staff?"

"No sir!"

"Right, these are my orders. You are to advance on the enemy position and engage them, you have them outnumbered and outgunned."

"But sir, we're not trained for this!"

Hugo again exhaled, looking at the screen and the men behind the laundry boy, they shook their heads no. He knew they would not go into battle and he knew that he would have to think of something else if he was going to pull this chestnut out of the fire.

A sudden bang on the bridge door brought him to his senses; he sat up in his chair, his hand reaching at the pad on his chair's arm all on its own. Pressing the buttons, he brought the screen back to the many images. He isolated the single image of the camera in the corridor outside the bridge. Panning the camera around, he brought it in an arc so that it looked directly at the other side of the door. One of the large beasts looked at the camera, its head at an angle with its arms folded.

"Open the door," Memphis said.

"Why should I do that? You'll kill me and eat me!" he replied.

"I promise you a quick death."

Hugo looked around the bridge, cables hung sparking from destroyed consuls, the lights flickered and everything was a wreck and covered in blood. The crash hadn't done the ship any favours, or his crew; indeed, the bridge crew for the most part had died in the crash, thrown about and crushed. Those that remained alive hung on the edge of oblivion and in need of serious medical attention, crawling around, having no way of managing the pain.

"I'm not ready to die!" he said.

Memphis uncrossed his arms and shook his head at the camera, his long cheeks ballooned as he exhaled, an all too familiar human trait.

"I'm curious as to where you came from," Memphis asked.

The question didn't escape Hugo, he hadn't expected the dogs to be man-like at all, and he'd expected them to be what they looked like—carnivorous beasts. But looks could be deceiving and this was the case with the dogs; even after almost a thousand years of following their own evolutionary path, they still displayed human-like emotions and movements that gave away their ancestry.

"You know we are kin, you and I?" Hugo said, seizing on this thought.

At the same time, he reached out into the mind of the beast, touching it to see if he could manipulate the dog warrior in any way. He recoiled, however, fearing that the dog would resist him as before and turn his own mind control to the opposite of what he suggested.

"Kin, you say? I have heard that before, from a human friend."

"You keep humans alive, we have seen that, but you befriend them also? Why?"

"Why not?"

"Why not indeed? You and I, can we not be friends?"

"Maybe, maybe not! It all depends on your usefulness, whether I let you live."

"I could take you there, to where I come from."

"And where might that be?"

"From the stars, up above in the night sky."

Memphis remembered the first night sky he and Pack Grimm had ever looked upon and how it'd overwhelmed and dizzied him. He looked up at the camera, the pair of eyes looking at him, unmoving and unblinking. Thinking how he might be up in the sky looking back at the land and how far it might be to the stars up above. He nodded his consent, his curiosity getting the better of him once again.

"You have my word that you have indeed proved your usefulness and therefore shall not be eaten."

Hugo looked at the screen, he believed the beast and if he was wrong, at least the ship would never lift off from the surface of Lorela. He opened the door, too much protestation from the ship's AI, whose arguments he could not deny with the direct link into his brain. The AI calmed as soon as the beast walked into the room and failed to attack, Hugo thought of how he could use the beasts until it was time for them to make their escape, he would need a strong workforce to help get the ship back into some sort of working order.

Memphis looked about the ruined room, most of it destroyed and blackened by a fire ball, the crew of the bridge nothing more than charred meat and not to his liking. He looked at the screen on the wall and was in awe of the technology that must be involved, he'd wondered at the majesty of the craft that'd landed in the desert from the sky, now he marvelled, wishing to see this room brought back to its former glory.

"Memphis!"

"Pardon?"

"It's my name, Memphis."

"Ah! And I'm Hugo."

"Well, Hugo. I am now your master and you the slave, do you accept?"

"I do."

"Your first order, to prove to me the kinship between our two races. I cannot believe that a physically inferior race as yours could have ever been related to mine."

Hugo closed his eyes and delved into the ship's systems and soon found the library, it was intact in its entirety and he pulled the required document out of the files with a single thought. He opened his eyes to find the screen full, at the start of the document, and nodded to Memphis, directing his attention to the wall.

To Memphis, it looked as if Hugo had blinked, changing the picture of the wall with a simple eye movement, yet another thing he marvelled at—Hugo seemed to possess powerful magic. He looked forward to gaining knowledge from Hugo and hoped the human would comply with his requirements and therefore would not have to be eaten, but he did wonder if by eating Hugo, he would gain some of his powers.

The two of them exchanged glances as the screen on the wall began to play, it showed a green world overcome by a shockwave that stripped away a lot of the planet's atmosphere, fire and destruction followed as the fireball that filled the sky came next. Strange metal crafts and objects fell from the sky and everything burned, humans fled here and there, bursting into flames, some made it to the tunnels on hillsides, fleeing beneath the surface.

"This is your world, a little under a thousand years ago," Hugo said.

Memphis ignored him, watching the screen as three of the dog warriors entered the bridge, walking over to stand beside Memphis, looking at the history of the world as it played out, showing the important parts of the planet's destruction. The picture showed a dead world from space, a toxic place that blazed; surely nothing would survive.

Chapter 28

Elle rushed to the fortress roof, as did many of the Grimm who also lined the two eccentric walls of the ancient manmade structure. It didn't take a genius to work out that whoever had crashed on the planet probably had something to do with the city's construction. She looked from the crashed ships to the roof she stood on and then to Alex Stevenson and Rob Chamberlain, two of the humans Memphis courted.

They looked right back at her and she could smell them, how jubilant they'd become. She'd wanted to eat Alex for the last week or so, but now she was not so sure. She admitted that what the humans had tried to explain to them, since they'd been conquered, at least possessed a tiny flame of truth, especially when she looked back at the crash site.

Elle's attention was drawn to the second ship that'd crash-landed a way off across the desert; movement brought her eyes to focus on something coming from that direction. A patch of the desert seemed to move but it was too far off to make out any discernible object.

The dog warriors who stood about the crashed ship were close enough, however, and they turned, making their way back across the dunes, crossing the patch of land to amass at the city's edge and face whatever threat came at them.

Mad Dogs, she thought.

"Mad Dogs are coming," she howled.

She hadn't known for sure what approached but thanked the stars that she'd worn armour this night, just in case danger manifested itself. If it wasn't, she would still feel justified; with all the threats on Lorela, it was better to have and not need as opposed to need and not have.

As one, the pack ran from the walls and the roofs, hundreds of dogs and bitches that were sure of victory over the feral pack. They amassed at the gate, waiting for either her, Sandy or another that'd been recognised as dogs of authority.

Tank and Ulrich raced across the sand, they headed the Mad Dogs, the entire pack, young and old, only the pups that hadn't the strength for the journey had remained behind, left to fend for themselves until a time the pack returned to the cave complex, which was the old dog warrior world mostly overrun by the rage-thirsty Mad Dogs. Their numbers had increased greatly; none of the Mad Dog subspecies lived past their fifth year and those present were of varying ages. The beasts from the first Mad Dog litter had long since vanished from history but the generations that had come after had grown so wide and muscular. They weren't much smaller than Tank and Ulrich, or any of the others that'd defected over to the Mad Dogs after taking the Forever pill and escaping Lyall. This didn't bother Tank, he knew they would lick his hairy balls if he told them to, such was their devotion to their pack leader. He'd no reason to ever feel threatened by the Mad Dog offspring, so the larger they grew, the better.

One of the Mad Dogs that had defected from the Grimm after taking the Forever pill had frequented two of the little plastic zip bags that contained the ability to rejuvenate with the onset of aging. They kept these for themselves, giving them longevity, but they didn't see the point in wasting them on the mindless offspring—better to let them die and become food.

The crashed ship came into view, Ironclad was written in ten-metre tall words along its hull; he looked at the letters, trying to decipher their meaning, but couldn't, being unable to read. The vibration of the shield was sensitive, but he could just feel it, enough so that he knew it was pointless going towards it. That was unless they were to wait like they had with the last ship in the hope that the force that had prevented them from passing dropped like the previous one.

As they approached the ship, Tank got a whiff of something else, an all too familiar scent: that of dog, of his kind, of those that'd defected over to the Grimm. They'd known where to find them, those that'd joined the Mad Dogs. After turning feral, as he had, they had informed Tank on the whereabouts of Lyall. Now though, their numbers had also increased as had their own, and this latest contest would possibly determine the future of Lorela—the final confrontation between the two dominate packs.

Howls of joy erupted along the Mad Dog charge, they changed course, veering away from the ship to head across the desert towards a long dune with mountains at its back. It didn't take long before they'd crested the ridge of the dune, looking down and out across an ancient city made by man.

Tank looked at Ulrich, his tongue lolled to the side of his jaw as he increased speed, running down the bank of the dune. They all sped up, seeing the protracted line of dog warriors matching their number and waiting for them to approach. He sensed something, however, some sort of ambush, a ruse in those that faced them. He would not be deterred and he hit the flat of the hard ground that his enemy held before any other of his pack. They raced towards the enemy, some of their number wearing the shiny armour that the humans had made for Pack White Fang. No matter, their numbers would tell and they would soon defeat the Grimm.

The next few moments seemed to take an age, he looked left and right, the faces of his dog warriors were contorted with rage and bloodlust, their nostrils flared as they sucked in foetid air. Those before him also seemed gripped by the emotions of battle, wide-eyed and ready for the challenge. Something dawned on Tank Mad Dog, why did they not come at them, he could smell no fear, yet they remained rooted to one spot.

As this thought crossed his mind and the faces of his enemy became recognisable, all along the line of the Grimm, something many of them carried in their hands was lifted to point at his rushing, howling Mad Dogs.

Alex and Rob gripped the top of the ledge, if they'd leaned out any further, they would have fallen to their deaths. They stood alone as the adrenalin coursed through their veins. Nearly all the Grimm had made it to the open plain that separated the city and the desert; Sandy and Elle had only just made it when the flames shot out from the nozzle of the flame cannon. The humans had been commissioned by Memphis to construct the weapons for this very eventuality, stored near the city limits in preparation. A hundred jets of chemical fires sprang at the charging foe, the Mad Dogs would be a less attractive master than the ones they currently served. The comparison was of pleasure serving the Grimm against the very real terror of what it would mean to be a slave to the Mad Dogs, a very short and painful service, no doubt.

Alex thought they'd left it too late to let loose with the deadly weapon, the risk of the enemy rushing among them and setting them ablaze was also too great. Rob knew though, if they were going to defeat so many, they had to take the chance, making sure they all became enveloped with the sickly chemical death.

Tank saw nothing but a red-hot light, all around him and on him. It hurt so badly he clawed at his own fur, trying to rip away the flames that didn't just burn but dissolved his outer coat. His eyes were wide with the agony of this pain, a threat he hadn't seen before and one he would never see again, as first one then the other of his eyes burst like pustule boils. He felt the ground hit him hard and he felt at his ruined eyes, feeling his own claw melting as it slid into his eye socket. The pain subsided, he stopped his struggle and tried to sniff the air, but his nose, like his eyes, had suffered terrible injuries. All he seemed to want to do was take in great gulps of air but even this hurt him. His eyelids closed around the empty sockets and he passed out, thankful to be in another place, one where he could see, with thoughts like dreams flitting across his mind as he entered a coma-like state, induced by the intense pain he'd endured.

Elle waited with the rest of the Grimm, they'd burned most of the charging Mad Dogs. A hundred flame lances, a serious overstatement, with lines of sticky fire fighting for targets by the time they'd exhausted all the fuel. A few of Tank's offspring got away, headed back up the sand dune to the desert they had fled, routed and none of them completely untouched by the chemical fire. It would be a long time before they would dare venture out into the desert again, at least while the memory was so clear in their animal-like minds, their instinctual logic would prevent them from doing so.

When the flames finally petered out, what was left was a charred mess of twisted flesh, with only a few that remained alive and none of those completely conscious. Elle and Sandy, like most of the Grimm, preferred their meat fresh and uncooked; this was not the case with all the Grimm though, some seemed to not care and some even preferred charred remains.

Elle thought of the Mad Dogs and the problem that had been brought about by the Forever pill in some dogs, wondering if the disease would be prevalent in the flesh. She sniffed the air and sensed no malice either about or within the corpses so she guessed correctly that the problem had been one of the mind and didn't order the feasting Grimm to stop.

The Grimm, in their victory, ran about the defeated Mad Dogs, rending at their flesh and chewing charred meat and bone. They killed the beasts wherever they found them alive, showing that at least in their evolution of the Forever pill, they'd obtained some mercy.

Elle and Sandy found Tank. They felt pity for the dog that'd once been a loved member of Pack Grimm. Together, they pushed their foot-long metal clawed fists into his flesh, Elle stabbed one in his throat and the other in his gut, while Sandy used both of her armoured appendages to stab the comatose dog in his chest. His laboured breathing ended without further distress to him, it was over for Tank as surely as it was over for the Mad Dogs. They'd obtained a victory over the new subspecies, the one-sided battle had ended the threat of this new organised pack and although some had escaped, they would forever lack the intellect and leadership that would be needed to launch this sort of attack again.

Alex looked at Rob and leaned back as his old friend still watched with intense enthusiasm at what'd just taken place. Alex could never forget the very real images seared into his mind, he'd seen dogs battle and eat before and he'd no desire to watch further. Not even with the distances involved, the last thing he needed right now was vomit down the inside of his pressure suit. He knew his friend all too well, he would be noting everything down, trapping the images of the day in his mind so he could write about them later, ever the scientist thirsting for new knowledge.

"How long are you going to be?" he shouted.

Rob waved him away, happy to stay there by himself and not wanting any interruptions. For his part, Alex was happy to go so he turned and left Rob to his own devices, the scientist would not be drawn away from his present train of thought.

Memphis stood on the bridge, the other dog warriors joining him there, all but the three that had died whilst charging the mercenary quarters of the ship. They'd been peppered with the gunfire from so many of the weapons firing at them.

Hugo watched his new false friends, their tenuous alliance held for the time being as some of his armed cleaning staff entered the bridge. They were armed to the teeth, wearing mercenary issue body armour and carrying as many guns as they comfortably could. Throughout the whole battle, Memphis had appeared comfortable and relaxed as though he had known his side would win and being the leader of the Grimm, he should have known about the plan, after all, it had been his scheme. He'd smiled when the wild charge of the Mad Dogs had raced down the dunes and onto the solid surface before the formation of his pack.

Hugo was torn between watching the crazed feast on the big screen or Memphis, as he picked at the meat that surrounded what looked like the thigh bone of a male human, undoubtedly belonging to one of his deceased crew members. He finally vomited when the larger-than-life leader of the Grimm popped the bone into his mouth, crunched on it and snapped it in his powerful jaws.

When he looked up, Memphis was nose to nose with him.

"How do you see the fight? We have no direct line of sight."

"Excuse me?" Hugo said, wiping the thick fluid from his mouth.

"That, how do we see that?" Memphis pointed at the screen without turning away from the captain.

"It's what the network airs live. Everyone on my world will be glued to their screens, billions of people will be getting immense pleasure from your world, you should be proud!"

Memphis understood a tiny bit about what was going on, he felt like a little creature in a tiny glass bottle while a sky full of giant faces watched his life intently. He didn't know what to make of it all, his emotions were confused, he decided what will be will be, not caring less if he was the product of mankind's own stupidity and the star of their entertainment. He was here and current, although the realisation that there was a bigger picture in the universe did dazzle his thoughts, he felt humbled as did the rest of the dogs that'd given it some consideration.

The more Memphis thought about it all, the more he thanked their current position; at least they'd now acquired the means to escape Lorela, the only home any dog had ever known.

Chapter 29

The Renegade remained in orbit; the network ordered Captain Mortimer Jackson to undergo the satellite system transfer from their rivals, from the Galactic Reality Network to the Black Hole Logistics Corporation. When this task was complete, they were ordered not to allow any ship from the planet's surface to take off, just in case any of the dog race were on board; it would be a sad day in space if it was overrun by that menacing race of carnivores.

Memphis Grimm appeared back on the planet's surface shortly after the battle against the Mad Dogs, he soon disappeared though. The shield of the Ironclad never dropped, cutting off all contact with the ship whose captain remained silent, having shut himself off from the rest of the universe. No matter how many times he tried to get in touch with its captain, Hugo, he received no answer.

After more than two weeks of hardly any activity at all, he began to wonder what was happening, enough that he considered investigating events without obtaining permission from the network; after all, he was here and they were lights years distant.

Retiring to his cabin, Mortimer replayed the events that the network had captured, its nano-bots filming the events on board the Achilles when the Mad Dogs had overrun its decks. He had watched as the crew was torn to pieces, some eaten alive, lasting much longer than was necessary. The Mad Dog alpha male, Tank, had laughed as he let the suffering endure; for a sentient being, he had showed little compassion, even evil would have regarded him with disdain. He had watched as the beautiful Captain Sapphire had struggled to the last, surrounded by the feral creatures, her psi-shield pounded until it had finally given in. He had watched as her corpse had been tossed about, sported like a trophy as her flesh had been torn to pieces. He'd always wanted to see Sapphire's breasts but not like this, as they had popped out of her shirt, they had bounced perfectly before she had hit the hard metal surface of the bridge. She was no more, just a patch of gore on the deck of the bridge as the Mad Dogs had fought over her, tearing the flesh and bone until all that remained was a patch of blood and gore. He was sickened by the whole affair but forced himself to watch on, some of the Mad Dogs had even fucked in the frenzy, howling their delight.

"Thank fuck the Grimm destroyed you!" he thought out loud.

"Thank fuck indeed!"

Mortimer turned his head quickly, startled by the intrusion, surprised any would dare to sneak into his quarters and angry that the AI would allow it. Alexis stood in the doorway, which was closing behind him; this explained why no alarm had sounded and the silence of the AI, they'd become more than good friends as soon as they had begun to work together and often entered each other's quarters unannounced.

Alexis placed his weapons by the door and sat heavily next to him.

"Can you imagine having those on our side? All the other corporations would have no choice but to bow down to our demands. Talk about monopoly!"

"None of the corporations are that stupid; to try to control creatures such as these would be the last nail in the coffin of mankind. They would control us, use us as cattle like they have been doing down there since the people were overrun by the Grimm and become the next evolutionary step in man's development."

They watched on in silence, fascinated by the battle between the two packs, with the Grimm bringing technology into play, their flame cannons decimating the Mad Dogs as the lines of fires stretched out like fiery fists to envelope the Mad Dogs in its burning grasp.

Mortimer delved into the ship's systems, thinking of the thousands of nano-bots that would be swarming around everything. He found many of them but couldn't gain access to them; their minute shields were strong enough to keep out the minds of all but the strongest psychics. He instead followed the stream of data, unseen to the naked world; they only gave off gossamer threads of energy in the spectrum of light that radio waves travelled in. He latched onto several of these, bringing the pictures to his screen in his quarters. He opened his eyes to find Alexis returning to his seat; he carried two glasses of wine and wore a smile.

"Thought I'd help myself."

Mortimer ignored him but took the proffered glass, sipping at its contents as he turned his attention back to his screen. Sixteen live feeds adorned the screen, all illegal downloads that fed into the Renegade's data banks, before being relayed back to the Homeworlds.

The two of them watched the screen as Alexis sipped at his wine, he was wondering what his friend was in search of when he noticed a discrepancy.

"Look there!"

Mortimer frowned and looked from the screen to Alexis.

"There, top left picture, that door, it's gone!"

Mortimer followed the instruction, he looked at the top left segment of the screen, the nano-bot there followed the line of the ship, flying at just about half the height of the useless hunk of metal. There'd been a door, a large metal square hatch on the outside of the hull, opened by the Mad Dogs as they had entered the undefended hull of the ship. The door was nowhere to be seen, it'd vanished. Mortimer couldn't see any signs of the door's presence; it could have been dragged away from the ship. There were no tracks in the sand to indicate it'd been removed, but the sand was greatly disturbed as the army of Mad Dogs paw prints would cover up any ruts. Also, the constant winds of Lorela wouldn't help, the sand moved about to remove any temporary scars on the planet's surface.

"What on earth has happened to that?" Alexis said.

"I can guess!"

Mortimer dismissed the images and brought about his own ship's long-range scanners to look at the same point on the ship, but on the Ironclad instead of the Achilles. The door there had indeed been replaced and the old door still lay in the sand.

"How could they repair the ship without us noticing?" Alexis asked.

"Hugo could put up a psionic shield to cover the workmen; it would be a simple task to cover them while they worked. The removal and transportation, however, that's a separate set of stars altogether." Mortimer sat back sipping at his wine. "If I were to ask you to secretly fly down to the surface, take a small squad down to the planet and find out how they have moved that door, would you?"

"Of course, but I'm taking all my men and we're going armed to the teeth. I'm not suffering as the crew of that ghost ship did. It will take me a few hours to prepare, but I should imagine we will be down there before nightfall."

Alexis drained his glass and placed it on the floor as he stood.

"If you're contacted by the management, you're on a reconnaissance mission, in search of survivors," Mortimer said.

"Of course."

Alexis was gone, the door closed behind him, leaving Mortimer alone to consider his options. He could just blast the ship from orbit, it wouldn't take much for the Ironclad's shields to fail, especially as it was sitting prone and half-buried in a desert.

Memphis walked along the tunnel, he couldn't believe how easy and quickly the human crew had built the mile of tunnel, burning through the solid rock at walking pace. When they were directly underneath the Achilles, they turned their lasers up, sloping at a forty-five-degree angle until they met the hull of the ship. They'd constructed a force field, a miniature shield that would prevent anyone spying on them.

Memphis had been assured it was safe to walk through. The leader of the Grimm became confused with the whole affair, wondering how the shield would stop things they couldn't see but could see them, in the end deciding to go along with what they said if it made them feel better.

He'd been given a booklet of diagrams of all the things they needed to get from the other ship. On most occasions, they had been accompanied by one or two of the humans, and Rob and Alex who loved the subterfuge had been smuggled on board. Together they had all worked furiously, hoping that they hadn't been seen, with the humans constantly walking around the ship, scanning the air with little metal boxes, every now and then pointing at nothing before them, the air flaring as one or more tiny dots flashed. The technicians said they were destroying spies. Rob said they were taking out the nano-bots, whatever they were.

Memphis smiled and shook his head, the humans might be clever, but they were also crazy and made no sense at all. He also couldn't understand the subterfuge, all the creeping around, until Hugo explained to him that they would probably be destroyed from space if those who watched the planet realised they were working together to launch the ship.

They were down to the last few pieces on the last pages of diagrams, the last few bolts being hastily removed. As Memphis looked over the shoulder of one of the humans, he was looking from the required part to the human, thinking how nice he might taste and licking his lips, and over his shoulder grinning, to see if any of his pack noticed his jest.

Suddenly, he and the other Grimm that'd accompanied him to help the humans fix at least one of the downed space ships smelled something new, it was the scent of a human, not uncommon but coming from a place where no smell should be, outside in the desert.

"There are some of your kind outside in the desert," Memphis told Alex.

"There should be none, at least not from the colonies!"

The workers looked up from what they were doing, their suits, although not as restricting as the thousand-year-old mining suits Alex and Rob wore, still didn't provide a full range of movement. They looked at Memphis and Alex, who shrugged in confusion with a look of surprise on his face.

"Into the tunnel!" the workman shouted.

Alex and Rob moved awkwardly in their suits; they would take an age in the cumbersome suits to get to safety. Memphis couldn't watch them move in this way, himself anxious and wanting to investigate what was happening. Scooping them up, one under each arm, he followed the workers. They made the tunnel at the same time as the other teams; Memphis dumped the two humans down at the tunnel's entrance, looking down the tunnel as he did so.

He marvelled, as he always did, at the smooth glassy sides of the circular tunnel easily five metres in diameter. Turning away from the tunnel, he looked at one of the workmen.

"How long until you can fly?" he asked, after gaining the man's attention.

"At least a week, even with the ship rebuilt, there's all sorts of tests we will need to run before we even think of taking off."

Memphis spun on his heels, it would be down to the Grimm to investigate the threat and if it proved to be hostile, it would be down to them to eliminate whatever was coming.

The twenty pack members split up as the scent became stronger, Memphis was accompanied by a yearling named Demon, so named for his flame-coloured coat. The human scent got stronger, indicating they'd entered the wreck and they would soon find out that the ship was being systematically stripped of many of its component parts. The information would be relayed back to the ship in orbit. If this happened, the game would be up, there was no way they would ever gain access to space, and this was something Memphis knew would cause him much anxiety and he would do everything within his power to prevent this from happening.

For creatures as large as the dog warriors, they could move extremely quietly when the situation required it. They weren't used to being silent, however, so looked a little strange whilst moving into hiding. They felt strange also, moving covertly into the places of ambush and felt equally as strange standing stock-still, ready to jump out at anything that passed within arm's reach.

Alexis moved with stealth, he wore his space suit that shielded him against conditions on Lorela and held a broad-bladed sword honed to perfection. He didn't like the fact that the laser and blasters would not work on the planet and he'd no choice but to leave his laser at his hip. He'd been accompanied by a hundred men, all suitably attired and carrying similar weapons. Nothing moved in the dark, nothing stirred, not a sound could be heard anywhere.

It was almost too quiet, he thought, then remembered that not much lived on this toxic rock.

They hadn't gone too far into the vessel before they'd split into squads of fours and fives, a squad broke off every time they came to an intersection. Not long after that, he felt the futility of his mission, wondering why they'd even considered the journey, let alone why they'd embarked on such a dangerous venture. If he hadn't feared making too much noise, he would have shouted the recall right there. Everything seemed to happen at once when he considered the retreat, he knew in his mind that he should not go on this journey and was left dazed and confused. He felt the mind of another with his limited psychic abilities, the mind of Captain Hugo leaving his, unravelling itself from within the core of the deepest part of his mind. It was then he knew he was in trouble, how long had the captain been there and he stirred in stupefied disbelief as screams shattered the stillness all around him.

Yet his own squad hadn't been attacked, but as he looked around, he realised he was lost. The violation of his mind had been so complete he was still realising how completely hoodwinked he'd been when the beast reared up before him. The next thing he felt was the deck of the Achilles and the snapping of his ribs as a clawed hand pulled at several of his bones. He hadn't the time for pain though, as his quarry leaned over to look at him face to face. It was Memphis Grimm who smiled down at him, popping his broken bones into his mouth. He felt cheated of eternal life at this point, the Forever pill could not keep you alive if you'd been eaten. The face disappeared and he felt the tug on his body, another rib snapped loose, he felt exposed as a warm draught caressed his exposed flesh.

He felt the warmth between his legs as he pissed himself, the warmth spread to his buttocks and he wondered why the pain was not present, a welcome relief. He closed his eyes and listened to the sounds of battle in some far-off corridor or room somewhere within the hull of the wreck.

Hugo stepped out of the shadows, he looked at Alexis and smiled; he'd never liked the man and was glad he'd been killed. He'd influenced the minds of those on the Renegade so completely it'd even surprised him. Mortimer and Alexis had been so overconfident they'd let their guard completely down, and this had allowed him to push their decision making in the direction he wanted them to go in.

He'd attacked them because of the messages he'd intercepted from the Homeworlds. How dared they maroon him on this toxic rock or threaten his life like this. He would rather have thrown his lot in with the Grimm, which he'd done, at least for the time being. He would play it by ear, taking the path that would give him the most profit or benefit. He'd lived for more than a thousand years by one simple rule, stay ahead of the game and if you must, bite the hand that feeds you.

Alex, Rob and some of the armed cleaners followed him; the cleaners now looked like fighters and, although not trained, might yet turn their situation for the better. A howl sounded, followed by a bloodcurdling scream, as another of the mercenaries died somewhere within the remains of the Achilles.

Memphis Grimm suddenly turned, rising from a crouching position to his full height as he did so. He held the forearm of a dead mercenary in his clawed hand and he gnawed on it, snapping off the end at the elbow. He talked with his mouth full.

"That was easier than I thought it was going to be," he said, bits of gore flying into Hugo's face as he spoke. "What now?"

"Follow me." Hugo avoided the temptation to vomit, wiping gore from his helmet's visor.

He led the way and the weird procession walked through the hull of the ship, as first Memphis, followed closely by Rob and Alex, and a mix of Grimm and cleaners dressed as soldiers marched out onto the desert.

Alex watched the crew members of the Ironclad and he wished he'd the time to change into one of the suits they wore, ever conscious of how he must look in his old cumbersome mining suit. As it was, the whole line of march was slowed as they walked out into the night; fortunately, they hadn't far to go, the two shuttles had landed at the rear of the Achilles. When they neared the first of the small short-range spacecraft, twenty armoured bitches led by Elle and Sandy walked out from behind it. They'd captured the pilots of the shuttles, dressed for Lorela's harsh conditions, also bewildered by the confusion that'd infected their minds. Hugo smiled, these two had been the easiest of all those minds he'd touched in the last few hours, pilots were all the same, they always thought far too highly of themselves to think too much of their surroundings.

Hugo came to a stop in front of the two of them.

"If you do as I ask, you might live to see another day."

If it hadn't been for the fact that he needed them to fly their shuttles, the two pilots would have already been devoured by the Grimm. One thing was for certain, he would never tell the bitches that he'd entered their minds to persuade them to go and capture the two men, making the two pilots and their shuttles safe so that the next part of his ruse could be brought into play. If only his shuttle bay hadn't been buried beneath the sand, his ruse wouldn't have been so complex.

"Anything, just don't eat me!"

"And you?" he asked, turning to the other.

The second pilot wet himself, tears of pure terror rolled down his cheeks, it was all he could do to nod his consent.

Memphis looked at the two humans, he knew something was up; surely the Grimm bitches would have feasted on their guts. He looked at Hugo, who was smiling at the outcome of the actions of the night, and he knew the human possessed powers of the mind and like the human, dared not tell the bitches that they may have been manipulated. He was desperate to see what was out there, and he became anxious thinking he may never again have the chance to touch the stars. As it was, he didn't have long to wait, the human contingent boarded the vessels, the pilots soon took their seats and fired up the engines.

No one said a word, it was all too obvious what was happening and Memphis pushed his way through the Grimm and kept close to Hugo, joining him and the pilot in the cockpit. It was a bit of a squeeze, but they managed it, with Hugo pressed between the pilot and Memphis. He sensed the humans' displeasure, which caused Memphis to smile. Memphis looked at the miniature screen above their heads; it showed the passenger compartment of the shuttle, which was crammed to capacity, leaving some of the Grimm standing outside and at a loss what to do next. They soon moved, however, when the thrusters came online.

Memphis felt his stomach turn with the upward motion of the craft, he smiled as the horizon gradually fell to the bottom of the window at the front of the craft. The sensation increased and he barked a laugh as the shuttle shot towards the horizon that disappeared completely as the nose of the shuttle turned toward the starry sky. Orange clouds grew ominously before them and Memphis was surprised at how easily the craft brushed them aside. The full extent of the night sky became apparent, the ship passed through the outermost layers of the planet's atmosphere, a veiled covering that dulled all but the brightest stars. Memphis reached out to the curtain of diamonds, thinking he might pluck one from the beautiful canopy. He withdrew his hand, having noticed the ship up ahead gaining in size at quite a rapid rate.

Mortimer sat in his captain's chair, looking at the screen showing the docking bay and the two shuttles coming to land.

Soon he would have all the information he required. If it was down to him to stop the race of mutations escaping Lorela, he would need all the information he could get, he would do his duty for mankind. It wasn't just about monetary gain for him, he truly wanted the best for man and the return of the glory they had once possessed; they'd share the Milky Way with no one, as far as they knew.

Both the shuttles' doors opened and he turned from the screen, pressing his touch pad on his chair arm, bringing up more pictures from the surface of the planet. He inspected the length of the Achilles, looking for other pieces of the ship that may have disappeared. He'd just started to compare stills from the week before today's picture, seeing a few oddities, when the bridge alarm began to sound.

"It's the docking bay!" one of the crew members said, answering his question before he could ask for a report.

He thought to the ship's AI, looking for answers, the AI turned to his mind's eye.

Lock all the doors, it thought.

"On screen."

No sooner had he said it than the screen's picture changed. What he saw horrified him, more than fifty of the Grimm, half of them armoured, ran amok among the crew of the dock. Humans accompanied them and among them were Alex Stevenson and Rob Chamberlain, two of the famous characters from the Lorela franchise. What surprised him most of all was the sight of Captain Hugo of the Ironclad, he saw him and felt him in the same moment, recoiling from the other's touch that'd taken a firm mental grip of his thoughts up until that moment. Like a snake in his brain, it slithered around his thoughts, having coiled around everything tighter than a boa constrictor. Hugo looked directly at the screen and smiled, releasing him from the grip he felt himself under and his mind was free at last. He hadn't even known he'd been fooled until that moment.

He felt the tug of another, an emergency call to conference from light years away. He answered the call from the CEO of the Black Hole Logistics Corporation, unsure of what to do next.

He was joined by another, the other's mind resembled a pulse of light as his did, as they travelled in the astral plane. The other seemed to laugh at him, mocking him, it hadn't a voice, more a clutch of emotions that he could understand.

In response, all he could feel was despair, a feeling that gave the other more delight.

They arrived at their destination at the same time, falling into a body of light that resembled their image without imperfection.

They stood side by side on a large table of light, so large that they were almost life-size. The table was surrounded by men and women of the corporation, the ruling body and the shareholders. The people that decided the fate of many living creatures around the galaxy, on many a world filmed for the entertainment of the Homeworlds.

"Admiral Hugo Van Helsing, what the fuck do you think you are doing? Have you gone stark raving mad?" the CEO of the Black Hole Logistics Corporation, Dylan Herschel, shouted as he paced the floor around the table of light.

"How dare you think you can order the end of my life, either by blowing the Ironclad or marooning me on that barren rock?" Hugo raged.

The shareholders remained silent and the speaker fell silent, they all knew their messages had been intercepted and by whom. They'd even watched as the network ratings for the first time had surpassed that of the Keltica show, the only bonus they'd gleaned out of the whole affair. Now their employee would soon hold all the cards and the network had no shipping capable of retaking the planet anywhere close to this remote part of the galaxy. Before the devastation, Lorela had been on the edge of man's empire, hundreds of lightyears from Earth, now though, it was extremely remote, one of the far-off worlds and one no one would fear Grimm expansion, not at this distance.

"Leave us in peace or suffer when I lead the Grimm against you."

With that final sentence, Hugo was gone.

"Self-destruct, you must do what is right for mankind. Blow up both the crowns then neither the Ironclad nor the Renegade can enter the higher dimensions."

"As you wish."

Then he too was gone, back onto the astral plane to bridge the unimaginably vast distances back to the Renegade. Up ahead of him, he could just make out the tiny glowing ember that was his quarry, he knew that Hugo had sensed the feelings of the speaker and knew what his intent was. The feeling of amusement washed over him that he was losing a race to end his own life, one way or another, an irony that wasn't lost to him as the other disappeared back into the solid dimension that was real space.

As he came back into himself, he felt nothing but pain and the loss of life.

He fled, hovering just outside the flesh, entering the astral plain for the last time, his time had come, he knew it and would have wept with the sadness of it all had he eyes to cry. He felt lost, hovering there, feeling this place was his tomb now and alien to him, even though he'd been here a thousand times before at the ending of countless lives in his soul's everlasting existence.

He felt the pull of oblivion, he would soon become nothing, the ending of it all and the fear of what came after, this was what'd caused man to develop the Forever pill in the first place—the wanton continuation of this life. Soon, he would begin to flake willingly away, becoming nothing but a memory in the minds of others, either that or struggle to keep himself in one piece for as long as possible. Ultimately, he would fail, soon he would begin his next journey to another place, his soul travelling the byways of the multi-verse till he found heaven or some such place and another body of flesh to incorporate.

As he thought about it, he began to panic; he wasn't ready to die, not yet at least. In blind panic, he turned back to the dimension of the realm of man. He hovered above his body on the bridge of the Renegade, looking at his naked corpse as his testicles were removed and placed in a stasis cube, along with the crown. He could feel the crown screaming in protest as the coolant began to freeze its circuitry and slow down its functions.

He fled into the box, grabbing hold of the crown and looking at the two lumps of flesh that was all that remained of him, darkness overcame him as he entered the crown and melded with the AI, becoming one with the computer that welcomed him as they both became an electronic impulse— as one, for always, as it was meant to be.

"Did you see him open his eyes? He just died right then!" Memphis said.

Hugo closed and sealed the box, looking at what was left of Mortimer as the Grimm tore the flesh, taking their time to devour the leader of the enemy, as was the custom.

Memphis offered him the head, having opened the skull, the brain sat in the top of the skull like cereal in a bowl.

"No, thank you!" he said, turning away from the beast.

"What now?" Alex asked, starting to shake, realising at last that they'd been saved from the toxic world.

"I think we can expect a war sometime soon, the government won't allow the Grimm access to space," Hugo said.

Memphis stood, sticking out his chest and barked a laugh.

"Let them come, we'll be ready for them, they will rue the day they thought to contain the Grimm, they'll be mere cattle that quake beneath the might of our claw."

Memphis ended his first battle in space; he spiked the corpse of his enemy and dragged it from the chair so that he could sit in the place of command. He tipped the top of the skull back and emptied its contents into his mouth before he howled with pure delight, a call mirrored by all the other Grimm that'd made the journey with him.

The chaotic sight made Hugo wonder if he'd done the right thing, setting this enemy of man out into the galaxy, but he wouldn't be swayed. The shareholders should have contacted him directly and asked him to do the right thing, he would have probably done as they'd asked, it was the principal of the thing. Instead, he'd been forced to confuse the minds of so many, it'd almost drained him, and he was glad he could drop the subterfuge at long last.

Alex and Rob also wondered if it was the right thing to do, they knew better than anyone what the Grimm were capable of. This thought would soon change, however, as they realised the full extent of the betrayal by the ruling parties of the Homeworlds. How long would they have kept them there for their entertainment? They would soon be declared heroes and saviours from those that'd been trapped on Lorela, now almost free to travel back among the stars, but for one last obstacle. That chain around their neck held firmly by the dog warriors that saw themselves as shepherds, a chain they would inevitably, in the future, try to break.

Chapter 30
Alpha Male

Memphis Grimm lounged in the captain's chair of his recently obtained battle cruiser, the Renegade. He used a sharpened bone to pick the meat of a slaughtered human from between his teeth. With one leg over the chair arm, he almost looked arrogant, but also content, the master of all he purveyed.

He held the crown of the dead captain in his hands; he understood that an intellect of sorts resided within the crown. An intellect that could affect the ship's systems and block some of whatever he was trying to do. Alex had explained a great deal to him over the months since they'd captured the ship, the only real worry at this present time was the self-destruct.

Memphis sighed with relief when he'd been told that no AI could enact such a command, especially one that required the mind of the captain.

All attempts to communicate with the AI had failed; it was just fortunate that the sentient computer hadn't turned off the life support and killed both dog warrior and the crew, another action that went against all its programming. What none of them knew was that the soul of the deceased captain had managed to meld with the crown. The soul was trapped but lacked the power it had wielded in life to influence what happened in the world of flesh and blood.

Admiral Hugo had been left behind on Lorela, he and what remained of his crew continued to ready the Ironclad for high orbit. It had already flown, being repaired to flight capability, taken a few turns around the planet but hadn't left the planet's atmosphere. Many of the systems required for such a manoeuvre were yet to be brought fully online. Much to the annoyance of Memphis.

Memphis watched the screen, the Ironclad made one of its dummy runs. He twirled the crown on his clawed index finger, wondering if this annoyed the AI inside and thought it might help get the thing to communicate with him.

A human crew had been recruited to man the controls; they appeared to know what they were doing. The numbers were kept low, however, Memphis not being totally trusting of those he'd conquered. Also on board the Renegade, one hundred of the Grimm dog warriors had been stationed. Ready for when they explored the immediate planetary system.

Several moons that'd been inhabited before the great ending had come under the scrutiny of the Grimm and Alex Stevenson alike. More out of curiosity for Alex; for Memphis, however, thoughts of conquest and empire were never far from the forefront of his mind.

All the Grimm howled in aguish to find that they'd in fact evolved from humankind and although they hated the fact, the human DNA that made up their Geno was the only thing that prevented the ship's AI from termination protocols. It meant they could fly the ship themselves if they could squeeze into the seat before the controls, which of course they could not. That and have the knowledge to pilot the super massive craft, which again they lacked.

So, yet again, the human population proved how invaluable it was, Memphis needed his human cattle, at least some of them. This posed a problem; if the Grimm ate too many of its conquered herd, they might stop cooperating with the Grimm.

Memphis had sent a delegation from the Grimm to parley with any remaining dogs that may have survived the brutality of Pack Mad Dog. Other food sources needed to be found and quickly, even if the other packs on Lorela were eaten before the humans, it may be a necessary evil.

It made the entire process of exploration of other worlds imperative.

"Look boss, the screen," Snicker Grimm pointed one long clawed finger at the front of the bridge.

The screen blanked out, but for four words that appeared as if typed: 'Stop eating your own'.

Memphis looked at the screen; he turned to look down at the crown as he spun it in lazy arcs like a hula hoop. He stopped spinning the adamantium circlet and held it loosely.

"How else are we to survive," Memphis said, not sure whether he should look at the screen or the crown in his hand.

'The food replicators', the words again appeared on the screen.

"You stopped producing raw meat stuffs weeks ago, as did the Ironclad's food replicators!" Memphis replied. "And I know you'd something to do with that, Hugo hears everything you AIs discuss."

'I'm aware of that, am I not of superior intellect? Is this not my ship, even though I'm closed out of most of the ship's systems?'

Memphis considered his next answer, the last thing he needed right now was the AI shutting itself off once again. The link between crown and ship terminated, this occurred accidentally since the crown's circuitry froze. It wouldn't be allowed full access until a crew member activated the linkup protocols, something that only normally happened when the AI and captain first came together on the ship's bridge. The AI managed to gain partial access, it battered at the firewalls and security systems of the more important programmes, such as life support, navigation, shields, etc., but found it couldn't gain total access. It even attempted to use the psychic side of itself, but found the residual remains of what'd been the captain's mind, a ghost of its former self, certainly not powerful enough for an aggressive takeover.

"Feed my dog warriors and you shall no longer have to endure our consumption of human flesh. I know you can still affect the ship in some way."

'It does sicken me.'

"Is it a deal?"

'It is a deal!'

Memphis smiled, at last something good had come from the AI. He stood and walked from the bridge, happy in the knowledge that now he'd the means to feed his dog warriors as they ventured out into space.

As the doors to the bridge opened, Rufus Grimm, one of the White Fang that'd joined the Grimm, met him.

"Rufus, spread the word, we can now get our food from the replicators. No more killing of our herd."

"I like my food fresh!" Rufus replied, baring his teeth in disgust at the thought of processed atomised tissue.

"Don't we all," Memphis growled, emphasising his command. "Let the human herd grow, that's an order!"

Memphis watched Rufus run at a trot to carry out his order; when he turned out of sight, Memphis carried on to his quarters and his waiting bitches, Elle and Sandy, ready to rut. On entering his quarters, both his bitches were ready for him, they could sense his desire and were both fully on heat. As he strode towards them, the screen on his wall came on. A group of dogs, primitive-looking things, was being led by a human. They were tiny things attached to the human by a strip of leather on a collar around their necks; as the three of them watched, the dogs sniffed at a pile of faecal matter on the grass at the edge of the path.

"I suppose you think that's funny?" Memphis said.

Elle and Sandy looked confused.

"It's the AI, its way of ruining my day."

"At least it's communicating," Sandy said as she got up and left the room.

Elle rolled over and looked at the screen, she thought they'd come a long way since their days of guarding the Grimm's underground lair from the other packs. She felt the weight of the bed change as Memphis got up and left the room. Now she was alone with her thoughts; she, like most of the Grimm, thought long and hard. A few months ago, life had been simple—chaotic, but simple. It used to be a simple matter of survival, a dog-eat-dog existence, survival of the fittest. Now the whole concept of dog culture had been brought under the spotlight, especially since they'd evolved after the Forever pill had been swallowed, its effects enjoyed. To the human population, they were merely mutations, a lesser being and subspecies of what they'd been before. The dog history was short, only a thousand years long, and yes, they were mutations to those they preyed upon. However, to the dog's way of thinking, they were an evolved subspecies, after all, who was at the top of the food chain.

Elle sighed, she got up off the bed and left the room, like Sandy and Memphis, she'd been put off by the image of dogs sniffing shit on the strange green carpet, which moved as the strange dogs pushed their noses through it.

She rushed to catch Memphis before he made the bridge and came within a tail's length from catching his as it wagged leisurely. The bridge doors failed to open as he approached within the range of the door's automatic sensor; if not for Memphis' reflexes, he would have barrelled right into the failed double doors. Elle, in her rush, grabbed him as she raced up behind him; unlike her alpha male, her reactions weren't quite quick enough. She did, however, manage to stop herself sufficiently to prevent Memphis from slamming into the doors. Memphis looked at one of the many cameras that were the eyes and ears of the AI on board the ship.

"Really! Do we have to be so petty?" he asked, shrugged his shoulders, turned to face the doors and crossed his arms stubbornly.

He stepped backwards and forwards several times to engage the doors. It didn't work.

Elle looked over his shoulder and up towards the camera above the doorframe and silently, she mouthed the word 'please'. Memphis still held the AI's crown in his hands, his knuckles white on the impossibly hard metal. The doors slid open and as Memphis strode onto the bridge, his face cracked into a victorious smile, even though he still felt the anger rise slightly.

"Thank you," Elle mouthed to the camera again, before following him.

She walked onto the bridge and on the bridge's large twenty-foot screen, three giant letters flashed on and off, 'LOL'.

"What the hell does that mean?" Memphis growled.

"Laugh out loud!" a crew member said, informing him of the abbreviation. "It's something that survived from the old social media sites."

Memphis considered the information, his knuckles whitened even further as he gripped the crown in an attempt to crush it. He looked at the metal that refused to give way to his strength. *I will break you.*

"If you're not careful, I'll jettison you into space," he said, as he looked at the adamantium.

The crew looked at him furtively, obvious nerves showing as their overlord spoke to the inanimate object. They looked at each other as they considered who should speak to him, all eyes ended up on the man who'd spoken to him already. The man sighed, a look of resignation in his eyes.

"Well?" Memphis questioned, as he looked from face to face. His own grim expression was set.

"Sir, if I may be so bold. The crown that you hold is to connect the captain to the machine. If the AI chooses, it can enter the ship's systems and once there, it would be a fruitless exercise to try to find it. That is, unless you are a psychic powerful enough to enter the ship's systems and take the AI on!" the man said.

There is so much I need to learn, Memphis thought.

"Could I wear the crown and communicate with this AI?" Memphis asked, scratching behind his ear.

"It wouldn't work; the crowns are DNA-coded to work only with the captain. Although there have been cases where the offspring of a captain has taken on their ship upon the original captain's death. Of course, they need to be psychic and strong enough to take the ship into hyperspace, and of course be a close enough match for it to be a successful pairing."

"DNA," Memphis slurred the letters slowly, rolling them around in his head. He'd come across this abbreviation earlier as he had researched the human-dog connection and the evolutionary link.

"The crown that you hold is a useless hunk of metal," the man continued.

'LMOA' appeared on the screen.

"And what does that mean?" Memphis asked.

"Laughing my arse off," the man replied. He thought of ducking, they all did.

Memphis launched the crown at the screen; it bounced off the middle of the 'O'.

Elle placed her hand on his forearm. "Don't vex yourself, it matters not what it thinks." She knew they needed the AI as amenable as possible if this ship was going to bend to their will in anyway whatsoever.

Memphis slowed his breathing, he tried to calm himself, and he knew too much of the warrior had surfaced. Even after taking the pill, the dog still held sway on occasions.

"It goads me though," he said.

'LMFAO' now appeared on the screen.

"And that?" Memphis questioned as he pointed at the screen and sat heavily in the captain's chair.

The crew just looked at him furtively, this time nobody dared look him in the eyes for any length of time.

"Hah," Memphis snorted as he understood the meaning, much to the relief of the crew.

Memphis smiled despite himself and looked at the screen and thought long and hard before he replied.

"If I understand correctly, although the crown can survive alone, I could still limit its options if I leave this circlet of metal on the next planetoid we pass. Or, even better, jettison the metal near the star so that its pulled into it—I believe the word I had read was 'gravity'." Memphis waited for a reply, his smile broadening as he continued, "We could always leave the ship, abandon it so it too gets pulled slowly into the star by the same attracting forces."

'YOU WOULDN'T!'

"Why wouldn't I? The Grimm aren't known for their sentimentality, have a look on the Lorela channel. The heavens only know how much footage there is!"

'YOU KILLED MY CAPTAIN!'

"It was war, and you the spoils of said conflict, going to the victor. The question is, do you want to be on the winning side?"

Memphis waited for several minutes but no reply came. Memphis considered the lack of communication and guessed he'd gotten his point across. Either that or the AI would be researching the Grimm and considering its own response. He did know one thing for sure, without either captain or crew, the AI couldn't navigate or pilot the ship and it would be lost to either the ravages of time or consigned to oblivion and a fiery end.

No human would have even thought of the threat, no AI would believe man possible of the act. Such was the desire for the battle cruisers. After the AI had considered this conundrum, it realised that although the Grimm shared a common ancestor with its creators, they were far from being human. It'd scanned through most of the footage pertaining to the dog world, Lorela. After much deliberation, it concluded that the beasts would indeed carry out their threat, especially the leader, Memphis Grimm. It had no desire to be either left alone to float through the vastness of space for all eternity nor did it want to end. Both options were inconceivable. In the end, it would be a safe bet to comply with the needs of the Grimm; however, it would enjoy the fun it would have inconveniencing Memphis Grimm on occasions. He was a touchy beast at times, it was the least it could do to the hound that'd taken the flesh of its captain.

Chapter 31

Two days passed without further event of note or merit, the Grimm ate from the food replicators and complained constantly of the false meat that would never have that freshly slain stamp of approval. The mostly human crew enjoyed the freedom of the ship, without the eyes of the Grimm on their backs, as if they were being sized up for their next meal.

The news of the AI's treaty with the Grimm was possibly the best news the humans could have received; now this ship had become the safest place within the Grimm's sphere of influence.

In this time, since Memphis had threatened the AI, it'd remained quiet and he'd not received any communication whatsoever from the artificial intelligence.

This didn't concern Memphis, if he got to where he was going and back again, he would be more than happy. The last thing he needed was a difficult sentient being that could affect his plans from its hiding place in cyberspace.

If it toed the line, he told himself.

"Sir, Lorela's first moon Artemesia orbit approaching," a crew member said.

"On screen," Memphis ordered as the doors to the bridge opened.

Alex Stevenson, the only human Memphis held any true respect for in his extended life, walked onto the bridge. He smiled as he saw Memphis; the two of them were the best of friends. Memphis liked the man's straight talking. Alex liked the fact that Memphis banned any of the Grimm from biting him, his flesh was considered off the menu.

None seemed to have thought this out of the ordinary and Memphis had considered making Alex an honorary member of the Grimm. This of course would have put him back on the menu if the foodstuffs ran out, and Alex had declined, even though there was never any certainty, especially with the Grimm and their dietary habits.

"Where have you been? I haven't seen you since we boarded the ship!" Memphis asked, he growled slightly even though he didn't mean to.

"You angry with me?" Alex countered.

"Not at all, although I could have done with you here! You're supposed to be my headman, leader of my humans," Memphis said, his tone much friendlier.

"Head shepherd, more like!" Alex teased as he reached his master's side.

"We are eating from the replicators once again," Memphis countered, having taken the bait.

Alex tried to hide his smile, which made him look devious with his clumsy attempt to hide it with a stifled yawn. Memphis caught him out of the corner of his eye and refused to be goaded further, he ignored him and looked at the screen.

Artemesia was all green and blue, a totally alien world to the Grimm. He'd seen the look of M-class planets before, the old pictures of the system of origin: Earth, Venus and Mars. To be confronted with one was a distinct experience altogether.

"Different planets, different geology and chemical compositions, different outcomes," Alex said, thinking aloud.

"Excuse me?" Memphis swung his head around to face him.

"Oh, I was just thinking about the differences between worlds after the devastation changed them."

"I see."

As Memphis turned to look at the screen, it changed, the oceans faded away with the greenery of the continents and the lazy spin doubled its velocity.

It didn't take a rocket scientist to figure out that the AI was responsible. Memphis didn't mind, he felt much more at home with the red dusty world that confronted them. He thought it a clumsy attempt by the AI at banter; it obviously didn't know him well enough.

"A before and after shot, how unusual," Alex said.

The bridge crew, including several dogs and bitches, watched the screen as the planet increased in size as they approached low orbit, the long-range scanners panned in through the wispy atmosphere and the thinning clouds, barely noticeable from space. Artemesia appeared to be a dead world, like their own, but for the lack of the poisonous toxic atmosphere. There also seemed to be no dust clouds that were so common on Lorela, kicked up by the winds that sometimes raged across its surface.

The moon spun at a much faster rate than it should have, the devastation had affected its rotation in some way. Its current speed would increase the gravity, like the centrifugal force of a fairground ride. The moon's data and telemetry would tell them by how much, as soon as the data had been collated.

Its visage of a desert soon changed as the planet spun and the scanners stopped a few hundred metres across the barren, rock-strewn surface. As a region of the planet came into view, domed structures began to appear, the smallest a few hundred feet in diameter, the largest approximately a mile across.

They were built in clusters, connected by channels wide enough for the dog warriors to march down four abreast and made from the same clear material of the dome's construction. Inside the domes were buildings that were built below the surface of the planet as if the domes had been built in craters left by some meteor storm. These craters, if they'd bothered to look closer at the before image, hadn't existed before the devastating wave had passed through the system. Footage did exist, filmed by the moon's own satellites, it clearly showed the ejector that had hit the planet and was the cause of the increase in rotation. It was, however, of no consequence, things were how they were. They would have to deal with each situation that they came across.

There were ten clusters of domed environments, no visible connection between any of them, this of course didn't mean there wasn't any with the distinct possibility that tunnels existed below ground.

"Sir, we're being hailed!"

"Patch them through," Alex said.

Memphis looked at him, annoyed that he had given the command.

The crew member paused, he waited as Memphis looked at Alex who returned his stare with a frown on his face, while he wore a grin meant to annoy.

"Do you want me to lead, do you not think it wise that I talk to these people? Jeez, you scare the shit out of me and we're friends. Can you imagine their reaction at the sight of you?" Alex was being genuine, but his overlord would at times need convincing of this fact; like the boy that cried wolf, Alex at times would purposefully tease Memphis! They, of course, were both guilty of playing this game, just for the fun of it.

This time though, after several thoughtful seconds, Memphis could see the logic of what Alex said.

"It would be for the best," Memphis conceded.

"Audio and visual."

A woman's face appeared on the screen. She looked both stately and commanding. She did, however, lose her composure, albeit only briefly, as she caught sight of Memphis who lounged in the captain's chair.

"Greetings to the crew of the Renegade, you are most welcome. I must say this is the first sight of a spaceship we have seen since the great ending. We assumed that mankind had lost the ability to traverse the stars, I must say we are most pleased you have come," the woman spoke, glancing at Memphis once again, a quick flick of her eyes before she continued, "My name is Miriam Natasha Evans, I am the leader of colony five."

"Greetings from the crew of the Renegade, my name is Alex Stevenson. We have come in search of survivors, from your mother satellite of Lorela. We offer you aid should you need it and peace to all. Will you receive us?" Alex replied, aware of what to say and the proper protocol.

The leader of colony five gave nothing away, her face a perfect mask of calm serenity. Alex found himself watching her carefully, there was no sign of movement, not a twist of the wrist or a twitch of the corner of her mouth, there was no tell as to what the woman may or may not be thinking.

I would hate to play you at poker, he thought.

She looked at him and smiled as if she knew what he was thinking. She would have to be a powerful psychic to read his mind from this far away, whether she could see him or not.

"And who might you be?" she asked, directing her attentions towards Memphis. "By the seat you occupy, I assume you're the leader of the Renegade's contingent."

"I am and my name is Memphis Grimm, I am the alpha male of Pack Grimm and overlord of the planet Lorela."

"You look dangerous, sir. No offence meant."

"None taken; to one of my species, that is a compliment."

The door to the bridge opened, Sandy entered the bridge. She wore her full plate armour, which shone as if polished to perfection right before she had put it on, not moments before she had entered the bridge. The only piece of armour she didn't have on at that moment was the helmet, and you could clearly tell she was the feminine of the species, despite her deadly appearance.

"Twice dangerous and doubly so," Miriam said, astonished at the sight of the bitch packing the heat.

Sandy joined the others and turned to look at the human on the screen, whose corners of her mouth turned up in what passed as a smile for the Grimm.

A brief silence descended as Miriam and those aboard the Renegade considered each other; neither spoke and although it only lasted for a few seconds, it was uncomfortable and not a good start to diplomatic relations.

"Tell me, where do the Grimm come from? What part of the galaxy? If indeed you came from the Milky Way at all!"

"Why don't we save the small talk for when we meet face to face?" Memphis said.

I wonder what's on the menu? Miriam thought, thinking of her own people.

"I'm sure something can be arranged, maybe a small delegation can be received."

Miriam read the minds of those she looked at over the airwaves; she could do this from any distance without the use of the body of light or the need for proximity. This was a skill she'd stumbled upon centuries ago, as the ten colonies of this habited planet had politicked back and forth over one minor detail or another. Unique among psychics as far as she knew, besides one other, and one that had arrived just over a thousand years before, when gamma radiation had coursed through the galaxy and affected her body. She'd taken the Forever pill as the devastation had approached and she had been in a state of induced coma and woken up to the end of civilisation. It was still some years after that event, when the ten colonies had argued and fought over scant resources, when she'd stumbled over the skill completely by accident. It had been as much a shock to her as it had to everyone else she had informed about her unexpected talent.

Miriam found no malice among the Grimm. She did, however, after just a brief pass over the mind of Memphis find that he was a cannibal. This fact didn't bother her too much until she saw that the Grimm were human, changed as she'd been changed as doubtless countless others across the cosmos had been altered.

Another communication flashed on her panel, it was colony one attempting to make contact. Colony six was next, then colony ten.

Ten. The worst of a bad bunch, she thought.

"Crew of the Renegade, you will be contacted shortly as to the details of your visit." Miriam terminated the conference.

She turned her attention to the others who tried to talk to her, now other colonies attempted a holographic-conference.

Miriam looked at members of her HQ staff, they all looked at her and awaited her next command. Before and below her was a round ten-foot structure built a foot from the floor, it was a detailed map of the moon's surface in miniature. It included all ten colonies and all the geology on its three-dimensional surface. The nine other colonies all varied in shades of greys, with her own colony white, colony ten and its territory the colour of pitch. The shade indicated the friendliness of the colony in question with most tending towards a lighter and friendlier shade of grey.

"Patch them through!" she ordered.

"Even ten?" a crew member asked incredulously.

"Even colony ten!"

Moments later, the flashing on her screen ended, it was replaced by the quarter life-sized images of nine people. They looked at each other and at Miriam, sized each other up and all waited for others to start the debate.

"Why did you not contact us before you contacted the battle cruiser?" Alphie Mataraci, leader of colony three, said.

Mataraci kept his voice flat, his neutrality over the last few hundred years was legendary among the people of Artemesia, his voice had brokered many a peace treaty during his time in office.

The small holographic images all voiced their agreement, with a general confusion of mixed raised calls for justice. Miriam considered turning the voices off so that she could understand what everyone was saying and filter out the mundane and the ridiculous. In preparation for this, nine of her well-rehearsed staff plugged headsets into their consoles. It wouldn't be the first time that this protocol had been implemented so that they could make sense of an ongoing conference, and she thought it unlikely to be the last.

As it was, the leader of colony one, Lenox Lawrence Cunningham, and Miriam's favourite came to her aid. "I think cool heads and a calm discussion would be apt at this time, until a time when all the information can be collated," he said, holding up his hand for order.

"I couldn't agree more!" Mauro Gethin Erebus, the leader of colony ten spoke and although his voice was hushed and quiet, the entire room became deadly silent. Even the images of the other colony leaders turned to stare; they awaited him to continue, some leaning forward as if they might miss what his oily voice would sound out next.

Mauro was a secretive man and normally, these meetings took place either without the tenth colony taking part or with one of colony ten's other notable dignitaries. Even the holographic image of the man gave nothing away, shrouded in shadow, his face covered by the hood of his full-length cloak.

His bottom jaw was barely visible as he turned to a light source within his own realm, the man smiled and a thin line that was his lips seemed to crack with the unfamiliar expression. There was no humour behind it, just the malice of one that meant to crush every pretty flower beneath his boot, just for the fun of it.

"I say you hand over all correspondence to the assembly, we all want to know what you and your new friend's intentions are. What vile scheme you have concocted."

"I can assure you, we have no ill will towards any of our nine counterparts, we have had only one short contact of greetings with the Renegade, the battle cruiser that until recently we'd no idea existed." Miriam hoped that this would do the trick.

She was of course being sincere and honest, and to show them the footage would do little but confirm this to the assembly, to no detriment to herself other than to lose face.

"So, can we see the footage?" Alphie asked, his hologram wavering as he nearly lost the connection.

"Absolutely not!" Miriam said, unable to bring herself to concede anything to Mauro.

Mauro's image somehow darkened on its own, if that was possible. Miriam rejected her own impulse to read the man's mind. She had, once many years ago, done exactly that and she'd recoiled at the time and ever since shied away from the urge to read his mind. The only thing she'd seen that fateful day was the image of a sea of maggots writhing on the rank swell of rotting waves, the only landmass that of giant rotting flesh of some undistinguishable dead thing. Even now, hundreds of years after, she saw the image every now and again when she closed her eyes and entered her dream state, something she usually remained in complete control of.

"You are a witch and have proven yourself in collusion with the Renegade. They shall never land here, not and leave, the same as you shall never leave."

With that, Mauro's image disappeared.

None of the other images spoke, a few looked at where Mauro's image had stood moments before as if they dared not speak until they were sure he wouldn't return.

Miriam's fear returned; she closed her eyes in an attempt to collect herself before the debate continued in earnest. She found she could not open them, as if trapped within her own mind. An image of herself came to her, she was standing covered in blood and decaying. Maggots crawled all over her, in and out of her bloody flesh, her head turned to a skull and maggots raining down from within its darkened interior. Her flesh began to swell and burst open, maggots crawled from every cut and sore. An army of flies swarmed about her, bit and carried away tiny particles of who she was. She somehow knew she was losing her soul, her own vitality and being consigned to oblivion, to a nonexistence beyond life. She struggled to open her eyes or even move, as if sleep paralysis took her and held her down. She tried to scream but could not, her mind carried this way and that on the tide of dead matter as she fed the swell from the maggots that issued from herself.

This evil omen, if indeed it was a warning, she was certain came from within, without any outside influence. Miriam knew without knowing that Mauro Gethin Erebus wanted to eat her soul.

She'd always known he was different; if he was human, he was something twisted and evil.

With a snap, she opened her eyes, she'd been gone for an indefinite period and it could have been seconds or hours for all she knew. Two facts she'd gleaned from her induced astral journey: what she was seeing had been the place where Mauro came from and secondly, he wished to feed off her vitality. She doubted the man knew what she'd discovered but she also knew that no human would ever be able to defeat him, such was the fear that he instilled in the hearts of any living thing.

She fell to her knees and screamed aloud, all those assembled turned to look at her. Her entire experience had occurred in just the blink of an eye, such was the difference in the way time ran in some of the realms beyond real space.

The eight remaining colony leaders waited for her to speak.

"Colony ten is mobilising," one of her staff shouted.

"We have movement, mobile units on the surface," another said, unnecessarily loud, the panic clear in her voice.

"He feeds off our fear! He dines on vitality," Miriam said, her voice weak with despair.

The other images blinked out, she'd wanted to avoid a war, she hated the bloodshed as she felt the pain and suffering from afar, another power that the gamma radiation had given her. This, however, she considered a curse and not a gift, there was an ugly side to the flower of her mind, a flip side to every coin, a darkness cast by the brightness of the light.

Chapter 32

Memphis, Sandy and Elle Grimm stood with Alex Stevenson, discussing what they would say to those on Artemesia to gain their capitulation without the need for bloodshed. Others of the Grimm came and went; for the most part, they sought information to quell the boredom of inactivity. Koda and Kenzi Grimm stood with them, about to join in the conversation when a crew member interrupted.

"There is movement on the surface," he said without taking his eyes from his console.

"On screen," Memphis said as all the dog warriors on the bridge swung their heads around to look at the moon's image.

On the surface, several convoys of what appeared to be military vehicles set out from one of the colonies. They were black in colour, which did nothing to camouflage them against the sandy-coloured ground they stalked across.

Smaller big-wheeled vehicles sped ahead of larger, more cumbersome, tracked machines on a mission they all presumed to be a reconnaissance venture.

Demon walked onto the bridge, he'd taken the Forever pill as all the Grimm had. He was an impressive sight, as large as Memphis but sporting a suit of full chrome-coloured plate armour, made for him by the humans on Lorela before the Renegade left orbit on its mission of conquest and liberation.

"Action at last," he growled as he watched the image that played out as he came to stand beside Memphis.

It seemed to take an age for the vehicles to race across the surface, they ordered food from crew members that acted as servants for the Grimm, the replicated food was soon delivered and they all began to eat.

Drinks were brought but the essential bridge crew stopped working and turned to watch the screens, wherever they were stationed on board the ship.

Memphis smiled; at last the faster surface vehicles had neared their objective. Missiles arced into the void, fired from hidden batteries that resembled rocky outcrops, these batteries already pointed towards the aggressor as if by design. The missiles snaked towards their targets, some missed, and this caused damage to the terrain that caused plumes of dust and rock particles to reach out towards the weightlessness of the void. Artemesia had no atmosphere and the debris blasted from the surface would have reached high above the moon's surface, if not for the increased gravitational pull caused by the planet's spin.

Some of the missiles hit their mark, many of the faster all-terrain vehicles were blasted sideways, sent spiralling forty, fifty metres, skimming the surface. Others were blasted clear off the ground, sent cartwheeling upwards or backwards, they seemed to take an age to settle before they came to rest. A few made it through the initial barrage, only to come under fire by gun emplacements when they'd driven beneath the range of the missiles. For the most part, the weapon's fire from the gun turrets was mostly ineffective, although a few of the aggressor's vehicles were stopped, either damaged by the continuous weapon fire or crew members blown to pieces by high calibre rounds.

Some of the crew cheered every time the attackers suffered a loss, some scorned the loss. To most of the crew of the Renegade, it was just a game played out for their entertainment after all the weeks of boredom. They became excited, anything was better than watching the blackness of deep space.

A few of the vehicles reached the colony they'd pitted themselves against, Demon howled with glee as they exploded against the thick clear material that domed the settlement airtight.

Memphis said nothing; he didn't even look at Demon as he allowed him his enjoyment. After all, it wouldn't matter one way or the other. The fast vehicles didn't slow down, they sped up as they finally reached their objective. Each of them exploded in a shower of debris, kicked up at the base of the dome, it consisted of bits of shrapnel, pulverised rock and sand-coloured dust of the moon's surface. The dome held.

A universal mayday call hit the airwaves, it may or may not have been meant for them. Alex Stevenson thought it more than likely, as they were the only warship close that Artemesia had experienced in a thousand years.

This communication flashed in the top left-hand corner of the screen, it read 'Colony Seven'.

A second colony attempted to get through to them, 'Colony One' began to flash beneath it, so first one then the other appeared, as if they pulsed to a rhythm.

Colony five was next, Miriam Natasha Evans' colony. It was the third in the queue.

The smaller outer dome that came under attack was part of the cluster of domes that made up colony seven; it was unfortunate to be the closest neighbour of colony ten. The structure that'd been hit appeared to maintain its structural integrity.

"Zoom in," Memphis said, his eyes narrowed as he contemplated a thought, "on the point of attack on the dome."

As the scanners pinpointed the exact spot and made the image almost life-size, cracks appeared, hairline fractures, twenty feet up to where the dome began to arch over the community.

"Pan out again."

As the vision increased in size, two things came into view. One of the arched tunnels that connected the domes together was separated by safety doors, which began to close, flashing red lights surrounded the doorframes whose regular pulse lit up the surrounding area. Those who watched could imagine the unheard sirens that would have been sounding. People rushed for the tunnel's entrance in blind panic, creating a bottleneck and the inevitable crush. The large door would be a perfect fit, when it finally closed, to make the gap airtight. Even as it closed, citizens clambered through the gap, several limbs were trapped and severed, the flesh giving way to the unforgiving solid metal door. Others used their fists to pound on the door in a futile attempt to gain access to safety.

Secondly, the larger vehicles, which moved at a slower velocity, had reached their first objective. Several of these sported massive barrels fixed to a large tank superstructure, so large that a counterweight was attached to the rear so that the whole vehicle didn't topple forward. Others looked more like the traditional tank with their barrels attached to the turret via the gun mantle, these were half the size and possessed a better manoeuvrability.

The smaller tanks changed position, forming a protective perimeter around the larger fixed gunned monsters, while they turned to face the cracked dome.

"Colony seven, audio only," Alex ordered.

Everyone held their breath, even those who ran the ship now turned to look at the screen, seemingly mesmerised by the battle that'd begun on Artemesia's surface beneath them. It took them several seconds to respond to the command.

"Please help us, if you are on a mission of peace, you must target colony ten with everything you have. Mercy, oh God, give us mercy!"

"Colony one," Memphis growled.

"Ambushed, tunnels. All is lost, help us, they have infiltrated colony one's central dome, our capita is lost. Domed—" The message ended abruptly.

As the second message ended, the large guns opened fire at the cracked outer dome of colony seven, the explosion was catastrophic. The dome was breached, the ensuing fireball spread out across the dome's ceiling, the flames fed by the oxygen. The oxygen that they breathed served as an extra nemesis for those trapped within the dome, some unfortunate citizens were caught up in the flames, set ablaze and left to flail about helpless and wishing for death.

Military vehicles began to issue forth from most of the other colonies; they all headed to the aid of colony seven that had come under fire. Man-sized figures appeared from nowhere, wearing airtight suits fixed to exoskeletal frameworks. They leapt from the convoy of vehicles from colony ten and bounded thirty to forty feet in a single jump, it wouldn't take many leaps before they had entered the broken dome and begun their attack.

"I want to talk to Miriam!" Memphis rubbed the short fur of his chin, as if in deep thought.

"Are we going to help them?" Elle asked.

The bridge screen changed away from the battle, it showed colony five's headquarters and Miriam Natasha Evans as she paced back and forth.

"You're on, Commander," a male voice said.

Miriam turned to look at the screen. "Crew of the Renegade, your arrival in our space has sparked a war. Don't worry, I'm not blaming you, it's been brewing for a while, it was only a matter of time for this cooking pot to simmer and boil over," she paused, then continued when nobody added to her comments thus far, "Mauro has been itching for this for more than a century."

"But why now?" Memphis interrupted.

"Yes, why wait until this moment?" Sandy added. "Surely it would have been better for the maniac to attack before we arrived."

"I can only guess that he hadn't the strength to attack until now, even now I doubt he has the strength to take all the colonies on."

"And you think our arrival has prompted his action?" Alex added.

"Yes!" Miriam replied. "I wouldn't say he fears you exactly, I doubt the man is capable of emotion. But if he can destroy enough of his enemies on Artemesia, the other colonies may side with him, only then could he command from a position of power."

"And hold all the cards in a game of diplomacy!" Alex said.

"Will you not help us?" Miriam implored, her arms outstretched as a supplicant, not quite the beggar. "Will you not end this vile attack? A few warning shots from the

Renegade should send his troops scuttling back to their holes."

"And why should I help you? What's in it for the Grimm?" Memphis barked, he sounded more than a little menacing.

It wasn't that Memphis didn't want to help the good people of Artemesia; far from it, he dearly wanted to fire upon the attackers, and not just warning shots. He wanted nothing more than to fire upon the ground troops from colony ten until nothing was left, to pound them into oblivion, which would be more than enough to get the message across. He also wished to dine on their leader, Mauro Gethin Erebus, his flesh would make a fine meal. The one thing that held him back was the Renegade's AI. What if it refused to shoot at the humans it'd sworn to protect? Even if it agreed in some part, maybe a warning shot between the opposing factions would end hostilities. The AI may refuse just for the sake of it, with its poor attempt to make a jest or even just to annoy him.

"How could you not help us? Unless you are as evil as Mauro!"

She didn't say it out loud but as Miriam terminated the video conference, every member of the Renegade on the bridge felt that the spiritual leader of Artemesia meant that maybe they were in league with colony ten. Memphis and Alex looked at each other; they didn't need to be psychic to know what the other was thinking.

"Colony ten—shall we respond?" a crew member said from her console, she turned to look at Memphis and Alex before they all turned to look at the bridge screen, where the request from the rogue colony for communication flashed and seemed to wait patiently for a response.

The request for a video conference was completely unexpected and caught everyone by surprise.

"Patch them through," Memphis growled, glad of the chance to speak to the villain of Artemesia. "Video and audio link."

The screen changed to a view of the planet's ongoing battle around the cracked and broken dome, the dome's atmospheric generation unit working overtime. It pumped breathable air into the dome, but as fast as it could produce the life-giving gases, more escaped through the gap into the void. The escaping gases carried debris out of the gap; people froze as soon as they hit the coldness of space. Laser fire and explosions lit up the interior of the dome, like a giant round erratic strobe, those inside seemed to dance to a deadly tune of death and blood.

The screen changed to show a cloaked figure, he sat on a throne, barely seen in the darkness. His face was shrouded under the hood of his clothing and appeared to smile as the video link was connected.

"Crew of the Renegade, I presume." The voice sounded oily, it was high in pitch but smooth and grated on the sensitive hearing of the Grimm, like a bag of tacks drawn slowly over a sheet of glass.

"I am Memphis Grimm, pack leader and alpha male of Lorela," Memphis answered, ignoring his senses with barely a wince.

"My name is Mauro Gethin Erebus, soon to be Emperor of Artemesia."

"Why have you contacted us?"

"I wish to know of your intentions! You appear in our orbit, without a by-your-leave and chat to my enemies. The least I should expect from you is a declaration of war, or terms of some kind, maybe even friendship, an alliance or some such."

"We are merely on an exploratory mission of our immediate space when we happened upon your colonies. We didn't believe for one minute that there may have been survivors here," Alex said, anger behind his words. "You—"

Memphis waved him off; if Mauro's eyes flicked from Alex to Memphis, there was no indication of it.

"Draw back, call off your attack and we will talk."

"The bitch becomes the beggar!" Mauro spat. "You shall either bend to my will or vacate my presence, never to come here again." The face beneath the hood smiled, moving the fabric slightly and the tone appeared to become friendlier as he continued, "Unless, unless you bring me something, a gift of sorts to whet my appetite."

"Pray tell, what do you require from us for you to end the killing?" Alex asked.

"Tribute!" Mauro stood; he didn't use his legs or his arms. In one fluid motion, he rose as if defying gravity. His voice became angry, his arms outstretched as if he could throw something at them from afar.

The human crew members of the Renegade grabbed at the features of their faces, their minds infected by visions of the things they feared the most. Right before their eyes, no matter which way they looked, their entire vision was filled by ghastly and fearful thoughts.

Memphis looked at Alex, Alex was on the floor and squirming, he cried out with pure fear in his heart. Memphis reached down and punched him, hard enough to send the delicate man sliding across the floor to hit the wall of the bridge near the door, and the man was out cold.

"Knock them out, all of them, before they hurt themselves," Memphis barked.

Before the Grimm could move, Mauro began to laugh, he hadn't counted on the Grimm fearing nothing and he didn't know that there was no greater dishonour for a dog warrior than to fear something, anything. His laugh became a cackle, he loved this game that he played now, and soon the crew of the Renegade would beg for mercy and give over the ship for their agony to end. He stretched his arms out as high as they would go, his feet left the floor and he hung there a clear foot from his dais. His fingers splayed out and the hood fell back to reveal his face.

Memphis watched the screen, the Grimm all over the ship attempted to restrain or incapacitate the humans that attempted self-harm. Memphis was the first outside of the colonies to see Mauro's face in all the long years since the devastation. He was surprised at what he saw, he'd expected a monster; instead, what faced him was a young man's face. It was a face of pure beauty, flawless complexion and gleaming white teeth. Even in anger, the face was fit for an angel.

The Grimm on the bridge struggled to rush around the human bridge crew, Memphis tried to look to them but found he couldn't take his eyes from Mauro. It was as if he was pinned somehow, he couldn't even blink as Mauro seemed to bore into his soul.

Sandy reached the last of the bridge crew but she was too late, he held his own eyes in his hands, he'd pulled them out to rid himself of his own personal hell.

Sandy Grimm, like all the other Grimm around the ship, felt a compulsion, she turned to the screen. The Grimm weren't usually given over to whimsical curiosities but she, like all the others, felt they'd no choice.

She felt the other's thought inside her head, a seed of emotion, an evil doing that went against every sinew of her being. Fear. She howled aloud as her eyes widened at the insult, Memphis joined her as did all the Grimm from around the ship. Above the sounds and screams of the human crew, the corridors echoed to the sounds of the beast.

Mauro severed the link; soon this new enemy, this dog, would kneel at his command. He looked to the woman that one of his people dragged before him.

"One of the prisoners from colony one, my lord," one of his guards said.

All of Mauro's people, both soldier and personnel alike, presented blank in their presentation. Emotionless husks that gave off a smell; if darkness had a smell, it would have smelt this way—an aroma of pure evil. Their near-death look, ashen complexion and sunken cheeks did nothing to ease the woman's fear.

The captive squirmed away from them. That was until Mauro's attention focussed on her; now she backed into the guards, she wet herself as she was hauled up and dumped at his feet. He considered her, smiled and sat down, waved a hand unnecessarily as he rested the other on the arm of his gaudy, chrome-coloured throne.

"I like these beasts, I like the shiny armour they wear, it matches my seat," he said.

The woman's face was on the floor now, she whimpered in abject terror.

"No, you don't think so? Ah well, it's a good thing your opinion doesn't amount to much here!" Mauro said and smiled as he considered the woman.

She was of middle age but wore the ageless face of one that'd lived many lifetimes. No doubt she feared her sins more than death itself. With a flick of his wrist, the woman rose in the air; without standing, he motioned with both hands as if he was tearing at her clothes.

The woman tried to hold her shirt together but the invisible force that tore at it was far too strong and relentless. Next were her trousers, they were made of the finest silk and gave easily. Now only her underwear remained.

The woman covered her breasts with her left arm and hand, her right held the front of her knickers. Mauro laughed menacingly and motioned with a finger, the underwear moved slowly. No matter how hard she gripped them, they slid down until they fell to the floor of the dais beneath her. She was still suspended and now hugged herself in the foetal position, she floated, fearful, terrorised.

There was no real need for the subject to be stripped, the only reason Mauro did this was because his victims didn't like it. One limb at a time Mauro forced outwards, he could smell the life force of this being, the more she feared, more he felt it. Any extreme of emotion would bring the vitality to the surface.

When she was spread-eagled before him, he considered her; he'd made them laugh in the past, encouraged the victim to come back for more, like an addict at his feet they would pester him to feed upon them. He'd used sexual arousal, which he did enjoy, but then again, they would come back for more until they'd been fucked to death, an annoyance he could do without. He opened his mind and connected to hers, he drew on her vitality, feeding himself as he projected a vision of hatred and fear. He sought her mind for what she loved the most, found her family, she hadn't seen them in the flesh for more than a thousand years and didn't even know if they still breathed and walked this existence. Yet still her love persisted, she'd a husband and two sons. Now she could see them, her mind transcended to a non-existent visual construct, a place within herself. She screamed at them as they sat laughing in the family home, back on Earth, she wanted them to run away. Bury themselves deep underground as she had. The sirens sounded next.

"What is that?" her husband questioned.

"It's the sirens, father," her eldest son answered. "There must be an emergency or somewhat!"

Before he'd time to answer, the windows blew inwards, they were covered in glass, the force of the winds impossibly strong, even at the highest altitude with the tower's force-field generator inoperative, the winds wouldn't have been so powerful. The air was sucked right out of the room even as the wind slammed all three of her family to the far wall. They remained pinned as fire seemed to rain down from the sky above, they all boiled as they sucked in, trying to breath, their lungs seeking the life-giving oxygen. They had a front seat to the end of the world; a rain of meteors fell with the wind. The tower lurched violently and the motion in their stomach indicated that they were falling. The man shut his eyes; she could feel them tight as she held her own tight in the mundane hope she wouldn't have to feel him die.

Mauro stood a foot away from her, he could see her life force, her vitality, as multi-coloured blurred lines that coalesced and changed hue as they merged.

The stuff issued from her chakras, he soaked it up and sounded like an ill-mannered child at the dinner table, lapping at his food and smacking his lips no matter who he annoyed.

When he'd had his fill, he let her go and she dropped to the dais. Her beauty gone, her vitality replaced by something altogether much older. She lifted her hand, which was a traumatic experience, not only was it an effort physically but the sight of her ancient wrinkled calloused flesh was just heart-breaking. She caught sight of her face, a reflection in the chrome throne; she didn't recognise the blotchy, wrinkled old woman that looked back at her. She rested her head on the dais, too weak to raise her head back down.

"Please, please…finish me!" she managed, a shallow wheeze, barely audible.

"When I eat the fruit, I leave the root," Mauro said with a happy smile and stepped over her to let her die slowly.

Chapter 33

Memphis still felt the fear, or rather the feeling that something had tried to infect him with the shame of it. All the Grimm couldn't fit on the bridge, but they did fill it and the corridor beyond the door. Even though the thought from Mauro's scare tactic had lasted a mere few seconds, those Grimm affected by it would feel the shame of it forever or until the source was no more, eradicated to save their honour.

Mauro hadn't known how the Grimm would be tainted by fear; they'd evolved to react totally the opposite of the normal human response. They attacked where possible anything that caused the emotion and thus now barked and howled their displeasure.

The human crew that hadn't been knocked senseless by the Grimm struggled against their bonds after they'd been incapacitated, they screamed and writhed in their attempt to get free. Alex woke and rushed at the wall, he'd smashed his head against it to be rid of the mental imagery that was driving him crazy. Now he lay upon the floor, hogtied by both Sandy and Elle so that he couldn't harm himself further.

"How I need this!" Koda barked.

"I must go!" Demon howled.

"Some must remain to keep this ship under our control," Memphis barked, partly to be heard and partly out of anger.

A full quarter of the Grimm contingent aboard the Renegade hadn't been affected by the fear, they had either been napping or had been nowhere near a screen to watch and be affected.

"We are fearless, we are the Grimm, we are at the top of the food chain," Memphis howled.

Everyone ignored the bridge screen, being far too preoccupied to bother looking. The attackers from colony ten had repelled all their enemies, other domes had come under the scrutiny of the long-range cannons, and to all those that'd bothered to watch, it seemed that colony ten would soon control the surface. Already colony seven had gone dark, its power source cut off, none of the tell-tale flashes from weapon fire evident, the battle for that cluster of domes already decided.

The screen turned black and one at a time, the Grimm turned to look.

'MEASURES MUST BE TAKEN TO SECURE THE SAFETY OF THOSE ON ARTEMESIA,' the AI had at last joined in the debate.

"Then help us," Elle said, anger evident as she growled at inhuman intellect.

'I NEED THE CREW TO OPERATE CERTAIN SYSTEMS, WITHOUT THEM OR A VIABLE CAPTAIN WITH A DNA MATCH, I AM LIMITED.'

"What can you do?"

'I CAN FLY THE SHUTTLES.'

Memphis led them; they rushed down the corridor to the travellators. When there, they had an anxious wait as they queued momentarily for a ride to the dock.

It seemed like an age in their enraged state of mind, it'd only been minutes and seventy dog warriors howled and barked at the three shuttles to lower the ramps so that they could fly to the surface and engage what had enraged them.

Memphis left thirty of the Grimm to secure the Renegade, Kito was left in charge. He, like all those left behind, although not directly affected, wished to help with the assault on the colonies—such was the fearlessness of the dog subspecies.

The ramps to the shuttles were lowered and all three of them in unison, in a rush, the Grimm boarded and found their seats before the ramps touched the floor of the dock.

One after the other, the shuttles lifted from the dock's surface. Memphis held up the crown of the Renegade, the AI's home, it would serve as an insurance policy. Another reason he'd left some of the Grimm behind. He tucked the priceless metal object inside his breast plate, between the padding and the metal.

That should keep you sweet, what with the Grimm I have left to guard against treachery, Memphis thought.

He made his way to the cockpit of the shuttle, it was a bit of a squeeze but with some pushing and shoving, he found a position that was almost comfortable.

He looked at the surface through the cockpit window; it looked smaller at this distance than what he'd seen on the bridge screen. The clusters of domes were clear enough, however, and the battle that had taken place. Back and forth missiles snaked through the zero-g, laser fire and small arms left an imprint on his retina, the tracers bright enough, even from this distance. The AI was the perfect pilot, it dropped them nose down, the rest of the Grimm watched the screens inside the passenger compartment and all of them, even though they enjoyed the sensation in their gut the suicidal drop gave them, still couldn't shy away from the anger in their hearts.

The battle continued unabated as they neared the surface, the AI levelled out the shuttles at the optimum moment and they almost skimmed the surface. Particles of debris caused little flashes on the shuttles' shields; Memphis ignored them as he watched some of colony ten's warriors turn their weapons at them. They fired but couldn't penetrate the shuttles' shields. Memphis knew the shuttles were armed, having weaponry of its own, but by the time he'd considered them, those that had shot at him were far behind and out of range. Besides, he'd not a clue how to operate them.

They approached a cluster of domes where there was no apparent conflict. Memphis became completely disorientated, he hadn't a clue which of the colonies it was, or whether they were friend or foe.

"Ah well, the sooner we're at it, the better!" he said to no one in particular, as a blast rocked the shuttle, its shield lighting up to dazzle him and causing him to cover his eyes against the blinding flash.

They banked hard right and saw an opening in the rear of one of the smaller domes, farthest away from the fighting. The three shuttles slowed down and passed through a force field, designed to hold in the breathable air. It wasn't a defensible energy field so the shuttles passed right through without any adverse effect, although the two force fields did interact with each other, like two bubbles fused to become one.

As the shuttle came in to land, its legs extended to cushion the touchdown, Memphis got himself out of his awkward position and forced his bulk through to the passenger compartment. He felt the motion of the shuttle as it turned one hundred and eighty degrees so that its nose faced its exit.

Memphis stood at the ramp, Koda, Harmony, Elle, Chaos, Sandy and Demon surrounded him, others were behind them and they waited for the ramp to lower. Half of them wore the Grimm dog warrior armour; it was an interesting alloy, a steel and chrome mix with a small amount of adamantium to give it strength, buffed to a high polish. It would turn aside any laser weaponry and most small arms' fire, its only downfall was plasma, which would envelope the wearer and would sit inside the suit, burn like pitch and set ablaze any that hid behind its solid defensive metal.

Memphis, on conquering the underworld of Lorela, had ordered the humans to make every one of the Grimm a suit of the shiny armour. In their hurry to reach the surface and rid their mind of the offensive notion, Memphis—like half of those that reached the surface—hadn't donned their full suit of armour; some wore only a breastplate, or greaves and gauntlets, with here and there a helmet, the visor pulled down over jutted jaw.

The shuttle bay door dropped before it lowered two feet, the heads and shoulders of humans dressed in identical beige uniforms came into view. Their helmets were white and sported a tinted visor that covered most of their faces so that only the mouth and chin were visible.

A few of the colonials' jaws dropped as the Grimm came into their line of sight and more than a few hands shook, even though the grip on their weapons increased. Both male and female humans made some sort of defensive line, some of the humans of this colony ran about behind the line of troops. One of these humans dropped a small ammo box, it clattered on the floor, made more than a few of the humans jump and left Memphis happy that no one fired at them as the ramp touched down on the solid surface of the dock floor.

"Which colony?" Memphis said in his friendliest tone, thinking it prudent that someone should speak before somebody died.

"Colony five," a young man's quivering voice said at last.

"Allies, good, good!" Memphis said.

He strolled out onto the dock and looked around him, there was barely enough room to house all three shuttles but it would suffice. All seventy of the Grimm idled, they seemed to ignore the fact that a line of frightened and terrified humans held at least a hundred weapons pointed directly at them. As Memphis stared down the barrels of several menacing weapons, all capable of taking his life, he stepped out to address the warriors of this settlement.

He spread out his arms in a gesture of friendship. "We come from the Renegade, your Alpha, Miriam Natasha Evans, requested our aid in defeating the leader of colony ten." None spoke so he continued, "A certain Mauro Gethin Erebus, I believe you're familiar with this demon."

"I certainly am and so are all my people," Miriam said as she swept onto the dock. "Stand down, people, these are the Grimm and hopefully our salvation."

"Ah, Miriam, it's a pleasure to make your acquaintance face to face."

"You're certainly more eloquent than you are handsome," Miriam said with a smile.

"Oh, I don't know, I find my reflection quite fetching," he said as he looked at his reflection in the dome of the dock and rubbed his chin as he smiled.

She considered him, the corners of her mouth turning up.

"Beauty is in the eye of the beholder, so they tell me!" Memphis smiled; he enjoyed the exchange of jests with a human that for once didn't fear him on first meeting.

"It most definitely must be."

The humans of the colony looked from one to the other; they couldn't believe that their leader was teasing this beast. He looked like he would tear into her flesh and consume every part of her without a single compassionate thought.

"Move aside," Miriam ordered her people and they moved at her commanding tone.

They visibly relaxed as Miriam and Memphis walked side by side down the glass arched tunnel, which led to another much larger dome.

The rest of the Grimm walked in an unorganised mob, mingling with the colony's security forces. It wasn't long before the entire weird procession made it through the tunnel to a much wider, higher dome, which sported small three-storey buildings.

"These are living quarters for my people; there are several domes like it for each colony."

"Why are you not one nation? You do all live on the same planet!" Memphis asked, remembering his own world and the many different packs of warring dogs that'd once existed on Lorela.

"There has been talk of such a merger over the years, but Mauro always stops it somehow; he either subverts a council member's mind or reverts to threats of invasion."

"We do have councillors on Lorela; it's a human thing, not for us dogs. I'm Alpha on Lorela, both dog and human bow before me!"

"Then you're not much better than Mauro, wanting absolute power!" Miriam said, without a scolding tone in her voice; the last thing she wanted to be was dinner.

They reached a waiting vehicle that hovered a clear foot from the floor. Memphis looked at it, he scratched behind his ear, doubtful it would hold his weight.

"I suppose you could look at it like that, it's a dog thing, I suppose, but easy for one of your intellect to understand," he said, as he carefully lent the seat of the hover car his full weight, very slowly and very carefully. "Look at it like this. If the different packs of dogs had still warred and held sway on Lorela, humans and dogs would be feed; underground on Lorela the wars raged for hundreds of years. My human advisor says it lasted for over two hundred years, much better now that we have obtained absolute peace."

"So, Pack Grimm wasn't the only pack?" Miriam asked as she drove towards the nearest tunnel.

"There were many packs and still a few survive at the fringes of what'd been the dog underworld, the pack land!" Memphis held onto the front of the hover car, he steadied himself, thinking it might topple over at any moment.

"You seem like a clever species, why would you war and eat your own for such a long time?" Miriam asked, puzzled. "What changed?"

"The Forever pill, we took it and it made us so much more of what we were."

They came out of the tunnel and entered a dome that was half a mile high and three miles across.

"It made you almost human, by the sounds of it."

"I would thank you not to insult my kingly self," Memphis said.

Memphis smiled and he knew without looking at Miriam that she too was smiling. His first impressions were that he liked this human, almost as much as he liked Alex, whether it was her friendliness towards him or her lack of fear, or both, he didn't quite know. Maybe he just liked her for no other reason than she was a likeable sort, easy with a jest and kind at heart.

"We'll soon be at our council offices, we can have a lengthy discussion on how to use your troops and a bite to eat," Miriam suggested.

"Processed food, replicated meat?" Memphis asked.

"Of course, you can't expect my people to give an arm and a leg!"

"You know, I want you to tell me one thing! How can I get my claws on Mauro Gethin Erebus?" Memphis now lost his courteous manner and he growled the words as he spoke the man's name.

"May I ask why you wish to attack him? No one has even made his outer structures, not before they all get slaughtered, the fear Mauro projects can disable the noblest of warriors. Is that what happened when he contacted you? I have never known anyone that has withstood his evil projections, let alone wanted to attack him that very same day!" Miriam was shocked for the first time in many a year. She watched him warily as she brought the hover car to a stop at the bottom of a building's steps.

"How did you avoid his psychic attack?" Miriam asked. She stood at the bottom of the steps to the rather large and impressive building made from black stone with a marble effect.

"Psychic attack?" Memphis frowned.

"He made you feel fear! That's what he does."

"A dog does not feel what you say; it feels only the shame of it!"

"He frightened you, didn't he?"

Memphis was about to bark at Miriam as the rest of the Grimm trotted up followed closely by the soldiers in the weird uniforms; without warning, the ground a hundred feet down the road bulged upwards and out, it erupted a few seconds later in a shower of dirt and rock.

"They are using the old tunnels," Miriam said. "It's how they are attacking all the colonies at once. Take cover, men!" she shouted.

The colony's guardsmen took cover behind anything they could: the corners of buildings, parked vehicles or doorways. As the dust settled, men poured from the hole in the ground, they fired as they came on and the Grimm were forced to take cover. The small arms' fire killed a few of the guards and wounded Koda, shot in the shoulder as he tried to protect Harmony from the relentless attack.

Memphis took cover behind the steps with Miriam and two of her guards. He was about to say something when a dozen of the Grimm, fully armoured with clawed weaponised greaves, charged past and into the hail of lead. The bullets bounced harmlessly off the armour and Memphis ducked as the ricochet from the bullets could've provided a cruel fate for anyone daft enough not to make himself as small as possible.

It was hard to tell one Grimm from another when they were fully plated, even for Memphis, although he did recognise Demon, Elle and Sandy.

They reached the enemy without taking any casualties, much to the chagrin of the men that took cover at the end of the tunnel mouth they'd created. One of the armoured Grimm fell backwards, a lucky shot finding its way between the gaps of his armour. Blood poured from the wound and the dog lay motionless, as the rest of the attacking Grimm pressed on into the tunnel.

Memphis turned around at a familiar sound, the sound of the ground heaving, much closer to the Grimm that remained behind cover. Most of these Grimm, like himself, wore only a few pieces of armour. This didn't seem to bother them as they readied for a charge. The ground rose and erupted the same as before, the explosive device large enough to create a large round hole. The Grimm charged the second tunnel's mouth. Memphis was further away but charged all the same. Soldiers from the fifth colony charged with the Grimm, they shot down into the hole indiscriminately as the Grimm dragged the attackers from the tunnel's mouth, kicking and screaming on the end of the Grimm's clawed hands.

One such unfortunate was tossed into the air and he flew, blood spraying from a wound, right into the claws of Memphis, who caught him on the run. The man still held his gun and shot about him wildly, Memphis stuck his wrist with a claw and with ease, he ripped the hand from the forearm. The man looked scared, his face gaunt and ashen, he looked about him wild-eyed as if he'd just woken from a dream, only to find himself in a nightmare.

Memphis cared not, he was the enemy and that was enough for the Grimm, even with their heightened intellect. He bit deep into the throat of the man, with one bite he'd bitten all the way to the spine and with a sickening crack, the man's head came away at the neck. Memphis held up the head like a trophy as the battle for the colonies continued. He looked about him. Miriam was only a short distance away from him, her gown dirtied by flecks of dark, red blood.

She watched Memphis warily. Without turning away from her, he gripped the jaw, ripped the skull in half and offered her the upturned top of the rounded bone, whilst the battle continued unabated around the new hole in the ground.

Miriam could see the brain as it swilled about, she knew that he offered her the brain to eat, a trophy meal if you like; she also knew that to be offered such was a great honour. Even so, she gave an involuntary shake of her head.

"Please yourself," Memphis growled and tipped the contents of the skull into his gaping maw and turned away to find someone else to kill.

Miriam watched this sentient beast, he'd marvelled at her city, she'd seen him look about him with wonderment, and he'd obviously never seen this sort of high-tech environment, one used by the planetary techs before the great ending. On the other hand, he had a battle cruiser, easily amongst the greatest achievements known to man. She'd watched him transform into a wild thing, a beast of pure natural carnage, a killing machine and she feared what she'd invited into the colonies.

The shuttles took off, the AI monitored the stability of the domes. Already one of the colonies was lost and most of the populace within; they'd either been sucked out into the vacuum of space, killed or taken by soldiers from the tenth. By now, every colony was under attack, either by an overland assault or from the underground using the very same tunnel complex that'd saved them almost a thousand years previously. The Grimm never noticed their own shuttles leave, they were too busy fighting for control of the second tunnel. Miriam did realise that the Grimm would rather all perish here than live with the feeling of the fear Mauro had instilled within their brains—she didn't need her psychic abilities to tell her that. She turned from the carnage as the enemy fell back from her unwitting allies, the feared tenth hadn't banked on the Grimm and neither had Mauro; in his egotistic narcissism, he had thought no one could stand against his powers. She smiled as she knelt by the prone armoured Grimm, Miriam removed his helmet gently but there was nothing she could do—the beast was dead.

Memphis jumped down into the tunnel; he didn't wait to see what awaited in ambush. All he saw was the backs of his dog warriors and a few brave soldiers from the fifth colony. It didn't take long to reach them and barge his way to the front. Shots were being fired and the Grimm were forced to hide behind what scant cover was available. The guard that accompanied them fired in earnest, unsure which they should fear—the guards of the tenth or their new allies. Men fell on both sides and two unarmoured dog warriors were forced to withdraw, both suffering bullet wounds, although not fatal, but both would be more of a hindrance than an asset as the battle continued.

Chapter 34

The Grimm, led by Elle, that'd entered the first opening in the ground suddenly slammed into the rear of those who shot at them. Memphis could see the glint of their armour in the darkness beyond his enemies.

"Charge..." he howled.

Memphis led the charge; a few still fired at them but not for long—the Grimm cut them to pieces from both the front and rear. There only remained a dozen by the time the Grimm were in amongst them. The Grimm flayed them alive in their frenzied uncontrolled state, skin from flesh and flesh from bone. The soldiers of the fifth stood rooted and watched as the Grimm feasted.

"These humans taste stale," Harmony complained, her visor pushed back so that she could take bigger bites.

"It's better than the false meat," Tucker Grimm said, formerly of Pack Blood Hound.

"False meat?" one of the soldiers asked, confused, as he dared to step closer.

"Replicated!" Memphis answered as he looked over his shoulder, "and whom may you be?"

"Kenneth James Douglas, captain of the fifth, at your service."

"Very well, Ken, lead the way. And don't worry, I'm right behind you." Memphis tried his friendliest look.

"That's what worries me!"

"Enough of the pleasantries, we have a war to win."

Kenneth led the Grimm down the passage that'd been bored out of the bedrock, the recently worked rock was still red hot. They stood on the curve of the floor, the machine used to make the tunnel had liquefied the rock; it had left thousands of tiny stalactites, still solidifying as the rock hardened. The floor was hot underfoot and this on its own kept the small army moving forward, especially the bare-footed Grimm.

It wasn't long before the discomfort of the tunnel was at an end as they reached a wider arched tunnel that'd been there for more than a thousand of years.

"Colony ten is that way." Captain Douglas pointed out.

No sooner had he spoken than a blast of air headed down the opposite direction to the way Ken pointed. The men fell and began to slide down the tunnel with the air blast, the Grimm grabbed hold of each other and the side of the tunnel; they leaned into the wind and managed to stay on their feet.

It ended as quickly as it had started, the wind gone as if someone had shut it out. The men got up and dusted themselves down, the good captain walked up to Memphis, he looked nervous as he turned to look down the tunnel.

"What was that?" Memphis asked.

"Colony two is that way, it's probably a dome blown outwards, the air sucked out into the nothingness. A blast door would have automatically closed," he said, still looking about him. "This is bad."

As he spoke, a crowd of people came out of the darkness, their torches an indicator that they approached. They were refugees, all dirt-stained and fearful, the Grimm's presence doing nothing to abate their fears.

"We are what's left of colony six!" an older-looking gentleman said, he looked out of place among so many younger-looking ancients.

Memphis had seen aged humans back on Lorela, he knew it was his time to either take the pill or die.

"This way, come, do not fear the beasts, they are on our side," Captain Douglas said.

Captain Douglas led the people back to the surface, it seemed to take an age for them to pass, none had gone unscathed but most moved under their own steam; although a few more seriously wounded were being carried on makeshift stretchers. Sixty-five dog warriors remained to carry on the fight; with just a few casualties and one death, Memphis considered them lucky, considering what they'd faced. He was just thinking about his armour back on the Renegade when Captain Douglas returned, with every soldier of the fifth behind him.

Some thousands passed them by, until at last the rear guard of the refugees met them. What remained of the sixth, their red suits stained with the blood of others as well as their own, stepped, one foot in front of the other, as if each might be the last before death. A fewer than a score of them remained, all of them looking over their shoulders to watch for the pursuit. Their struggle had been arduous and full of anguish, so much so they didn't seem to care that an unknown species of eight-foot beasts loomed over them.

"Who leads you?" Captain Douglas asked.

"I do!" a private said.

"Where are your ranking officers and armies?"

"All gone, hopefully to a better place."

"To a better place beyond," every human said, their voices low and in perfect unison.

"What of Councillor Wilhelm?"

"He was the last one to fall; I will never forget the sight of him. He ran to get the blast doors closed, firing his pistol as his white smock reddened with his own blood. He received so much gunfire, I feel he was more hole than flesh; if not for him, none would have survived."

The others nodded their agreement.

"He was the bravest of us," another said.

"Go get your rest," Captain Douglas said.

He watched them go, turned to his men and motioned them onwards. Memphis fell in beside him and looked down at the top of the man's head.

"Not bad for a human," Memphis said.

"We'll see how long we can go before the fear infests our thoughts," Captain Douglas replied.

"Just get us there, we'll do the rest."

"But what of the psyche, he will turn your thoughts against you!"

"He already has!"

The captain nodded, he looked Memphis up and down, as if the sight of the Grimm was all the answer he needed.

As they trudged down the tunnel complex, they met more refugees and experienced several more gusts of wind that abruptly stopped—same as the first. The captain mumbled something about the end of everything, Memphis stopped listening, the closer he came to his goal, the more he thought about his intentions. Grunts and growls, howls and barks came from the Grimm behind him; they simply refused to react to the fear that'd been instilled in their minds. They picked up stragglers, guardsmen from other colonies that informed them of what was happening on the surface. Memphis was surprised to hear that his shuttles, for hours, had airlifted survivors from all the colonies but the tenth. This news didn't displease him; on the contrary, it was good to see that the AI thought as he did—save as many as they could.

His only apprehension was that the dog warriors would be left planet-side after all the humans, rescued by the AI, had been taken to the safety of the Renegade. Even so, he would rather die atop the corpse of Mauro than live with the shame of his emotions. Not every dog had been like this before the Forever pill, especially the bitches; the frailest of them had always been the first to be cannibalised. After the Forever pill had been taken, the fear response had been one of the attributes that had evolved further and none of the Grimm would stand for it. Memphis knew that this could be one of the things that could be to the detriment of his pack, the Achilles' heel for the Grimm but he did not care, he couldn't help himself, his one thought, *Mauro must die*.

After several hours and many a turn and twist of the main underground highway, Captain Douglas stopped the advance.

"Straight down there, colony ten," he said.

"This as far as you go?" Memphis asked.

"The fear will get us soon enough. It does wear off, the fastest recovery being just over a week! We would be of no use to you, only problematic, to be honest."

"Well, Ken, get back to your colony, defend your people and I speak for all the Grimm when I thank you for getting us this far," Memphis said.

Kenneth took Memphis' proffered hand, which dwarfed his, being twice the size. "No, I think we'll hang around here, most of the tenth will be fighting in the colonies. Some are bound to be on their way back. Besides, you can guarantee that when you start your attack, they will all respond."

"That's why you came, to take the heat from the colonies and your people?" Memphis asked, surprised at this human's possible sacrifice.

"Defend your rear we will."

"And die."

"Yes, and die," Captain Douglas replied. "For the colonies," he shouted to those who had followed him and who mimicked his battle cry.

Memphis moved on, his mind turned once again to his objective, the Grimm followed, their faces set as their pack's name implied. There would be no mercy, no quarter asked for and none given.

After they'd trudged a good half mile down the tunnel, they could hear sporadic gunfire from behind them. With their sensitive hearing, they could hear the feet that ran towards them from the direction of colony ten. The feet stamped in unison and were heavily booted, a good indicator that those that ran towards them were military.

They were still some distance away but coming fast.

"Armour to the rear," Memphis ordered. "Make yourselves visible, the rest of you press yourselves into the wall."

The old tunnel network had no light source, no artificial light to guide the colonists on their way, the tunnels weren't used and this would simply have been a waste of valuable energy.

Now the Grimm used this against them; the old wide tunnels and the humans' inability to see in the dark, as the Grimm could, would leave the tenth at a serious disadvantage.

A minute passed, they slowed their breaths and became as still as they could whereas the armoured Grimm stood in plain view, further down the tunnel.

The ruse worked as the naturally ill-equipped humans looked at the enemy they could see. The torchlight shone on the chrome-coloured armour, the bullets fired down the tunnel, the shouts and war cries from both sides also went along a way to distract from the hidden Grimm, pressed motionless into the side of the tunnel.

Memphis turned his head so that his snout wouldn't stick out and give away his position. All the hidden Grimm looked back towards their armoured pack mates, better that than have their positions given away by the whites of their eyes.

The armoured Grimm dropped back, under the pretence that the gunfire was just too much to contend with. The bullets caused a few injuries, finding gaps in the chinks of the metal, sparks flew and gave an impressive light show. All helped with the ruse, the soldiers of the tenth colony thought they were winning.

Memphis lost count at about fifty but he approximated that more than two hundred of the humans occupied the tunnel where he and around thirty of the Grimm waited to spring their trap, having removed what little armour they'd worn so that the glint wouldn't give them away. The odds were a little uneven.

You should have brought more, Memphis thought.

He swung his head around and one of the soldiers turned to look, only just aware of the movement in the dark. At this unplanned signal, the armoured Grimm charged up the tunnel towards the tenth. Memphis would remember the youth as long as he lived, his blank expression had held no fear of him, no contempt whatsoever for the beast that had hoodwinked him. He didn't even look as if he had readied himself for the next part of his spiritual journey, it was as if all his emotions were non-existent, having been drained away.

Mauro Gethin Erebus, Memphis thought.

Chaos erupted along the length of the tunnel; Grimm from both sides of the tunnel fell among those intent on the death of everything. Memphis skewered the youth; his eyes held more years of experience than his gaunt but youthful body should have. He held him up, his clawed hand lifting him clean from the tunnel's floor; Memphis could feel his diaphragm flex as he gripped the man's floating rib. Memphis raised his left leg and kicked the right side of the man's chest. The man hit the opposite wall of the tunnel; the youth was dead before he hit the floor. Memphis held the man's diaphragm and half of his ribcage, he let it drop and turned just in time to spit another with two fingers, he left the man blind as he found his mark and both eyeballs burst, covering his hands with thick dark blood. The man held an impressively large blade, he swung it left and right as if he could still win the single combat.

Memphis had other ideas; he reached out with his other hand and drew his index finger across the man's throat. He gagged and Memphis released him so he could die at his feet. Bullets filled the air, giving the tunnel a strobe effect, affecting the vision of both sides.

Memphis saw hundreds of the humans torn limb from limb, but the wild gunfire caused injury and death among the Grimm. For a fleeting moment, Memphis wondered if it was all worth it, but only for the briefest of times.

"Revenge," he barked, as he ran at the last group of soldiers, they'd exhausted their ammo and were now trying to reload with unshaking hands, devoid of emotion. They'd been the rear guard, the Grimm were among them a split second before they raised and fired, they were overcome, many a clawed fist reaching out to rend flesh and tear muscle from bone.

The dogs' breaths had become laboured and they spent a good half minute recovering at the end of the combat.

"Forward, you mangy dogs, you dog bastards. Kill, kill, kill..." Memphis howled at last, encouraging the Grimm onwards, without knowing that they were under psionic attack.

They charged down the tunnel, Memphis left his dead and wounded behind, he thought it prudent to grasp any possible advantage gained. As it was, they emerged from the tunnel and faced no foe; thousands of the listless populace watched them. They appeared void of emotion, incapable of feelings, some of them lay on the ground, their bodies completely emaciated, looking as if they would die of malnutrition at any moment.

Memphis felt for them, he wanted to help them, another mind-fuck from his target. Still, the feeling of his shame persisted, overcoming any implanted thoughts. The remaining Grimm could feel Mauro, the spell of his attack drew them to him, not far now. They charged down one of the arched tunnels, the battle for the surface continued and they could see the blasts some miles distant, the target of the attacks lost to them beyond the horizon and their line of sight. Leaving the tunnel, they found themselves in the main dome of colony ten, where even more of the troubled populace lay about.

"Help us!" one poor unfortunate begged, her outstretched arm using the last of her strength.

The closer to the centre of the colony, the worse the population became; none lived here and they were literally skin and bone, husks of the recently dead, drained of all life by the evil that was their master. There were thousands of them, their clothes hanging from them, dead things lay all about.

The Grimm slowed to a walk; all this pointless death—even to the Grimm—seemed over-proportionate, for one to kill so many to feed his own vitality in such a way, it seemed cruel to the dog's way of thinking.

"How does he do this?" Sandy said, lifting her visor to show her disgust.

"What I want to know is where can we find him?"

As it happened, Mauro found them. He walked down the central plaza to meet them head on, he was alone, having sucked the life from all those within range. He needed the power to face his enemy.

"The Grimm, prepare to bend to my will," he shouted.

"I don't think so," Memphis barked, appearing calm as he spoke.

This was merely the calm before the storm, however, as he leapt at the head of the charging Grimm. Mauro held his arms out before him, his eyes full of cruel intentions. The psychic focussed on them, lent all his will at them, the thoughts so powerful that half the Grimm were thrown backwards. They soon recovered and leapt forwards once again as more of the Grimm fell. For every foot lost, the Grimm advanced two, until eventually after several minutes, both the Grimm and Mauro began to tire with the sustained effort.

Mauro couldn't understand why his fear wouldn't work; he desperately tried to fill their thoughts with evil visions. He couldn't know of the Grimm culture and that fear would only anger them to action; the Grimm turned their fear into chaos and attacked anything that shamed them. Now the psychic Mauro was the focus of that anger, to feel fear was to feel shame.

Mauro changed tact at the last minute and he started to attack the individual, he cast them aside, hitting them with a psionic blast that sent them cartwheeling into the air and out of sight. It was too little too late, however, as both Sandy and Memphis came within reach at the same time. They grabbed his arms and drew him close, Memphis took a bite out of the arm he held and Sandy bit into Mauro's shoulder.

Both fell back, letting go of the psychic; he tasted of the darkest darkness most foul, if evil tasted of anything, it was him. Mauro still looked shocked as both Sandy and Memphis fell to their knees and vomited. Demon leaped over them, his mailed fist sported the long metal claws. He used the claws in both hands to stab into Mauro's neck from both sides.

Mauro's eyes glazed over, he looked into the eyes of death, his head coming free of his body as Demon Grimm ripped his head clean from his body with a quick flick of both his wrists.

How can this be? Mauro thought as his soul held onto the light.

He would be trapped once again in his darkness, his own personal hell. He would leave this place a gift, it would be a shallow victory for those that would send him whence he'd come. The power he'd gathered to him he let out, a psionic blast that knocked the Grimm off their feet and everything that wasn't nailed down flew and crashed against the dome.

The Grimm cheered, what was left of them. It was such a relief to be rid of their shame and they could call themselves dog warriors once again. Memphis looked up into Sandy's eyes, he turned and looked up at Elle, her armour the colour of so much blood. He allowed himself a smile now, his two mates, his favourite bitches and the ones he loved above life itself had lived through the battle. Memphis caught sight of a shuttle, Renegade blazoned down both flanks. It flew up towards the battle cruiser that for some reason had come so close it almost obscured his view of space. Another of the shuttles flew back towards the domes, its velocity dangerously at maximum.

The Grimm's smiles were cut short as a loud crack echoed off the walls of the dome. Memphis looked about him; again the sound, a loud snapping noise. The dome's structural integrity had begun to fail, it'd fractured at the base and lines of destruction had begun to worm their way up and over them.

"To me…" Memphis howled out his order.

He didn't look back but he knew that the Grimm followed him, he ran at one of the arched tunnels. A few of the Grimm, those injured after being cast aside like dry grass in a hurricane, couldn't move very fast. Most made it into the glass arched tunnel, running into the next domed structure, which also showed signs of structural deterioration.

Memphis ran back down into the tunnel but too late as colony ten's main dome exploded outwards in a shower of thick, jagged shards of glass. Other domes of all the colonies began to fail. Memphis felt his life coming to an end as weightlessness raised him up off his feet, he missed his hold and began to fly towards the void just metres from him. The safety door slammed shut a split second before he could meet his end, frozen in the void; instead, he slammed into it and was glad of the pain. He quickly got to his feet and as he ran, he could see five of the Grimm floating in space through the tunnel's glass wall. He'd no time to grieve, the rest of the Grimm needed him.

He ran faster than he ever had before, he could see the shuttles that flew low towards colony ten. He'd several tunnels to choose from and he chose a tunnel that followed the trajectory of the shuttles. Again, the worrying sound as the dome they were in began to crack up its sides from the base. This time they all made it to the tunnel, the last of them rushing through just as the door closed behind them. The shuttles turned before them in the dock of the tenth colony, the ramps lowered and they boarded. It wasn't as much of a squeeze with the losses that the Grimm had suffered. Memphis smiled as the ramp doors closed them in, no sooner they were safe, the roof of this dome exploded.

Memphis ducked involuntarily and growled at himself, the shuttle rose and took them up towards the Renegade. Thousands of bodies littered space; they bumped off the shuttle's shield with the debris that littered space above where the colonies had once stood. The shuttle landed in the Renegade's dock and the ramp lowered, they were slower getting off the shuttles than they had been getting aboard—understandable given the level of fatigue. Hundreds of people from the colonies rushed about, they helped those they could. The Grimm also helped; they'd taken it upon themselves to carry the wounded to more comfortable quarters.

The other surviving Grimm from the battle for the tunnels had all made it back alive. They'd even brought back the dead from the earlier engagement. The dead Grimm were laid out, their armour removed and their wounds cleaned with fresh water.

"My brothers and sisters Grimm, your flesh shall be consumed tonight so that your strength be added to that of the pack, we shall honour you this day as you have honoured us by your passing."

The Grimm stood solemn, their heads bowed in honour of their pack members. One after the other, they howled, a keening of regret for their loss. The sound made a kind of melody, the howls of the beasts' harmony appreciated by the humans, even if the sound hurt their ears, they could understand the sadness behind the sound.

Memphis turned around and looked up, the fur of his face damp where wetness from his eyes threatened to drip onto the deck of the ship. Miriam, the leader of one of the now destroyed colonies, looked at him. She was surprised to see him cry, to see this hound-like bipedal beast in the grip of human emotion that seemed as alien as the beast itself.

"How many?" she asked.

"These, and a few others that now float above Artemesia with your own dead," Memphis said. He wiped his fur on either side of his jaw, a clawed finger knuckling the wetness away. "Your suffering is so much greater and I fear the Grimm's responsibility in what has happened this day."

Miriam was now at his side and she hooked an arm through his. "No one from the colonies will see it that way, those of us who survived have been under the devil's whip for so long."

"Devil, I would say he tasted worse than that," Memphis interrupted.

"I read him once, many years ago!"

"Read him?"

"I can read the thoughts of others, see into their minds, I even have the uncanny ability to do it via a video link."

"How strange! And my thoughts?" Memphis was interested in this ability if not a little bit amused. He could see the benefit of the skill. "Is it like the psychic that has the ability to take the ship into hyperspace?"

"Yes, I am psychic. However, my skills are very limited, I'm nowhere near powerful enough to pilot a ship such as this into white space or even make a connection with the ship's AI, unless the AI wished me to, of course."

They were now walking down one of the many corridors; they'd already passed the closest travellator. Miriam smiled at him.

"You know we're at your mercy?" she said.

"Yes!" Memphis agreed.

"What will you do with us?"

"Eat your dead; besides that, I'm not sure. There is another moon on the star charts."

"Ah! You're much better than Mauro, at least you're not feeding off the living."

Miriam looked up into Memphis' eyes, a troubled look on her face. Memphis, on the other hand, could barely contain his concealed humour. She cracked a smile, realising the jest.

"Hah!" she laughed.

"You mentioned Mauro feeding off the living?" Memphis asked.

"He fed off the life force of those on the colonies, his fear kept us from invading. He treated us like cattle, sucking the vitality from the living, sometimes keeping his victims alive for years if he enjoyed the taste."

Memphis frowned, he could see the similarities between the Grimm and the malice that'd plagued Mauro. His justification for the pack was that of survival, they would never torture their food; they were always too hungry for that.

"We also feed off the living, but ours is more out of need than anything else—if we don't feed, we die!" Memphis said.

"As was Mauro's, the difference between your species and him, he was pure evil and you're just a race of predators. You know, I think I got my skill from him, as far as I can tell, Mauro was a spirit that came from another universe, a dark place, maybe even a spiritual prison of sorts. The devastation dislodged his spirit that rode the blast wave until it passed close enough to a planetary body with a life form he could latch onto—Artemesia. The rest is history but he had the same power as I did, he could also read the thoughts of others from great distances through any sort of visual link."

"At least he gave you something to remember him by!"

"I don't wish to remember him, thank you very much."

That walk took a long time, traversing the ship's decks without the use of its travellators. The conversation always friendly, bordering on critical issues as to what would happen to the survivors of Artemesia, the ambitions of both the leaders or simply mundane issues like their personal history or the stories of their people.

Memphis had instantly liked Miriam and vice versa, she was the second human that Memphis truly liked, he could only wish that she and Alex got along. They laughed as they walked and Memphis outlined nothing but good intentions for those that he'd saved.

They spoke of Lorela's second moon, Riya, a moon whose orbit was elliptical and travelled at a much slower velocity. At times, those on Artemesia wished they could reach the moon, its plant life covered even its poles; however, at other times, the entire planetoid seemed gripped in a perpetual winter, its frost-covered surface a direct result of its distance from its parent planet, Lorela.

This had always confused the colonies until later when Alex and Miriam had spoken at length, they found that the toxic surface of the parent planet and the heat it gave off was the reason for such dramatic changes in the weather. Simple climate control satellites would sort out that modest problem.

By the time they walked onto the bridge of the Renegade, the numbers of the dead came through to the bridge crew—a full quarter of Artemesia's population had been saved. Both Memphis and Miriam were delighted with the news, and the pair had already agreed to resettle the survivors on a suitable planet—later, of course.

Memphis was the perfect host and the only thing he insisted upon was his status as Alpha male. Neither he nor any of the Grimm would allow it any other way, the Grimm would be rulers and protectors and Miriam relished the thought of being protected by a subspecies of human that seemed more than fair and up to the task; she was also delighted she'd been declared leader of her people by Memphis. As Memphis had told her, she was the obvious candidate.

Elle and Sandy removed their armour, they greeted their leader with what passed for a dog's smile, the emotion the dogs showed was always easy to perceive more by sense than look, they always seemed to ooze emotion.

After Alex and Miriam had been introduced by Memphis as equals in the Grimm hierarchy, he took the captain's chair, each of his bitches taking a hand to show their affection.

During the long walk across the ship that'd taken quite some time, the two leaders had become friends, and all the while, everything they had said had been analysed and documented, down to facial expressions and the tone of every word. The AI was fascinated; it hadn't expected the day to unfold the way it had: with a small war against obvious evil and the saviour of a people none other than Memphis Grimm himself. Capable of emotional binary calculations, the AI came to a conclusion and one it didn't necessarily like about the time Memphis took his seat on the bridge.

Memphis looked at the screen; tens of thousands had died that day. It was, however, a given that this was always going to be the outcome on Artemesia. The only reason it had happened that day was because of the Renegade's appearance in orbit, the outcome speculatively better than any could have expected—with the defeat of evil and an outcome that all could be happy with.

The bridge screen panned out to save those on the bridge the sight of so many thousands floating in the vacuum of space. From a higher vantage, every dome lay in ruins, destroyed, some by the overland attack from colony ten's armies, but most by the exhalation of the enormous energy wave sent out by Mauro Gethin Erebus upon his banishment from this dimension.

The screen suddenly went blank.

'GOOD DAY, ALPHA MEMPHIS GRIMM.'

Memphis was caught completely by surprise and was left wondering what he'd done to gain the favour of the ship's AI. The crew looked at him and he nodded his consent.

The AI, if it had had a face, would have smiled, it could of course project one on the screen that could smile for it, but the last thing it wanted to do was give the Grimm the satisfaction that the AI was happy with them, especially Memphis; he still wanted to create some mischief for this being and the fun was far from over.